# Margot's Secrets

# Margot's Secrets

by
Don Boyd

Published by Ziji Publishing
www.zijipublishing.com

Distributed by Turnaround Distribution Services Ltd.
Telephone 020 8829 3000

ISBN: 978-0-9554051-5-0

Printed and bound in the UK by CPI Mackays, Chatham, ME5 8TD

To Hilary Boyd

# PROLOGUE

## THE MARTYRDOM OF SAINT EULALIA
### A Videogram for the internet created by Domatilla Milliken and Paolo Lorca.

*(Screenwriter's note: The shooting style in digital video will pay crude homage to the great American film experimentalists of the 1950's and 1960's who worked isolated from any commercial infrastructure).*

### Title Card:
*"I want to die from longing, and never live in boredom.*
*I want there to be in the depth of my soul, a hunger for*
*love and beauty."*
### Khalil Gibran 'Love Letters in the Sand'

EXTERIOR. DAY. BARCELONA. DAWN

Images of mediaeval Barcelona culled from the city as it is now. The Cathedral interior. Some shots in the Barri Gotic area of the old city – its ancient streets, its old churches and squares. Nothing modern. All mediaeval or later. And in the Jewish quarter – its cramped houses, and a synagogue.

Walls. Stone. Statues. Paintings. Gargoyles.

All of these images form a patchwork which will be integrated into the text of this story of our Catalan heroine, Saint Eulalia.

TILLY is sitting outside the Segrada Familia, Antoni Gaudi's great unfinished modernista celebration of Catholicism.

The camera circles around the body of this young woman. A close up – her strawberry blonde curls hug her face which is photographed in the style of a Pre-Raphaelite painting.

### TILLY (VOICE OVER)
*This is my story. This is the story of Eulalia. She is my spirit.*
*She was I and I am she. I live through her and she lived in*
*the certain knowledge that within centuries she would live through*
*me. She died for me and I will die for her...*

\*\*\*\*\*\*

# Chapter One

Sunday mornings in early Spring were usually spent lazily rustling up brunch for friends on the terrace of their Montjuic apartment with its magnificent view of Barcelona's harbour and its old city. Margot's American culinary roots and her husband Archie's quirky British breakfast obsessions were creatively integrated with the Catalan delicacies they ferreted out from stalls at the Mercat de la Boqueria off Las Ramblas. But on that Sunday, St. George's Day, April 23rd, the English ex-patriot community were celebrating their patron saint with an exclusive lunch to honour Eusebio Casals, a renowned Catalan artist. This annual event was traditionally just a good excuse for a raucous alcoholic binge and some light-hearted jingoistic patriotism – hardly reasons to cancel a treasured weekly ritual. But Archie's status as an eminent professor at the university and a fine art consultant for Sotheby's made it obligatory, yet he was grumpy at the prospect.

"Why don't you go on your own, darling? I'll be perfectly happy moping around here."

Still in his huge, ruby red dressing gown, Archie was immersed in the Sunday newspapers. Like a Pasha in the library of a nineteenth century oriental Palace, he was clearly bemused at the thought of abandoning the cosy four walls of their large drawing room with its leather-bound first editions and his two beloved, original Pre-Raphaelite oil paintings. A light Mediterranean breeze wafted across from the French windows – this was Archie's taste of paradise. But Margot was shy socially and very reluctant to attend parties on her own. She was determined to muster some enthusiasm from her entrenched husband.

"Don't be such a curmudgeon!"

She continued with a charming barrage of witty repartee and affectionate mockery from the bathroom where she was luxuriating in an extravagant pseudo-Victorian bathtub, submerged in bubbles. All of it fell on deaf ears. Archie was buried in the magazine section of the Catalan equivalent of the *National Enquirer*. In exasperation, she reminded him that his favourite young god-daughter, Tilly, would be there with her boyfriend Paolo, the artist's stepson.

"You know how much she makes you laugh."

He was still unmoved. "I suppose Tilly is an exception. She's special. But the rest of that crew are all so insufferably smug. Spoilt brats; they seem to stay out of all the turmoil, whatever murky happens to the rest of us. They remind me of the reasons why I would never want to live in England again."

Margot wasn't letting him off the hook.

"They're not so bad - they probably think the same of us! I'm sure that we're going to have some fun. I thought you liked Eusebio... Stay grumpy, if you must... or you can come and have a swim in the lovely pool, or talk to Robert... flirt with Stella. They'll be there."

Archie was not impressed.

"Stella is staying in London this weekend – since her bank went bust, she's had to work a little harder for her bonus. I 'phoned Robert to tell him that our brunch here was off today. Eusebio doesn't count, he's a Catalan. But you're quite right," he sighed, "I do love seeing Tilly and Paolo. They make me laugh. Teenage love can conquer all. How old is she now? Eighteen?"

Margot knew that she had finally won the day as Archie shuffled off to change out of his striped flannel pyjamas, muttering to himself about the handicaps of marrying a woman twenty-five years younger than him.

Margot giggled like a naughty schoolgirl as she waddled over to him and planted some soap suds on his forehead.

They really had no alternative but to forego their usual Sunday luxuries and make their way down from the Montjuic. They walked across Barcelona's harbour towards the Arts, a tall, post-modern tower dwarfing Frank Gehry's copper and steel lattice Fish sculpture, which playfully overlooks the Mediterranean Sea. It was a magnificent spring morning and the sandy white beach glistened in the sunshine. The palm-lined promenade was already full of skinny kids in multi-coloured tee-shirts on roller blades and skateboards. Neither Margot nor Archie were in the mood to talk much, which suited Margot who was now lost in thought. She was going to come across some of her clients at the party – an inevitable occupational hazard in the small, close-knit, English-speaking community which defined their social life. She tried not to rationalise the tenuous nature of these public encounters. Even Archie would have found it difficult to identify who were her 'patients', as she called them, although he would probably have been able to hazard a good guess. She discouraged anything except the slightest of innocuous banter with her clients, particularly at large social gatherings, and Archie was sensitive enough to notice this nuance and respect it. Only Tilly and Paolo, also clients, had been able to break through her professional barrier.

She was also feeling a little vulnerable and lonely. Although she was very popular amongst Archie's university friends, she had no pals of her own age in Barcelona who might have an inkling of her way of life in her home state of California, and who could provide a more frivolous balance to the heavy academia of her husband's coterie. As much as she adored Archie and her new life in one of Europe's great cities, she was beginning to yearn for some of that easy-going, intimate banter that had been the feature of all her peer group friendships at home in La Jolla during the few years she had lived there after college. She had tried e-mails and video phone lines to establish communication with her cultural past, but they proved poor substitutes for the real thing. She missed frivolous chit-chat sessions over cocktails in the evening, and longed for an indulgent milkshake gossip after the yoga class. For all his other considerable qualities, Archie was no substitute for a girlfriend or confidante of her own age.

None of this had been helped by one over-riding problem: for nearly a year now, she had also been inadvertently denied one of the essential aspects of all qualified practising psychotherapists – regular sessions with a supervisor. At the time that Archie had come into her life, Margot had felt no further need for a regular supplement to the intensive analysis she had undergone during her training, but she knew that however professionally qualified she was, there would always be a need for a mentor from within the psychological arena. Very much for this reason, the Institute that gave her the necessary qualification to practise insisted on providing supervisors to monitor the work in progress of all their members. Margot had resisted their imposition at first. She hadn't rated the reputations of any of the therapists fielded towards her and turned them all down. But she then had a stroke of luck; Marie-Christine Traille, the only supervisor prescribed by the Institute living in Barcelona, turned out to be extraordinary. She was a wonderful and wise French woman whom Margot had met coincidentally at an American Psychological Association junket when she had first arrived in Barcelona.

As would be expected of an eminent Freudian, she had unpicked Margot's childhood with such clarity. Many of the anxieties she had been harbouring about her marriage to a man the same age as her father had been to a large extent mollified by Marie Christine's perceptive worldliness. Fluent in English and sensitive to Margot's 'fish out of water' tendencies, she had helped Margot navigate the treacherous waters of European vocal cynicism about America's damaged cultural and political status, particularly in the wake of the war in Iraq, which had been so vilified in Spain. In university circles she had been shocked by the incessant jibes about the country she loved in spite of its flaws, and her sessions with her therapist had bolstered her self-confidence in this treacherous, hurtful arena. Just as important to her, Marie-Christine had also been helping her understand her role with her ex-patriot clients. Immensely well read and informed, she had encouraged Margot's natural brilliance with her own witty brand of intelligent rigour. Her influence had provided Margot with a strong humanistic balance to the often stifling analytical process and this had prevented her carrying around her clients' illnesses hour by hour, a tendency when she had first started practising professionally.

Finally, Marie-Christine became her 'best friend', the confidante she had longed for. Their meetings had often been conducted away from the stuffiness of an office or consulting room and as such she had been the perfect tour-guide. One week they would amble around the exquisite mediaeval frescoes at the MNAC and sip frappoccino in the Picasso museum. Another week they would hang out in the dives in the heart of the Raval, and eat butifarra and white beans at the counter of Pollo Ricco, one of the cheapest restaurants in the world. Margot would tease Marie-Christine with the notion that she must have been Mrs Thomas Cook in a previous life. And of course, Margot could discuss all those secrets she couldn't begin to share with Archie, in the absolute knowledge that they were safely harboured.

But Marie-Christine had developed breast cancer six months ago and had retired to her home town in the Languedoc with her husband, to try to fight it off. When they said goodbye to each other on the very beach she was now ambling past on her way to the Arts with Archie, Marie-Christine, a devout Catholic, had given Margot a tiny silver cross she had owned since childhood. Margot thought then that she would never talk to her again, let alone see her, knowing that her friend would become too ill to continue even the slightest telephone relationship.

She had failed to find a suitable replacement. Qualified therapists are required to have supervisors who monitor their work. In desperation, Margot had tried a couple of 'long distance' internet replacements but the efforts of electronic conferencing communication had been frustrating and impersonal. The only woman she had vaguely connected with lived in Boston, and had announced that she was taking a sabbatical. This compounded Margot's feelings of isolation and emotional vulnerability: nobody else could fill the spiritual void created by this cruel separation from Marie-Christine. Even Archie's eccentric, almost paternal encouragement, which usually helped her sustain her rigorous professional commitment to her clients, had its limits.

As they made their way up from the beach to the raised garden terrace at the back of the hotel, which had been bedecked with the red crossed flags of St George, Margot took Archie's hand and clung to him like a frightened schoolgirl.

"I love you, Archie darling."

Chattering throngs of ex-patriots epitomised one of her greatest anxieties: that a client of hers, or worse still the husband or wife of one of her clients, might confront her with an embarrassing public manifestation of secrets they had only shared with her in the privacy of her consulting studio. This heightened her professional paranoia and weakened her characteristically robust social skills. She liked to get out to meet people and have fun but there was always that lingering knowledge that if she came across a client, she might ruin months of careful psychological rehabilitation with a careless slip of the tongue. For this reason, at parties she liked to use Archie as a protective shield. He understood and enjoyed the sensual flirtatiousness she used at moments like this when the easy-going luxury they enjoyed within the private, protected world of their domestic life evaporated in the public arena. Margot's beauty had always been a source of pride for Archie and he wore it elegantly. Her public displays of physical affection contributed to his self-confidence.

"I'll stay close but you know how shy I can be."

Margot knew that he was probably the least shy man in the room. She laughed away his reply and broke away from his hand to take a couple of glasses of ruby red Cava from the silver tray proffered to them by a uniformed flunky. Sipping the cool bubbly wine, they gingerly edged their way into the throng of people who were hovering around, awaiting the celebrity guest. Coincidentally, St George's Day is also celebrated in Barcelona, and more enthusiastically than in England – La Diada di Sant Jordi. To symbolise their love and mutual respect for each other, Catalan lovers exchange gifts. Boys give girls red roses, girls give boys a book. And so, rather over-dressed for a Sunday morning, an elite selection of the great, good and the bad of the city's English-speaking, ex-patriot community were mingling with an equally chic Catalan equivalent. Few of them were paying much attention to the artworks dotted around the immaculate lawn. Only Margot, tall, beautiful, short-haired and wearing a white tee-shirt with Eusebio's name hand-painted on the front of it, and Archie, grey-haired and distinguished, were now diligently inspecting each sculpture with any sort of serious aesthetic appreciation.

Eusebio finally arrived at the entrance to the hotel in a black, open-topped, vintage Porsche. Three liveried men surrounded his car as if royalty had arrived. With an effortless demonstration of physical strength and old-fashioned gallantry, he lifted Tilly out of the back seat while Paolo, a dark-haired Adonis, leapt out to join them. In sharp contrast to Eusebio's immaculately groomed silver white mane, Tilly's strawberry blonde ringlets were straggling across her teenage face. She nuzzled into his elegant frame. Her boyfriend Paolo grabbed his stepfather affectionately around the waist, finding Tilly's hand to hold at the same time. This exotic trio, with infectious joie de vivre, giggled their way into the glass elevator, which whisked them one floor up to the Arts Hotel's poolside garden terrace.

Margot was stroking a simple abstract structure made of mahogany, a subtle cross between a figurative Rodin and one of those bronze abstract statues, which peppered the Soviet Union before it collapsed.

"Do you think he might give me one of these? Tilly told me that Eusebio needs as much filthy lucre as he can muster. He's looking for another wife. He once offered to give me a piece in lieu of payment, pleading aristocratic poverty."

Archie laughed. "Filthy lucre, indeed! I can just hear the old devil trying to pretend that cash doesn't matter. The idle rich. Always skint. Go for his throat, if I were you. His work goes at auction for thousands."

"I told him that he shouldn't come to see me if he can't afford it. He's one of my oldest clients and I'm American, remember... always after those big bucks! Whisper to him that I rather fancy this piece here for our hall. I'll offer him a year's free therapy? He certainly needs it!"

Archie chuckled infectiously. "There's my girl. I'll have a word. Judging by the money dripping from the bods on this terrace right now, if a bomb dropped here and you survived, you would lose most of your best clients. I never know how you get away with hobnobbing with them like this. I can see at least half a dozen of them right now. What's your secret?"

"Who wants to fly to London twice a week to see some over-rated Freudian in St. Johns Wood when they can have me? I'm the perfect alternative, cheap at half the price... and very careful to keep what they tell me to myself."

Archie laughed at the defensive tone in her voice. "Keep your hair on! I'm only teasing you, darling. They're lucky to have you, whoever they are."

Margot kissed him gently on the lips. "I wish they would hurry up with the speeches and houha. I am dying for one of those waffles over there. Their buffet brunches here are the best."

Margot had a charming, childlike enthusiasm which Archie so clearly adored.

Eusebio, Tilly and Paolo finally emerged from the aluminium and glass-housed atrium which housed the hotel's first floor reception area. The elite throng broke out into rapturous applause. The manager of the Arts was awkwardly trying to shepherd his distinguished guest through the hordes of welcoming friends towards a makeshift dais with a microphone, but Eusebio was stopped, kissed and given a book by every woman en route. Each of them had a rose in her hand. Paolo couldn't resist a jibe at his stepfather's expense.

"You old goat! How do you do it?"

Eusebio laughed and winked at Tilly as he collected at least half a dozen books on his way to the platform. He paused only once, for Margot. Scurrilously disregarding the rules of their professional relationship, he kissed her on the mouth and then hugged Archie.

"My favourite tee-shirt on my favourite wife! So typically American. I love you for it... Stay close, I need you to calm my nerves and taunt your husband."

"Bless you for the St. George's rose, Eusebio. Archie was so jealous."

Archie was chuckling again. He was used to his beautiful wife's flirtatiousness.

"He's Scottish! Their patron saint is St Andrew!" quipped Tilly, who was playfully air-kissing Margot, who then in turn hugged Paolo. Tilly's natural exuberance was infectious.

"Where's your brother, Tilly?"

"Hugo's changing into his state of the art Speedo. He has challenged Eusebio to a swimming race and wanted a warm-up swim in the pool over there. He's been training for weeks."

They all laughed. These unscheduled interruptions in their regal procession were beginning to irritate the hotel manager who was keen to start the official ceremony. Eusebio was finally strong-armed towards the stand.

After a brief welcome from the British consul, which was greeted with braying whelps and shouts, Eusebio came to the microphone. He was in his element, among this community, his cultural stamping ground.

"Thank you so much, everyone, gracias. I am so moved. Gracias... I want to tell you about the Sant Jordi tradition in Barcelona. Sant Jordi, your St George... When Sant Jordi killed his dragon, the blood from his enemy spilled into a beautiful rosebush. He gave a red rose to the beautiful princess he had saved and rescued. April 23rd. Did you know that this is also the day in 1616 that both William Shakespeare and Cervantes died? England and Spain. Books... Love... Spring... Fertility..."

The guests cheered. When the noise died down, Eusebio's voice went quiet. "I have an important contest to announce. Tilly's brother, Hugo, has challenged me to a swimming race. After lunch I will be Hugo's dragon, maybe? And my blood can be a thousand rose bushes."

More raucous braying and applause. He raised his arms. "But now, so that you can also think of your lovers and mistresses, and beautiful roses, and Don Quixote... Falstaff, and dancing the sardana tonight in the Plaça St. Jaume... and making love all night... I want to sing a song for you to say to all of you, 'T'estimo', 'I love you!' All of you!"

And then, putting his finger to his lips to silence their euphoria, this debonair man in his seventies broke into a beautiful rendition of a haunting Catalan love song, which brought the house down. Archie put his arm around Margot, whose eyes were brimming with tears. They walked over to the buffet brunch. Archie had regained his sense of humour.

"He's such an old goat, but I can't help loving him. Can you see Tilly and Paolo anywhere? They have vanished."

"No, but they are probably at the pool watching Hugo warm up for his race. I'm starving. Let's have brunch with Robert. Where is that mad hack?"

Archie muttered, "He'll be charming some pretty young girl, probably a client of yours. Not that I would know one, of course..."

Archie's best friend, Robert, in his dishevelled, grey-speckled, tweed jacket, light grey trousers and worn-down old sneakers, was already tucking into a plate of waffles and scrambled eggs at a wooden table under one of the white-brimmed umbrellas which surrounded the terrace. He was alone and as if he had heard them, he bellowed out, "Eusebio will win. He's a brilliant swimmer."

Margot remembered that she had a date with Robert at the opera the following evening, who was bringing along a mysterious friend he had wanted her to meet.

A new lover, perhaps?

# Chapter Two

Ciutat Cooperative is an industrial zone to the West of Barcelona's international airport. It is a bleak wasteland in sharp contrast to the seductive beauty of the city it serves. Portacabins are strewn around irrigation channels and temporary construction ducts which crisscross clusters of brown-painted, corrugated iron sheds, sleek, single-storey warehouses and a myriad of yellow and lime green containers. Even bald young palm tress planted to add some decoration fail to give any charm to this unfriendly landscape sprawling from the Mediterranean to the mountains which straddle the Costa Brava coastline.

Occasionally, at dusk in the spring, the winds coming from the sea are strong enough to create a light dust storm. A portly, middle-aged man dressed in the khaki uniform of a night watchman, was cycling through this dusty mist along one of the many makeshift construction site paths. He parked his bike in front of a large brown hut next to the security gates of a parking lot littered with modern engineering equipment, some of it covered with tarpaulin sheets. The hut housed a sophisticated security system within a neatly arranged bed-sitting room and kitchenette. He flicked some switches to activate the eight television monitors, which then swept his patch with a series of surveillance cameras. Satisfied that all was in order on his site, he flicked another switch, which closed the system down. He then walked across from his hut to an old black sedan car, parked in front of a sleekly designed, aquamarine-coloured modern warehouse across the parking lot. He looked around furtively and then bent down at the front of the car and took an envelope from the top of the left tyre. He opened it and while counting the bank notes inside, he walked hurriedly towards the sliding doors of the silver warehouse. He stuffed the money into the back of his tatty uniform, tapped a code into a security locking pad, and went inside. Negotiating a labyrinth of palettes and makeshift storage areas with a flashlight, he arrived at a larger open space and fumbled for a switch. Several fluorescent tubes clamped to what looked like photographic lighting stands flickered on to reveal what he had come to inspect. He took it in with more than a passing sense of curiosity. Painted on three large screens, which were laid out like the set of a stage play, was a three-dimensional reproduction of the walls and piazza of a mediaeval city flanked by its Gothic cathedral. In the centre of the stage area was a large, old wooden barrel, a mound of broken glass on what looked like a funeral bier, and two planks of wood arranged in the shape of a crucifix. The floor had been covered with several canvas tarpaulins.

To one corner there was a lengthy, rectangular, glass-topped table strewn with digital paraphernalia: a wireless mouse – shiny white, comfortable. A sleek black laptop, its seventeen-inch screensaver radiating a crisp, well-defined digital reproduction of the famous Victorian painting of Shakespeare's suicidal Ophelia – an exquisite, red-haired teenager drowning amongst the water lilies. Near to this laptop were two expensive mobile phones with liquid crystal display screens glowing in the shadows. One of them was attached to the computer by a sleek grey cable. The other was vibrating almost noiselessly. A few feet away from the table was an old Sony High Definition Z1 video camcorder perched on an aluminium tripod. Its screen flap was open but blank. The tape loading mechanism of the camera had been ejected and was empty. The baffled night watchman finally decided to pick up the vibrating mobile 'phone and clumsily managed to answer it.

"Si?... Si, Paolo!... Si, vale, vale... Adios!"

He turned off the phone with awkward unfamiliarity, placed it back where he had found it and hurried out of the warehouse, back across to the brown shed where he began to settle in for the night. After stripping down his bed, he took a plate from the tiny fridge and placed it just outside the door of his hut, and stood there looking out towards the dark warehouse. The black sedan car had disappeared. He listened to the soft hum of the Mistral and the intermittent screeching of a pack of hungry wolves. There was no moon. He chuckled as he went back to his bed and a dog-eared copy of La Vanguardia.

# Chapter Three

*To whom can we entrust our darkest, deepest secrets? A priest? Hardly, even if you're a Catholic... A drunk in a bar? Our immediate family? Maybe a sister or brother at a pinch. Certainly not my mother; she would tell my Dad, for sure! And then there are our husbands and lovers. Lovers are about as discreet as second-rate gossip columnists. Husbands? We need secrets to keep our marriages alive and Archie and I have our past to hide from each other. Therapists, like me? We thrive on discretion in the way that Swiss bankers and doctors are supposed to. In my book, once you have told somebody a secret, it stops being a secret. Your confidante knows and even the pretentiously discreet live on in the knowledge of their new information. Tell a best friend about the withering terminal disease persistent in your family medical history, and you can be sure that there will be a pregnant pause in the conversation when you let slip that you are about to have the obligatory medical examination to qualify for a life insurance policy. Those desperate precarious moments when we feel the need to expel the burdens of childhood anxiety or the need to confess some hideous crime of passion are the catalysts for tragedies of Shakespearean proportions. But these secrets are my stock in trade and I revel in them on so many different levels. And they allow me to help my patients to live their lives more comfortably. Something I love doing.*

***

Margot's conventional childhood in La Jolla had been very happy and so the stories she was told by her eclectic collection of patients fascinated her just as much as they inspired her to help them cope with their strange, uncomfortable lives. That Freudian, 'evenly suspended attention' she diligently indulged in these damaged people as part of her job, she combined with a familiar and overwhelming private excitement which comes half-way through watching a great film when the characters and story are so enjoyable, we don't want it to end. The lives of Margot's patients, or clients as they would have preferred, always seemed to her like never-ending movies and ever-persisting nightmares. But like great dreams, when great movies end, we have to make our way reluctantly back into the baffling vicissitudes of our humdrum lives. In that sense the exotic and outrageous sagas about abusive parents and incestuous siblings which are standard psychiatric milestones for the damaged children of the rich, Margot had to put into the context of her professional responsibility. She took her job very seriously. She possessed a rare ability to put everyone at ease and along with an infectious laugh, she managed to blend her natural charm into her rigorous 'no nonsense' manner when her work demanded a tough approach.

Early every Monday morning, Margot relished her walk down from her apartment on the Montjuic, Barcelona's highest vantage point. After winding her way past the modernism of the Olympic stadium and away from the pseudo Classicism of the great museums surrounding it, she would alternate her route to the harbour according to her mood and according to her first client of the day. That morning, she chose to amble through Raval, the ramshackle, impoverished old brothel district still inhabited by the same families which had been the engine room of Barcelona's great mercantile empire. Nowadays, these families are joined by the North Africans, Pakistanis and Indians who have colonised it with Internet emporiums, mobile phone shops, cheap cafes and shabby hairdressing salons. Some of the late night bars, still haunted by the ghosts of Cocteau and Dali, who had immortalised their seductive seediness, stay open to serve breakfast to the human remnants of desperate alcoholic nights and sordid encounters.

Her first session that day was with, of all people, Robert, who was strictly speaking not really a client. After a psychological campaign of gargantuan proportions which had included abortive referrals to other eminent therapists in Barcelona, and at first on the mutual understanding that their time together could never be defined as a professional relationship, (she was jeopardising her licence to practise by seeing him), Margot had very reluctantly agreed to allow him one hour every Monday, as a friend. This should have been a taboo for any self-respecting clinical psychologist and therapist like Margot. But he had pleaded so desperately.

"You are the only person I can trust, Margot, and you don't have to talk about me to Archie, do you?"

She had succumbed to his emotional blackmail and this tenuous arrangement had worked out, certainly to Robert's satisfaction.

As part of the raison d'être for adopting a lifestyle in sharp contrast to the more familiar English shires of his childhood, Robert regularly indulged in the faux romanticism of the Raval in all its seedy glory. Margot used her dawn journey through its narrow, moody streets to orientate her mind into his bizarre psyche and environmentally prepare herself for her weekly exposure to its perverse intricacies. On one occasion, she had bumped into him sitting outside a seedy bar, much the worse for wear after a night of drunken debauchery and entwined with a girl less than half his age. As was Margot's custom on such occasions, she pretended not to recognise them – the girl looked horrifyingly like Tilly. Later that morning during their session, when she confronted him with his behaviour, he had told her that he had wanted to die. Perhaps the melancholy sky and the multiple *copas de Cava* which had fired his fertile fantasy, had been factors in his gloomy mood? Perhaps his doomed affair with this teenage nymph had finally alerted him to inevitable mortality? Margot patiently harboured this secret and reminded him gently about the other women he was also sleeping with. Robert had a very dark alter ego.

When she finally emerged on Las Ramblas, her favourite newsvendor was busy arguing with a couple of hung-over English tourists. The avenue was littered with red roses, and the bookstalls from Sunday's La Diada di Sant Jordi were being dismantled. The vendor handed her *The International Herald Tribune* with his customary smile and a wink. She then walked down towards the sea and crossed the square southwards, over to the Colm, Philip II and his Queen Isabella's famous homage to Christopher Columbus. The azure Mediterranean sparkled behind the gleaming stone statues heralding Spain's vainglorious maritime past.

She loved walking around this tall, rather vulgar statue which proudly celebrates Barcelona's connection with the New World. Christopher Columbus had sailed five hundred years ago into this harbour to be greeted by his reluctant but now jubilant benefactors, the King and Queen of Spain. Like so many proud Americans, Margot had a powerful and sentimental attachment to the Europe of her forefathers. She had been thrilled when Archie had mooted his stint as a visiting professor at Barcelona University.

"It's about time I went back to my European roots. After all, I spent the first ten years of my career teaching there. I have been hiding away in the Windy City now for far too long. And one of my friends from my teaching days in Scotland says it's now the best city in the world."

When she asked him what she was going to do while he was at work, her Spanish being poor at best, he laughed: "You can learn Catalan, and you can set up as a shrink for the ex-pats! I'm sure that they are all as fucked up as the rest of us, and will welcome someone with your special qualifications!"

His jocular, half-serious suggestion had made so much sense. She could continue her work as a psychotherapist, combine that with fantasies of Catalan citizenship and luxuriate in the bourgeois indulgences of urban tourism. She had never imagined that the therapeutic territory would be so fertile, especially in the treatment of sexual problems, which was her speciality. Much to her amazement, even her research work into recondite sexual practices proved useful and helped increase her professional reputation. Within weeks she had established a dozen regular clients – and the extra money came in handy. The academic network of American psychology had led her to Marie-Christine who, as her supervisor and personal therapist, became a vital building block for the serious analytical work she was keen to pursue within this hybrid, rather effete community. They had become such firm friends. She was now missing her more than ever, and at least as much as she missed her parents in La Jolla.

Her final destination before going to work this April Monday, like every weekday morning, was a small, dark bar hidden in the shadowy cobbled streets of the Barri Gotic – the city's crammed and haunted mediaeval quarter. Heaven and a haven. Margot used to be embarrassed to ask for her café solo in the poor American Spanish she had learned at high school in California. But Elvira, the wise beauty who owned the bar, put her straight. She explained, in the simple unpretentious English she spoke with the lilt of a Catalan accent, that Barcelona prospered in the eighteenth century as Spain's pre-eminent imperial city because the people of Barcelona had explored, plundered and exploited the Americas. She was proud to have her American friend there every morning.

Elvira's family had lived in the same terrace of loosely connected, timber-framed buildings since the Wars of the Spanish Succession. Fiercely proud of her Catalan roots, she would tell Margot a new story every day – often about the myriad of her descendants and relatives over the centuries who had been hemp importers, cardinals, revolutionaries and executioners – the garrotte had still been in use late into Franco's regime. On occasion she would let her into lurid contemporary stories about the darker criminal side of her beloved city. Her husband Carlos's role as Barcelona's most celebrated police inspector gave her a special insider's track. By way of reciprocation, Margot matched these yarns with her own graphic tales of psychopathic criminality stock-piled during her time at Chicago University's legendary Department of Psychology.

Elvira was no substitute for Marie-Christine but she had become a vital part of Margot's life. They kept their husbands and families away from their friendship and Margot trusted Elvira in the way that she might have done a favourite aunt. They had carefully delineated and respected boundaries. And so, as she entered the bar that morning and was not greeted with the customary hug with quite as much of the usual amount of enthusiasm, Margot knew that something was ruffling Elvira's feathers.

"You have a young friend waiting for you upstairs."

The bar had a spiral staircase, which led up to the toilets and a tiny private room with a couple of tables. Elvira's eyes told Margot that she was somewhat irritated by this intrusion into their cosy friendship.

"A friend? Not many people know that I come here."

"I will bring up your solo and orange juice."

Margot noticed that the two priests who were also habitués of Elvira's emporium were arguing. She smiled and climbed the staircase to find Tilly sitting forlornly positioned so that she could watch the customers coming into the bar from the balcony, which overlooked it. She jumped up immediately and threw herself at Margot and held her for an unnecessarily long time. Margot was bemused but she noticed that Tilly had unusually dark shadows around her eyes and was clearly distracted.

"I thought I was seeing you tomorrow?"

"I know, Margot! I know you are strict about this, and I am so, so sorry but I can't wait. I had no other person to see. I have to talk to you. I can't wait until tomorrow."

"You could have 'phoned."

"I couldn't take the risk of missing you. I've seen you skip through your messages."

Margot laughed. Her answering machine drove her crazy at times.

"I always pick up my messages. Especially important ones from clients like you."

Elvira arrived with Margot's breakfast, and another cup of Americano for Tilly, who smiled appreciatively.

"How did you know that I came here so early?"

"Paolo knew, somehow."

"Why is he not here with you? In all the time I have known you, I have never seen you on your own."

Tilly paused. Her eyes welled up, she was fighting back tears. She sipped at her black coffee.

"He has told me that he doesn't want to see you anymore. He said that if he comes back to you he only wants to come alone. Separately.

And he said he always hated the feeling that you were learning things about me he didn't know. Sitting outside your room, waiting in the corridor."

"If?"

There was a quiet desperation about the way that Tilly was talking. Margot had always known that the day would arrive when the uneasy nature of counselling these two lovers at the same time would cause problems. Margot's professional relationship with Tilly's boyfriend had been excellent and he had always been very friendly whenever they met socially. In the spirit of guardianship, Archie had occasionally invited Tilly and Paolo to their apartment, not just as an extension of a longstanding friendship with Tilly's parents, but because he and Margot loved their company. Their natural enthusiasm for life was infectious and they always brought along some kind of entertainment as their charming way of 'singing for their supper', either a couple of scenes from a Shakespearean play which Paolo had used his considerable talents to distort into a Catalan fantasy of his own, or some Catalan love songs Tilly had learnt. She had a particularly beautiful voice. But except for these idylls, and the occasional sightings at ex-patriot functions like the one at The Arts, Margot had managed to restrict her work as their therapist to the twice weekly meetings. They would come together but see her separately – a condition she had insisted on from the start which they had been thrilled about – and although much of the work was very raw and emotionally charged, they had never indicated that they wanted to change this. They came together, saw her privately – sometimes Paolo would go outside into the square below but Tilly always stayed in the corridor reading Margot's movie magazines – and when Paolo emerged, they would leave hand in hand. They had only broken that arrangement once.

"Have you had a fight with Paolo?"

Tilly had tied her long red curls into a bunch behind her shoulders. She had teenage freckles and incandescently blue eyes. Her beautiful face, now exposed and streaming with tears, was silently begging Margot to help her out of her misery. Her adolescent vulnerability had obliterated any vestige of the professional rigour which Margot might have used to delay giving Tilly all the help she so obviously needed away from her studio.

"We never fight, as you know. But we argue. Usually we come to some agreement to be different. We like to have different opinions."

Margot had heard this a thousand times before. Paolo and Tilly adored each other, of that there was no question. But they had different temperaments and were never afraid to voice their opinions to each other, very vigorously and occasionally for hours on end.

"But last night after the party at the Arts, we went down to the square in front of the cathedral to dance and he seemed different. Robert danced with me which made him jealous and then he disappeared for an hour... he wouldn't tell me where he had gone."

Margot remembered the graphic stories they had both so earnestly told each other about their adolescent sexual experiences. Every detail had been scrutinised as if their brains had been under some hypersensitive neurological microscope. But she had also remembered that momentary feeling that Tilly had been with Robert that morning in Las Ramblas.

"We have always had two rules. No secrets. No lies."

"We all have secrets, Tilly. You know that. We need a secret or two..."

There was a pause. Tilly sipped her coffee.

"Paolo was... Paolo wanted me to... I was angry. He had been hiding something..."

She hesitated. Margot took her hands.

"Paolo is one of life's treasures, Tilly. If I had met him when I was your age, I would have fallen in love with him too. I would have trusted him. I would have wanted him forever, but I wouldn't have wanted him to be put on any pedestal. And that is what is so refreshing about your relationship. It has developed so that you both can be individuals. Very special people with your own way of going about the world. With love and respect for each other at a level that is quite rare. I so hope that this is not in jeopardy because of me?"

Tilly didn't really take much of this in. She was pre-occupied.

"We have never argued about you before. We only told you things that both of us were happy to tell each other. Yeah, and of course there are things we have kept to ourselves. Our own secrets..."

Margot was trying to work out where all of this was leading. She knew it was not strictly connected to her professional relationship with Tilly and Paolo, but Tilly was obviously holding back. She seemed almost frightened. Anxious.

"...but Paolo, Paolo had one very big secret. We now both have this big secret. Dark. Weird. He wants me to be part of his past..."

Tilly suddenly broke off and, switching her mood, lurched over to a straw bag which had been hanging over the chair at the neighbouring table.

"Oh my God! I totally forgot to give Archie his book yesterday. I've brought it for you to give to him. He sent me a rose on Sunday morning. I always give him a book on St. George's Day."

Margot couldn't help laughing – Archie only ever sent one rose out and she was used to Tilly's charming ability to deflect her anxieties or discomforts with a convenient, completely irrelevant diversion.

"He would have had a sleepless night worrying about it."

Tilly rummaged through her bag and produced a slim, dog-eared paperback. She kissed it and gave it to Margot. It was a volume of Catalan love songs.

"This is my only copy. It was the first gift I received from Paolo. I know all these songs now by heart, words and melodies. I want Archie to learn them too, and then on my birthday, I want him to sing them to you. They are just as lovely as those fabulous Neruda poems he gave Paolo last year... I think Archie loves Paolo as much as I do!"

And with that Tilly suddenly stood up, kissed Margot affectionately, and flew down the spiral staircase. Margot was flabbergasted. She sprung up and watched her from the balcony. Just as she was going out of the make-shift, multi-coloured and beaded curtain which masqueraded as the door, she spun around to blow a kiss to Elvira. For some strange reason she was wearing a long, flimsy black coat which became caught up in the beads. One of the priests rushed up to help her untangle it. With an unforgettable smile she shook his hand gratefully and called up to the balcony as she left the bar.

"See you tomorrow!"

The priest glanced up at Margot and rejoined his colleague. Margot stood there, leaning on the balustrade for a moment or two, and then left the bar as quickly as she could without seeming rude to Elvira.

She hurried down the tiny streets of the Barri Gothic, crossed the square in front of the eleventh century Cathedral, wound her way almost impatiently through a couple of alleyways and reached a set of large, wooden gates. She squeezed through the tiny door and ran to a narrow interior staircase and her consulting room which overlooked the faded grandeur of the Plaça de Reial.

*Maybe I am a sort of Madame, running a psychological brothel. Take Robert, for example. Tall, thin-haired and with a face which is a cross between a bloodhound and an ostrich. This distinguished, intelligent man has been known to hide during the lunch hour under the desks in the open plan office of the Catalan newspaper where he works, blubbing his eyes out. He never tells anybody why he is so unhappy and yet he spends an hour a week describing his complicated and perverse sexual proclivities to me – particularly in the context of his cloistered childhood in Oxford where his parents had the dubious privilege to play out their lives negotiating the eccentricities of antiquated academia. (I had made the mistake of telling him once about my PhD thesis at Chicago which explored the treatment of sexual perversions; this had piqued his desire to tell me much more about himself than I had ever wanted to know!) Giggling like a naughty schoolboy, he recounts the duplicitous and mendacious manoeuvres of his love life, which revolve around at least three unsuspecting mistresses. There is his bored divorcee, recovering from her marriage. His ambitious young work colleague in love with his Englishness. And finally there is his man-eating, teenaged English language student who targeted him specifically to initiate her into the rituals of sado-masochistic sex – she caught him emerging from a brothel one afternoon after school and realised, opportunistically, that there was more he could teach her than iambic pentameters. (Tilly perhaps – God forbid!). He pours out all of this to me (prurience doesn't have a comfortable definition in my dictionary), in the full knowledge that he also enjoys a weekly game of squash with my husband, his best friend. As if this perverse need to advertise to me that his omnifrenic existence isn't enough for him to survive comfortably, he is almost religious about joining us at our Sunday brunch rituals with Stella, his wife of twenty years, who flies in most weekends, from London where she works as an investment banker.*

*I can always recognise his polite, slightly guilty cough as he winds his way up the ancient staircase that leads to my office. His throat clears and his warped mind switches into a completely different universe as soon as his angular frame settles in front of me.*

Margot's studio apartment was split into three areas. She looked around at every corner of the studio, a ritual she practiced every morning. She liked her patients to absorb the layout with the similar comfortable familiarity that they might in the favourite room of their own home. She walked down the narrow corridor which had one small stool with a side table covered with film and gardening magazines. This reception area had one rather eccentric abstract Escher drawing on the wall, and led to a small but very modern, fashionable shower room with a toilet and a bidet. She noticed that the soap was depleted and replaced it with a new bar from the stash in the closet. Off this arterial corridor, and directly opposite the entrance, was an oak door leading to a small office area with a large window overlooking the square. In the centre of the room was a beautiful old desk cluttered with the inevitable laptop computer and telephone. Without sitting in the perfunctory office chair, she pressed the answer phone – only one hurried message from Tilly. Behind the desk, in the far corner, sat an old-fashioned Dickensian armchair and against the wall was a sofa-bed decorated with a floral rug which she unravelled and neatly arranged around the black velvet cushions. Next to the sofa-bed was a very modern corner bookshelf and on the walls were some exquisite David Hockney illustrations, Grimms

Fairy Tales. She straightened the largest of them. Rumplestiltskin.

Checking her watch, she then walked out of the office area through a beautiful patterned Linda Bruce fabric, which acted as a makeshift partitioning curtain, and into her consulting area which was affectionately referred to by Archie as the Priest Hole. This area was sparse. White walls. A Charles Eames chair. In the other corner, a black velvet chaise-longue ominously decorating the latticed French window which led out onto a balcony – no doubt reserved for those patients brave enough to go beyond the fifty minute, twice weekly shrink's hour. And of course, next to the comfortable orange 'patient's armchair', was that staple of every self-respecting modern therapist, the square box of tissues discreetly propped on a tiny glass side table. She rearranged the box – it had to appear fresh and unused. One last glance around the studio and she settled into the Eames.

Robert was more than a little dishevelled that morning. He, like Tilly, had turned the St George's Day party into a saga that had lasted through the night. The rims around his eyes were swollen and his face was sweating. His breath stank of stale cigarettes and alcohol as he bent down to kiss Margot before stumbling away from her and, quite uncharacteristically, lying down on the couch instead of sitting in the armchair which was his preferred resting place in the room he affectionately called, 'Margot's Lair.'

"I am not going to fall asleep on you, I promise..."

Margot waited. She liked her clients to set the agenda. But Robert was still a little drunk, certainly hung-over, and she would normally have been very reluctant to carry on with him in such a state, but the nature of their friendship demanded that she stuck with him for at least a beat or two.

"...and I don't think that you are going to fall asleep on me this morning either," he continued.

She resisted reminding him that it was barely ten o'clock and that she had never once in her entire career even so much as dozed off. However, seemingly irrelevant asides, innocuous observations and the most trivial of chit-chat were often building blocks for her more incisive analysis. Especially with Robert. His stories were very rarely boring – he had the journalist's knack of being able to spin quite a yarn, so whatever he had in store that morning, Margot was preparing to provide him with as much of her insight as she could muster.

"I have never needed one of these here before," he said, as he wiped his sweat from his forehead with one of the tissues. It was true. Although Robert was known to blub like a baby at the drop of a hat, he had never once cried in Margot's consulting room.

"Last night I did something I am deeply ashamed about... I deliberately set out to see if I could seduce Tilly... and if I failed to seduce Tilly, I was going to try to seduce Paolo... as it is, I didn't seduce either of them but I caused the most appalling fight between them... And then I behaved very badly indeed."

Margot laughed. "Robert, you are slurring your words. What made you imagine for one tiny second that either of them would have found you even remotely attractive enough to have succeeded?"

Margot was now very anxious that she had failed to understand how desperately Tilly had needed to talk to her earlier. She had often talked about Robert, and although she thought he was funny and attractive to be with, she had never for a moment thought he was sexually alluring. As much as clients hide and disguise the truth, Margot was absolutely sure that the only man that Tilly had eyes for, physically, was Paolo. Much more worrying, was their fight.

"What kind of fight, Robert?"

"She kissed me and told me that she found me... attractive, irresistible!"

"I don't believe you!"

"Well, perhaps I am exaggerating... a little. She did allow me to kiss her, and I told her that I found her irresistible!"

The conversation had moved away from being in any shape or form a session of therapy.

"Margot, you are supposed to be helping me here. Not giving me a hard time."

Margot was gentle.

"I can't treat you that easily like this, Robert. You're still drunk. I just can't take you seriously. Why don't you go home? We're supposed to be seeing each other tonight at the opera. We can talk then."

She desperately wanted to question him in order to shed some light on her conversation with Tilly, but she knew she couldn't do that and expect a truthful answer. She waited again. Robert began to whimper like a child. She continued to wait.

"I have never seen Paolo in such a horrible mood. He screamed at her. We were in that square in front of the Cathedral where they hold the dancing. Tilly was a little tipsy and she kept telling me that Paolo had betrayed her. She said that he had lied to her."

"Betrayed her?"

"He hadn't told her about an old lover. I think that she was flirting with me to pay him back. It was all very childish. They are so young. And being in love when you are that young is always a nightmare! I was in love with Stella when I was his age but I am not in love with her now. I think that I am in love with you, Margot, and I did such a stupid thing last night. I told Tilly how much I love you..."

"I don't think you were telling Tilly anything she didn't know, Robert...

and I am sure that she took it all with a pinch of salt."

Margot knew now that she would have to send Robert home. He was too drunk to be properly coherent. Thankfully, Robert did the job for her.

"You are quite right. I must go home and sleep it off. I do love you so very, very much!"

He stood up and kissed her clumsily on the mouth. She ushered him to the door.

"I can find a cab in Las Ramblas. See you tonight. It's Lucia. My favourite!" He spluttered his way down the steps.

Margot walked back to her desk, sat down and fingered the book of Catalan love songs Tilly had given her. She dialled her number. Out of service. She dialled Paolo's number. Also out of service. She decided to look through her notes about Tilly.

# Chapter Four

When Domatilla, or 'Tilly' to her friends, was eight years old, she looked like a clichéd personification of Tenniel's illustration of Alice in Wonderland. With curly, strawberry blonde hair which she neatly bunched up with a red velvet ribbon, her freckled face was almost always buried in a book, and because her mother and father ignored her at the expense of her irritatingly pretty brother, she hid her precocious intellect from almost everybody except their butler, Stephen. He realised that behind that innocent façade lay the mind of a mature adult, schooled on everything she could lay her hands on from the lewdest of Boccaccio's stories to the most romantic of Rimbaud's homoerotic poems. She would amuse Stephen for hours with the plots and characters from every single one of Shakespeare's plays, and she knew the difference between a dildo and a dirk. Stephen was a tall, intense, scholarly man with a superb memory, and although his understanding of poetry was limited, he gave her the attention that wasn't coming from her weak, hen-pecked father.

Tilly's family home in Oxfordshire was still anachronistically run like an Edwardian manor; butlers, cooks, maids! And in the manner of the Edwardian family, she and her brother were hidden away from the main drama of adult life and lived life in the nursery and 'below stairs'. Or what was known as a nursery. In fact it was like a room in a Natural History Museum. Butterflies and moths were encased in glass frames on the walls. Cabinets with dead snakes. Stuffed frogs. The children hated this oppressive reminder of their family's eccentricity. Even the blackboard displayed representations of flora, fauna and lepidoptera carefully linked to their scientific names so that when the children's grandmother made one of her infrequent visits, Hugo and Tilly could elicit the old boot's approval with a parrot-like recital of their Latin labels.

Stephen was the major domo amongst the servants who were all known as 'under the stairs staff' or 'serfs'. His status allowed him special access to the children, away from their parents. Tilly would escape from this hellhole of a schoolroom to the kitchen where she and Stephen would tell stories to anybody who wanted to listen. Their performances would last late into the evening and then Stephen would ask their nanny to take her to bed, hinting at the promise of a late night story from him to send her to sleep. Hugo slept in his mother's bed, leaving Tilly a large bedroom to herself.

Stephen would arrive, usually when she was all but asleep, and then gently read her a long poem. Her favourite was *Christabel*, an erotic romance about a beautiful virgin who is all but raped in the forest by a mysterious knight, who then haunts her life forever. At first, Stephen would sit on the bed reserved for Hugo. Respectably distant. But as their friendship developed beyond conventional boundaries, Tilly persuaded Stephen to sit at the end of her bed. Before long he was sleeping in the room. And on one extraordinary night, Tilly came back from the bathroom, naked, and slid in beside her own mysterious knight. The innocent glass of milk had become the excuse for a passionate and illicit love affair – an abusive relationship which began innocently enough and within time became obsessive and needy.

At night, Tilly yearned for Stephen's thin body and the sweet smell of his cheap after-shave lotion. He would whisper to her. Stories about his childhood, his favourite Shakespearean plots and Keats. She would make up fairy tales and bury herself in his smooth arms or stroke his hairy back, which made her giggle. These nocturnal visits lasted into puberty and Tilly finally lost her virginity to him. He was gentle. Loving. This poetic idyll came to an abrupt and hysterical end when her mother made her only visit to Tilly one cold night when Hugo had begged her to ask Tilly to tell him a late night story. The police were called. Stephen was arrested for rape (charges were later dropped) and the family ostensibly left their English stately home for a life of tax exile. Tilly cried herself to sleep every night for the next two years.

Living between the family ski chalet in St Moritz and an eccentric Victorian mansion outside Dublin might have seemed an attractive alternative, and of course fun for her hedonistic parents, but Tilly hated the disruption as much as she loathed the ghastly people her parents mixed with in this new existence – the rarefied equivalent of what the family called a 'two centre holiday' for the rich. Barely had she become used to the peculiarities of her specially imported tutors in Ireland – they were regularly fired or replaced – than she found herself having to make friends with the rather dull girls in her class at the best convent school her father could find in Dublin. There was never any consistency in her life, either in the area of her education through her teachers or in the arena of friendship with her peers.

The tutors who replaced the disgraced Stephen in Tilly's strange, increasingly hermetic universe were perversely recruited from the lists of those Oxbridge students who swotted or blagged their way to a good degree. They came for a few months before joining the ranks of the institutional classes for which they had been educated. Algebra and Latin lessons for Tilly were the least of their priorities, and the alcoholic advances from her mother Sabrina, which they either gratefully accepted or indignantly resisted, always led to the sack. One way or another.

The girls in her class in Dublin fell into two categories. The boring swots who were not nearly as clever as she was and yet tried in vain to match her formidable intelligence. Or the precocious mini Lolitas who couldn't compete with Tilly's beauty, or for that matter with her highly developed eccentricity. When it came to dealing with the boys on offer outside school, she swatted them off with elegant disdain. The one friend she made, the brother of one of the girls in her class, a very pretty mixed race boy whose parents were tax exiles, disappeared half way through Tilly's second term along with his sister. It turned out that their father was a Jamaican drug dealer, a Yardie on the run, whose business running a fanciful Dublin art gallery had been a cover for his dealing exploits amongst the artistic bohemia of Dublin society. She gave up trying to make any more friends after a tea party her mother gave which ended when she bloodied the nose of an annoying girl with big teeth and a hideous crew cut. The throng took against Tilly and she was ostracised, which suited her down to the ground. Friendless and handicapped with the combined attributes of a fierce intellect and startling beauty, Tilly ignored the opportunity to integrate. She did exactly the reverse: she played truant, and truant of the most sophisticated kind. When she was at home she read obsessively from her father's considerable and eclectic library. And when she turned fifteen, she began to balance her literary passion with a highly sophisticated gift for the manipulation of her parents.

First, the bouts of phoney headaches, migraine attacks. Six in the first month in her carefully plotted campaign designed to undermine any medical attention which would come her way.

"She's faking it," was her mother Sabrina's shrewd conclusion.

And so the migraine moved into bouts of depression – she refused to leave her bed in the morning.

"No! I am staying in bed!"

43

"You will be late!"

"I can't get up!"

"Why? Are you sick? Shall I call the doctor?"

"I don't know... why?!"

Her mother didn't normally surface until after lunch anyway and so her father's vain attempts to take her to school were undermined. He gave up after a week's worth of perfunctory kisses and one disastrous attempt to arrange for the doctor to see Tilly. She had locked her room and pretended to be asleep.

Tilly then began the third phase in her campaign to manacle the attention she so desperately wanted. No food. Anorexic behaviour – no more communal eating. And the Internet. She spent day and night pouring over her keyboard and computer screen, bug eyed, surfing obsessively.

"What on earth are you spending all that time on the computer for? It's not good for you. Bad for your eyes. And anyway, what happened to reading books, for God's sake?"

"Mind your own business, Dad! I don't ask you what keeps you awake all night long."

Tilly knew that her father was an insomniac. Tarquin listened obsessively to spoken books. Everything from Mickey Spillane to Stephen Fry's reading of Harry Potter. But he was also something of a whiz on the digital keyboard and had managed to hack into her Yahoo account when she was in the bathroom. And he had taken a peek at her hard drive.

"Tilly, you don't read Japanese, do you? Manga? What's Manga?" he shouted. "Swahili? Comic Books?"

The following morning, after a night lost amongst the pleasures of Stephen Hawkins' astrophysical universe, Tilly's father, Tarquin Milliken, decided to investigate his daughter's private world with more than his usual benign fatherly curiosity. And the shock came within a couple of clicks of her mouse: Tilly had been downloading Japanese animated pornography. Smiling old Samurai with massive dicks were pleasuring nubile sixteen-year-old Geisha girls, and evil-eyed gangsters enjoying fellatio from huge-breasted Japanese transvestites. This was too much for Tarquin.

When Tilly finally emerged from her bedroom that morning, her hair a bright orange, two of Tarquin's employees, 'serfs' as they were called by Tarquin (with no irony), were there to accompany her to a chauffeur-driven Mercedes. She was quite literally frog marched by them into the surgery of Dublin's most prestigious therapist's office, accompanied by an ashen-faced Tarquin. And so began phase four: the failed suicide attempts.

The psychiatrist, an old-fashioned, strict Freudian whose usual clientele fitted the Dublin demographic of the more elderly, the more conventional and the new breed of online entrepreneurs and Irish Eurocrats, was clearly at sea faced with this clever, manipulative and uncooperative teenager. Tilly knew exactly how to make her father look silly.

"He's over-reacting! I downloaded that stuff by mistake. I don't take any of it seriously anyway... it's harmless."

She categorically refused to have even one session on her own with the poor baffled Freudian, and Tarquin ignominiously apologised to him for his 'over-reaction' by writing him an unexpected huge cheque. As for Tilly, she was now in pole position to renegotiate her adolescent right to privacy. As part of the deal to keep her computer and the vital freedom of access to the Internet, she agreed to return to the local school, from which had been suspended after her last round of excessive truancy.

Being a Catholic convent, the teacher nuns also had a tendency to expel anyone they thought might have a corrupting influence. Tilly fitted that bill and was now on probation.

She was a very good artist and could write, rather poetically. And so her prowess in art classes and English lessons, combined with a massive donation to the school's swimming pool fund from her father, had been just enough to satisfy the reluctant Mother Superior that any disruption she would probably cause in all the other classes would justify giving her 'one last chance to redeem herself'. Even when Tilly turned up on her first day back with black lipstick, her bright orange hair now jet-black and her nose pierced, the teaching hierarchy decided to indulge her as the school's one eccentric.

Alas, not so her compatriots in the schoolrooms. They continued to brutally ignore her clumsy renewed attempts to socialise with them. Even the smoked salmon sandwiches proffered from her specially-crafted, sterling silver lunch box (a present from her grandmother) were scoffed at. Branded as the school weirdo, even when she turned up with cans of Coca Cola, chocolate cup cakes and bags of Walkers cheese and onion crisps to distribute, she was ignored. The reality was that Tilly had a heart of gold and most of her peers were spoilt brats who had learnt how to conform just enough to get away with their nasty brand of insidious bullying.

All this frustration was reported back to her mother to no avail. Sabrina had long given up on Tilly, having decided that her son Hugo had inherited the family genetic genius. She left Tilly to her computers with a sigh.

"Make sure you eat at least once a day, Domatilla!" was the sum total of any maternal anxiety. But Tilly's phase five was about to go into operation. Without much effort and no provocation, she was able to move on to her ultimate weapon of control: she was going to pretend that she no longer wanted to live.

Until then, Tilly had loathed cigarettes. She walked out of any room if there was even the faintest hint of stale cigarettes or a dirty ashtray. Oddly enough, cigars she tolerated and had been known to puff on her father's post-dinner Havana without coughing. She sneered at the bike-shed puffs on offer at school and shouted at people who smoked in the streets, so her request for a lighter after dinner one night was met with horror. The family were sprawled around their drawing room like a litter of dogs. The debris of half-eaten pizzas, stale chutney bottles and abandoned bottles of wine littered the carpet and picnic table they used as a dining surface. The ghostly chiaroscuro of family ancestors stared into the void from within the ancient frames of nineteenth century paintings – some of them priceless. The huge television was glowing silently. An American golf tournament.

"I thought that you loathed cigarettes, Tilly."

"I did! I like them now."

She blew the smoke into the air above her, helped herself to a large brandy and flounced out of the room.

Within ten minutes the house was echoing with the screams and moans of a madwoman. Tilly now had this phase firmly and successfully in operation. Her first suicide attempt was in full swing and working gloriously. Even her mother now appeared anxious and exasperated: the fire brigade was called! Tilly had climbed onto the slate roof of their rambling Victorian mansion and was shouting across the neighbouring red rooftops towards the sea and the twilight of Dublin Bay. A mixture of Turner's light and the crazy desperation of a Munch painting had been her plan. And then the terrible dialogue: her deliberate attempt to appeal to her father's intellectual sensibilities.

"I want to die. I hate it all. There is no point. It's all so absurd. I am an existentialist manqué. I hate my mother. I hate my father. I hate you, Hugo. I hate life. Hugo! Hugo! Hugo!"

The shrieks and wailing never really approached operatic heights. They came over as what they were – pathetic melodrama. If anybody had really paid any attention, the use of Hugo's name should have given the game away. Secretly Tilly absolutely adored her brother, and he had loyally repaid her genuine love with regular sneaked visits into her bed late into the night. These moments of sibling passion were the bedrocks for a solitary expression of a robust familial connection. But her parents had been fooled. Hugo wasn't brought into play during their ridiculous attempts to persuade her that life was worth living after all. Coerced into the arms of a ruddy-faced fireman, wrapped in a blanket and carted off to the local hospital in an ambulance, they all sobbed into the palms of their hands.

Her family were now exasperated, and genuinely anxious about Tilly's desire to die. They indulged her every whim during her recuperation. Like a hermit, she began to spend almost all her life in her room with her eyes glued to the computer screen. She emerged occasionally to take possession of new electronic and computer equipment she had ordered online with her father's credit card. Something was stirring in her complicated mind. She was moving on. Her hysteria and desperation had been turning into a powerful self-motivational force. She seemed to have found a solution, a remedy, salvation. She hatched such a bold and credible plan that Tarquin and Sabrina, cowed into acquiescence, clutching at every straw available, allowed her to present her new found condition without much explanation, with mind-boggling simplicity.

"I am in love with Paolo!" she announced to them suddenly, and proceeded with a startlingly simple manifesto. "He wants me to come to live with him in Barcelona! I am going next week. I want to fuck him all night. I want to make love to him for forty-eight hours without stopping. We are going to watch each other all night between now and then on our web cams. I am so in love. I want to die."

Her mother fainted, quite literally. When that particular drama, including a visit to the hospital, had been obliterated and Sabrina had recovered, somewhat miraculously, Tarquin asked Tilly for Paulo's telephone number and his e-mail address – if he couldn't reach him on the phone he would find him online.

"You can Skype him!"

"Skype? What on earth is Skype?"

"I can't believe that you haven't heard of Skype, Dad. It's an online 'phone. Cheap. Come up to my room and I will show you..."

Tilly ushered her father into her room and proudly showed him how to log on and communicate with her beloved Paulo with her computer's equivalent of a telephone system and file-swapping device. She repositioned her tiny web cam in front of her father and a small square window popped up on the computer screen showing both her and her father sitting there looking a little nervous.

"That is what he can see of us on his big screen! I am Skyping him now. You must know about Skype, don't you, Dad?" And before Dad could answer, they were both face to face on screen with the new love in his daughter's life. Paulo's beautiful face stared at them with the clarity of a Richard Avedon portrait – stark features against a white background.

"No colour?" Tilly's father asked, a little sheepishly.

"We prefer making love to each other in black and white. I can switch it if you would prefer."

"No, no. That's fine... Hello, Paulo. My name is Tarquin. I am Domatilla's father."

"I know who you are. Tilly has sent me a few movie files of you on her website. I wanted to ask you why you were given such a peculiar name?"

"How fascinating. This technology is still really very new for me. I have been resisting it. Probably a bit perverse." He had deflected Paolo's question.

Tilly was already regretting her invitation. She had always been impatient with what she was sure was her father's exaggerated technophobia. She suspected that he was more competent than he pretended and loved to play a game by disguising his knowledge. After all, he had only recently hacked into her computer to discover her pornographic Manga. But she humoured him.

"He wanted to talk to you and I suggested Skype. He's pretending that he doesn't know about it but I found his profile on Facebook and I know that he has an avatar on Second Life."

"That's cool. The Emperor Tarquinius was one of the subjects of my dissertation at university in Barcelona. He was a brutal murderer and his son raped Lucretia." Paolo's serious expression vanished and he replaced it with a startlingly beatific smile. Tarquin was now mesmerised.

"Do you live in Spain?"

"No, I am from Milano. But I am studying in Barcelona. Latin and Greek."

"Classics!"

"He got a first at Balliol last year, Dad. "

"Very impressive. I read history there... Forty years ago." He was still nervous. Awkward. But polite.

"Wow! Did you meet George Orwell?"

"Yes!"

"And WH Auden?"

"No!"

Paolo began to recite a couple of stanzas from an Auden poem about the Spanish Civil War.

"'The conscious acceptance of guilt in the necessary murder!' Orwell rather disapproved if I remember correctly..." Tarquin mused.

"Your Dad is so cool!"

Tilly winced but the remark softened her father. He said a hesitant 'goodbye' to Paolo and began to shuffle out of the room, bemused.

"Maybe you should go to see him after all, Tilly." She ran after him and hugged him and within minutes, Paulo had booked Tilly's flight to Barcelona online before the end of their session.

"I want to sing you a song," Paolo announced as Tilly was setting up the web cam so that she now had it trained on her double futon. Paolo gestured to her.

"Please do!" he replied, and Tilly began to remove her clothes.

"What on earth are those marks on your legs, Domatilla?" She didn't reply. Her legs and arms were scarred.

Paolo was now warbling a very beautiful cancon, "Adeu Petita Rosa, rosa Bianca del mati..." Tilly was naked on her futon.

Tilly whispered as he blew her a kiss and smiled at her wistfully. They fell asleep watching each other on their computer screens.

The following morning Tarquin was in the kitchen preparing his cereal when Tilly surfaced. She sat there fiddling with a glass of water as he ate.

"I am sorry about the fire brigade, Daddy!" And she began to cry: she had fallen obsessively in love with Paulo. This wasn't the issue for Tarquin, who realised that his daughter really needed to sort out her mind, and he devised a plan of his own.

Tilly's request to see Paolo in Barcelona became another opportunity for negotiation. The new bargain was simple. A passport, tickets and money on the strict understanding that she should have twice weekly sessions with Margot for six months – Tarquin had been at university with Margot's husband Archie. They had kept up with each other during the years Archie had spent climbing the academic ladder in Chicago after they had both shared long stints teaching at a Scottish prep school, before Archie moved his career to a more collegiate environment in the States at the Univeristy. The British patrician's tradition of the old boy's network was not the only factor at play: they shared a powerful, trusting friendship and regularly wrote to each other.

"A condition of me paying for your trip is that you agree to spend two hours a week with Margot and an hour with a psychiatrist; you can rely on her implicitly. She is your godfather Archie's young American wife. Great fun and very clever. Like Archie, only much younger."

This was unashamed bribery but Tilly seemed very happy. Although she had only really met her godfather at family gatherings, they had immediately bonded when they had discovered a mutual passion for Pre-Raphaelite art. He had also taken her to Lords to watch cricket and there had been the occasional opera visit. She met Margot at a theatre visit and had liked her, too. Tarquin knew all this and immediately wrote to Archie enclosing a cheque to cover the costs of Tilly's sessions with Margot. A drip feed was the phrase he used to describe the equation which was to provide Tilly with money and the psychiatric help she so needed.

From the day she arrived in Barcelona and set up life with Paolo in his small apartment, Tilly's life was transformed. She gradually began to blossom intellectually, and any of the perversities of her adolescent behaviour began to disappear. She and Paolo managed to fit into each other's lives as if they had been created for each other. Tilly made no more emotionally charged demands of her parents. She lived within her meagre allowance, and she and Paolo worked and studied obsessively. They were very popular amongst their small group of friends and the ex-patriot community in general. Margot was seeing them regularly and was able to focus on repairing the emotional and psychological wounds of their dysfunctional childhoods – a common bond. All that awkward confrontational behaviour which had so characterised Tilly's life in Ireland was slowly being replaced by simple, enthusiastic, youthful charm. They were very happy together.

The encounter in Elvira's bar and Robert's story about her 'fight' with Paolo had been the first signs of any serious cause for anxiety about Tilly in months.

*Have I been missing something? Have I been duped by Robert? I wish I could remember whether the girl he was with that day in the Raval had been Tilly.*

# Chapter Five

The Gran Teatro del Liceu, Barcelona's great nineteenth century opera house, sits regally half way down Las Ramblas opposite the Metro station. It took Margot only five minutes to walk there from her office. She tried to reach Hugo and Eusebio to talk about Tilly, but their mobile 'phones were both switched off and the home number was permanently engaged. She had then 'phoned Archie to remind him that she would be late back that night. Archie told her a very funny, frivolous joke about a rabbit and a butcher. He succeeded in cheering her up and made her feel much more comfortable about going to the opera. She changed from her 'work' clothes into a stunning short, red dress.

Margot looked like one of those thin beauties in a Goya painting. Her short dark hair advertised her neat, geometrically proportioned shoulders. Her tiny nose and a witty seductive mouth opened out invitingly, especially when she threw back her head to laugh. She needed no make-up to look not a jot older than twenty-five, but she would apply a little pink lipstick when she went out in the evening. On this evening she had decided to wear a very simple silver necklace, a gift from her husband on their fifth wedding anniversary. It was warm enough to carry a diaphanous, hand-painted silk scarf to cover her bare, elegant shoulders. As she left her building and walked down the narrow street, away from the palm tree in the tiny square in front of it, she inhaled the balmy Mediterranean breeze with sensual anticipation. *Lucia di Lammermoor* was her favourite opera and Robert was usually a wonderful companion. His breathtaking knowledge of the opera canon verged on the annoying for anybody less passionate about music than

Margot, but she adored all his anecdotes about sopranos of the past and first night catastrophes. She loved his obsessions – the coloratura of Donizetti was one of them. Wallowing in the excitement of the early evening atmosphere wafting from the outdoor cafés on Las Ramblas, Margot had also completely forgotten about his mystery guest. She even broke a rule and threw a coin at the mime artist posing on the sidewalk. An elaborately costumed Harlequin.

Barcelona's chic bourgeois greeted each other with elaborate air-kisses in front of the neoclassical façade of the Liceu, as Margot slid through the foyer, up the white marble staircase flanked by stucco and bronze, and into the magnificent, red velvet splendour of the auditorium via the curtain of Robert's regular box. She had arrived early because she loved to sit beneath the gory, flamboyantly painted ceiling, faux Tiepolo, and watch as the audience filled the theatre. She relished the syncopated strains of the orchestra tuning their instruments. One of the cellos was picking out some bars from the sextet. The percussionist gently stroked his timpani. Did she hear a soprano's voice wafting from the wings? But Margot was thinking about Paolo and Domatilla.

Robert arrived, flustered and sheepish. He kissed her on the lips a little less zealously than when they had last seen each other, and his breath was back to normal. Margot smiled to herself like a small child at a treat as the fake candle-lights and candelabra in the auditorium began to fade.

"I am so sorry about this morning. I got home and crashed out. I felt awful when I woke and realised what an ass I had been. I have completely recovered."

"Where is your date, Robert? I thought that you had someone joining us," she whispered.

"I have no idea! And by the way he's not my date, he's yours!" he replied as the conductor entered to applause.

"My date! I keep telling you. I am very happily married, thank you very much."

"So am I! And how is darling Archie?"

"Shut up!" she snapped firmly, with her hallmark girlish and flirtatious giggle. "Archie sends his love," she hissed. And then Donizetti's powerful overture to *Lucia di Lammermoor* allowed Margot to wallow in the seductive passions of nineteenth century melodrama at its most palatable.

Boxes in opera houses are invariably disappointing. They restrict the view from one side of the stage and the seating is rarely comfortable, and their position fails to enhance the music. But one delightful advantage is that when the mind needs to wander away from the opera, or if the music becomes turgid or impenetrable, the orchestra pit provides a plethora of interesting characters to indulge some wild fantasies. The tenor on this occasion was fat and too old despite his magnificent Ukrainian voice, and Margot's concentration uncharacteristically wondered off towards the bewigged contra bassoonist who seemed to be flirting with one of the young cellists.

She had begun to think again about Tilly. Tilly was unique. She realised that despite the nature of their professional relationship she had come to love her as an older sister might have, or a special godmother. She had tried so hard to give her the benefit of all her special psychotherapeutic skills. This had meant tears and moments of severe antagonism but these more difficult elements in their relationship had been balanced by other, more celebratory moments, like the day she had arrived with Paolo and they had performed their Catalan rendition of the Pyramus and Thisbe comic tragedy from *A Midsummer's Night Dream*. Tilly was a great patient in that she had understood the needs for creative interactivity and unconditional trust. She had also responded so positively to Margot's insights. They had developed a fruitful bond and the handicaps caused by the utter craziness of her early life were slowly being replaced by a poetic and exciting sense that Tilly was on the verge of offering the world something very special. Especially in the world of art. Despite this, Margot was still haunted by her encounter in the morning, and her anxieties about Paolo and Tilly.

While these musings blended with the cadences of the music, Margot became aware of a new mysterious, warm and welcoming presence. She began to feel that somebody else was participating in her ruminations and the sense took hold that, both in her mind and in her body, another spirit was sharing her sentiments about Tilly. Unlike any unwelcome or threatening intrusion, this new emotional and physical presence was seductive and irresistible, her destiny. She was reluctant to come to terms with it physically but the music had begun to conspire with her mind. Instead of being a diversion, its powerful cadences began to overwhelm her, sexually. The soprano, a very beautiful, dark-haired Catalan, scantily clad and enveloped in misty moonlight, began to sing the opera's most celebrated aria, *'Regnava del silencio'.* A movie screen behind the set evoked her vision – a naked nymph, as if in a water ballet, submerged in a luxurious pool of aquamarine.

Margot could sense her nerve ends and body fluids beginning to provide that unmistakeable sensuality that came from the early glow of sexual excitement. Her lips were soft and moist, her nipples firm. She glanced furtively over to Robert – but he was caught up in the bosom of Lucia who was by then recalling the ghost of a mistress past. No, Robert could never have inspired the fresh, mysterious atmosphere which now so powerfully enveloped her. This was unique. As the diva's voice reached the climax of Lucia's dark nocturnal forebodings, a hand very gently brushed her face from behind, in a gesture designed to help wipe the tears which had been rolling down her face. She didn't jump up or resist. At first she ignored it – she wanted to continue to enjoy this sensation. She finally turned slowly and smiled: a dark-haired man had come through the velvet curtain at the rear of the box and was standing over her. The soft, reflective light from the stage was enough to allow Margot to register that he was tall, with bushy eyebrows which embellished a pair of kind blue eyes. He smiled back and sat down in the empty third chair directly behind her.

In what was no more than a millisecond, Margot's mind and body had moved out of that familiar, realistic space which had characterised her life until then. She had suddenly been overtaken by something so profound and unexpected, so much so, that even what might have been quite reasonable hesitation or normal reticence, evaporated immediately. All those moments that she had treasured as magical or spiritual and had been special for her – her first kiss, the joy and pride she felt at her parents' excitement when she had graduated, her wedding night with Archie and the happiness she had felt when she woke up on the first morning of her honeymoon in the beautiful dawn light in Ocho Rios in Jamaica – all the emotion and ecstasy connected with those beautiful memories were immediately transcended by the sensations aroused when she looked so fleetingly into this stranger's face. It was as if he had seen into her soul in a way that no one ever had before.

Margot was now spiritually and physically overwhelmed, and powerfully connected to this man she had never met. He had silently exploded into her life. She could hear him shifting in his seat. She could smell the clean cotton of his shirt. She could feel his knees very gently and accidentally touching the back of her dress; he moved them so slightly to avoid the contact. She turned to give him her programme, which had dropped to the floor. He reached down to retrieve it for her. He was impeccably dressed in a dinner jacket and black tie. His hair brushed almost imperceptibly against her legs as they both bent down to retrieve the programme. Her body trembled, as if close to an orgasm. She had never been so aware of her sexuality. She had never felt so exhilarated and uncharacteristically discombobulated. She fumbled for Robert's opera glasses on the ledge at the front of the box and tried to re-engage with the powerful spell of the Bride of Lammermoor on stage. Mercifully, the orchestra and singers' crescendos climaxed and the curtain fell. Margot was oblivious to the rapturous applause until Robert tapped her on the shoulder and gestured to the back of the box. The lights in the chandeliers in the magnificent theatre faded up and Margot was formally introduced to Xavier.

"That is the first time I have ever known you to use my opera glasses."

Margot giggled nervously. "The Lucia is so beautiful!"

"More than can be said about poor old Delgardo."

Xavier was immediately defensive. "But he has a gorgeous tenor voice!"

Again Margot giggled. "Gorgeous!" And smiled at him, shyly.

Intervals during operas have always been opportunities for social intercourse. At the Liceu, a nineteenth century reconstruction of a theatre which had been host to Handel, Rossini and Albinoni during Barcelona's pre-eminence as a rich trading port, each floor has a circular corridor which articulates society's bourgeois tendencies to this day. Like a post-modern Tower of Babel, from the over-dressed peacocks who inhabit the promenades on the first two floors, to the hoi-poloi whose more modest passions are concerned more with the love of music, excited babbling tongues intermingle with surreptitious hushed declarations of passion and lust. Robert's regular box, a Christmas gift from a rich friend, was in a prime situation on the first floor and allowed him, and his guests, both the privilege of privacy within it and the opportunity for lascivious flirting amongst the cosmopolitan rich and powerful. He loved to go to the bar and collect the champagne he had ordered; he loved the throng. He left his guests in the intimacy of the box and the emptiness of the auditorium.

Margot and Xavier sat in silence. She was almost breathless. She had taken in the physical presence of this brooding stranger before she had looked at him. The rich, reflective red of the velvet walls had given his face the appearance of a moody chiaroscuro portrait. His penetrating, dark blue eyes twinkled mischievously from behind the shadows cast on his dark eyebrows. He smiled, lifted her left hand and raised her wedding ring towards his pink, full lips and at the same time gently, almost imperceptibly, caressed her fingers. Skin on skin. He lingered just enough to send an electrifying tingle from the tip of her finger to her left nipple as if it had been gently tweaked.

"Who is the lucky man?" he asked her.

His voice was mischievous. Margot laughed nervously again and returned his smile. Her body almost exploded and she began to stumble with her words.

"Archie? He's my... my rock...!"

She casually fingered her wedding ring again. He took her finger gently, admiring the ring, and then smiled. She pulled her hand away.

"So beautiful."

"Thank you."

Robert had returned with a silver tray and began to peel the silver paper from a bottle of Cava. He was quick to fill in.

"He is a 'gorgeous', brilliant, funny Scotsman who combines a job teaching Spanish history at the university here with a business buying and selling beautiful paintings... He works with Sotheby's in London and New York."

"And what about you, Margot?"

Margot seized her chance to disguise the overwhelming physical attraction she felt for Xavier with professional banter.

"I spend my time talking to psychologically damaged ex-patriots. And they are not all rich Americans hiding from the embarrassments of their ill gotten gains... pretending to be on some sort of modernista grand tour... or a handful of desperate trustafarians from Notting Hill who dabble in video art."

"Xavier is an ex-pat, and an artist of sorts."

Robert was trying to break the palpable sexual tension. He had effortlessly prized the cork out of the bottle and was now pouring the Cava as pedantically as a restaurant sommelier.

"No, no. I am an amateur! I can't even draw."

"I don't believe you. You must invite Margot to see your apartment. It's a shrine."

"A shrine suggests something religious? Are you a priest?" Another girlish giggle.

"I have a very quiet private life rather like a priest's, I suppose!"

Xavier chuckled as Robert gave him a glass. The Cava glistened on his lips. Margot wanted to kiss him gently, and run her tongue across those lips.

"May I have some too, please, Robert?"

"That's a first. You always say that it sends you to sleep."

"It won't tonight. Too much on my mind."

Robert poured, and they chinked their glasses. Margot and Xavier locked eyes and almost as if she felt guilty, she repeated the gesture for Robert.

"I am hardly a priest but I am passionate about the work made by all those American sixties artists who are enjoying a bit of a revival here in Barcelona."

"You mean painters like Andy Warhol and Roy Lichtenstein?"

"As much as I like them, no! I mean performance artists and the early, experimental filmmakers. Video art."

Margot began a private fantasy where Xavier had moved into her arms and had begun to unclasp her silver necklace, unzipping her dress. She so wanted to kiss his eyes and his lips.

"Andy Warhol made movies and organised happenings," Robert chirped in, oblivious to the sensual foreplay Margot and Xavier were now enjoying, thinly disguised with their frivolous chit chat.

"True, Robert, of course. But there were others... I'll show you my studio tomorrow, if you like? After lunch?"

His eyebrows had moved enough to suggest that unless she had a very good reason, Margot had no alternative. They were going to be lovers.

"I'd like that."

They settled down to watch the boulevardiers return to their seats. A violin was picking out the chords of Lucia's suicidal aria, as the percussionist gently adjusted the timbre of his kettledrum. The conductor entered to applause and the lights went down.

Robert reached out for Margot's hand. He squeezed it but she drew away and moved her chair back to within an inch of Xavier's long body. She looked behind her and he smiled again. This time, he looked into her luxurious and inquisitive eyes. She smiled and whispered:

"I know very little about video art!"

Margot noticed that Robert had been looking at his watch regularly. He began to fidget, uncharacteristically. During the sextet, usually a scene which, if performed well, earns rapt, silent attention from the audience, Robert leant back and whispered into Xavier's ear a couple of times. As the audience erupted into tumultuous applause, he shot up, apologised for leaving early, kissed Margot very peremptorily on her cheeks, and left, whispering that he would see her at her office in the morning.

Xavier moved into Robert's seat and within a minute or two the sexual charge which had been interrupted by Robert's departure reignited. The guilty pleasure returned and Margot quite literally and physically had to control the outward expressions of a powerful, internalised orgasm. When she had calmed down, Margot resisted any further flirtation. She almost ran from the box like a scalded cat when the curtain came down, making a flimsy excuse about a dinner date with her husband.

Xavier laughed. "*Cal Maño* in the Barceloneta. One o'clock tomorrow!"

Margot had lied about her dinner date. She all but ran to the ladies' toilets and locked herself in a cubicle. While she caressed her hard nipples and massaged her soaking vagina, she rang Robert on the mobile and left an ironic voice message.

"Roberto! What are you playing at? Where did you go? You abandoned me to a wolf. You will have to come up with a very plausible excuse. Ciao, ciao!"

# Chapter Six

Margot walked slowly through the boisterous nightlife of the Raval, and wound her way up the steep, small street which led home. She opened the front door as silently as she could, but Archie grunted her a greeting.

"You're early. I thought that you were going to have dinner with Robert?"

"He rushed off. I walked home."

She went into the kitchen and was boiling a kettle when Archie appeared in his pyjamas. She jumped up with a shout.

"Lost in my thoughts!"

"Come to bed, Margot."

"Soon, darling... I promise!"

She poured a cup of hot water and sliced a lemon for it, avoiding his eyes. He kissed her goodnight from behind and shuffled off. Margot was beginning to feel guilty. She poured her drink down the sink and tiptoed down the corridor to the bathroom, shedding her clothes. After a very speedy mouthwash, she climbed into bed next to Archie. He was snoring.

She closed her eyes.

*I love Archie and wouldn't want to be married to anyone else. He is in so many ways an ideal husband; so funny, so quaint, so energetic, and so clever. I will never forget the moment I realised that I wanted to go to*

bed with him. He was sitting at the end of a table in a small restaurant near my campus with a couple of very pretty girls on either side. He was ignoring their slightly annoying attempts to persuade him to flirt with them. He is a handsome, quirky looking man and at that time he was in his early fifties and had made Chicago, or the Windy City as he insisted on calling it, his home for some years. Despite this he had retained his rather eccentric European accent. Overweight and bald, but in no way self-conscious about it, he was using his magical talent to make us laugh. He told a great story about having a passionate and complicated affair with Peggy Guggenheim in the Venice of the 1950's when she was at least twenty years older than he was – I had wondered later if this had been his subtle attempt to flirt with me. He is twenty-five years older than myself, and the moral of his story was quite clear: older women (and men) are wonderful lovers.

He followed that story with a witty anecdote about Salvador Dali – apparently he once appeared in the dining room at the Carlton Hotel in Cannes in a fur coat and a black tie and refused to allow the waiter to remove his magnificent mink until he was seated at the best and most prominent table in the room. He sat down and proceeded to regale the hotel for its silly policy of insisting on the wearing of ties in the restaurant. He then beckoned imperiously to the exasperated maitre d'hôtel and told him that he was now too hot. He insisted on removing his fur and in a grand theatrical sweep of his arms, he revealed that he was wearing nothing except the bow tie. He then parked his completely naked, corpulent body back in the seat at his table. In the company of two stunning prostitutes, one a tall Algerian man and the other an Italian nymphet, he ordered two lobsters, washed them down with a bottle of champagne and announced flamboyantly that he was going to fuck them both.

*How true the story was didn't matter. Archie told it with such wit. His language was peppered with arcane peculiarities and his Venetian accent, tinged with a light Scottish brogue, was so compulsively sexy. His mischievous, enthusiastic laugh was a very powerful aphrodisiac. Within weeks I had begun to sneak into his Spanish History classes – they were de rigueur for the cognoscenti at Chicago then, and I plucked up the courage to ask him to dinner.*

*"Only if you marry me!" was his reply.*

*Our wedding took place in Barcelona's Santa Maria Catedral and until now we have had five years of happiness, the like of which most married couples might only experience for a couple of weeks during their honeymoon. He is very proud of his chair at the University in Barcelona. "I am a Scottish Italian ice-cream maker's son, for Christ's sake! Who could have guessed that I would become the foremost authority on Catalan history?" And he takes his responsibilities there very seriously.*

*He also has a powerful homosexual charisma and he relishes my harmless flirtatiousness as much as I enjoy the outrageous way in which he uses his sexuality to charm his young collegiate in the classroom. Of course we have secrets. Of course we flirt with others. But the notion of infidelity has never once entered my head and I am absolutely certain that Archie decided to completely curb the promiscuity of his complicated love life in Chicago after we became lovers. We made an early pact to reduce long confessionals about the sins of our past lives.*

*Who could resist a man whose idea for a weekend birthday treat to London involved a costume re-enactment of Pushkin's duel on Hampstead Heath, a swim in the mixed pond there, picnic lobster lunch, sex in Claridges and This Is Spinal Tap at the Everyman?*

*What I adore about Archie is that he can abandon his flamboyance without ever losing his sense of humour. My birthday present to him last year was a new bicycle. He insisted on joining a tourists' bicycle tour of the city pretending to be, by tactful arrangement with the organisers, the tour guide. Never for a second either pretentious or patronising, he explained to the lucky, unsuspecting throng of backpackers that the new bike was his birthday present and this tour was the perfect way to break it in. He explained that if they felt dissatisfied with his services, which would include Catalan, Castilian and English translations, they would receive a refund. Little did they know how erudite and expert a guide he would prove to be. We used their enormous tips to buy a celebratory brunch at The Arts.*

*Our small apartment in the Montjuic overlooking the Barcelona harbour is a haven for our very select circle of special friends and our sanctuary, away from the pressures of our professional lives. I rarely discuss my work with Archie and he never asks me about the time I spend away from him, except in the most superficial way. (For instance, he knows about my Platonic friendship with Robert, and knows that I have a favourite breakfast café in the Barri Gotic from which he is barred). In all other respects, we have separate lives during the working week. I live a somewhat schizophrenic existence, embroiled as I am in the complexities of my patients' minds. He combines his work at the University with his passion for Spanish art and his beloved Pre Raphaelite painters about whom he knows more than the most anal of Victorian art historians.*

*As such, our marriage is primarily acted out and enjoyed when we are cocooned in the haven of our apartment or when I make the rare forays into Archie's academic world at those university functions involving wives and families. More often than not, the ensuing socialising revolves around the politics of the university, and almost always involves people of Archie's generation and status. I play the part as much as I can, but Archie is usually smart enough to know that he can't take me for granted. He never insists that I pitch up or participate in much of the conversational banter and so is always forgiving when I bow out or sneak off early for an evening on my own at home. I would feel much more selfish about this if I didn't compensate with my 'hostess with the mostest' persona, which I provide when we entertain his friends and academic colleagues at home. I stay quiet when they hold court, and reconciliatory when the inevitable after-dinner philosophical discussions descend into the aggressive banter which can lead to fisticuffs at dawn. And when they have gone, I love to unpick the subtext of our guests' lives for Archie's considerable amusement using my analytical skills, spinning sometimes fanciful theories about people we hardly know. In that sense it has all been working rather well, but recently I had begun to realise that outside of my group of patients and Elvira, I had made no new friends in Barcelona of my own age, and I seemed trapped, anachronistically, in a world of a bygone era when it comes to our social life. Even our evenings at home alone tend to be dominated by his obsessions.*

*The plethora of experiences which Archie has always so generously shared with me tend to revolve around his subjects – European and Spanish history. In recreation, his fields of expertise and passion are again in elitist and rarefied arenas – Victorian art and baroque opera. At first, there was an exoticism which fascinated me about all these subjects, which were so refreshing and diverting for a woman caught up professionally in the neuroses and dysfunctions of her clients' lives. I relished it all and gobbled up all the knowledge I could, gratefully and lovingly; Archie is so entertaining in that sense. But something has recently begun to bother me. What had previously been almost magically alive was becoming stale and dull. Everything Archie was interested in seemed to be rooted in the past. And, of course, his own terms of cultural reference as a young man were all hinged in an era at least two decades before I was born. I had increasingly noticed that I was completely out of touch with the cultural tastes and fads of my own peer group, my generation. In a round-up in the foreign edition of The Guardian of films, music and novels created by artists of my own age, I was appalled to discover that I had almost no knowledge at all of the names of the creative people who were part of my generation, let alone any exposure to their contemporary work. This niggled me, frustrated me. But there was also another suppressed and alarming new phenomenon about my life with Archie. And a potential catalyst for a disaster I was determined to avoid.*

*When we first met, sex had also been a delightful part of our after dinner-party ritual. I have always found Archie physically attractive and loved this part of our marriage. Sex had been great, even if, on the whole, it had been somewhat unadventurous and conventional. This had never bothered me. I fancied him and he satisfied me physically. But Archie's sexual appetite for me during the first few years of our relationship in Chicago had gradually begun to diminish here in Barcelona. It wasn't as if he didn't desire me, didn't want to have sex with me, but when we try now to reach the heights of passion which had so characterised our early relationship, he seems only able to satisfy himself, and I lie there afterwards listening to drunken snores (another unpleasant trait he has developed), feeling somewhat short-changed. I rarely reach my climax, for example – unheard of in the first years of our sexual life – and quite often Archie's penis is now too limp to enter me. I made a light joke at breakfast once about his homosexual inclinations and he nearly bit my head off. "I am the most heterosexual man I know," he quipped in an uncharacteristically defensive tone.*

*Of course, I feel bad but I have begun to fantasise and have cravings for some uncomplicated, compensating balance. I want to shift my fantasies into some sort of comfortable reality which won't disturb the otherwise perfect aspects of my life here. Too much of my social life revolves around Archie's friends, and I miss physical interaction with younger, more virile men of my own age. Flirting with Archie's older friends is hardly a substitute. The opportunity, the need, to discover that life has something else more desirable, some other pleasure to offer, which could be indulged without harming or prejudicing my marriage, has finally become more than just a temptation. It has always been feasible on the practical front. Is it now finally irresistible?*

*In the context of my experience at the opera house, Xavier and all that he represents could become an exciting complement, and need not be a perverse threat. I can be joyously in control and passionately out of control. Xavier will be my most exquisite secret. A taboo to be transgressed which can reinforce the taboo. In that sense, am I dangerously close to opening that Pandora's box of the perverted and heightened sexuality which has characterised so much of the deviant lives of my patients? Deviant sexual behaviour, which has until now only been the object of my professional prurience.*

# Chapter Seven

The night watchman had telephoned the emergency services. He had been asked to look around for something which might give some tiny clue as to the identities of the victims. On a chair close to their bodies, he found a red document folder. It contained a neatly typed film script. He had told the officer on duty that he could hardly read it. English. He was Catalan. He managed to pick out the words St. Eulalia from the first two lines in very broken English and he read out a Barcelona address which had been printed below the title on the front cover.

✳

Sirens...

At break-neck speed, a strange motorcade sped through the empty streets of the Diagonal – Barcelona's perfectly proportioned modernista district. Guiding two police cars and two ambulances towards the city's outskirts, was a lone rider on a Vespa, like a latter-day Horseman of the Apocalypse, also in police uniform. He signalled every direction change, ominously slowing down and waving his arm emphatically, dangerously. At one corner of the industrial estate they had begun to penetrate, he drove his scooter so tightly around the bend that the wheels were touching the ground horizontally. When he finally stopped, he leapt off the bike, gesturing towards the nondescript aquamarine of a small, modern warehouse. At first, nobody knew where to go or what to do. No sign of the night watchman. Inspector Carlos Mendoza, the senior police officer on duty, shouted something in Catalan about procedures.

Finally, the younger policeman who had led them there wrenched off his helmet and pointed towards what looked like a make-shift area, partitioned away from the abstraction of the commercial storage units which proliferated the untidy floor of the warehouse.

Underneath the crude temporary strip lighting which bathed the centre of the room they had entered, a blood-soaked futon was positioned on a pallet. Above the futon was a crucifix in the style of St. Andrew's cross, and nailed to the cross, a beautiful, dark haired and olive skinned boy, no older than twenty-one. Paolo. His mouth was crammed with a blood-soaked cloth. Slumped and tied like an animal at the foot of the crucifix was the limp body of a red-haired girl, a few years younger than the boy. It was Tilly. Next to her tiny frame was an expensive professional digital video camera, a computer, a mobile 'phone and a smaller amateur camcorder. The room looked like the aftermath of some ghastly re-enactment of a religious scene from a bad Hollywood sexploitation film. There was still no sign of the night watchman.

One of the younger policemen vomited. Carlos had now reached the girl's body.

"For fuck's sake!" he shouted. "She is still alive."

He screamed at the group around him who had been numbed by this horrendous tableau.

"Take him down!"

Carlos was now shouting in Spanish and Catalan. The policemen awkwardly began to disassemble the crucifix.

"And don't touch anything without gloves."

It was clear that Paolo was dead.

Three anorak-clad porters rushed Tilly out on a gurney and Carlos followed into the back of their ambulance as a doctor administered intravenous medication. Tilly was mumbling. She seemed to be begging Carlos. Insisting.

"Hugo… Hugo… my brother… Milliken… please, call Hugo. I must see Hugo."

And she finally bleated out an address in the Diagonal, and a phone number, as they sped away from the warehouse.

The ambulance crew and Carlos had a quandary: would she survive the journey to the hospital and to what extent was the ambulance equipped to save her life? Nobody knew, so they decided to split the motorcade. Tilly would go directly to the nearest hospital at the seafront while Carlos fetched her brother from the address Tilly had managed to bleat out. He tried Hugo's phone number unsuccessfully.

More sirens…

Hugo wound himself reluctantly out of Emma's sleepy embrace. Her dark, waist-length hair had entrapped his creamy-white, aquiline body. The persistent whine of an approaching police siren would not normally have bothered Hugo, but the blue light now flashing around the speckle of dawn which bathed his room had been enough to drag him out of bed. He gently kissed her pink lips.

"Come back, I want you inside me," she sighed.

"Greedy! Some idiot is ringing the doorbell. Maybe it's Eusebio. Coming in from the celebrations. He said that he was going to stay in the city last night."

"No, he's back. I heard him come in late."

Wrapped in his silky, red and black dressing gown, Hugo stumbled through the wood-panelled corridors of his labyrinthine apartment and opened the heavy, oak door which led to the magical staircase of this beautiful Gaudi building. Emma slipped out of bed and went into the bathroom.

"Good morning! It's five in the morning! Dawn!"

Shyly combing his blonde hair with his long fingers, he forced out the greeting with a languid, reluctant drawl which pinned him into the anachronistic ghetto of the English upper classes. In his perfectly inflected English, Carlos, a large, craggy-looking Catalan wearing an ill-fitting, dark blue uniform and white shirt, apologised politely for waking him so early and showed his Mossos D'Esquadros credentials.

"My name is Inspector Carlos Mendoza. Is your name Señor Milliken? We need you to come with us urgently. Do you have a sister called Tilly... or Domatilla...?"

Within a couple of minutes of Carlos' very sparse but effective explanation, Hugo, Eusebio and Emma were pinned tightly into the open-topped Porsche, following at speed another strange police motorcade which made its way to Barcelona's Hospitale de Mare. When they arrived at the white, post-modern buildings which look out over the Mediterranean, the ambulance which had carried Tilly was waiting outside the main gates. Its doors were open and the same three, anorak-clad porters hung around, smoking. Carlos looked into their faces. One of them shook his head as Carlos went over to talk to them. The decision to make the trip to the hospital had not saved Tilly's life.

Another ambulance arrived as if to signal some sort of hope. Emma tugged at Hugo, who was still in his dressing gown. She looked like a Pre-Raphaelite mediaeval fantasy – almost naked in a diaphanous slip, vulnerable, ravished and about to confront a sensual and prophetic apparition. She clung to Eusebio. They were all bewildered. Numb. The doors opened and another gurney was wheeled out.

"Paolo?"

The body passed them on its way to the hospital morgue. Hugo lifted the makeshift shroud which was soaked in blood. Emma's screams of recognition were terrifyingly unpoetic. In sharp contrast, her beloved brother's pale face had the lifeless beauty of a Christ in a Botticello.

"No sense of urgency!" said Eusebio.

"No point!"

Hugo wept pathetically as they all fell into a prolonged embrace.

# Chapter Eight

On her way down the Montjuic, Margot had heard the early morning police sirens, but these were familiar urban incursions, and like most of us she usually took no notice. A green and yellow ambulance, followed by a peculiar motorcade which included two scooters, one of them a policeman, whined its way around the column towards the empty boulevard which stretched away from the Barri Gotic towards the Barceloneta – a reclaimed peninsular of tenements and a beautiful beachfront promenade. For some reason, Margot watched this bizarre and isolated clump of vehicles speed past. Some desperate attempt to keep someone alive, no doubt. Too many cars for a premature delivery. And then, as usual, she crossed over to the centre aisle of the Colom.

Tuesday mornings in the studio were always kept aside for Tilly and Paolo. They were usually punctual. They loved to tease her about the strict routine of their two, fifty-minute, consecutive periods. Paolo called them the 'shrinking hours' – on one occasion he brought a stopwatch into his session which he kept checking every ten minutes. She left messages for both of them on their mobile 'phones as she ambled along Las Ramblas towards Elvira's café. The same message for each answering service.

"I love you both. I can't wait to see you as usual today."

*Perhaps Tilly has persuaded Paolo to come with her after all.*

Elvira was very busy. She welcomed Margot but rolled her eyes as she continued to serve the clutter of two very exotically-dressed families that had crowded into the bar that morning. Apparently, there was to be a civil wedding in the Plaça St. Jaume. The bride, a pretty curvaceous

German in a pink tutu which looked like a reject from the costume department at the Liceu, was playing one of the fruit machines with her two younger sisters. Her tall groom, smoking nervously with his father at the bar, was a very elegant young Nigerian. They were dressed in white suits. Margot watched the families that hovered around them, trying to come to terms with each other. High-pitched laughter mixed with awkward silences.

She really wanted to tell Elvira about Xavier. In the absence of her supervisor, there was no-one else she could confide in. She tried to reach Tilly and Paolo but again there was no response. This was very unusual as they always returned her calls quickly. Feeling anxious about them, she decided to go to the studio earlier than usual. She air-kissed Elvira, wished the bride and groom good luck and hurried out. When she arrived there were no messages for her on the answering service, except one from Xavier reminding her of their date. She rang Robert and left a caustic thank you message: "You hurried off. Hot date?"

After taking a shower, she lay back in the chair usually used by her clients and dozed off, not waking until nearly lunchtime. She fixed her hair, sprayed a little perfume around her shoulders and rushed out into the bright sunlight now bathing the square below her studio. As she hurried along the harbour front towards the beach, she tried Tilly and Paolo's mobile 'phones again. This time, neither phone delivered the usual answering messages (they had recorded simple messages in English. Paolo for Tilly and Tilly for Paolo: "Please leave a message for us and we will get back to you!"). She rang Robert again. "Do you know where Tilly is? She didn't pitch up this morning. Nor did Paolo."

⁜

Xavier was already seated when Margot arrived. They had decided to meet in Cal Maño, one of the small old fish restaurants in the Barceloneta. At first she couldn't find him – the tables were crammed into two tiny areas with the open kitchen adjacent to the back room. The old proprietor marshalled his clients haphazardly and there was no preferential hierarchy, but he recognised Margot and showed her immediately to a small table near the fruit machine in the front. She waited anxiously, watching the chaos with detached amusement, and then decided to go to the tiny bathroom, which was no more than a broom cupboard. Xavier watched her negotiate the gaps between the tables and the sweaty chefs who were preparing their production line of cheap cuttlefish, red mullet, aubergines and bean soup which had made this restaurant so popular. But he made no move. When she had closed the door of the cubicle, he beckoned to the nearest waiter who nodded and immediately brought him a bottle of white wine, some bread, mineral water and two menus. This was obviously a familiar routine.

Margot finally emerged and saw Xavier, who seemed to be preoccupied with a newspaper. He stood up, helped her efficiently into the chair opposite him and poured her a glass of wine. They sat looking at each other and he finally broke the silence with a broad, welcoming smile. Margot uncrossed her legs and in doing so, found that his legs were wide apart on either side of hers. Her dress was riding high. She inched her chair closer to the table and her naked right knee lightly brushed his left thigh. As if to register this, Xavier kissed her ring finger. No wedding ring today. She looked down and up again to his eyes. It was Xavier who spoke first.

"I don't normally drink at lunchtime! I don't normally drink at all, but I do make the odd exception for very special occasions. I am so sorry. I was being rather presumptuous..."

"No, no. Perfect. Thank you. I have had a rather strange morning. I dozed off in my studio. Two of my clients failed to show. Very rare. "

"I can't imagine anyone letting you down deliberately. I would imagine that you are the kind of person who inspires compulsive behaviour. I am sure there are good reasons."

"I am sure, but thank you."

She drained her glass quickly and he poured her a second. She prolonged each sip of the dry white wine, allowing its crisp, chilled texture to linger on her palate. Her lips glistened, her skin was alive. She could feel her nipples hardening and the tip of her clitoris was tingling with anticipation. Her vagina was soaking wet and she smelt of sexual excitement. She was enjoying every new sensation, and surreptitiously moved her hand to within inches of Xavier's arm which now rested across the table. Margot fished pathetically for a way to temper the sexual atmosphere with some clever conversation.

"This reminds me of my favourite Marguerite Duras story about a woman who can't help returning to the scene of a crime which took place in a bar, a murder, with her small child, and she keeps knocking back glasses of red wine..."

He laughed: "Why did she do that?"

"I have absolutely no idea!"

Another pause. She took his hand and kissed his fingers as if to give him permission to do whatever he wanted to her.

"I have ordered."

"Are you always so self-confident?"

"I am."

She laughed. The waiter brought some grilled squid and fried tomatoes.

"I like to play elaborate games."

"What sort of games?"

"Games which involve a modicum of danger combined with an enormous amount of sexual pleasure."

"Danger? I've never played games like that before. Sexual pleasure, maybe..."

"Would you like to start?"

"You'll have to teach me the rules as I go along."

They began to play with each other, marking time.

"You're an immensely beautiful young woman, Margot."

"You say that to all your conquests."

"No, I don't. Are you a conquest?"

"Not yet..."

Silence. Someone laughed rather loudly in the kitchen.

"They smoke while they cook here and nobody seems to mind."

"The food is delicious. Thank you."

"I hope that you'll allow me to initiate you into our first game this afternoon."

"You are an immensely beautiful and very dangerous man, Xavier."

"How can you resist that?"

"Impossible!"

They laughed while the waiter brought their soup. Xavier poured Margot more wine and sipped his glass of water. By now, Margot had become totally unaware of the environment – the clatter and chatter, the eclectic crowd, the smell from the kitchens and the general mayhem encouraged by the waiters within. She could see only his mouth and his eyes, and occasionally she looked down at his craggy hands. They were very expressive and he peppered his conversation with occasional, disarming bursts of laughter. He paid her compliments and asked many questions about her life and her relationships. Margot enjoyed his curiosity, and his intimate analysis. She told him about her relationship with Archie, and with Robert. He was gentle and attentive.

"I'm not used to talking about myself."

"Don't worry. It is very charming. I was listening carefully to your voice at the opera house. Your accent still has strong traces of its Californian origins. But the language is obviously beginning to be very mid-European."

"My clients expect me to engage with them as if I was their friend as much as their confidante, but I never really allow many of them to have much of look-in, a glimpse of my own life. Certainly not in any intimate way, although I am sure they have their theories! I am necessarily very secretive in that sense. I've told you more about myself today than even friends like Robert really know about me."

"Do you think that they tell you the truth about their lives?"

"Not always. But I probe. 'What is truth said jesting Pilate and would not stay for an answer'. One of my Dad's favourite quotations."

"Alexander Pope?"

"No! Francis Bacon!"

Xavier laughed again. More silence. Looking slyly into her eyes, he discreetly moved both legs to circle hers and tightened them firmly around her right thigh while he squeezed her left arm with his fingers. Margot had been captured, kidnapped, seduced, overwhelmed. She drained the bottle of wine.

"There are a few important rules for this afternoon's game and they are very simple. You can start the game when you choose to, you can indulge it for as long as you want, you can play hard, play fast, play slow – you set the pace and, most important of all, you can stop play whenever you choose."

"Like a referee?"

"No! Good referees know all the rules!"

"Do you think that I might be good at this?"

"Absolutely no question about that."

The waiter brought the bill and Xavier stood up to pay. He pulled back her chair and gave her a card. "This is my address in the Barri Gotic close to the Santa Maria del Pi. I will see you at my apartment in an hour."

"Where are you going?"

"My secret!"

"But I am drunk. I will never find it."

"Of course you will."

"I have to be back in my office at five."

"I live two minutes away."

Margot smiled. "An introductory game?"

He ignored her. "See you in an hour and if you don't turn up you will never see me again."

He kissed her lightly on the lips and walked out towards the toilet. He looked around and laughed. All Margot's senses were now as responsive as they had ever been. She felt as if she was going to explode. She looked around the restaurant. Margot often came across people she knew in her favourite places in Barcelona. She and Archie had a very wide circle of friends. And so she became self-conscious. Nervous. Furtive. The proprietor noticed this and offered her a digestif.

"Non! Non, graçias!"

She blushed and stumbled out to the street. It was a stunning afternoon. Margot remembered reading somewhere that the crisp air and light atmosphere of cold sunny days in the early spring were very powerful aphrodisiacs. She inhaled deeply and went back to her consulting room to prepare for Xavier's rituals, whatever they were to be.

Almost by default she went to her answer 'phone and casually prodded it into action. The first message was a 'please return my call' plea from Carlos Mendoza who explained that he was Elvira's policeman husband. She paused the machine, kicked off her shoes and began to undress. Carlos had never called her before. They had never met. Part of her pact with Elvira was that they kept their husbands out of their friendship. She scribbled down his number with a frown and listened to the next missed call: a suggestive, lascivious message from Robert, making some sly comment about the sexual frisson which had so obviously existed between her and Xavier at the Liceu. And no, he didn't know where Tilly and Paolo might be. "Why should I?" Surely no connection with the call from Carlos?

Now naked, she dismissed that idea, punched at the off button of the machine and walked quickly to her shower room and washed her hair, keen to prepare for her encounter with Xavier. While the warm water poured over her skin, she gently probed and massaged every erogenous zone on her lean, perfectly proportioned body. She sprayed her vagina with Chanel. Her nipples were still erect. Her breasts firm. Her lips soft. Her legs apart. She then slid into a simple, short, red summer dress. No make up. A leather belt and a long, black, soft velvet coat.

Normally, a walk along the streets across the Plaça Reial into the patchwork of ancient buildings behind the Santa Maria del Pi is a pleasure Margot associated with her passion for drinking the gooey chocolate served in a café hidden within a stone's throw of the fruit and vegetable market off Las Ramblas. This afternoon she shook with a mysterious combination of carelessness, fear, lust and guilty conscience. Even her customary wave as she walked through the little hole in the wall leading into Elvira's bar was a perfunctory gesture. Elvira was a devout Roman Catholic and would have been horrified to know that her *amiga americana especial* was about to commit *adulterio* with a man she hardly knew, within fifty yards of her neighbourhood church. But Margot had made her decision. She wanted Xavier and wanted to play his game, and damn the consequences. Peculiar and mystical influences seemed to be swirling around her life, which added to her determination to indulge herself, to extend, to take risks. She was already addicted. She craved her first 'fix'.

Xavier answered the intercom with her name and she pushed the heavy glass and wrought-iron, art deco door into a large, warmly-lit hallway with a marble staircase to the left, an old wooden framed elevator opposite the doorway and a dark corridor to the right. He was standing at an open door. He had changed into black jeans and white cotton shirt. Margot noticed that his feet were bare as she walked towards him slowly, deliberately luxuriating in the excitement and anticipation.

Nothing that anybody could have described to her would have matched the extraordinary environment he had created for his living space.

"You must see my frogs and then I will give you a guided tour."

"Frogs? Are they part of our game?"

"They watch. And listen."

He removed her coat and kissed her lips very gently. "Come!"

They walked through what could be loosely described as a studio area, then through what appeared to be a workshop and out into a terrace. The afternoon sun penetrated the entire space through beautifully designed skylights which had been constructed above a raised bedroom area. This was cluttered with objects. Statues. Old projectors. Video installations. Old lamps. Antiquities. Photographs. Paintings. An easel. And computers everywhere. She noticed a gurney and three or four trolleys of differing heights and sizes – medical trolleys and the kind of aluminium trolley you might see in the kitchen of a modern restaurant. There was even a wheelchair placed behind some electronic paraphernalia that Margot recognised from her trips to the optician.

"Don't worry, I will show you some of this later; I want to introduce you to my frogs first!"

In the 'garden', which was also cluttered with antiquities, was a small fountain in the centre of a pond, around which sat several enormous frogs. One of them jumped into the pond when Margot spoke.

"I have never seen such huge frogs!"

Xavier laughed. "I feed them well! Do you like my arboretum?" he was referring to the myriad trees, palms and plant life which contributed to the clutter.

"How do you keep it all alive during the winter?"

Xavier walked to the side of the terrace and pushed a button. A glass canopy appeared silently from within the tiled roofing above the extension he had built, which extended behind the building. The terraced area outside was now completely sealed off like a greenhouse.

"All of Barcelona's buildings extend generously behind their façades," he explained, as if to anticipate her curiosity. Xavier obviously had some access to two floors which allowed him what was effectively a two-storey extension.

"This is amazing, Xavier. Do you own both floors?"

"Yes, I do!"

Margot floated around his strange space with no real sense of time or space. Robert had called it a shrine, implying something religious.

In that sense she felt like a nubile nun, about to be initiated by the High Priest into a ritual which would transcend any previous religious experiences.

"Shall we can begin our little game? It is a variation of a children's game called Snakes and Ladders. But instead of the dice, we use our imagination. And instead of a board, we have my apartment. You roll the dice in your imagination and tell me what number between one and twelve arrives in your mind. And I correspondingly guide you to the next stage on the playing space. Metaphors. Concepts. Fantasy. At each spot that your number has led us to, I prescribe some behaviour which we must both indulge in. We will begin at the beginner's level. Nothing too extreme. Do you remember my rules?"

"No," she lied. But she was happy to obey them, whatever they might be.

"You can start the game when you choose to, you can indulge it for as long as you want, you can play hard, play fast, play slow – you set the pace and most important of all, you can stop play whenever you choose."

Margot smiled and closed her eyes. He kissed her again and on this occasion she parted her lips and gently kissed him back, allowing her mouth to open just enough take his tongue and play with hers. He took her in his arms. She whispered to him. "I have just rolled my dice. Seven!"

Xavier paused for thought and pulled away. "Seven? Interesting... Seven Brides for Seven Brothers."

He took her hand, kissed the nape of her neck, her ear and then led her by the arm inside to the workshop area. He pulled a large carpenter's trolley from below a work surface to reveal a range of what looked like ancient farm implements. Obscure, unfamiliar, dangerous, sharp. Some of them were rusty, some gleaming steel or aluminium. Some of them were made in wood. One of them looked like a corkscrew, yet another had some leather around two cylindrical handles and some rope. Xavier had begun to kiss the nape of Margot's neck again, and then her lips.

"I must now prescribe some behaviour..."

Xavier invited Margot to finger the objects he began to describe. The knives and axes were sharp and mysterious; the complicated, ancient farm implements were in mint condition. She combined her physical curiosity with the thrill and excitement of an experience both seductive and dangerous.

"What do you want me to do with these? What are you going to do to me?"

Xavier continued to be obscure, evasive, but he was also gently forcing her to explore the texture and physicality of each and every object as if they had some sacred significance. The more he teased her, or confused her, the more she was aroused. Her fingers caressed the blades he passed to her for inspection and he wrapped her hands around the wooden handles he was rubbing against her cheeks. She squeezed them gently at first and then with the encouragement of his strong hands, she tightened her grip. His hands wandered around her body, but his voice was beginning to sound a little imperious; he was in control and Margot was happy to be submitting to him in every way. When he clasped her body from behind, she could feel his hard, erect penis.

"Now, you must go through to the kitchen, find and open the fridge, pull out a small bottle of champagne, and bring it back to me without opening it."

Margot laughed softly to herself, temporarily coming out of a trance.

"Was that a snake or a ladder?"

"A ladder."

Margot went through to the kitchen area, adjacent to the workshop. On every wall were posters advertising some sort of political commitment. Some of them were old posters from the Spanish Civil War, revolutionary calls to arms. There was the inevitable poster of Che Guevara and what looked like an Andy Warhol Chairman Mao. All were neatly framed. Even the slogans were carefully mounted. She easily found the old American-sized fridge and the half bottle of Cava was positioned prominently. When she returned to the workshop area, Xavier had disappeared. Bewildered and exhilarated, she shook with anticipation. She looked around.

"I need another roll of the dice. Come through to my studio," he replied.

Margot looked outside into the garden area but there was no sign of him there. She went back to the kitchen, a little confused, and then backtracked to a bedroom area – a large double bed with a white duvet. No sign of Xavier.

"Where are you, Xavier?"

No reply as she left the bedroom and walked back towards the kitchen – the apartment was a labyrinth of rooms. And then she realised that she had missed the studio entrance, which was disguised by a makeshift screen. She went through the gap and into another large, darkened space, in which there was a huge, flat TV screen and an array of computers. Xavier's face was glowing behind the largest screen in a corner at the back of the room. He emerged from the flickering shadows.

"Eleven!"

Margot gave him the bottle and kissed him, biting him gently on the lips. He opened it and poured the bubbly wine into two exquisitely proportioned glasses which were on a desk.

He gave her a glass, chinked his and drank it in one long uninterrupted gulp.

"To Marguerite Duras! And the number eleven."

Xavier then clicked the mouse of the nearest computer and the number eleven appeared on the screen. It changed into a ten and then a nine as if it were the leader introduction to an old film and at the end of this numerical countdown there was a stunning, photographic close-up portrait of Margot's beautiful face. He clicked again and the image was on all the screens in the room including the large one. She was flabbergasted.

"Where on earth did you find that? Who on earth took that?"

"Does it matter? What do you think I was doing during the hour after lunch?" he sounded a little irritated, almost unpleasant. This was proving to be a theatrical performance as much as it was a bizarre seduction. "But I haven't prescribed any behaviour for you yet."

"I am waiting..."

"You must now go to the downstairs bedroom area, take your shoes off and your jewellery including your earrings, your panties and sit on the side of the bed and wait."

Margot did exactly that and Xavier pulled down a series of blinds to darken the area from the brooding, approaching dusk. He then wheeled towards Margot the sleek metallic instrument she had noticed earlier, a very modern, optician's electronic eye-testing device which now looked like a small friendly robot. He told her to sit still and look straight ahead, gently pushing her thighs wide apart so that her dress rode up leaving her wet cunt exposed, and then wheeled the machine between her legs. The hard, vertical central column nudged her clitoris. He placed a heavy pair of oculist's spectacles on her face and then positioned the protruding vertical arms of the electronic device firmly around her face. The black metal was cold but surprisingly sensual. Without touching her body, he began to inspect her eyes in the way an optician might – laser beams of light shone into her pupils, red and green lenses slipped in and out of the holders on the right and left of the spectacles. While doing this, he intermittently slid his fingers skilfully though her hair. Occasionally he brushed her lips with his fingers.

"These are very, very imaginative eyes."

"Thank you! How are we doing? How is our game progressing?"

Margot felt anxious, but the experience was so beguiling and intense that she was going along with it with total abandon.

"What now?"

"Another number!"

"Five."

He clicked a nearby mouse.

"I am afraid that you have guided me to a snake. And the game must move onto a much more eccentric, more dangerous level."

Xavier was now pulling another trolley towards him. A pristine medical trolley. On top of this was a tray full of a series of surgical knives and scalpels.

"This is weird, Xavier! Very weird... What are you going to do with these?"

"You have to trust me."

She shook her head. Margot had a client whose sexual exploits had included controlled rape fantasies, and her Chicago training had provided her with some truly unpleasant examples of perverse sexual violence. These had all been in the context of abuse by one person to another, but she had never understood the acquiescence of the victims. Surely she wasn't beginning to manifest within herself an attraction for the sado-masochistic games and perversions she had spent so much time studying?

"Remember the rules."

Xavier was almost irritated, as if anticipating her reluctance. Margot had become his puppet, shaking with sexual excitement.

"What are you prescribing next?"

"I won't hurt you. I will go up those stairs to my mattress area and you must follow me with one of these knives... Don't undress, keep your clothes on... And then I will tell you what to do..."

Margot moaned in anticipation. Breathless. "Are you joking?"

"I can only promise you that if you do exactly what I say, it will lead to an experience which will transcend anything you have ever done before."

Margot stood up and paused. She was at a point of no return. She was now intoxicated with the charismatic sensuality of Xavier's movements and behaviour. She was out of her depth both physically and emotionally, her body pulsating with excitement. The darkest of her fantasies had become reality and all her customary bourgeois preoccupations about sexual boundaries seemed superfluous; trite. Xavier had moved the optician's device aside and was climbing up to the raised bedroom area. Margot sipped her champagne and looked at the gleaming knives. She gingerly chose what looked like a scalpel. She felt the blade. It was obviously very sharp. She tested her dexterity on the hem of her red dress. The blade was also very efficient. She then climbed the wooden staircase to his sleeping area like Marie Antoinette on her way to the guillotine.

"What do you want me to do with the knife?"

When she arrived in front of him, he knelt opposite her on the mattress almost as if in prayer. Margot sat watching him for what seemed like an hour. He pressed the knife into her fingers.

"I want you to slowly and carefully cut all my clothes away from my body."

She smiled and, as carefully as an experienced seamstress, began to cut at his sleeves and then down the line of the buttons on the front of his shirt. He stood up so that the waist of his jeans was close to her mouth and she cut open the flies. He was magnificently erect. She instinctively kissed the slightly moist helmet of his circumcised penis. He gently took away the knife and helped her slide his jeans off his legs and away from his tanned body. He then slowly sliced circles from her dress around her large erect nipples, which were thrusting tantalisingly against the silk of her dress. He teased them with the tip of the blade before cutting through the dress around her wet cunt which he skilleted like a surgeon during a heart operation. She was now completely naked. He then placed the knife carefully on a bookshelf above the bed, parted her legs, which were still partially covered by remnants of her silk dress, and then entered her as if he owned her body and had known it for years. She gasped as her back arched. The pace of their lovemaking was slow and progressive. Xavier was a consummate lover. He knew how to deny and he knew how to be almost violent without ever seeming dangerous. He fucked her cunt, her arse, her breasts, and her mouth. She exploded, moaned, screamed and again exploded, repeatedly. His cock remained hard throughout. Finally he came, deep inside her.

And then they lay there quietly while he stroked her nipples, caressed her thighs, kissed her cunt, drinking the fluids from her wet vagina, bringing it to her lips with his mouth. The bell of the Santa Maria struck the quarter hour.

"I must go!"

While Margot manipulated her coat over the shredded red dress, he put on some music – the slow movement from a Beethoven violin

sonata. She smiled to herself. Somewhat corny. He came over to her
from behind, cupped his hands around her breasts, turned her around,
opening the coat and pushing the silk upwards pressed his erect penis
up against her moist vaginal pudenda. She kissed him and gently
pushed him away.

"I don't want to go, but I must."

Without kissing him again or saying goodbye, she wrapped the coat
tightly around her dress, hurried out of the building and ran back to
her office.

# Chapter Nine

Margot slept at her studio that night as she often did during the week. She woke early, walked to the elegant public swimming pool at the end of the Barceloneta for a swim – thirty brisk, icy cool freestyle laps in the lane which straddles the plate glass window and its magnificent clear image of the early morning Mediterranean – and then ambled in for her usual breakfast at Elvira's bar.

Before Margot had time to settle in her usual stool in the centre of the bar for her shot of dark, strong black coffee and the juice from two squeezed oranges, Elvira beckoned her over to the tiny table next to the fruit machine. The regular couple of young priests were gossiping to each other quietly in the opposite corner close to the bar counter. A man with a paunch was nursing a brandy and stirring his solo obsessively. Elvira squeezed Margot's juice and hurried over with the coffee on a small, aluminium tray. She was very agitated and was whispering. Her voice was normally strident and jovial. This was the first occasion in three years of her friendship with Margot that this elegant woman had narrowed her blue eyes with more than just worldly-wise anxiety. That morning Elvira's husband was the source of the story which Elvira knew would profoundly affect the lives of many of Margot's friends and clients. And of course, as Margot knew so well, she was married to Inspector Carlos Mendoza, one of Barcelona's most prominent and respected policemen, a source of considerable pride.

"Carlos called again to check your 'phone number. He needs to speak to you urgently – he's looking forward to meeting you. He knows we're friends. We have no secrets. I told him about your job."

Margot smiled. She was used to that moment when a friend would use her analytical talents to help them out with some family saga which might benefit from a therapist's professional slant.

"No, don't smile! He is very upset. My husband is a tough guy. He is very strong..."

Margot looked around. The priests were paying their bill.

"Yesterday morning he left our bed at four o'clock. He was called and was very angry. Normally he doesn't go to the scene of a crime but, he was called by the officer who deals with the ambulance service. He was out late night the night before, drinking too much Cava. Our son graduated..."

Margot jumped in: "How wonderful. Congratulations! What fun!"

Margot couldn't help smiling again. She had often wished that her own social life might have included a wild, drunken family celebration or two. But the smile was quickly wiped from her face with Elvira's news.

"A young Englishman and his girlfriend were found dead. That is why Carlos wants to see you as soon as possible."

She passed a slip of paper with a telephone number. "Is this correct?"

Margot nodded. "Yes, that's right. That's my number; he left a message for me yesterday... Dead? Who are they?" Margot's heart beat faster.

"He didn't say, but he has this crazy thing that this may be a double suicide? Romeo and Juliet." Elvira loved a good drama.

"Suicide? I only have three young English boys and none of them are likely suicides. I would have known. I can't even guess."

"We can never know what is going on in the minds of the young. Even you, my sweet Americana."

Margot was used to her friend's simple aphorisms. She didn't bother to follow that line of philosophical enquiry, and whatever Elvira was going to say, she was not going to change her mind. None of the three English boys Margot treated would have had the guts to kill themselves, let alone in any form of pact with their girlfriend. And only one of them had a girlfriend and Robert was her only client whose suicidal tendencies ever came to her small, tidy room. And Tilly, of course, but so long ago.

Margot stood up abruptly and gave Elvira an affectionate hug.

"Tell Carlos I am looking forward to seeing him, that I will see him earlier, or whenever he wants me to be free. He knows where my office is. And you can tell him that I am absolutely certain that he has a murder on his hands. Not suicide."

Robert was sitting on the last step at the top of the stairs that led to her studio. Tears streamed down his face as he lumbered up to welcome Margot, and he fell into her arms like a child. The telephone was ringing in her office as she gently pushed him aside while she fumbled for her keys.

"Robert, Monday is your morning. Today is Wednesday." But she knew why he was there.

"Paulo and Domatilla are dead!" he bleated. "Paulo and Domatilla seem to have killed themselves!"

Margot dropped her bag and stared at him incredulously. Elvira's information had been correct. If it hadn't been Robert imparting the news, she wouldn't have believed it.

She didn't want to believe it.

"Paolo and Tilly? What do you mean by 'seem'? There is absolutely no way that those kids would have killed themselves."

Margot resumed the process of finding the keys, emptying the entire contents of her bag onto the cold stone floor. No keys. She sat down. Robert knelt down and picked a set of keys from the debris.

"How? Maybe this is a grotesque mistake?... Who told you?"

"A policeman rang the news desk at the magazine early on and then I rang Hugo. He was still at the hospital." Robert seemed to be so informed.

The answer-phone had clicked into action but the 'phone rang again within seconds. Margot led the way across the small corridor which she used as a waiting room and ignored the black, old-fashioned telephone beckoning her from the beautiful sixteenth-century Italian writing bureau which dominated the high-ceilinged studio – the desk had been a thirtieth birthday present from Archie. She drew the green chintz curtains which divided the studio in half, and sat down in her Eames chair – Margot's psychiatric throne. Her face had drained of colour.

"Paulo and Domatilla?"

Robert sank into the deep and comfortable orange armchair opposite, her client's refuge, as she finally answered the telephone. It was an unfamiliar voice and she hesitated.

"Who is this, please?" And then she realized; it was Elvira's husband. "Carlos! How silly of me! Buenos dias, Carlos!"

She listened and then reached for her diary.

"Of course you can. I can be free at five o'clock this evening but I have another client at six... yes. Domatilla, too... was... Five o'clock? OK. Five! See you this evening, Carlos. Adios."

She dangled the handset in her hand for a few seconds, replaced it abruptly and wrote a note in her diary.

"I am so sorry about this, Robert... I am not sure I can go on with this. And I know how much Tilly meant to you. They were very special. Therapists are not supposed to have favourites but they were like that for me."

"I know what they both meant to you, and Archie, of course..."

Robert stared at her for two minutes without uttering a sound. She stared back.

Margot was used to these pauses. On a couple of occasions Robert seemed to be almost asleep. His eyelids dropped and he seemed to be in a trance. Today she lost her usual concentration. She was absolutely devastated by the news about Paolo and Domatilla. She had grown to love them in the way that parents do. Margot and Archie had decided not to have children, and Paolo and Tilly were as close as it came to a substitute.

Robert broke out of his trance. He shot up rather abruptly, kissed her and hurried out like a recalcitrant schoolboy who had been spared a punishment. Margot continued to stare at the empty orange armchair.

⁕

*Ethical questions inevitably arise, especially when death interrupts the psychiatric relationship. For instance, do members of kith and kin have any rights of access to the notes and records of every session? I have always been clear about this issue. These are secret while my patient is alive and they will remain secret when they are dead or stop coming. Barring the period proscribed by law, I usually destroy all my notes as soon as I can, and have only made exceptions when there has been a clinical or academic reason to write up a case study. All good therapists keep their records carefully locked away and disguise the identity of their clients if they present a case publicly in order to protect their anonymity. But what am I going to do about the Spanish police? They have obviously come to the wrong conclusions, and what if they have a killer on the loose?*

*The clients' right to confidentiality is a vital element of all good psychotherapeutic practises but do I have a conflict when crime is involved? Professional ethics and the law in the US put the onus on us to inform on any harmful intentions we might know about. But this is not the situation here. Technically, the police here have absolutely no rights to my notes. And, anyway, Tilly is a British subject which makes it even more complicated, legally.*

*Robert rushed off. Not his usual style. Maybe he feels somewhat responsible?*

※

To say that Margot found it difficult to concentrate on her work that day would have been a ludicrous understatement. She paced around her tiny studio. She washed her hands a couple of times. She sat silently in her patients' chair. She turned the radio on and off. She closed the shutters only to open them a couple of minutes later. This would have been one of the two days that she would have seen Domatilla and tried to review the numerous, detailed notes she had written about Tilly. She nearly broke down on a couple of occasions.

Only two 'phone calls came through. One from Archie – Robert had called and asked him to break the news to Tarquin. His broken, baffled voice finally provoked the inevitable cascade of tears. She sobbed like a child. While she tried to recover, he told her that Paolo's funeral had been rather hastily arranged for Friday morning and that he was going to pick up Tilly's parents at the airport that day. He had offered to shepherd them around. Margot asked him if there was anything she could do to help – book a hotel, or arrange a driver? Archie seemed to have taken care of most of the necessary arrangements. He suggested that she should out of courtesy call Hugo and Eusebio. Archie, as always, so wise and sensitive.

She hung up on him, very reluctantly. She was trying to control herself. And then Laura called, a very brusque Englishwoman who demanded to see her urgently. Margot slightly reluctantly made an appointment for an exploratory meeting at midday the following day. She had another simple rule about her roster of patients. She would only take someone on if she felt that they genuinely needed her kind of simple analysis. She also insisted on their commitment to the process of psychotherapy. They had to believe, at least at first, that the ensuing process with Margot as their psychotherapist, would eventually have a positive impact on their lives. Their commitment to the process had to be as earnest as hers would be to their well-being. She had no interest in anybody who just wanted to use his or her time with her as an opportunity for any complicated emotional or psychological game. Women who merely wanted a diversion from the humdrum nature of their lives, or men who wanted to flirt and tease with a beautiful woman, were swiftly despatched or politely referred to other therapists. For this reason she had built up her limited but select range of clients with people who genuinely wanted her help and who could benefit from the years of her broad-based apprenticeship in the USA, which had included stints at shrines in her field at the University of Chicago and at the Chicago Institute of Psychotherapists. Most of these clients had been coming to see her for many months, and in some cases many years. She invested an intense, emotional commitment to her 'patients', as she sometimes called them, and could therefore only cope with, at the most, about a dozen at any given time. She tried to spread appointments evenly through the week, and in some cases she would see a patient two or three times a week. Most of them had been loyal and consistent and she reciprocated that with an intense sense of responsibility, bordering on obsession. She had been seeing Domatilla with Paolo for many months. Their relationship had become so important that Margot had imagined that Tilly would always have been part of her life. When it dawned on her that she would never see Tilly or Paolo again – she broke down and sobbed once more.

Her two clients that morning, a young mother of two called Audrey and an older businessman called Clive, spent most of their counselling time discussing the murders. It seemed that everyone in the world already knew something about them. Margot tried to discourage this but the ex-patriot community is so small and in terms of the analysis they were going through, their reactions proved useful. Thankfully, neither of them knew the extent of Margot's relationship with Tilly or Paolo, although they probably knew she had been seeing Tilly as a client. Margot guessed that all their information was inaccurate hearsay, probably gleaned from the early editions of the Spanish newspapers and live newscasts on television that had been running lurid headlines about the way they had been found. Apparently, the police were still treating the incident as a 'double suicide', a fact which led to a serious discussion with Audrey about the nature of obsessive love.

Clive was more interested in Barcelona police procedures – apparently there had been some criticism. Why had the police not taken Hugo, Emma and Eusebio out to the scene of the crime? (There had been a genuine belief that Hugo might have been helpful psychologically –

Tilly had still been alive when the bodies were discovered). Why were they releasing Paolo's body so soon?

Margot refused to take fees from either client. She admitted that she herself had also been somewhat pre-occupied and less focused. To say the least. She had also been thinking about Xavier. She gingerly tapped his number into her 'phone and then cancelled it. She left a message for Robert, thanking him for the opera ticket, (she had forgotten earlier), and asked him to call back before lunch. He returned her call during her session with Clive but he had gone out to lunch when she tried to reach him again. She also began to wonder why Robert had left their box at the opera house so suddenly.

# Chapter Ten

Before Carlos arrived, Margot had time to look at her notes about Paolo. Clients' notes were a strange medium. At college she had developed a style which served to record the vital clinical information she needed to help her satisfy her supervisor's monitoring process, and at the same time helped her integrate a personal aide memoire. She smiled. At times they were so badly written, and read rather like an idiosyncratic, awkward school essay. At other times her cryptic, barely decipherable scribblings became the catalyst for the entire thrust of her therapeutic philosophy. One of her supervisors had teased her so much about this that she had stopped sharing them with anyone. In that sense they had became her intensely private diary.

Thinking back, she shouldn't have agreed to see Paolo as a client in the first place. But rather like Robert, his arguments had been so forceful and charming. And he shared everything with Tilly.

"You are the only person Tilly trusts. There is nobody else!"

Nobody else was as qualified.

※

*June 23rd 2008*

*Paolo 'Lorca' McAlpine - brought up in Seville. Father, older, Scottish merchant aristocracy. Killed in car crash. Mother (née Lorca, no relation of poet but much coveted family name), young, Spanish. Three husbands including McAlpine. Aged eight – packed off to a remote, second-rate (?) boarding school, Scotland. (Which one? Archie taught at one many years ago. Must ask him about this one day. He never mentions it.)*

*Tape recorder requested – his request.*

Margot clicked the small tape recorder she occasionally used. She didn't really like taping her sessions – certainly Freud and Klein would have disapproved, but she made the odd exception. In this case, Paolo had been vehement. For some reason, he had wanted his story documented in the way that he was going to tell it.

"Will you promise to make a transcript?" he begged.

A transcript somehow implied that one day somebody else should read it.

"This could destroy our secret bond, Paolo?"

Paolo laughed: "I don't care!"

While I was hunting for a fresh tape, he explained that when he was a boy, Guy, his prep school housemaster who had doubled as his Spanish teacher, had mesmerised him.

*Tape recorder (his request). Transcript of Paolo's story about his Spanish teacher.*

"I don't feel ashamed anymore. I don't feel any need to hide it all away now. I want to talk about it, talk about all of it, so that maybe somebody might learn from it. I want to move on, move on in my life, without a horrible secret which I haven't sorted out. I want to cry about it. I want to love without feeling that I have to find and give good sex to be loved..."

"Sorry, Paolo, can you stop for a moment, please. I must check this recorder."

*Short break while I check that the machine is working properly. While I do this he tells me that he is in love with Tilly. And that Tilly has met Guy. Tape recorder his request. Notes for transcript: he talked slowly and fished for the words to describe everything.*

"There I was, one of the more 'fêted', yes *fêted* specimens, of this 'special' Scottish institution. There I was, masquerading as a respectable recruit of Scotland's establishment! Trussed up like a grouse hen in my weekday uniform – tweed jacket, blue serge shorts, red stockings, and on Sundays, in my Royal Stuart kilt, formal black dress jacket, tartan 'trews' and stiff, studded Eton collar piercing my neck. Superior? Elite? Privileged? This ludicrous fancy dress! We were forced to wear it. It summed up the hypocrisy. This idea that we were better than everyone else. We weren't even allowed to talk to the local boys – they were called *keelies*.

"We loved him... Guy! I will call him Guy but that isn't his real name. Spanish classes were like street theatre with him. He was a kind of brilliant leading man, master of ceremonies. We could only speak Spanish in his classes – he was very strict about this. We all had Spanish names – animal names. I was *el mono* (the monkey). As soon as he rounded the corner of the building near to his classroom, each class would burst into a Catalan song. This was the beginning of our favourite lesson of the week. This ditty started with the lyrics 'Adeu petita rosa' and we would elongate these syllables to be in time with his entrance into the classroom. He was like a king or a rock star. His open tweed jacket would sweep by our tiny wooden desks, his red neck scarf swishing by – *'Rosa blanca del mati'* – I can still hum the tune.

"The first task of the day was a ritual he called *'Las novas'* (the news or information of the day), which we would write in Spanish on the blackboard before he came in to the room. We would write, in Spanish always, the date, the weather, which we would copy from the BBC website which one of the richer boys found on his Mac (even then, we used email; only the needier kids walked around with handsets), and other, naughty schoolboy stuff: *'el mono està en apuro'* would signal that I was in trouble and would be due a beating that day; it was still legal then in private schools.

"All of us... eagerly... would wait for one special ritual Guy would perform every Spanish lesson. On reaching the top of the classroom, hands suggestively in his pockets as if he was feeling his balls, our tall, handsome, elegant *profesor* would call up one of the boys to the front and help him very slowly and sensually to rub out *las novas*, leaving certain letters on the board. We laughed so much: *'FL'* would be picked out of the words now rubbed off the board: *(French letter, which is apparently what he used to call condoms when he was at school)* and then *'ST'* elicited a gale of treble voiced hoots and giggles *(sanitary towel)*, 'VD' equally a winner. Venereal diseases, even in post-Aids days, got huge laughs. As the blackboard was lowered to rub out these 'infantile transgressions' as he would call them, a long piece of wood propped there deliberately would fall to the floor for our leading man, our superhero to scoop up. This was *'Carolina'*, a crude sculpture of a naked woman, with breasts, red lips and a bushy vagina which had been clumsily carved onto the plank of wood with a penknife and coloured chalk. We were ten or eleven years old. We laughed without really knowing why and yet we somehow knew what this was all driving at.

"The first act of Guy's performance would end with the boy who had been 'naughty' enough to leave the suggestive letters on the board receiving a very tame spanking in front of us – we loved this. He would be hugged for his spanking before walking proudly and glowingly back to his desk. I so wanted to be that boy. One of our handsome leading man's chosen few. Guy was so good-looking, almost woman-like. Witty. Worldly. We were all lonely... precocious... impressionable... vulnerable... and pre-pubescent. We all wanted to be one of his special boys. Especially because he was the best... he was the best Spanish teacher in Britain, bar none."

*Lonely, precocious, vulnerable, pre-pubescent and more. He dug deep for those words. El mono's parents were thousands of miles away in Seville. Unlike los otros animales, he didn't hear from his parents by telephone, or e-mail or text messages; he couldn't take advantage of Sundays out with Mum or Dad. El mono hardly received any letters – the mail was distributed on a table in the common room every morning after breakfast and he would scour the envelopes for a sign of the telltale aerogramme from Spain. No luck for the monkey. El mono was fortunately pretty good at games – this kept him apart from the bullied boys. He was as good at arithmetic as he was at Spanish, of course, and French, English and History. And he was desperate to be liked. El mono wanted a mother, a father, and a playmate. He wanted to be singled out. And so, of course, el mono wanted desperately to become one of "Guy's" special boys.*

*Tape recorder – his request. Transcript. Paolo's words verbatim:*

"I pushed myself towards this. Being one of his special boys. Not only was I allowed to rub out *Las Novas* but I would also find myself favoured with goodies – with Guy's special jar of garlic salt at table in the dining room. I would be the first to be invited to come his room to listen to his favourite singers, faded pop stars from the fifties in Spain and France – Concha Velasco, Rosalia, Edith Piaf, Charles Trenet, and to smoke dope. My hero had a seductive, shadowy study – he loved all that smoky sentimentality of wartime European culture, particularly the iconography of Spain during the Spanish Civil War. All this was so much for me, as I was then. Impressionable. A bit frightened. Like a child. I won the prizes he doled out for perfect marks in his Spanish lessons. Quarter pound boxes of *Black Magic* chocolates. I won a bottle of *Kia Ora* orange squash for the best-kept cricket-scoring book in the summer. (A way to keep us watching the school match more seriously then – Scottish prep school cricket is crap) and, of course, I was always the quickest to conjugate Spanish verbs. I was brilliant at it.

"In the early stages of I sort of hero-worshiped Guy... I had absolutely no idea of what he had in store for me. I loved it. Innocent, well-deserved attention. I laughed, as all of us did, at the sexual jokes – none of us knew what they meant. We even joked about our suave hero's love affair with one of the pretty female teachers. We were, after all, beginning to know a bit about sex. Some of us were masturbating. *Sex was rearing its seductive head*. We were shown 'naughty' mags in his study: *Playboy, Private Voyeur* and *Titbits*. This made our visits there so exciting – for all of us, not just me. He was so popular. We all loved him. I loved him unconditionally.

"And I couldn't help beginning to notice that I was his favourite. And all at the expense of another boy who was a couple of years older than me. I liked this boy very much and I had always preferred being with boys older than me. Being a bit ahead of my age group in my studies made that easier. Callum was his name. He had become my friend and this made it a bit difficult. At first I thought that Guy's favours were because I had an unusual advantage over Callum. Mum is Spanish and I spoke fluent Spanish in a way that even the smart boys like Callum couldn't. But other factors crept in. For instance, when it came to punishment, I wasn't beaten properly in the way that other boys were. On one occasion, Guy pretended to cane me, yet I knew that the other boys had been caned brutally. Callum showed me the stripes on his bum in the tub room – this was the last year of legal beatings, and for some nasty reason this had increased the number of punishments. The dreaded pain, this was… superseded… by an overwhelming sensation of sexual excitement when he hugged me instead of caning me. I was standing in his study in thin white games shorts and a flimsy rugby jersey. My Spanish teacher was holding me tight, close to his body. I could feel his penis. It was hard. Gradually I began to get a message, which made me realise that there was more to the 'special' relationship than just a brilliant teacher/pupil rap. A new dynamic crept into our relationship. Repeated, subtle references to his bedroom began to crop up – it was all very hush-hush, secret – other boys who had heard through the bush telegraph that a visit to his bedroom was the ultimate accolade for 'special friends'. Callum seemed to be in on this. True acceptance as a 'special friend' was a visit to Guy's room. These rumours were made stronger by the occasional, almost casual, hint from my superhero that I might like to visit him 'upstairs' one evening, for a 'session'.

" *'What is a session?' I asked."*

" *'Very secret',* Guy replied, smiling with a naughty, naughty smile as he raised his long finger to the ruby lips of his handsome, rather louche face. I had to find out more. I asked around and got blanks. Extra tuition it wasn't! A beating – no. Sex education possibly? Titters of ignorance. I finally made a decision. One evening in his study I told him that I would be interested in the prospect of a session. I had been told that I was to become Head Boy the following term. I was old enough. He explained that I had now become a *'special friend'.* He emphasised secrecy. Discreet was one of his favourite words. He embellished the invitation with a hint of the dangers of being caught. He played on a sense of trust. He relied on the knowledge that to become part of this special club was as dangerous for a newbie as for himself. And so he fixed a time for my *induction*. No text messages, emails – too risky. I knew that this was going to be my first proper sexual experience. I was twelve years old. I had fallen into Guy's deliberately orchestrated trap. I was about to visit his lair. And what is horrifying to think about now is that I wanted this more than anything in the world. I had been primed! I was a willing victim... Of this man's determined campaign to seduce me into his world of illicit homosexual sex.

"I can hardly remember my first visit to his bedroom, although I can remember many aspects of these sessions over the four years. The 'sausage between your buttocks' sense of buggery. The putrid smell of sticky male cum. The whiff of gelatine cream (KY, I think), which he used to make entry easier. Fumbling. And his low seductive voice, yes, gentle encouragement as I was introduced to each new facet of sex between a man and a young boy. His room was very neat, with combs and brushes laid out neatly on a small, makeshift dressing table.

"I will never forget seeing his erect penis for the first time and gasping... I was petrified. It was huge. He asked me to fondle it and put my mouth over it. I never quite understood, and still don't to this day, why he was so excited by me. I wore glasses and was hardly a Greek God to look at. My own penis is not huge, sort of average. But I clearly got it on for him. I found doing it itself fairly revolting, although I enjoyed coming in the way that you might imagine a young boy who is doing it for the first time might enjoy coming. I hated the taste of his semen. I loathed the pain. I could smell the slightly effeminate, perfumed aroma of what I assumed was his after-shave. I hated that, too. And yet, I became a member of his highly secret club. Regular. My initiation into this club – sophisticated... exotic... this secret world, seemed to make it more important for me to be one of Guy's 'special friends'. I was at last receiving some proper attention from a man I really admired. It was exciting. I felt privileged. And so one session became two, and two became...

"And then something truly hellish happened which increased my own need to be loved and cared for. My friend Callum had decided to leave school early before taking his 'A' levels. Nobody really knew why – he was very clever and would have definitely gone onto Oxford or Cambridge. He was a strange, rather emotional boy but I liked him. Loved him. Like me, he had enjoyed a special relationship with another master at the junior school when he was very much younger, many years before I had arrived. A brilliant teacher, older than Guy, but with the same gift of the gab. Callum had worshipped him. And quite suddenly, this man had left rather abruptly, under a cloud. Forced to resign. Some hushed up scandal. No proof. This had profoundly upset Callum. He told me that he had been to blame. I never really found out why, as Callum refused to talk about it. The only thing he did tell me was that it had all happened after he had been off sick in the 'san' and been examined by the school doctor. Callum's secret! My secret! But he did tell me how he had felt, and that he had nursed these feelings for months and had been very depressed – guilty, lonely, traitorous, isolated. I was his only friend. He told me that he used to cry in his bed at night and had been bullied by the other boys in the dorm. That Summer term he didn't show up. He lived in the Highlands where his Dad owned a small deer-stalking estate. I think he was an only child. I assumed that he had persuaded his Dad to let him go to a local day school to sit his exams. They are pretty good in Scotland. How wrong!

How stupid! I was flicking through *The Scotsman* one Sunday and came across his familiar face, splashed across two pages. One night during the summer holidays, Callum had hidden himself in the gunroom of his ghillies' home and shot himself in the head with a twelve bore, double-barrelled shotgun... I felt so bad. As if it had been partly my fault..."

*Paolo went very quiet. I asked him if he wanted me to turn off the tape. He was silent. He shook his head. Callum's secret?*

"Guy was especially comforting to me about Callum. When I moved in the winter term from the prep school to the senior school at Strathalmond, I thought that our 'sessions', as he called them, would have to stop. Apart from the shock of Callum's suicide, I had enjoyed my term as Head Boy and my Common Entrance results had been good enough to put me into the 'A' stream class, which meant taking my first GCSEs while I was still only twelve, with boys who were nearly two years older than I was. This required fitting into a new, more competitive environment at Strathalmond's upper school, meaning that all this exciting stuff, sex, would have to stop. And yet, of course, there was a culture of public school homosexuality at Strathalmond. Even in a mixed school. The girls were taken for granted and kept largely to themselves, while the boys had rampant sex with each other. I began to obsessively nurse the secret of my relationship with Guy and get on with normal life at this horrible place. Beatings from prefects – secret and illegal but they were happening. And mild flirtations with pretty boys being every public schoolboys' substitute for teenage sexual experiment. Strathalmond had this system called the 'Top Ten'. The top ten most desirable boys at school were favoured creatures who all provided fantasies for the rest of the mostly heterosexual guys.

Their photos were posted on our special Internet site, which had a secret password. I fell in love with a peaches and cream boy then like everybody else. I even had the occasional masturbatory homoerotic experience with fellow dorm boys. But out of school I began a long career of rampantly heterosexual experiences. I thought that Guy was firmly in my past, a very, very secret rite of passage. But I was soon to discover that 'special friendships' do not necessarily cease, and that what had begun as a powerfully organised campaign of seduction disguised as good, clean, harmless fun, was going to go on into my teens and dominate the rest of my life.

"Guy rounded on me after chapel one Sunday at the beginning of my second week in senior school. He invited me for a session on the following Thursday after prep. The ease with which he explained how I could wangle this without being caught, suggested that he had obviously organised similar visits from other 'special friends'. Clearly this was not a club for one member. All week I would be excited at the prospect of seeing him again. From the seconds after our short, sly exchange outside that very beautiful chapel, while the rest of the kilted pupils filed meekly out of our two Sunday church services, and that millisecond of my cry of sado-masochistic pain as his large circumcised penis entered my tender, teenage, well-lubricated buttocks, I would nurse a sexy, exciting, all-enveloping sensation which would not go away until after I had clandestinely crept out of his small bedroom, close to the tub room on the top floor of his boarding house, and taken the short, ten-minute walk back to the main upper school gates. This was Strathalmond School, one of Scotland's most prestigious 'public' boarding schools.

"I had sung the treble solo at the carol service in front of the stained glass window of that church. Within months of singing an innocent adeste fideles, I was committing the sin which should have earned me perpetual damnation, six brutal strokes of the cane and the summary expulsion which almost certainly would have been my fate had I been caught. And yet the fear of this kind of disastrous punishment didn't put me off. I slipped off secretly to continue a relationship which I now know was one which allowed a man to commit a crime which he should probably have been locked up for."

Margot stared at her handwritten notes:

*This man is a criminal in the eyes of the law and he is an evil manifestation of a peculiar British phenomenon, which for so long has characterised the institutional elite. These more disguised predators are just as culpable as Guy, just as culpable as the Welsh priests serving jail for their child abuse offences, just as guilty as the men serving sentences for abusing children in the 'care' homes of our social welfare system. Or the Catholic priests in Boston. Has the public school system mysteriously protected itself from a terrible history of child abuse for too long and if so, why has it got away with it all for so long? These are just a few of the issues which crop up in analysing Paolo's case. On a personal level, the idea that anyone I know – cousins, godchildren, friends' children, anyone – should fall prey to such a monster is too hideous. Where is this all leading to, I wonder?*

*I must ask Archie about his experiences in Scotland. It's a small country and the school community there must be rife with gossip and secrets.*

Margot stopped the tape, and made another note to ask Archie about Strathalmond. And then she turned on the tape again:

"I was manoeuvred by Guy into out of school activities, making it easy for him to continue to sexually abuse me. He was so wily. My brother and I went on holiday in Austria with him my last summer at school – my parents' marriage had become alcoholic and violent and they were heading for a divorce, as Mum had fallen for Eusebio by now. Dad thought that we would be better off away from home on that holiday! We stayed in St Gilgen on the Wolfgangsee and in Salzburg during the music festival. Fabulous operas. And who was our chaperone on this perfect idyll amidst the Salzgammergut? None other than Guy. Between bouts of Mozart and the Marionetten Theater, between rubbers of bridge and visits across the lake, Guy forced me into two or three sessions for old times' sake. I went along with these very reluctantly – I had developed a major crush on a very pretty chambermaid who flirted with me every morning after breakfast. I looked at girls on the bus. I was beginning to realise that I was heterosexual and that Guy was something completely different. And yet our friendship thrived. He seemed to like my company. Was this the early stages of some sort of careful monitoring process? Had he gone too far with me? Was he anxious? When I finally began my foray into the glam world of London life, Guy arranged an apartment for me. But I had made it totally clear that there would never be any more sex with him. I was adamant. He seemed less interested and was happy to take me along to the races at Goodwood – horseracing was his other grand passion. I had graduated from pupil to 'friend'. It seemed that at school he needed to have these two identities. But in the real world, I was no longer *el mono*; he was no longer Guy the entertainer.

"My only contact with him after this was at a chance meeting in the Café L'Accademia, you know, that one near the Liceu Metro in that square with the beautiful little church? I thought that I would never see him again when I learnt that he had been sacked from school. That was until I had heard once more this unmistakeable, prolonged, rather phoney laugh, his laugh. I was sitting at the counter where you can have a cheap lunch. I was with Tilly. We love that place. Dark and sexy, it serves the best Catalan lunch. They throw in a glass of wine with your food – an old tradition dating back to the industrial unrest of the late nineteenth century. At first I thought that I may have made a mistake, so I peered around the wooden columns which separate the counter stools from the normal tables. And there he was. I shuddered and went white with shame and fear and pretended to Tilly, who was anxious, that I had heard a laugh which reminded me of someone I once knew. For some peculiar reason I just had to go over to his table and say hello. For all I know he may have seen me. He looked sheepish – he was with two rather beautiful older women who were clearly hanging on all his witticisms and charm. He insisted on schmoozing over to meet Tilly but her reaction to him must have told him that she knew something about our secret. Tilly was the only person I had ever said anything to about him. And then he took me aside and, holding my arm tightly, told me in a whisper how good it was to see one of his 'special friends' again and that we should be in touch soon! I so stupidly gave him my mobile number and scribbled out an address. Tilly threw him a look, which must have got to him because he all but ran back to his table."

*Paolo burst into tears. I (very gently) tried to find out why. He refused to talk. Session ran out of time. Next client had arrived.*

Margot's notes ended here. She shivered. Paolo had clammed up. He wouldn't tell her any more, and she would never see Paolo again. To ask him all the questions she now desperately wanted to ask him. She knew that he had more to tell her. Margot was ashamed. She felt guilty. She knew that he was not 'cured', as he put it. She had missed this golden opportunity to help Paolo. She hadn't probed enough. If she had, she might have helped to save his life. Tilly's life.

# Chapter Eleven

Detective Police Inspector Carlos Mendoza loved gadgets as much as his wife, Elvira, hated them. At home he was denied the opportunity to show off his considerable knowledge of digital technologies. It drove his wife crazy, not simply because she was a technophobe, but because all his waking thoughts were directed towards the obsession which had taken over their domestic life. She forbade him to use his mobile telephone and banished his elaborate computer equipment to a tiny room, which looked like the storeroom of a second-hand hi-fi emporium, at the back of their apartment. None of Elvira's hysteria perturbed Carlos. He ignored her remonstrations while scouring the Internet for bargains to supplement his extraordinary collection of state-of-the-art gadgetry.

"One day, you will see. All of my digital dexterity will pay off with a case which will be solved with my equipment!"

Elvira ignored him.

At last a case was providing him with an unusually rich opportunity to justify this indulgence, and his visit to Margot was to be the trial-run for the opening salvo in a display of technological prowess unrivalled in the annals of Barcelona's famously efficient and modernised police force. Elvira had provided him with some background about Margot without stepping outside the boundaries of her friendship with her American friend. Although they had never met, Carlos had a strong idea of her character but very little idea of the life and the world she inhabited. He had discovered from his inevitably limited police enquiries within the Spanish psychotherapy hierarchy that she was a brilliant and highly qualified psychologist and he knew that she had considerable experience treating patients in extreme forms of sexual behaviour.

When he arrived, he apologised. He hoped that his appearance had not in any way disturbed her working day. Margot found him to be as delightful as Elvira had described.

"Absolutely not, it is my pleasure. I think of Elvira like a sister. She has told me what a special man you are!"

"I wish she would tell me that one day!" he chuckled, and politely asked Margot to pull down the blinds. Then, on all fours, he negotiated her room with at least half a dozen wires.

"What on earth are you doing down there, Señor Mendoza?"

"I need you to see something. In the best way, as it was intended. And call me Carlos, please," he mumbled from below the table.

"Why me in particular, Carlos?"

Carlos didn't answer and went about setting up a couple of monitoring screens, a quartet of speakers and a computer. Margot was baffled. She didn't really understand why Carlos hadn't asked her to come to his office in the police headquarters which were five minutes away, just off Las Ramblas. And he was behaving a little like an amateur projectionist in a cinema club with a new toy.

"Please, sit down," he asked her, and then pressed a button or two on the console in his hand and all the screens exploded with a set of brightly coloured bars, and the speakers screeched with a long, penetrating sound tone.

"Pardon me, señora!"

The tone disappeared, and the coloured bars faded into black. Carlos smiled sheepishly.

The film began with one long, uninterrupted shot of the great

Gothic Cathedral of Santa Maria in the centre of town, as if someone were entering the church. The camera finally settled, looking up at an effigy of a saint. A hand came out in front of the lens and lit three votive candles, placing them neatly to illuminate the effigy: a woman. The camera moved to an inscription in Spanish, "St Eulalia, martyred for her beliefs, 12th February 304 AD."

The voice on the soundtrack was Tilly's. Margot knew very little about this Catalan saint but she remembered something about the local legend connected with her pallbearers – they had apparently struggled with her coffin as they bore her remains to a new prized spot in the Santa Maria. When they investigated, it turned out that her heart had turned to concrete. Why had Tilly not told her about this film? Let alone mention the saint who was so obviously the object of an obsession.

"Where did you find this?"

"This is the film we found on a back-up file on the disc drive of the computer next to their bodies. We also suspect that it has been posted on an Internet website."

The effigy of Saint Eulalia faded away and a black title card came onto the screen.

*"This film is dedicated to Margot, the only woman who might be able to understand it!"*

Margot was aghast.

"I am not sure I do understand. Is this me?"

"There are very few Margot's in Barcelona and as far as I know you are the only Margot known by Señora Milliken. Domatilla Milliken... The film is a replica of the script we also found at the crime scene."

The policeman's English was much better than he pretended. Margot felt that she understood him; Elvira was right to be proud and protective.

But Margot was also transfixed by what she was looking at, and as Tilly began to take her through the life of her saintly heroine, she wondered if the entire exercise had been mounted for her benefit. Perhaps Tilly knew that she was going to die when she began to make her videogram. Perhaps the film is a cipher, a *cri du coeur*, or some sort of weird electronic suicide note... Carlos lit a cigarette and then realised that this was probably a no-smoking room and put it out. Margot smiled and continued to watch.

Paolo was now digging a hole in the sand on the Barcelona beach. This was very cleverly staged: poetic landscape shots, intercut with mini-sequences of Tilly as if she was a Saint in a painting by Fra Angelico. Vivid turquoise featured heavily, as did The Cross of St. George. Altars. Angels. Monks. Monasteries... these were all visualised without, as if in a very accurately-designed period film – no cars, satellite dishes, modern buildings. She was preaching, kneeling, reading, sleeping, eating, praying and in the last of these paintings she seemed to be in a jail.

"This is so strange... weird. It's also very unsettling, Inspector. It's difficult to believe that she didn't mention any of this to me. I thought I knew her so well. She was so open."

"I am so sorry it is upsetting you..."

The next image was a sustained shot of MACBA, Barcelona's celebrated museum of modern art. Tilly's voice began to describe a recent visit there and then explained her enthusiasm for an artist called Günter Brus. Tilly's voice:

*"How can we possibly come close to understanding the agonies that martyrs like St Eulalia were put through during their trials, torture sessions and eventual crucifixion? Clues might come from the experiences chronicled by an Austrian artist called Günter Brus. He*

*was one of the most important artists working in Europe during the early sixties. His vibrant early paintings were macabre self-portraits whose roots lay in both Goya's darkest work, the work of Antonin Artaud, known as Theatre of Cruelty, and the work of some of the American abstract impressionists of the 1950's. He began to develop the notion that pictures should no longer be simply two-dimensional objects executed objectively by an artist, but that they should become 'events', and should be kinetic. Rather than be in any way representational and just show the world, the work of art should be part of the living world. He soon became one of the most influential pioneers of an art form popular then, known as 'happenings' or 'Action Painting'. After some experiments with his wife – she became a living painting – he produced his most revolutionary works in 1964 and 1965, Selbstbemalung 1, Self-Painting 1 and Sebstverstummelung, Self-Mutilation 2. Brus announced that his own body was the sole source of artistic expression and he presented it, like a still life, along with piercing and cutting objects to highlight its fragility. In time this led to his two greatest challenges to conventional art – Sheer Madness and Breaking Test. His public performances and the films he made from them provoked such a furore that he was arrested, tried and imprisoned."*

During this period of commentary the film showed a series of simple pictures of what was presumably examples of the illustrative work – a photograph of the artist in some sort of plaster caste with what appeared to be a large bloody scar stretching from the back of his bald head, down through his face, and ending on his throat. Adjacent to this image was an axe. But at no stage in this section were there any moving images, movies. After this, a long, very smooth tracking shot into an image which was clearly supposed to represent St. Eulalia.

Tilly's voice began to take on an almost supernatural texture, speaking in another language.

"This is ancient Catalan. She is saying that she is becoming St. Eulalia!"

"Thank you, Carlos."

Margot was now transfixed but her engagement with the film turned to semi-hysteria during the next sequence, heralded with a stark title in black and white that read:

*This is my story. This is the story of Eulalia. She is my spirit. She was I and I am she. I live through her and she lived in the certain knowledge that within centuries she would live through me. She died for me and I will die for her...*

A large white space. Tilly, sitting cross-legged on the floor, naked. Various objects scattered around the floor: a large pair of surgical scissors; a pint-sized beer mug; a bucket; a chisel – again gleaming like a surgical instrument. Off camera, a male voice then gave a command in what seemed again to be ancient Catalan. There was an English subtitle for this command. Tilly reacted to the command obediently and slowly took a knife and began to quite literally mutilate her body with light lacerations to her skin...

"I can't take this anymore, Carlos..."

Something about the voice disturbed Margot more than the fact that someone else had been involved in their exploits. Its tone was familiar but she was at a loss to work out why. Had she heard this voice before?

Margot rushed from the room, projecting herself onto the floor of the adjacent bathroom. She threw up, violently. Pale-faced, she returned to her room and sat in the chair usually reserved for her patients. Carlos had switched off the DVD machine and was standing at the window with his back to the room. Silence between them. A child was laughing in the communal courtyard below. A bicycle bell.

"I have done some research into the work of Señor Brus. There is even some of his work at MACBA now. He did indeed spend time in a prison in Vienna. I will spare you the rest of Tilly's film but I must tell you that at one of his performances in 1965 he openly defecated and smeared faeces all over his naked body, and masturbated while howling out stanzas from the Austrian National Anthem. In another performance which became a much celebrated underground film from that period, Brus donned women's underwear, cut himself with razors, danced around as if in some mad trance, urinated into a watering can and then drank his urine. Tilly's performance is almost identical."

"Carlos, I just cannot square what you have shown me with the girl I was sure had begun to sort herself out."

Every shot of the film she had just viewed contained elements which renewed all her intense feelings about Tilly's predicament at the time when she had first met her. Had Tilly tricked her into a false sense of security? She had also sensed, with some unease, that some of the rituals and atmosphere of the entire film had an altogether different resonance, but she was unable identify the reason. That off-camera voice still bothered her but again, she couldn't place it.

"The DVD corresponds to the script we found but they had filmed only half of the story. St Eulalia believed, apparently, that she was the female embodiment, or the re-incarnation, of Christ. In the script, Christ becomes Eulalia at the moment of his crucifixion."

Margot shook her head in disbelief, although Tilly's last visit to see her in Elvira's café now took on another dimension.

"I can't believe they didn't share all this with me! I was seeing them at least twice a week. And I just find it impossible to accept that I could have been so wide of the mark about Tilly and Paolo, so out of the loop from their reality. Paolo was strange and damaged, sure. They both were."

"I think that both your clients were being manipulated. I don't think that they came to all this independently. I think they were being encouraged."

"Encouraged! Manipulated, abused? But by whom...?"

Margot's mind baulked at the idea that anyone could have encouraged them to perform these awful acts. For a moment, she trailed off into the darker areas of her mind.

"Someone they must have trusted. Someone who knows a lot about art. Someone who speaks ancient Catalan – the voice on the film, the one that gives the commands, is the voice of a man in his forties. I need you to help me."

"I am not a policewoman."

"You know more about this group than anyone else in Barcelona and according to Elvira you saw Domatilla Milliken on the morning of the day she died."

Margot was taken aback. His voice had become as hard as nails. She became very defensive.

"I am just not qualified," Margot raised her voice, as Carlos began to pack up his home cinema equipment, "and I have a professional conflict of interest. You know that, Carlos."

He shrugged and smiled.

"If you won't co-operate, I will have to insist that we interview you at headquarters. And I will have to interview your husband."

"My husband. Why? He was Tilly's godfather." Margot was genuinely shocked.

"What is your English for this? — No stones unturned? - Adios, gracias, Señora. My wife sends her compliments. It has been a great pleasure to meet you finally."

Margot had decided that she didn't like him as much in his official capacity as she might have in a social sphere.

"Adios, Carlos! I will try to help as much as I can. But only within the strict boundaries of my professional ethics."

Margot waited for him to come out into the courtyard and cross it to the vaulted arch leading out into the front of her building. A police siren rang out, but Margot knew that Carlos was walking back to his office at police headquarters building, a stone's throw away. She also knew that Carlos had sensed that there was more to learn from Margot about Paolo and Domatilla. He knew that she was almost certainly harbouring something significant about the victims' lives, something which might prove useful to his investigation. But had he sensed anything else? Her feelings of guilt about her behaviour with Xavier, perhaps?

*I can't talk to anyone about this, which makes me so uncomfortable! Oddly enough, in this situation, I don't think that I have broken any of the rules I try so rigorously to apply to my work. No names. No pack drill. No gossip. And certainly no police informing. I never talk about my clients and would not have told Carlos anything he couldn't have found out himself. I suppose my reactions were enough. He was lucky I didn't vomit all over his DVD player!*

*Tilly was trying to tell me something I didn't know. She was unusually anxious. More like the vulnerable girl I first met. What was she trying to tell me about Paolo?*

*And Xavier? Why am I at this time going along this primrose path to that everlasting bonfire? He has pierced the armour of my well-protected psyche. What is happening to me? Have I been protecting myself from my own problems with all these years of professional prurience? Am I a sexual deviant, a victim like my clients, and is Xavier a manifestation of this?*

*And then there is Robert's peculiar behaviour... does he speak good Catalan? Archie? That Archie could have anything to do with this, is surely too preposterous, even if he is an art expert and does indeed speak Catalan...*

# Chapter Twelve

That night was very hot. There was a trace of a Mediterranean breeze blowing gently through the open windows of their perfectly proportioned, nineteenth century apartment in the El Parallel district on the foothills of the Montjuic. Margot, perversely perhaps, cooked paella for Archie. Like their Sunday brunches with Robert and his wife Stella when she came to Barcelona, this was another favourite ritual that they normally indulged alone, and in the first years of their life in the city it had led to an hour or two of very sensual and romantic sex. More often, nowadays, Archie would play some music and Margot would read a book he had given her. The ingredients of the paella, even the tomatoes, had to be bought from exactly the right stall in the Boqueria. The shellfish ingredients had to be very carefully prepared before going anywhere near the rice. The olive oil and garlic had to be local. And then every prawn, each piece of fish was individually cooked with the kind of care and attention a master chef might give to his favourite dish. And Archie always bought the same wine – a very expensive Catalan white wine from his friend who owned a small vineyard near the coast. Archie had picked up some rather pedantic cooking techniques from a brilliant Catalan philosophy professor he had bonded with in a bar one evening – Archie loved to engage with people everywhere, often to Margot's irritation. She had always been more private.

✳

Margot didn't eat much that evening but she sat quietly, twiddling her fork and sipping the delicious, slightly chilled wine while he talked about his latest enthusiasm – the music of Purcell. They had avoided talking about Domatilla until Archie brought it up. He had always been particularly fond of her. He had been a conscientious godfather and had agreed to deal with the formalities of the process to send her body back to London after the inevitable autopsy.

✳

"There was a very polite and slightly over-friendly policeman in charge of the investigation. Eccentric. A sort of Catalan Poirot… Complicated here, because Catalan law is different to Spanish law, which in turn is different to British law. He told me that he had to persuade a judge to agree to his investigation before beginning any surveillance and making any arrests. And he needed a 'victim' to begin the process. Someone who was alive. And so he has roped poor Hugo into it again."

Archie tossed up some banana fritters. Margot stared at hers. He wolfed down one of his, greedily, almost as if he had something uncomfortable on his mind. Nervous eating.

"I haven't really known Hugo so well, but of course he must have suffered from those loopy parents as much as Tilly. Hugo and I had lunch together after he had formally identified the body. He is as baffled as we all are. He thought that Robert might have been involved somehow – apparently Carlos is going to pull him for questioning. Ridiculous. Batty. He then rang Tilly's mother, his mother, and passed the mobile to me. She was drunk and railed on. She accused us, you in particular, of 'shrinking' Tilly. I passed the mobile back to Hugo when she started shrieking but she had hung up. Silly woman. I never did understand why Tarquin married her."

By this time Archie had eaten his fritters and was tucking into Margot's.

"I am used to being accused of shrinking. God, I so loathe that word... but Robert? He wanted to have an affair with Tilly. He was in love with her. We all know that. But, maybe we have all missed something about Robert?"

"That was Hugo's point."

"He is going to interview you and Robert. No stones unturned as he put it! Rather smugly!"

In one sense, Archie was as involved in the saga as Margot herself. She mentioned almost casually that Carlos had come to see her but they then agreed to try to stay away from the subject.

"I was reading through my..." she began, but Archie cut her off.

"Please, can we give it a break? I just can't deal with it anymore. Do you mind, darling?"

He hugged her and changed the subject rather abruptly. She had wanted to ask him about Paolo and Strathalmond.

"What does seventeenth-century British baroque music have in common with exquisite Catalan food?" Archie asked, rather self-indulgently.

"Nothing whatsoever!"

She was thinking about frogs.

"I am going to prove you wrong! The court of King Arthur and an exclamation of admiration and awe! *What power art thou!* à la that glorious English composer, Purcell."

Archie loved a challenge. He jumped up and almost ran to his vast CD collection filed neatly on shelves above their Bang and Olufssen, a wedding present from Margot's parents. Margot was now staring out at the orange glow of the bay just as the daylight was disappearing.

Magic hour! She was spectacularly disinterested in listening to Purcell, or anybody else, for that matter. And then Archie's music exploded from the six tiny speakers he had placed around their large open-plan kitchen and dining area. Archie, by some accident of fate, had let loose an aria which quite literally was the inspiration for vaginal flood – a mini climax. Margot blushed. She was thinking about Xavier again.

An exquisite, sensational, high-pitched baritone voice (which had been somewhat amplified) was evoking a series of very carefully constructed and repetitive chords which then transformed into what was almost a soprano or counter tenor voice – and became the vocal equivalent of a long, sustained female orgasm. The harpsichord accompaniment was uncharacteristically restrained and the voice had a passionate and breathy desperation, enhancing its sensuality. Archie returned to the table and kissed Margot suggestively on the mouth.

Within seconds he had coaxed her into their bedroom. The fan provided them with some cool air and for the first time, Margot altered her usual pattern of vocal sexual responses. In place of the quiet restraint to which Archie had been accustomed, her orgasm was prolonged, passionate, deafening and her spectacular sexuality echoed in crescendo across the small square underneath their apartment building. When she finally calmed down and began to relax, silent again after the screams and moans of her climax, a congenial smattering of appreciative applause and affectionate laughter echoed back from the restaurant opposite their bedroom window.

Archie and Margot couldn't help laughing aloud by way of response. They laughed and laughed and laughed. Hysterically. And then Archie asked the question she was dreading.

"Where did *that* come from?"

Margot didn't really know the answer and kissed him gently by way of a non-committal reply.

"I have hidden depths which I have been saving for your old age!"

"I see. I am a wasted old man, am I? Some people think that I am a closet queen!"

"If tonight's performance is anything to go by, I hope you continue as such. Nobody else can turn me on like that!" she lied.

Archie was all but asleep now. He moaned an inaudible reply and Margot kissed his back as he inched slowly over to his side of the bed. Within seconds he was asleep. Margot waited a minute or so, and then slid very carefully out of the large bed, put on her silk nightgown and walked quietly over the cool, tiled surface of the corridor floor, into the spare bedroom at the other end of their apartment. She opened the shutters and looked out over the rooftops of ancient Barcelona and towards its harbour, now glowing with twinkling fairy lights and the neon nightlife of the Barceloneta. The tower of the cable car, which during the day ferried tourists across the bay to the Montjuic and the Colm, were both resplendent in floodlight. The distant outbursts of drunken mirth from a late-night dinner party were mingled with the crickets and cicadas echoing around their beautiful villa. The bitch owned by their neighbour in the apartment below began to whimper and whine. A dog barked back intermittently, and Archie had begun to snore.

Margot shivered. Archie had sensed that she was hiding something from him. How much had he guessed? Of course, a guilty conscience can be the catalyst for unnecessary anxieties. But they can also spark subconscious, uncharacteristic signals. He was a clever man and their emotional connection from the beginning had been both visceral and intellectual. They shared erudite word game jokes about 'finishing each other's sentences'. Silly jokes about 'ut' clauses in Latin, which end in verbs. He had even taught her the rudiments of cricket, that most poetic of English sports – another of his obsessions. They had never lied to each other. There had been no need. Of course, they kept secrets. Who doesn't? Particularly about the emotional landscapes of past transgressions. Archie had always been particularly unforthcoming about his early professional life but then it had never really featured as being that important. But Margot's new secret was going to lead to a series of lies. Lies about her behaviour. Lies about her feelings. Lies about her whereabouts. Dangerous lies. Unacceptable lies in the context of their precious marriage. Betrayal.

She slid out of her nightgown, placing it neatly at the end of the bed, and walked through to their bathroom with its enclosed and luxurious shower room. She turned the cold tap to its extreme. The water was icy and powerful but after a few seconds of shock, Margot began to relish it as much as if it had been hot. Using the hand-shower element like a cheap vibrator, she allowed the force of its jet to vibrate against her vagina and began to masturbate. She brought the shower back to her face, and then again down to her now hard, erect nipples. She lay down on the floor of the shower and stroked her body, squeezing her breast with her other hand. Methodically, she placed the hand-shower back in its rest on the wall, turned off the tap, wrapped herself in a huge towel and then walked slowly back to Archie. She kissed and bit his lips, and then slid her tongue down his back. Within seconds he had stirred and turned on his back. She mounted him, softly massaging his half erect penis, and then guided him into her cool body. He opened his eyes.

"Paradise! The Dream of a Ridiculous Man! Rape!"

They tried to make love for what seemed like an hour or so, but was probably only a few minutes. Their bodies became too sweaty. Awkward and uncomfortable. They were trying too hard. Neither of them was satisfied.

"I am too hot, I am going to shower and sleep in the spare room. Good night, my darling!"

He kissed her and went back to the shower.

"I want to ask you about St. Eulalia tomorrow... I am treating you to breakfast?" she called after him.

"St. Eulalia! The martyr? Wonderful. I look forward to it. Sweet dreams."

Margot was now certain that Archie knew that she had been unfaithful to him. What he didn't know was that she was determined to be so again.

She fell asleep wondering how to deal with Xavier. The risks to her marriage seemed irrelevant. She knew that she was out of control in every sense of that phrase and that she was as excited as she was petrified.

✳

*What am I going to do about Xavier?*

*I have had patients who have been sexually obsessed. How have I handled them? The standard, almost formulaic, unpicking of their motives and neuroses is the route towards identifying simple links with obvious emotions – fear, for example. Am I afraid of Xavier? Does he excite me because I am afraid? I can't analyse myself. I so miss Marie-Christine. Is there anybody else I can talk about this with? Archie? As sophisticated and as worldly as he is, he would be devastated. Appalled. It would destroy our marriage. His life. My life. Jesus, I have been so stupid! I feel so ashamed. I have never dreamt of being unfaithful. I have never had the need...*

*Let me think this all through. From the get go, Archie always said that we should have no secrets between us and he knew from the start that I would never discuss my clients. Or very rarely, and then only with codes. And I have always told him that I would only tell him about an infidelity because it would be by definition threatening our marriage. And that I would no longer be in love with him. I never imagined that such a devastating, animal-like, physical compulsion would come along which has nothing to do with my love for Archie... Do I want to see Xavier again? Can I resist him? I am behaving like one of my more desperate clients.*

She dreamed that night of her childhood in La Jolla, California, and her mother and father who had been married for forty years.

# Chapter Thirteen

The two priests were huddled in their usual corner. Low voices, although this didn't look like an extension of some religious dialectic, more a conspiracy. Margot ushered Archie next to the Timba slot machine – its gaudy lights flashing as if it, too, wanted a breakfast of noisy Euros from some sad hobo, to start its day. They sat while they waited for Elvira to bring their solos from the grinding coffee machine, and two glasses of freshly-squeezed juice from an even older and noisier machine. These machines intermittently drowned the silly giggles of an overweight woman, sitting at the bar nursing an early morning bottle of beer. She held a tiny electric fan to her brow.

Margot tried to occupy her mind by analysing the crude iconography of the bar: she would normally have laughed with Archie about them. A *Schweppes* plaque depicting a goddess draped in a late nineteenth century velvet wrap. *Old Red Fox Kentucky Bourbon, Lucky Strike* and 1950's *Coca Cola* clock. Elvira flamboyantly threw a sugar pack towards the goatee-bearded man in the yellow and brown check shirt before sweeping the solos and the juice onto a tin tray.

"Buenos Dias, Diego," she smiled, as a grey-suited man with sweptback hair ambled into the bar as if he was about to close it down. He hunched his frame onto a barstool. Elvira nodded at Margot.

"Carlos told me he came to see you. I am so sorry. The funeral of Paolo is tomorrow. They are flying Domatilla back to England today."

Archie took the tiny black coffee glasses, Margot the orange juice.

"Thank you, Elvira. Archie has a meeting at the assembly today. He is going to give me another history lesson over coffee."

Elvira understood perfectly.

"I now see why Margot kept this place as her special secret all this time," Archie smiled at Elvira, who was obviously delighted.

"You will be there tomorrow at the funeral?"

"I had known Domatilla since she was born. Her father is one of my oldest friends."

"I loved her too..." She crossed herself.

Archie whispered to Margot as Elvira went over to the priests, wiggling her perfect bottom suggestively.

"Did she know him well?"

"I introduced Paolo to this bar... He loved the bar and adored Elvira. Tilly loved it as well! "

"Okay. St Eulalia. And then it will be your turn to tell me a story."

"I am a hopeless storyteller!"

"It won't matter."

"Not today."

They smiled awkwardly at each other and he leant over to kiss her but she avoided him.

"The St. Eulalia lecture and tour!"

"Two hours to the minute – I have a client at twelve!"

Archie, methodical when it came to sharing expertise, had planned to combine his careful academic speaking style, as if Margot was his PhD student, with a guided tour of the key locations associated with Barcelona's famous mediaeval saint. Margot tried to goad him out of being too stuffy with a series of sly questions, prompted by some of the scenes in Tilly and Paolo's DVD.

"In fact, there may have been two Eulalias. The one buried in the Cathedral La Seu just around the corner from here, is St Eulalia of Barcelona who was martyred in the fourth Century, on the February

12th, 304 in the year of our Lord. She was thirteen. According to a variety of sources, she was a particularly precocious young woman, incensed at the Roman emperor Diocletian's persecution of Christians. She was forced to confess her faith publicly in front of a pagan consul who, legend has it, ordered her public deflowering. She was thrown into jail, continuing her invective against her persecutors where she was subjected to thirteen tortures, one for each of her years alive. The last being nailed to the cross in the Angel di Barcelona in front of what is now the Cathedral. There are all kinds of other stories about her. Her miracles, for instance. A well ran dry and her tears refilled it. An angel is supposed to have appeared to her in a wood of cypress trees and told her that she would one day be patron saint of Barcelona. There is one silly myth: when her bones were finally discovered and identified about a century later, a dozen men tried to move them, when in the short journey from the place of execution to the burial ground, the bones temporarily turned into stone. Her remains are supposed to now be buried in the crypt of Santa Maria. Some people think that both Eulalias are one and the same person, the mythology blurred over the centuries. One of the great Pre-Raphaelite paintings is a powerful and highly sexually charged depiction of St. Eulalia's death. It was painted by Waterhouse, John William Waterhouse, who was like me, half Italian, although he spent most of his life in England."

Margot's heart skipped a beat.

"What does she look like in his painting?"

"She looks as if she has just been raped. She is naked from the waist upwards and is covered scantily with a simple cloak. Her hair is scattered out above her body. Why are you so interested in her, Ms. Wilkin?"

Archie never used her name in this way, and his soft, Scottish-

Italian accent had deliberately exaggerated the English phonetics. Even when he had been lecturing to her in classes at Chicago he had always called her Margot.

"Will you continue your story, Archibald, please? I want to know who she was, why was she murdered, what had she done, and how old was she?"

Margot was feeling a little giddy, the tone of her voice both insistent and anxious.

Archie laughed nervously. A measure of their intimacy was their ability to be easy-going with each other in almost any situation. Margot's behaviour was far from normal.

"Sadly, that painting is in the Tate, but there is a portrait of Eulalia here in Barcelona at the Cathedral... According to the fourth century Spanish monk, Prudentius, Eulalia was a twelve year-old girl who refused to denounce the Christian faith and was tortured ruthlessly by a local pagan Diocletian consul. In the story, she was left in the market-place at the foot of a crucifix, bleeding to death. Her body was then covered by an extraordinarily mysterious fall of snow, which became her shroud. All of this Waterhouse incorporates and much more."

"What is the colour of her hair in his painting?"

"This has something to do with Tilly, doesn't it?"

"It's red?"

"More red than auburn. She is very, very young! And Waterhouse gives her a bracelet of rope – a remnant of the crucifixion or the torture. The painting has a sado-masochistic atmosphere."

Margot gulped down her orange juice. She was transfixed. Archie drained his solo and they began to leave.

"Let's go to the cathedral right now. I want the guided tour. Do you mind, Archie?"

He laughed again. "But you have been there hundreds of times before. There is going to be a payback moment, you realise that, don't you? You are going to have to explain yourself. I feel like a character in a murder mystery."

"Archie, you know my rules about clients. Total secrecy."

Strictly speaking, Margot could have told him about the DVD, but she held back, using her work as the usual smokescreen. As Archie walked out of the café, Margot waved at Elvira.

"See you tomorrow. Where is the funeral?"

"At the Cementiria del Sud-Est, the new cemetery which looks over the sea... in the morning. We can walk; it is on the Montjuic, near the sea."

When Margot walked out to find Archie, he had disappeared. She walked along the narrow corridor which masqueraded as a street, towards the Plaça Reial. Archie was flicking through the local newspaper.

"Nothing!"

"Carlos would have kept the story out of the press."

As they crossed the square towards the Cathedral, Margot realised that they would pass directly by Xavier's apartment.

"Let's go the long way around, Archie. I love these old streets. It will give some colour to your story."

The Barri Gotic has so many routes, part of its appeal. Archie was used to Margot's whims about how they walked around.

"We can walk through the Jewish quarter. Did you know that the synagogue is the oldest surviving synagogue in Europe?"

Margot giggled. Archie was echoing an old private joke between them, which harked back to their first few weeks in Barcelona when they had been invited to dinner by a friend of Archie's, a Catalan philosophy professor, who had taken a rather lecherous shine to Margot. After a raucous alcoholic dinner he had insisted on taking them on a very late-night guided tour of El Call, including the old synagogue. He hadn't uttered a word of English all night until he led Margot by the hand in front of the synagogue, announcing aloud in perfect English: "This is the surviving oldest synagogue in Europe!" and then whispering into her ear, with a lascivious nibble that they should "make wild love with each other one evening". Margot hadn't been able to resist telling Archie about this at home later on, and so the episode was the catalyst for a family joke. Archie was not a possessive man but when Margot mischievously wielded her considerable sexual charms with a little innocent flirtation, he would evoke the old lecher's broken English phrase. Margot allowed his harmless dig to ride and disguised her relief that they were taking a different route to the cathedral with a mock chaste kiss.

# Chapter Fourteen

Unlike her previous visits to the Santa Maria, which had been not much more than the enjoyable diversions of an American tourist, this excursion had the atmosphere of an historical, religious investigation. Amongst the many artefacts in the Cathedral directly connected to Barcelona's patron saint, including the tomb in the crypt above the high altar which is supposed to house her remains, there is a small, gothic cloister where the monks keep thirteen white geese. Although she had seen these before, she hadn't really attached any particular significance to them. Margot immediately realised that they were the same geese in Tilly's movie. They had been lovingly filmed and their symbolic relevance had been interwoven into the narrative structure of the lovers' film. It would not be difficult to explain to Carlos the origins of ideas in the intense and disturbing script found by the night watchman. Clearly, all the humiliations which Tilly was shown to endure in the film were re-enactments of St Eulalia's tortures. Many of them were shown in the high relief sculptures on the choir stalls of the cathedral. The X-shaped St. Andrew's Cross she was lashed to, her flagellation tied to a stone column, and her body on a bonfire.

"Is there some connection between Tilly and Eulalia? Perhaps I can help if you...?"

"Archie, please, just tell me everything you can about the painting and the history behind it."

She was verging on being irritated with him. She almost snapped.

Archie paused. Margot absorbed this, but she was pre-occupied on a scale much greater than Archie could have expected from anyone merely horrified by the brutality of the Diocletian persecution of Christians. Facts she would have been well aware of, as an avid amateur historian.

Archie continued, in full professorial mode. In tandem with his expertise about Spanish art, he knew a great deal about Victorian painting – it had been one of his ambitions to write a book about the Pre-Raphaelites.

"Waterhouse put a conventional cross in his Pre-Raphaelite painting, presumably to avoid any confusion with the cross of St. Andrew. The fifteen doves around her body are almost certainly his whimsical reference to the mythology that during the final stages of her horrendous ordeal, a dove flew out of her mouth. The story goes that she was so defiant when the flames began to engulf her that she drank those same flames like water. After the Romans had untied her from the cross, it began to snow. The centurions were so enraged by the shroud the angels had provided for her, that they stuffed her body back into the barrel full of broken glass that they had tortured her with, and rolled it down a street now known as the Baixada of St Eulalia. Baixada being Catalan for a barrel."

Margot lit a votive candle under the haunting portrait of the teenage martyr, the last artefact Archie took her to as he concluded his story. She couldn't help remembering the images in Tilly's film, and became tearful. Archie noticed this and hugged her, but she pushed him away, gently. As Margot stared up at the innocent virginal eyes in the haunting face of the faded cathedral painting, she could hear only Tilly's voice:

*This is my story. This is the story of Eulalia. She is my spirit. She was I and I am she. I live through her and she lived in the certain knowledge that within centuries she would live through me. She died for me and I will die for her...*

A combination of the Waterhouse painting, the cathedral and some very well-researched, Diocletian history.

"Thanks, Archie, I have a client. I need to go to my studio. I don't want to be late."

"Do you want to meet for lunch? We can talk. You need to talk."

"I can't! They were my patients and I don't want to talk about them to you any more."

"Oh, Margot, that's silly. You know how much you can trust me."

Margot didn't answer. As they walked down the steps of the cathedral, a dove flew past.

"Tilly!" Margot cried out.

Archie stared at her.

"Are you going home now?" she asked, when she had recovered herself.

"I am going to the college. I'll take the Metro at St. Jaume."

They kissed quickly, and as he walked away from her, he tripped on his shoelaces and fell. She ran over and helped him to his feet.

"I am okay, thanks. My double knot became a single one! I was in such a rush this morning!"

He tied his laces and all but trotted away, embarrassed. Margot watched him, waiting for him to turn back with his characteristic valedictory wave. Another small, affectionate ritual they enjoyed, but today he seemed reluctant. She waved back and blew him another kiss but she was already thinking about Xavier.

Margot found a seat at a café on the square in front of the cathedral and tried to make some sense of what had been turning over in her mind. As far as she knew, neither Tilly nor Paolo were knowledgeable about the finer aspects of religious iconography and they were hardly experts in Pre-Raphaelite paintings. Neither of them had ever shown any evidence of this knowledge in their therapy sessions. Yet the references in their film were too sophisticated, there must have been another mind at work in the creation of that script. The voice was familiar. Xavier. Could Tilly and Paolo have met Xavier? The English-speaking group in Barcelona is certainly incestuous. It was possible. At a private view, perhaps? Or with Eusebio? Surely they would have mentioned him?

Margot tried to find every excuse she could to avoid her emerging, uncomfortable suspicions about Xavier. Perhaps she had been too hasty. Lust and passion are never useful allies when lucid analysis is required. Tilly had never mentioned him. Why? If she had met him, even once, surely she would have mentioned it, especially in the context of Paolo's abuse, which she certainly knew all about. It had been the subject of most of their therapy. Although desperate to revisit her notes and recordings, she felt that she owed Elvira an apology and decided to drop in on her friend as she made her way back to the studio. The bar was empty except for Elvira.

"Solo, por favor, Elvira!"

"You have been crying!"

Elvira poured her a brandy, and another for herself.

"Yes, Elvira, I am so sorry about this morning. I wanted to go to another bar but Archie insisted on breaking our rule. He wanted to see this bar I had been talking about for so long. He was suspicious."

"Maybe he thinks that you have a lover!"

Margot laughed nervously. "Archie is not the jealous type."

"All men are jealous. Carlos says that the men who come here want my body more than they want breakfast... especially the priests!"

"He's probably right! Shall we go to the funeral together?"

"Vale, bueno! Nine o'clock tomorrow after breakfast. I'll close the bar. Adios!"

As she dipped her head to leave, Margot was confronted by the unmistakeable figure of Xavier, walking across the cobbled street. He was wearing jeans, a dark pinstriped jacket, an open-necked, white shirt and a brown, felt hat. And he was walking with someone who looked remarkably like Archie. Margot immediately recoiled. She looked towards Elvira, but she was emptying the cigarette machine. She balanced herself against the wall for a beat and then walked out in the opposite direction to that used by the two men.

Archie had never mentioned that he had known Xavier, or anyone like him. Was this the product of an over sensitive imagination? An extension of her guilty conscience?

She rushed back across the bar, up the staircase leading to the balcony and into the ladies' toilet where she threw up, violently. The idea that her new lover had come across her husband accidentally was bad enough. The more serious notion that they had some relationship she knew nothing about, was appalling. She waited above the bar until Elvira was serving another customer and sneaked away out of its emergency exit. The blinding Mediterranean sunlight impeded her ability to adjust to being outside, and so she stumbled against the bottle banks blocking her speedy exit. Two cats were fornicating noisily, but other than that there was no one around. She ran through the narrow streets of the old town like a frightened child negotiating a maze for the first time.

# Chapter Fifteen

When she arrived at her building in the Plaça Joaquim Xirau, a police car was parked in front of it. Carlos Mendoza eased himself out of the driver's seat and kissed her rather awkwardly on both cheeks. Margot ignored the pungent aroma of his very expensive after-shave. She pulled him towards her and held him close for more seconds than would be normal, which seemed to embarrass Carlos; she needed some human contact. Carlos handed her a brown envelope.

"I have brought you these. Please will you have a careful look to see if there are any clues for us? I will see you tomorrow at the funeral; Elvira just rang and told me that you were going to come together. Buenos dias!"

He then shook her hand more formally, as if he now felt that the more intimate way that he had greeted her earlier had been inappropriate, and clambered into the car in a rather odd, unbalanced way, body first. He sped off with two of the wheels of the car on the pavement.

Sitting in half-shadow on the ornate staircase was a striking blonde woman in her early forties. Margot's observational skills were an important part of her job and every detail of dress, each nuance and behaviour, especially in first encounters, were all primary assets in the therapeutic process. She immediately observed that this visitor was expensively dressed – a simple short black skirt, a plain, white, open-necked, short-sleeved silk shirt and red, high-heeled shoes; on her left wrist she wore a gold Cartier watch. Her eyes were very blue and her short, cropped blonde hair had been neatly cut. She carried a mobile phone in her tiny left hand.

Margot took a deep breath and looked at her watch. At least a quarter of an hour before midday. This was obviously Laura MacLean, her new client.

"You must be Laura. You are very early!" she said, almost by way of admonishment. Therapists have strict rules about time and they hate clients to bump into each other by way of an overlap. Arriving early for an appointment made that possibility much more likely.

"I am so sorry. I was so desperately in need of you that I couldn't wait to get here."

Margot might have laughed at this to deflect her apparent anxiety, but she didn't feel inclined to do so. She suppressed a smile at the irony of the situation. She was being asked to help someone with an emotional need at the very moment when her own need in that respect was greater than it had ever been. There was arrogance in the tone of Laura's voice that Margot didn't like. New clients are a strange phenomenon. They came mainly because a trusted friend has talked glowingly about the therapeutic process and they came to Margot in Barcelona because she was the only English-speaking shrink in town with American qualifications and specialist knowledge in sexual behaviour. This created unique problems. The ex-patriot community was small and inevitably incestuous. They all knew each other – the university, the consulate and the large corporations based in Barcelona all had British contingencies. They were usually well-heeled and socialised with each other in the more expensive restaurants, clubs and bars. Adultery was rife.

Margot noticed that Laura was wearing an expensive diamond engagement ring next to her gold wedding band. She surmised that Laura was an adulteress and that was why she had come to see her, and so she didn't really need to hear her confession. It would probably be full of the usual clichés, the familiar emotional 'highs and lows,' but these were cues to explore, and engage. Especially with a new client.

Margot had unlocked the front door of her studio and gestured to the waiting area.

"Why don't you wait here a moment? Please feel free to use the bathroom, which is along the corridor just past my consulting room. I will be with you in ten minutes. We therapists are very pedantic about our psychiatric hour, I'm afraid. Fifty minutes precisely. That gives us ten minutes to make notes and prepare for our client."

Margot would often have used that time to notice exactly how her new client was negotiating the same set of circumstances that all her clients had done in their own way. This was another useful stepping stone, one which could provide early insight without delving much into the psyche. But she had noticed that her telephone answering machine was blinking to tell her that her message tape was nearly full. Cancellations, no doubt – they would all be going to Paolo's funeral, abruptly arranged for the following day. She closed the heavy door of her office. A prohibitive soundproofed door was the first and only change that Margot had made to the interior of her apartment when she had bought it.

Once alone, her first act was to open the brown envelope that Carlos had given her, with a bone-handled paper knife, another gift from Archie. When she had cut her finger rather unpleasantly on a staple, Archie, as ever, had found his way of turning her mishap into an opportunity to show his affection. Margot had always enjoyed his pampering - but the memory of his sweet gesture irritated her this morning. What had he been doing with Xavier?

The envelope contained a slim document, titled *The Martyrdom of St. Eulalia*. She recognised it as a replica of the script that the night watchman had found at the scene of the crime. And a DVD in a white sleeve. A copy of the film Carlos had shown her. She immediately slid the DVD out of its sleeve and loaded it into the drive of her laptop. She noticed in the film-like introduction – a *ten, nine, eight* leader identity announcement before the film started – that there was a website address in the bottom left-hand corner. Margot jotted it down. The film viewing would have to wait until Laura had gone, so she slipped the DVD out of the machine again. But she couldn't resist logging on and putting the web address into her search engine. The site was a home for experimental videos made by and for art students, juvenilia mixed with pretentiousness, but clearly from the site's home page she could ascertain that this was the brainchild of someone with a very fertile imagination. A *YouTube* website for art students. To register membership it was necessary to have a specific username. Margot used her slightly clumsy and self-taught computer knowledge to begin the process, but she was continually rebuffed. Annoying messages appeared, telling her that she did not qualify for the site. She tried every combination of username and the most obscure, five or six times. In each instance she was denied access. She gave up, logged out and gathered her appointment book – the only accessory she ever took into her sessions. Laura waited next door. The digital clock on her desk, another Archie present, gave her two minutes. She sat motionless.

Xavier. And then she picked up her mobile 'phone and dialled. Her face was passive and then his voice. Silence. And then, with some diffidence: "How did you know who it was, Xavier?"

With some relief: "D'accord! Trois heures après midi. Chez Café L'Accademia. Oui! Cette après midi."

And shy: "À tout à l'heure... Je t'embrasse!"

She clicked off. She sat motionless, breathing heavily. Her decision had been made; she was beyond return. Her nipples were hard. She moistened her dry lips with her tongue, then closed her eyes, opened them, and let out a sigh of contemplation. Then she laughed very lightly to herself.

"In French, for God's sake! I am fucked!"

Margot had made the decision to see Xavier again, come hell or high water. It couldn't have been Archie with him and anyway, if it was, it could only have been a chance encounter, a coincidence. She was hooked.

The digital clock clicked into midday and her Blackberry emitted an irritating, persistent click. She silenced it and went to the door like a priest who didn't ever want to hear another confession. Unlike the priest, Margot couldn't hide her face in a confessional box.

"I was very reluctant to come here..."

"Reluctant?"

"Yes, I didn't want to admit that I had any serious problems. I have never really believed in 'being shrunk' as my husband calls the process. He doesn't know about this."

Laura's eyes were searching for Margot's.

"I normally use the first hour to find out whether we can work together. This is a process. A relationship. There is no point in going down this precarious path unless you and I can explore and investigate. I need to know why you have come to see me. What you expect to get out of it? And this first session is free, of course. I don't charge you for today's exploration but I expect to be paid in future at the end of each session. I charge one hundred and fifty Euros for each hour."

"I can afford you, if that is what you are worried about."

Margot was irritated by Laura's thinly disguised smugness. And she loathed that use of the word 'shrunk'.

"It really isn't anything to do with money, although I insist on payment at the end of each session, it's more about commitment. I don't want to waste your time and I don't want to waste my own. I also need to know what you want out of me. Why have you come to see me?"

"I am a lawyer for an international bank. They pay me well. And my time is important, too. Is this a bit like an actor's audition? Do I have to do a party piece?"

Margot instinctively wanted to tell her politely to leave, but her professionalism kicked in and she restrained her annoyance.

"We don't have to be best friends. For this process to work, to be valuable for you, there has to be some basis for our relationship, an empathy. But I try to discourage too much emotional investment, especially outside the consulting room, which doesn't always work. They tend to come back."

"Unless they are murdered!"

Margot stood up. She was very rarely outwardly angry but she remained calm, dispassionate, and she tried to be as sympathetic as possible. She wanted to tell Laura to leave at once. Her cheap shot was unnecessary and insulting, but it was also presumptuous. Laura had no reason to know anything about Paolo and Tilly beyond what the papers had told her.

The coldness in Margot's voice was unmistakeable.

"I would love to know what prompted you to say that to me? Do you have any idea how cruel that was? Why are you being so aggressive? I have no real idea why you want to see me, but I am here to try to help you. That is my job."

And then Laura screamed at her. "Well you fucking well should, you cold-hearted cow!" And after the scream, she was in floods of tears.

Margot watched this display analytically. She had seen many other outbursts. Was this an act or was this some kind of manic call for help? She gave Laura the benefit of the doubt.

"I am so, so sorry. I really am. I had no right... I will leave in a minute. Please forgive me. I am so tense. Frightened. Desperate. Please forgive me... This Paolo thing. I met him and his sister once, when I came to this city..."

She was hysterical. Margot went to the bathroom and poured a glass of water for Laura, who was trying to wipe her mascara-stained face which now looked like a porcelain doll with a black streak leaking down each cheek. She stood up as if making to leave.

"Stay, Laura, please!"

Laura was in Margot's arms now, crying like a child.

"Let's start again."

Laura sat down, gingerly. "Eusebio Casals said that you were one of the most wonderful women he had ever met!"

Margot knew too much about Paolo's step-father to take anything he said that seriously. But she accepted the compliment gracefully and sat down.

"Eusebio? He probably says that of all the women he has tried seduce but I love him to pieces!"

She laughed and then realised the significance of what Laura had just said to her. "Of course, he must be absolutely heart-broken. He tried to be a good replacement father to Paolo despite all the complications. And he adored Tilly."

Laura managed to eke out a small smile. "I know what you mean about Eusebio but, yes, he is obviously very upset. He wanted to be my lover too, for many years. I have a wonderful flirtatious friendship with him."

"Are you married?"

"Yes... but..."

Margot waited. The inevitable confession.

"I don't know where to start... I am married, yes, and until six months ago, I was a happily married woman. Faithful, loyal, all that stuff... even the sex was good. I have two beautiful children; a six-year-old called Tom and a nine-year-old girl called Terry... Teresa... the two T's..."

"And Eusebio?"

"We flirted over the sculptures in his studio once and that was it... and there were other temptations... but I loved, love Reggie, my husband... we have known each other since childhood!"

Laura took another sip from the glass of water and pulled another tissue from the box of Kleenex Margot religiously had at easy reach. She blew her nose.

"Can I be a client? Please! I so need you."

Margot was firm and gentle. "Let's take it slowly... I promise to help you out, even if it is just to listen to your story."

"I need more than that."

Laura looked desperately lonely.

"Don't worry, we'll work something out."

Margot was still recovering from Laura's outburst.

And Laura, as if reading Margot's mind, said quickly and quietly, by way of a defence, "I never scream and very rarely swear! I am so sorry. My job requires it."

"Okay, Laura. Let's give it a go! Do you want to postpone this until we meet again?"

Laura's face immediately transformed and she sat back. "Thank you so much. No! I need to tell you my story..."

Margot laughed sympathetically. Laura looked at her watch. "We only have half an hour left. Is that going to be enough time?"

"No. Not nearly enough. You are right. We shouldn't rush. Let's leave it... until after Paolo's funeral? I can see you then, here at five."

Margot remembered that she needed a good excuse not to attend the wake. She hated wakes and wanted to avoid a confrontation with Tarquin and Sabrina.

Laura seemed surprised. "Are you sure...?"

"Yes. Quite sure." Margot smiled. Laura looked relieved, grateful.

"Five o'clock, after the funeral. By the way, he's called Reggie... my husband. Reggie. We are going to come with Eusebio and his family."

They stood up at the same time and looked at each other shyly. Laura went to the bathroom, emerging immaculately with a pair of sunglasses to hide her reddened eyes, and when Margot had finished writing the time and date for their next session in her appointments book, Laura crushed a wad of notes into Margot's hand with a very embarrassed and awkward lunge.

"The custom, I believe."

And before Margot could reiterate that she didn't expect to be paid at the first visit, Laura was running down the staircase. Her high heels echoed heavily around the elegant stonework and her footsteps lingered in Margot's mind like that sound effect in an episode of an old American radio serial, when the producers wanted to emphasise the vamp-like characteristics of their femmes fatales.

Margot returned to her old desk and watched Laura as she crossed the small square in front of the building. She sat down and neatly put the notes Laura had given her into a small cash-box in the top drawer of the desk. She reached for the handset of her 'phone and dialled. The answer machine silently continued to remind her that it was full. She pressed the play button and gave up after about eight apologies of cancellation and several hang-ups.

The machine fast-forwarded to the last message, which was from Archie, apologising for his strange mood, earlier. "I love you, my darling Margot. I have left this message on your mobile, too. See you at the funeral tomorrow."

Nothing else of any significance.

She opened her laptop and logged on. There were hundreds of unanswered e-mails; she often left them for three or four days at a time. This had always annoyed Archie, who didn't see the point of late e-mails. Only one old one caught her attention. It was from Tilly. There was no subject line, and no message. Just a web address and the words, 'with love from Eulalia. xx'. Margot clicked on the underlined address which was highlighted in bright turquoise...

# Chapter Sixteen

*St Eulalia: http:/www.videogramaticca.com*

Margot clicked the web address, which had been pre-programmed to automatically log her into the site. But she needed a password. She reached over to a shelf behind her and picked out one of about a dozen black, hardcover notebooks. These were her most recent case notes from her sessions with both Tilly and Paolo. She flicked through it, pressed the pages down and returned to her computer and its browser.

*Home page. Clips. Contributors. Upload.*
*Register. Log In. Password.*
*Clips. Play List. The Martyrdom of St. Eulalia. Search.*
*QuickTime Player.*
*Play.*

Domatilla and Paolo's DVD had been uploaded, perhaps the last act of a dying woman. Margot couldn't face watching it again but she gave it a five star rating – its first. She trawled down the long list of clips on the playlist. Hundreds of video clips. Mostly rubbish. One or two clumsy and blatant movie promotions posted by Hollywood studios desperately trying to woo the Internet audience. Fatuous comedians. Amateur videos. Nothing pornographic. She logged out. And then wrote in the notebook...

*Xavier? They had never mentioned him. But why had Robert never mentioned him? Why did he leave the opera so abruptly on the night of the murder. Robert?*

Margot closed the notebook and laid it on the side-table next to her chair with an air of finality. She continued to sit there, and began to think about the games she had played with Xavier when they had met at lunch for the first time. The sex. And the unthinkable. Could there be any correlation between that encounter and the deaths of her young friends? The paraphernalia in his apartment alone was reason enough to be wary of him, and yet she had been perfectly happy and finally comfortable about everything that happened. He hadn't been threatening. He had gone out of his way to make sure that she wanted to go along with his games. He hadn't seemed remotely violent or murderous! She forced that horrendous possibility from her mind.

She thought again about Xavier's physicality. His voice. His body. His eyes. His taste. His hard, beautifully proportioned cock. Margot's physical excitement at the thought of another encounter with him had so unbalanced her presence of mind that she began to behave like a pre-pubescent teenager on heat. Rather than triggering any normal feelings of grief and remorse, the horror of the murders had perversely heightened her sexual appetite. She tried to feel guilty about this but her sexual urges overcame her. Luxuriating in the cosy, seductive privacy and personal comfort of her consulting room, she moved her left hand inside her pink shirt, unstrapped her bra, and with her thumb and index finger tweaked her hard, erect right nipple and massaged her breast gently with the rest of her fingers while her right hand went down to her knickers, and with her forefinger she probed deeply into her tight but very wet vagina. Stroking her hard clitoris gently, she slowly and methodically brought herself as close to an orgasm as she could without having a climax. Closing her eyes and moaning as if in a trance, she slouched back into the soft leather of her Eames chair like a lifeless doll. She stayed like this for five minutes, until the church clock struck a quarter of the hour. She leapt up like a guilty schoolgirl who had been caught behaving badly, settled her clothes and walked back into the office area of the studio.

Margot pulled down her blinds, gulped down a contraceptive pill and changed her clothes. White dress, black leather belt. No underwear. Same perfume. Cheap Swatch. No jewellery. Flat, pink shoes. Very faint pink lipstick. She pulled off her wedding and engagement rings, hiding them guiltily in a secret compartment deep in the belly of her beautiful, late Victorian bureau desk – another Archie indulgence. The thought did occur to her that she might bump into him at the Academia, but Archie was almost certainly buried amongst his students and anyway she often removed her rings – to swim or to play badminton. (What other reason would Margot have had to take off her wedding ring?) She then sent Archie a text message to say that she was going to spend another night at the studio. "More early morning clients".

✳

The Café de L'Accademia is one of Barcelona's most popular restaurants for those who live in the city, and it was Margot's favourite haunt for lunch. Tucked behind a secluded Plaça opposite the tiny mediaeval church of Sant Just, it serves very simple Catalan food to both its small loyal local clientele of cognoscenti and to a steady stream of tourists and foreign businessmen savvy enough to have conducted their gastronomic research. The kitchen is miniscule and the small counter area offers a cut rate set lunch – a Catalan tradition which dates back to the turn of the nineteenth century when a law was passed by the Catalan parliament insisting that as part of their licence, the city's workers could eat lunch at an affordable rate at all the city's restaurants.

Margot was five minutes early, and because the first sitting of customers had shuffled off for their siesta, the counter area was temporarily empty. Margot told the small, pretty Catalan waitress that she was reserving one of the bar stools for a friend. She hadn't seen Xavier tucked into a corner at the back of the room under dark, oak-beamed ceiling. He came up behind her and sat on the stool next to her. She jumped off her stool when she realised that he was there.

"Where did you come from? I have been watching the door."

"Snakes and ladders."

He kissed her on both cheeks, lingering perhaps just a millisecond more than was customary. Margot noticed and leant into him by way of acknowledgement.

"You have the knack of appearing from nowhere. It was like that in the box at Le Liceu."

"I have never been one for the grand entrance and anyway I beat you to it first time around; you should have known I like to be early for lunch. What shall we eat? I always have the menu of the day with its free carafe of wine – red this time. I think that you should do the same. There is usually a choice between fish or meat…"

Margot agreed. It happened that she did exactly that when she came here alone, anyway.

"I was hoping that you might be wearing the same delightful clothes you wore the last time we met," Xavier said, mischievously.

Margot blushed.

"I had to throw my dress away… We didn't really learn much about each other, did we?"

"I learnt a great deal about you."

"I doubt it. What did you learn?"

And then he leant forward over the bar and whispered lasciviously into her ear, "You don't scream as loudly as some of the women I know! I want you to scream louder than anybody else for me." He almost cackled as he picked an olive from the small bowl in front of them.

"I see. Have I disappointed you? "

"Not at all. I felt that I had failed to take you to those unimaginable heights."

"You certainly managed to do that! Look, we can't talk about some things here and anyway, you are being much too presumptuous." She hit him with a fake laugh.

"I will try to behave myself."

The restaurant was relatively quiet, which of course inhibited their conversation. Rosa the waitress smiled at Margot as she greeted Xavier with a question about his choice of food. For some reason, he had merited her immediate attention. Margot agreed to go along with what he ordered.

In a deliberate attempt to reduce the sexual tension, she told him a little more about her ever-so-happy marriage to Archie and the privileged, protective childhood she had enjoyed in La Jolla before she went to Chicago. He asked about her sex life.

"A couple of very chaste teenage obsessions. A boring boyfriend who fumbled his way around my virginity. And one lover who taught me about the naughty bits but turned out to be gay! That was it before Archie! Goody two-shoes!"

He was attentive and parried with some witty stories about his encounters with the parents of the boys he had taught at the private school where he had worked in Scotland. Margot let these stories ride without any reaction. She had decided to suspend her anxieties. Xavier's spells were working. He recounted how one very rich Portuguese woman had invited him to Rio de Janeiro for a two-week holiday, ostensibly to give her son Spanish lessons. When he arrived he realised that she had really wanted him to be her sexual playmate. She lived alone on a small, self-sufficient island off the coast of Brazil, which included huts full of white rabbits bred and killed to provide a special skin graft used in cosmetic surgery – her husband was a plastic surgeon and spent most of his time in Hollywood. Margot half-believed his stories and laughed at the graphic descriptions of his escapades.

"I'm not sure that I should come back to your flat again, Xavier," she lied.

"That would be a disappointment. I wanted to show you something I have prepared especially for you."

"I bet you say that to all your lovers."

"You used the same line before. I only have one lover at a time," he remarked.

"Is this the start of another game of Snakes and Ladders? Or is it a little more adult than that? Dungeons and Dragons, maybe?" As a teenager, Margot had loved role-playing fantasies of wizards and monsters, heroes and beautiful damsels in distress.

"Nothing so tame!"

He threw his head back with a powerful laugh. The restaurant reacted with a sudden moment of empty silence, bar the clatter of plates in the kitchen. Xavier asked the waitress for the bill.

"On y va, ma chérie!"

"You go ahead. I am going to sit here and enjoy another glass of wine... I will come by in about half an hour."

Margot had almost imperceptibly lapsed into the American conversational slang of her childhood to counterbalance his pretentious command.

"À toute à l'heure, Margot, but remember that if you don't pitch up you will never see me again!"

He planted a peremptory kiss on both cheeks and with smooth insouciance walked slowly out of the restaurant as if he had just said goodbye to a junior business colleague.

*

*The trouble with my job is that I have to suffer in silence. There is no alternative. Why would a woman who would seem to have everything which could allow her to lead a happy, stimulating life, be on the verge of triggering an appalling, apocalyptic personal tragedy? Have I had too much happiness? I have been spoilt... Perhaps that's it. All those simple pleasures and special treats, and yes, those luxuries that only a very few privileged elite can enjoy: were they just apples in a basket of fruit which was now going to throw up something rotten?*

*Unpicking the fucked-up psyches of my clients had been such an easy process. I could see them in the context of my own spectacularly contrasting childhood experiences. During the many years of training, my own therapist had despaired. She used to say, with no sense of irony, that she had never before been confronted by such a blank sheet of psychological blemishes – my past contained precious little meat and drink for any self-respecting therapist! She had been desperately reduced to examining in minute detail, those nigh-on perfect moments in my childhood as her clumsy attempt to uncover any recurring, carefully disguised flashpoints which could balance the almost sickening perfections of my upbringing in suburban San Diego. Even the pink stucco architecture of downtown La Jolla had been scrutinised for potential iconographical references! I* used to laugh out loud at her frustration, especially when she resorted to exploring a girlhood visit to the mall as a pretext for a deeply buried psychosis. I actually adored the process of shopping in the supermarket there. The people, the air-conditioning, the ordered and manipulated lay out, even the laughable regimentation of the check-out provided me with amusement values, but they denied her any clues which hinted at my need to go into the deep analysis she so wanted to subject me to. Sickening perfection is what I called it.

My father and I loved to play chess together. We still do when we meet; always sitting opposite each other, pouring over the same beautiful table in our den at home. Black ebony and white ivory chess pieces brought back from a trip to Kenya. Simple wooden board. When he started to teach me, he would allow me to win the games because he didn't want to sap my confidence while I developed strategies. On one occasion, I noticed that he had varied a favourite opening ploy with a move of staggering stupidity. I smelt a rat, pulled him up and he let out a belly-laugh of Dickensian proportions – he is a large, portly man with very bushy eyebrows and beautiful blue eyes. "Ok! I am going to win this one!" he warned, proceeding to demolish me in about a dozen brilliant moves, after which he began to teach me notation. I was humbled and inspired, and hugged him when he came to say goodnight.

My mother, correspondingly, had a quiet, perceptive intelligence. When my breasts began to grow, I noticed that they were not as big as many of the other cheerleaders that I had been hanging out with before and after the big football games. I loved the exuberance, the discipline, even the superficial glamour of it all; and the fun. Mom used her own adolescent sexual experiences as the vehicle for gentle explanations of the glories and pitfalls of burgeoning sexuality. She took me though these in detail and we were able to obliterate any unnecessary neuroses I had *been starting to harbour about my body size.*

*Of course, there were mishaps along the way. A cycling accident which resulted in a scar on my knee. Tragic? Life threatening? Traumatic? Hardly. The death of my paternal grandfather, aged eighty-three, gave me a moody few months but he left me with so many wonderful funny stories about his Russian Orthodox upbringing in Manchuria. They continue to serve as a spiritual legacy whenever I need to smile. Eccentric stories about farting priests, adulterous rabbis and an alcoholic carpenter who killed himself swigging a bottle of methylated spirits one dark night, when the power had failed him in his makeshift workshop at the bottom of the garden, and he mistook the poison for his tipple of sloe gin!*

*Perhaps the most significant familial influence on me, and certainly a relationship my therapist dwelt on for months, was my love for my Uncle Ian. He came to live with us when I was eight. He had squandered his fortune and, as I learnt later from Mom who was his favourite sister, like my grandfather's carpenter friend, Uncle Ian was an alcoholic. Of course, I didn't pick up on this until much later on and I adored him on sight. I was only eight years old. Like granddad, he used to tell me some very funny 'naughty' stories which later in adolescence fuelled the curiosity that I developed in people's peculiarities. He also involved me in his own secret – the stash of 'sherry', (whisky probably) which he used to hide in my bedroom. Finally, Mom threw him out – he used to become belligerent and vent his alcoholic paranoia on her. She didn't want her cosy life disturbed. For all I know he became a tramp. When he died of cirrhosis of the liver, I shut myself up in my room for a week and refused to go to his funeral. I was so angry with my mother. But she explained it all to me so sensitively that I had to forgive her. Marie Christine, my supervisor, said that it was my 'love affair' as she called it, with Uncle Ian, which had almost certainly led onto my need to 'help' or 'nurse' people.*

*To make them better. I had always thought that it was more to do with my father's academic work in theoretical anthropology.*

*And here I am, hanging myself with the noose of my professional expertise, my over-educated sophistication. Apart from the trauma of Uncle Ian, my childhood had been full of Dr Seuss, the Wizard of Oz, of the Muppets and Mary Poppins, too. And when I ventured into the darker areas of the Brothers Grimm and anything approaching the Nightmares on Elm Street, Dungeons and Dragons or the ghosts and ghouls of forbidden fruit in Hollywood horror movies, I did so in the certain knowledge that my parents would provide me with balancing and revelatory wisdom which diminished their potential conditioning influences. Even the horrors and shame of the Vietnam War, which had defined their youth, were given their historical context.*

*But every action has a reaction. Every experience created a psychological corollary. In therapy I have always methodically allowed my mind to inspect the latent power of minor trauma. Those moments we discount as harmless or irrelevant. The history of psychology is crammed full of a deluge of evidence supporting the existence of those sneaky, unfathomable, undetectable cerebral poison darts which appear as mysteriously as a lethal cancer cell and are just as deadly. I had a friend who tried to warn me about the impact, for instance, of indulging 'dangerous' arts forms. I found his fatuous ideas about the potential dangers of subconscious conditioning so annoying, so glib and yet I had to take his ideas seriously enough to refute them intelligently. He approved of censorship, and advocated some sort of code which would steer us away from the risks of mental pollution, as he called it. His silly, neo-fascistic theories about the impact of subversive art served to consolidate my own sense of proportion in that respect.*

*But now that I am on the brink of quite willingly experiencing what can only become a major trauma, where has this self-control and philosophical perspective disappeared? Whence does my newfound latent hunger for perverse and dangerous self-abuse spring? Surely not from those relatively superficial studies I made at college on the machinations of the Marquis de Sade? Surely not triggered by the studious fascination I indulged in the philosophies of Wittgenstein? Or those nightmare visions of Dante evoked by William Blake? The Circles of Hell.*

*Until now, I have exercised supreme self-control and maintained a balanced perspective whenever confronted by anything extreme or unnatural. But I am beginning to feel a bit like poor Laura now. For example, I absolutely adore the short stories of Alberto Moravia. They often centre around the behaviour of a strong, fascinating woman in a simple familiar setting. They are always reminders of the quirkiness of human behaviour and they always have an ironic and witty warning about bourgeois smugness. Maybe I am just a simple bourgeois slut who is finally receiving her share of payback to balance a lifetime of stifling and excruciating complacency? Or maybe I am manifesting the same instincts which led Eve out of Paradise and into the clutches of Beelzebub? John Milton would not approve of my alacrity and he would have cast me on the side of Satan in all those battles for the soul of his brand of puritanical Christianity. What a case study for a psychiatrist he would have made. He was blind, of course.*

Blind.

# Chapter Seventeen

Margot woke up, thinking that she had been having an erotic dream, but when she felt the tension of the cord which tightly secured her wrists and feet to the brass railings at both ends of the top of Xavier's raised sleeping area, she realised she was beginning to live a form of reality which would have been as perverted as the wildest of her clients' fantasies. Fantasies she had only indulged before from the comfort of her studio. The silk scarf covering her eyes smelt faintly of an expensive French perfume. Her legs were spread out and her ankles were tied to opposite ends of the mattress at the end of the platform. She could hear the frogs mingling their croaks with the distant voice of an opera singer, practising a Donizetti aria. *Regnava al silenzio*. The apparition in the lake.

"Xavier?"

Silence! She raised her voice above the initial whisper.

"Xavier!?"

Louder and firmer, with a hint of frustration. Still no response. A baritone had joined the soprano. A duet. She pulled at the cords, trying to loosen them; they were very tight.

Her vagina was pulsating. Almost a dull throb. Xavier had stroked her pudenda so softly: "Imagine what I am going to do with you when I return." He kissed her lips and passed his hand and fingers very gently, almost like a butterfly's kiss, over her long, dark nipples, which were rigidly erect, before climbing down from the platform. His valedictory gesture was a treat that Margot hadn't experienced since childhood: he read her a poem. He had a beautiful, soft, mellow reading style.

Somehow, he managed to prevent what could have been a pretentious and laughable farce, transforming it into a beautiful, soporific interlude. Margot's vagina was like a torrent of spring. The last sound he made had come from the double locks of his beautiful ancient oak door – from the outside.

When was he going to return? Would he ever return? It didn't seem to matter. Margot was in an 'altered state'. Within three minutes she had an explosive, sensation-full orgasm and all her fantasies before and after it had been exotic and extravagant; worthy of the worst and best indulgences of a second-rate European art movie: Tristan naked on the mast of the boat in The Wreck of the Hesperus, watched by Isolde in the guise of a Carthusian nun; Héloise raped by the Sabine women in a modern porno movie; Joan of Arc with a giant penis; Freud and Mahler making love to each other to the strains of Albinoni; Don Giovanni in Hell surrounded by a score of masturbating lipstick dykes; and Xavier as St. George – slaying the Minotaur in a Dali-like landscape. Paintings, literature, music, poetry, religious iconography. She effortlessly conjured a plethora of fantastical sexual stereotypes and experiences while she waited for his return.

And then she had another seismic orgasm, gasping with pleasure as her body shuddered with sensual excitement. Freud called this kind of vaginal orgasm 'mature' and the clitoral one immature. Margot had never quite understood this descriptive distinction until now. Her mind was occupied with the dawning realisation that her theories about Xavier's intentions towards her that afternoon might have been totally wrong; her pleasures had been his objective, not his own.

When she had arrived, he had set up his ancient Italian 16mm movie projector on a table close to the French windows which led to the garden area. He rolled down a large, cleverly-hidden white movie screen which rested against the back wall of his kitchen area. "My computer screen is much too small."

He had then pre-laced into the projector's grey spools a black and white film made by a 'celebrated' Canadian animator. Called *Pas de Deux*, it was an exquisite, abstracted ballet enacted by two very beautiful dancers in sensual white body-stockings against a black backdrop. The minimalist soundtrack was as seductive and repetitive as a brilliant John Adams tone poem. The cinematography was manipulated so that multiple images of each carefully-choreographed physical movement seemed to have been repeated by a spirit or ghost. Against a simple abstract background on an empty stage two dancers enacted the traditional rituals of a conventionally staged pas de deux – simple and sexually-charged balletic lovemaking. After the film was over, Margot and Xavier talked about it and then he had asked her what she would most like to do with him. All her earlier suspicions had been obliterated by his charm and the gentle, relaxed atmosphere which he had so subtly engineered for her.

"What about those Dungeons and Dragons?"

She bleated this out like an over-excited child. He smiled.

"I didn't want you to think that I was always some sort of kinky pervert. I feel that you are open to all kinds of experiences with me. I love that and want to take advantage of my ability to surprise you."

"I want to indulge all my fantasies!" she said, with a coquettish smile. Xavier had devised the simplest of plans, which had left her for hours, tied naked to the mattress on his sleeping arena. Alone and blinded, like the poor hero of Milton's *Samson Agonistes*, one of Margot's favourite poems.

※

As she lay there hours later, the first vestiges of panic crept into her disoriented mind. Had she covered all her tracks? Before his improvised ritual had started, Margot had rung her answering machine at home. She left another message for Archie, explaining that she wanted to ensure that he knew she would be out for dinner and would sleep in her studio another night, but she would see him at the funeral – she would walk there with Elvira. She wondered if Archie might think that she seemed to be unusually concerned that he should know every movement. Margot had always guarded her need for time off 'for bad behaviour'. He teased her about this but respected her need for independence as he, too, enjoyed time on his own.

Margot wriggled her feet around. Tight. The blindfold was comfortable to wear but she was beginning to hate the dark. Shutting her eyes made no difference, blue and red blobs, yellow contortions. But finally a black void. What if Xavier intended to leave her there indefinitely? The sound of his key in the oak door finally obliterated this far-fetched anxiety!

"Margot?"

His beautiful voice and the sensuous memories of her two orgasms replaced any extraneous practicalities. Her body still tingled. She was still moist, and immediately she was drawn straight back into her sensual trance by his voice – an altered state so persuasive and irresistible.

Music: the smoky, high-pitched, mournful voice of Nina Simone singing *Solitude:*

"...In my solitude you taught me with memories which never die..."

Margot laughed. "Thank you, Xavier. Very funny."

He was soon above her, but fully clothed. He made sure that she could feel his jeans against her legs. He then peeled a banana and a cucumber, allowed her to feel them, to taste them, to smell them and then using them inside her, together on occasions, gently with the banana, hard with the peeled cucumber, brought her to orgasm, twice. Then, feeding the banana to her lips, he slowly unbuttoned his jeans and thrust his hard, drizzling cock deep into her cunt. She moaned and screamed, with almost unbearable pleasure. He came twice without interruption, driving his hips deep into her vagina. His semen was warm and soft, his climaxes prolonged. She exploded again and again. Afterwards, he kissed her lips gently and removed three of the cords, cutting them free with a small, sharp knife. The fourth, now separated from the railing he had used to restrict her, he quite deliberately left on her right wrist. Margot lay there, wondering what he was going to do next. She would have allowed him to do anything.

But when the blindfold had gone, and Xavier had turned on a small, pink neon light which glowed over her naked body, she realised the horrifying significance of the remaining cord bracelet: it was a replica of the one which Tilly had worn in the recreation of the Waterhouse painting of St Eulalia. She tried unsuccessfully to loosen the knot. Any vestige of the spectacular and sensational sexuality which had overwhelmed her for hours, vanished within a millisecond.

Without saying another word, Margot climbed down into the well of his strange apartment and dressed in the locked bathroom, alone. While she sat on the toilet seat, trying to work out how she was going to deal with him, she fingered Xavier's seemingly innocent gesture: the remaining cord bracelet. Perhaps this was just a coincidence? A cord bracelet is a cord bracelet, but all her anxieties had returned. She was trembling. Nina Simone continued from the apartment.

"I sit in my chair. No one could be so sad... I sit and I stare... I know that I'll know that I will soon go mad... in my solitude... dear Lord above, send me back my love..."

When Margot emerged from the bathroom, Xavier was sitting on a bench in the kitchen. There were two glasses of wine on the table. She sat on the bench on the opposite side of the table from him as he pushed a glass gently over to her. There was an interrogatory air about his smile, which she ignored.

"I feel a bit like a zebra or a gazelle in the veldt, who knows that a beautiful and powerful lion is watching her every move, luxuriating in the prospect of a sumptuous meal, and waiting for the inevitable moment when he is going to spring into action and devour her."

"A lion indeed! Now that we have established a modus operandi for lots of games, why don't we give each other the name of an animal as our means of secret communication? And we can use the animal's Spanish name. I can be el Leon and you could be la Gacela, the gazelle!"

He smiled.

Margot's blood ran cold. Paolo's abusive Spanish teacher had used exactly the same game. There could not be two men who use exactly the same, and unique, teaching technique. Could Xavier and Guy be one and the same man? Her stomach churned. She felt sick. She deliberately forced out an innocuous reply. "La Gacela it is, then."

Paolo was the leopard. Un leopardo. She wanted to leave as soon as she could without implying any change in her enthusiasm for their new relationship. Almost without thinking, and with the need to see if she could engage him in a subtle element of amateur detection, she asked him a question which could have given away to Xavier her newest and most deadly secret.

"O quizás un leopardo?"

She realised that she may have made a stupid, precipitous mistake. The seductively chilled red wine had gone straight to her head, which now reeled with her discoveries. Xavier laughed.

"My animals and birds are my secrets."

He hadn't noticed anything. He had absolutely no reason to imagine that Margot had made any connection about his nicknames, or would have known about them. Margot pushed it further.

"It's Paolo's funeral tomorrow. Did you know Paolo Lorca well?"

"Yes, I did. Rather well. The ex-pat community is somewhat incestuous in Barcelona, isn't it? As it happens, I have been teaching him Catalan here. He was brought up in Scotland."

Margot had to repress the screams now echoing throughout the darkest chambers of her mind. Could this man, that she had just allowed to tie her up and use her body in any way he chose, the man who had just provided her with sexual ecstasies on a level that she had never imagined, could he be the same man who had seduced and raped Paolo when he was a child? Had he also officiated at Tilly's horrifying and fatal re-enactment of the death of St. Eulalia? Was that Tilly and Paolo's secret? Perhaps it was Paolo's renewed friendship with Xavier that Tilly had been hiding from her.

Margot tried to stay calm. She was determined to deflate Xavier's presumptuous smugness and hide her immediate sensation of revulsion and self-disgust. He had clearly noticed a change in her mood.

"Are you coming?" she asked.

"I am not sure that I can. I would like to."

She hesitated, trying to find a question which would reiterate what she had learnt, and confirm what she suspected.

"Did you know Tilly?"

"I met her once or twice. She was stunning."

"So was he..."

He looked quizzically at her. Chit chat.

"The rumour mill has been working overtime. Robert rang to tell me that there had been some evidence of an accomplice in the staging of their macabre suicide. The police have been questioning him."

"Robert called you. Suicide? Robert knows that it was a murder. He must do."

Margot was trying to stay composed.

Xavier continued, volunteering information. "I had a call from a policeman investigating their death and at first he seemed to think that they had killed themselves in some sort of *Romeo and Juliet* style ritualistic game."

He was so calm, so casual. Margot tried desperately to suppress her rage and disgust.

"They were clients of mine... As bonkers as they undoubtedly were, they were not about to kill themselves. Certainly not when I last saw them, which wasn't so long ago."

He moved his hand over to the bottle to refill her glass.

"No, thank you, Xavier". She stood up to leave. "I must get back to Archie."

"Ah, your husband, Archie!"

"Do you know Archie?" Margot feigned surprise.

"I met him; many years ago. In Scotland."

"I wonder why he has never mentioned it to me."

"It's so long ago. We hardly ever meet. A different generation."

"He was showing me around the cathedral this morning..." Margot had decided to take a risk.

"Really? Why?"

Xavier sat there while she found a pair of scissors in one of the drawers and cut the cord off her wrist. She placed it neatly on the table near her wine glass.

"St Eulalia!" Margot whispered.

And at that moment, they both knew each other's secret. Someone was screaming in the distance. The frogs were silent. A cock crowed. Up until that moment, Margot had been in the special situation of knowing so much about this man's life, while he was unaware of the extent of that knowledge, apart from the most superficial details. In the clumsy assumption that he might have been innocent, and in a moment of stupidity, she had accidentally played into his hands and ironically enough in doing so, he would unwittingly reveal his guilt to her, and confirm her worst suspicions; that Xavier, her new lover, had been involved in the deaths of Tilly and Paolo.

"Will you stay for another drink, Margot? Please! I want to tell you more about Archie."

He sat there pathetically, as if all the sensual power he had manifested physically had suddenly drained from his body. Margot was almost drawn back to him. She shuddered.

"No, I must go."

And she let herself out, hurriedly.

As she walked through the corridor that led to the main front door of the block, she heard a strange, prolonged, muffled cry of anguish from his apartment. She walked back a few paces, and listened. Xavier was crying and moaning, like a desperate, overgrown child. She hurried along the dark corridor and out into the balmy safety of the Plaça Santa Maria del Pi. She shivered. The church bells were peeling early morning matins. It was dawn. There was no breeze but the crisp blue sky and cool air felt like a cold shower on her skin. She stood enjoying the tiny ray of sunlight beginning to prod its way over the Tibidado. The square was empty except for what looked like an old-fashioned police car, sitting discreetly in the small side street next to the Church, a black sedan which hadn't been there the previous afternoon. Margot hesitated, and then walked quickly away towards the narrow *calle* which led to her own beloved Plaça.

At that time in the morning, the narrower *Calles* of the Barri Gothic ooze the atmospheres of their sleazy histories. Pushers and prostitutes still ply their trade before their clients stumble out of the chic, and not so chic, hotels that have replaced the crowded tenements of its mediaeval past.

Margot felt like a woman with a terrible hangover, sheepishly trying to escape surreptitiously from a one-night stand in one of those hotels. A one-night stand that she regretted. She hurried past Elvira's café which was opening up in time for the early morning stragglers.

*"Damn it,"* she thought.

Surely Elvira would have been closed today? But of course, Elvira wanted to serve at least a few of her regulars before closing up for the funeral. Margot tried to slip by.

"Margot!" called Elvira from the doorway.

"Oh Elvira! In one hour Elvira... Una ora per favore! I will come earlier!"

Feigning innocence and surprise, she had shouted without stopping, backing down the street into a half-run. Once back in her studio, she showered obsessively. Cold. Fresh. Temporarily cleansed. She went quickly to her desk and retrieved her rings from the secret compartment. They were an awkward fit, her fingers having swollen in the heat. She changed into a neat black suit, opened the shutters and, avoiding Elvira's *calle* this time, hurried along a couple of blocks to sit at her favourite café in Las Ramblas. She was the only customer and her regular waiter, a Pakistani, hovered around the porn emporium where a clutch of transvestites was trading their stories of the night with him. She needed to think in as public a place as she could find. No associations. Anonymity. The area around this particular stand had a seedy liveliness, which she had always enjoyed. It made her feel safe and protected. It was also within yards of the gates of the largest and newest police station in Barcelona. The Mossos D'Esquadros headquarters. Carlos's office.

She ordered a Coca Cola, accepting with a limp laugh the inevitable innuendo about her body. She then waited for her fix of sugar, watching the newsagents laying out their magazines and newspapers. As she took the tall glass of Coke from the silver tray, she moved away to a table with a view of the bay. Christopher Columbus was posing as majestically as ever. What was she going to tell Elvira she had been doing at six in the morning in the Barri Gotic, dressed in the same flimsy white dress she had worn on the eve of her wedding day, five years ago?

She rang Archie. His answering machine. Slightly needy.

"Darling, it's me?... pick up, sweetheart... Archie?..." And then, in a rather quieter tone, "I just wondered. What are you doing after the funeral? Are you going to the wake because I have a new client to see then. Please ring me. I am on my cell. Are you still going to meet Tilly's parents at the airport? I need to talk to you."

There was still the faintest hint of desperation in her voice. Archie would pick that up and call her, she was sure of that.

*How blind indeed. Archie...*

# Chapter Eighteen

Five years ago, almost to the day, the café where she was sitting in Las Ramblas had been the first staging post for Margot's 'hen night', a peculiarly Western proto-feminist ritual which has begun to rival the stag night as embarrassing evidence of humanity's innate bestial and moronic tendencies. Archie and Margot had few friends in common at the time – even in Chicago they had kept their social lives separate. His position as a senior Professor had made that necessary – relationships with students are always discouraged. And Margot relished some independence. Most of Archie's friends were from his generation and many of them were rich and successful enough to be able to afford to fly to Barcelona. Apart from her parents who pitched up from La Jolla, of course, Margot's invitation list was by contrast much younger and poorer. No old boyfriends, mainly her large clutch of good girlfriends. And so only a small and predominantly female group, those who could afford the fare to Europe, showed up. About half a dozen Californian friends, including two fellow Cheerleaders dressed to the nines, three of her room-mates from the University, her Chicago-based psychoanalyst and an interloping but much adored gay friend who said that he could join the throng dressed as Penelope Cruz. They were an eclectic and entertaining group, intoxicated by this God-given opportunity to indulge their wildest Mediterranean fantasies in the setting of Margot's favourite Pedro Almodovar film, *All About My Mother,* filmed only a year or so previously in that city.

The dress code for the hen-night had been to dress 'Almodovar' and all were asked to rent a car for the night. A set-piece of the evening was a carefully-planned restaging of the fabulous 'prostitutes' car circle' scene in a field in the suburbs of Barcelona. Margot had bribed half a dozen of Las Ramblas' finest studs to join the party – as many Xavier Bardem equivalents as she could find. And the girls were to be prostitutes for the night, silly but enormous fun. At five in the morning, Margot was carried head high into the first floor lobby of the Arts Hotel by gorgeous Catalan transvestites surrounded by her drunken friends who were now singing her favourite Doris Day song *Que Sera, Sera*. When she was finally placed ritualistically on her huge king-sized bed, in the hotel's honeymoon suite on the top floor of the hotel, it was dawn. The girls tiptoed out giggling. She awoke a couple of hours later, surrounded by six gorgeous, naked men. All dead to the world.

Still dressed in her flimsy white dress, she wandered down the corridor to Archie's smaller suite two doors away. She couldn't resist sharing the moment. He followed her meekly back to the suite. It was empty! Her Almodovar fantasy had vanished. Undeterred, she led Archie into her bed, ordered a massive breakfast from room service and gently made love to him. He had been the only man she had ever wanted to be with.

In contrast to Margot's modest clutch of guests, Archie had characteristically invited everyone he had ever met to their wedding ceremony and reception, which he had set up to take place in the gardens of the then newly-built Arts Hotel near the Olympic village. The raised garden terrace at The Arts has some very simple beautiful wood sculptures, in sharp contrast to the giant bronze, magnificently garish steel, lattice fish, created by the American architect Frank Gehry, which separates the hotel complex from the sea. Archie had been determined to make Margot feel at home in Europe and chose this hotel very specifically. Its tall steel structure sits majestically at the end of the bay that the Barcelona Olympic committee had transformed artificially in 1992 by blasting a sandy beach, which now has one of the finest modern esplanades in Europe. Its architecture and interior design deliberately cock a snoop at the modernista influences of Antoni Gaudi and Lluís Domenech Montaner, whose artistic spirits pervade most of the other grand luxury hotels in the city.

"Modern California meets the Med, and I don't mean mediaeval!" is how Archie joked by way of apology for his choice. He had been amused at the thought of all his more stuffy academic friends mingling amongst its predominantly chic international clientele. "Let's sweep them into the twenty-first century!"

Margot began to piece together the elements in her marriage since her wedding which might give her some clue as to how to deal with her betrayal of the one person who deserved her unconditional loyalty. She was also trying that most impossible of psychiatric exercises, the agonising process of objective self-analysis. But what she most wanted, was to find a way to escape the mess she was in. Perhaps, in the absence of Marie-Christine's sorely-missed wisdom, she needed to talk to someone reliable, who could understand the extremes of her behaviour. One of her clients, perhaps? She decided to use the wedding and its guest list as her starting point because many of her new friendships had started then, and they were the conduits to most of her clients and the backbone of their social life. Archie's eclectic group of wedding guests had introduced Margot to a new milieu – that most bizarre and rarefied of all ex-patriot communities, the British in Barcelona at the end of the Blair era. Most of her clients came from this peculiar mixture of bankers, carpetbaggers, academics, playboys and playgirls. They ranged in age from the teenagers like Tilly to the over-sexed, eighty-two year old sculptor who had been married five times and was thinking of marrying once more, a girl sixty years his junior. Surely, amongst this very neurotic hybrid collection of eccentrics and misfits, she would find a soulmate who might offer her the advice she so badly needed. The intimacy of all her professional relationships, especially when they were in analysis, had allowed her the privilege of trust. A trust that was, in her case, mutual. Their secrets were her secrets. Perhaps her secrets could be theirs, too? In the absence of Marie-Christine, she desperately needed someone to turn to. Hideously unprofessional of course, but an indication of her isolation. She knew their secrets, perhaps one of them could share hers?

The second Coca Cola arrived. Lemon and ice. A massive white cruise ship was sailing silently out of the port. If only...

Rather desperately, she played along with the game, and began to sift through the vast database in her mind which had been the willing receptacle for so many of the weird and wonderful problems of her clients. On the surface, all of them in some strange way possessed some of the necessary qualifications as confidantes, and if they had been friends, might have been candidates to help her deal with the situation with Xavier. They all had a deep love and respect for Margot, along with a crucial understanding of her need for secrecy.

Her first client had been Anthony. He was very poor, and had been Margot's conduit to the transvestites of Las Ramblas and as such was a guest at the wedding in his own right. He had quite specifically modelled himself in life on the character Eusebio in *All About My Mother*, so Margot's fantastical scenario for the hen-night had been a form of reality for him.

Anthony?

*When he had arrived in the city as a teenager, he had fallen for an older trans-sexual woman he had met in the Mercado over a café solo. She had a light moustache and was overweight but dressed and acted like an Italian movie star. He loved Italian movies of the 1950's and 1960's. Gina Lollobrigida, Sophia Loren and the sublime Monica Vitti. He renamed her Monica. For a time they lived clandestinely in a tiny apartment overlooking the beach on the Barceloneta. She earned her living at that time cooking paella in a small restaurant nearby. He worked in a bar in the Universitat. But soon they were in debt and to escape they eloped to Brazil. Within weeks he began to earn his living as a rent-boy and they lived a strange but happy life within Rio's narcotic sub-culture. But everything turned sour when she was murdered in a tragic case of jealousy and mistaken identity. Devastated, he had no alternative but to return to Barcelona, knowing that he could ply his new trade on the streets of La Raval where he began to accumulate a small band of friends. One of those friends was Robert, who had tried to pick him up in a late night bar.*

*I had taken him on knowing that he wouldn't be able to pay me anything, but his profile was fascinating and I felt that he would give me some psychological keys into the minds of a subculture I had never experienced. I told him this and he seemed happy about it. He certainly provided that in spades and what was at first an unlikely fit has become a very special friendship.*

But Margot felt sure there was something Anthony had been hiding from her. No trust.

Asif?

*Asif was, by contrast, my first wealthy client. A successful author, oozing with louche charm and slightly self-manufactured charisma, in his youth he had been a very beautiful man to look at but as time and fame took their toll, he had been spoiled by the indulgent lunches during his time as a copywriter at a famous American advertising agency. Half Indian, a Sikh, his problem centred on his appalling need to cheat on every woman he had an affair with. He had chosen me as his mother confessor principally because he had wanted to fuck me, as he put it so poetically (and as he declared to me after a couple of sessions). Undeterred by my brutal rejection ("Don't be silly, Asif!"), he began to trust me slowly and finally revealed what he believed to be the nature of his problem: his rather desperate Pakistani father was a bitter man. Feeling that he had been a failure in his life, he became disproportionately jealous of everybody who seemed to be thriving and then when that jealousy became directed towards his son, Asif, by way of psychological self-protection, increased the pretext for this obsessive paternal jealousy by achieving at a level his father had only ever dreamt about. His international success as an author, his strong, mainly white, middle class collegiate of friends and his stupendous success with white women drove his father to a form of alcoholic madnesss, and he resorted to taking out his frustrations on Asif's poor, very English mother. This led to a painful conflagration which ended in a terrible public fisticuffs between father and son, worthy of Sohrab and Rustum, the Persian pair who fought to the death in the Assyrian desert to settle a war between rival potentates. Asif allowed me to unpick the clear-cut Freudian aspects of his psyche but spent large amounts of our time trying to seduce me. As the rejection became more pronounced, so his friendship deepened and his sessions now are as much a meeting of minds as they are therapeutic. But he wouldn't be able to handle my sexual passions for another man, especially as I used to tell him that my first and foremost sexual loyalty was reserved for Archie.*

And then there was Robert; of course, Robert might have been the obvious first port of call because he was not really a client in the strictest sense and had introduced Xavier. Knows him.

*The idea is preposterous. Robert would be the last person I could ever confide anything to, especially under these circumstances. He is a British journalist – this puts him into a special category as far as trust is concerned. From top to bottom they are quite simply the most unreliable confidantes in the world. It is an inbred phenomenon.*

*But queens in love with transvestites and self-important novelists are equally unreliable... This is all so, so silly; desperate... However intimate I may have been with any of these people, I am there to help them. I cannot reverse that situation.*

Realistically, Margot knew that as a collegiate, her clients were not a good pool of confidantes in any way at all. In fact, they were disastrously inappropriate from a professional point of view, and unacceptable options personally. As much as she would have liked the process to be mutual and a two-way exchange, the harsh reality was that all of them were in some way or another self-obsessed and did not have the capacity to exercise that evenly suspended attention which would be so necessary for her. She managed a wry smile at the thought. The rest of her list read like the wish-list for an unimaginable daytime reality television show. Eusebio, the seventy-year-old sculptor, a serial adulterer of monumental proportions; Kim, the recovering alcoholic in love with his sister; Leslie, the obese kleptomaniac; Suzie, the bulimic heiress bent on suicide; Donald, the impoverished film director with a myriad of masochistic obsessions; Russell, a classical cellist with a long grey beard who was a reformed child molester training for the priesthood; Lydia, the fetishist international lawyer who liked to be dominated and humiliated; Simon, a married ex-BBC executive prone to curb crawling, serial masturbation and threesomes with his wife dressed in military uniform; Gottfried, a very young and very fat merchant banker whose father was embezzling his clients; Hilary, the married owner of a Barcelona 'English as a foreign language' school, in love with a Roman Catholic bishop who had fathered two of her children; and then there was Tilly, with Paolo! Oddly enough, Tilly would have been the only candidate amongst this bizarre bag crammed full of deranged frogs who would begin to understand what she was going through. She smiled wryly at the mysterious metaphor her mind had conjured. Xavier's frogs!

She drained the glass and walked slowly back towards her studio. She was dreading the calls from the clients she had let down the afternoon before, along with the calls she was going to have to make. To cancel her one morning appointment, for example – an oversized Italian woman desperate to deal with her obesity. Anything to delay all this. She felt so vulnerable, trapped within the irony of knowing that the people she had secret confidential and intimate relationships with were an impossible refuge for her crisis. Trapped, knowing that she couldn't talk to Archie. And trapped, because Xavier had wriggled himself so severely under her skin and into her mind. Elvira's bar was of course one possible temporary haven. A last resort. What she really wanted, was to call the woman who had been her supervisor, her former mentor, Marie-Christine.

Apart from Archie, she was the only other person who had ever persuaded her to feel completely safe. At first, what began as purely a technical relationship, had blossomed into an intimate and profound friendship. Margot so desperately hoped that she would be well enough to talk to her. Her last conversation with Marie-Christine's husband had been cautiously optimistic but he had discouraged any contact. This, however, was an emergency.

Margot guessed that Marie-Christine was probably still very ill but her need to talk to her transcended any guilty feelings of unnecessary selfishness about bothering an incapacitated woman. Could she call France to try to arrange a visit to see her at some stage very soon, even if it meant hunting her out by just pitching up? Or beg for an hour or so on the 'phone, maybe? Marie-Christine had never really liked the telephone conversation as the means for any serious therapeutic interchange but maybe there was no alternative now? And of course, for all she knew, Marie-Christine might be dead, or in a coma. She had been through some very serious chemotherapy as part of her treatments, but Margot was desperate, and all of these factors were fracturing her usually crystal clear powers of deduction, or any sense of decorum. She decided to try to reach her at her home 'phone and her husband on his cell phone. She dialled and listened to the sustained tone of the French telephone service. She pictured her friend's wise face bulging out of her tiny frame. Hardly five foot tall, a tiny woman from the Languedoc, Marie-Christine looked like a very thin China doll. Before her illness, she had always planned to retire with her equally miniscule husband to their secluded villa in a converted Carthusian monastery in the Mid Pyrenees near Toulouse. They would grow organic vegetables and make organic wine. They had agreed on a modus operandi for sustaining their relationship if one or other of them should have to leave Barcelona for whatever reason – regular visits revolving around the changing seasons. Margot would pay for her 'therapy' by working the land. But Marie-Christine's chronic breast cancer had scuppered these fail-safe plans earlier than they had both anticipated.

No reply to either number and no answering machine. Maybe they had moved. Or maybe she had died.

# Chapter Nineteen

Investing trust in Elvira seemed to be Margot's only, somewhat desperate, means of immediate mental sanctuary. When she arrived at the café, Elvira was arguing with a drunk, one of her morning regulars, who was trying to persuade her to give him another free early morning cognac.

"You can have an orange juice!" she scolded him. He eventually gave up and Elvira began to pull down the shutter of the front entrance. Margot sent a text to cancel her morning appointment.

"I am going to close now! We can talk here. I know you want to talk."

Her intuition was comforting. Margot sat on a barstool. The noise of the coffee machine drowned out the barrage of drunken Catalan expletives which the disgruntled drunk hurled from the street. When the coffee arrived in front of Margot, the café was quiet, except for the faint hum of the slot machines.

"I need your help!"

"I know!" Elvira smiled and took Margot's hands in hers. "I love you, Margot. You are my friend. But I am married to a very nosey policeman. Nosey? Is that the word in Americano?"

"English, Elvira. English!" Margot managed a laugh.

Elvira waited for her friend.

"Elvira, I know that you are a devout Catholic..."

"Practising," Elvira interrupted, with a wink.

"I hope you can behave towards me like a mother confessor. Omerta is the Italian word. Whatever I tell you must be between us."

"Carlos?"

Margot thought about the implications. A secret stops being a secret once it is announced as such.

"Okay, Carlos!"

"I tell him everything. Well, not everything. He is so jealous about my customers."

"With reason, Elvira." Margot allowed herself to laugh once more.

Another awkward silence.

"I want you to tell me whether you have ever felt so physically drawn towards a man that he quite literally takes you out of yourself. He takes you into a state of mind which is uncontrollable."

"I feel like that when Carlos is making love to me."

"Carlos. But he is your husband?"

"I love him. And in bed he is like a hero for me. But he is also like an animal. And he frightens me sometimes. But I love him."

"He frightens you?"

"When he pushes my hands behind my head and clasps them together, like a pair of his police handcuffs, and his large body is inside me and on top of me, I have no power. He is powerful. He is like a rapist. I am his victim. But I want him there. That excites me and he gives me many, many orgasms like this. He never hurts me, he never hits me, he is so beautiful but I feel frightened. Weak. But it is very exciting. In that way I am 'out of myself', as you say. I never tell my priest about this."

Margot had listened as carefully and as analytically as she might have to a client, and realised that Elvira was describing a phenomenon which is common to most women who have good sexual relationships with men they trust and men whose sexuality they are happy to indulge and enjoy. There was nothing in her description of her relationship with Carlos which could be compared to what she had experienced with Xavier, of course. Was it familiar, as far as her sexual relationship with Archie was concerned? To a certain extent it was. Not quite as passionate and as Mediterranean in its characteristics, but familiar, all the same.

"You are a very lucky woman. Archie is not as strong as Carlos but I know what you are describing here."

Elvira giggled. "Carlos is a very lucky man."

They laughed and then Margot began to tell Elvira about her sexual experiences with Xavier.

"Why do you think this is so unusual? I have many friends who have secret lovers. Dangerous lovers. They play games like this, too..."

"But I have no control over him. He is like the devil. He is evil."

"He is not like the devil! Of course you have control. You don't have to see him again and if you must, you don't let him take you too far."

"I feel so guilty about Archie. I am sure that he knows."

"You must never tell him. Men are weak. Archie is no different. You know that."

"I have to tell him."

"We must keep some secrets. You love him. He loves you. Why spoil this? It will ruin your marriage."

"Elvira, what if I think my lover may be a killer, and that my husband may be involved?"

Elvira pitched her head back and laughed. Margot was quiet and calm.

"Your husband? Never!"

"Elvira, if he isn't the murderer, I think that this man and Archie may know who killed Paolo and Domatilla."

Painstakingly, she took her friend through all the elements in her relationship with Xavier which had led to this conclusion, including the fact that she had seen Archie with him. There were too many coincidences. The animal names. The secret abusive relationship with Paolo. His predilection for games involving sado-masochism and violence. His knowledge of digital filming technologies and finally, and most damningly, the cords on her wrist.

Elvira listened without saying a word. Finally, she asked a question.

"Why did you see him again if you suspected any of this?"

"Elvira, I had no choice. My mind and body... I cannot really describe to you how much I wanted him again, and still want him."

"Carlos will say that he will need evidence. Proof."

"I know."

Margot began to cry and Elvira came around the bar and hugged her.

"You must talk to Archie."

"I have tried so hard to find a way to explain to myself how this all happened. Why now, and to me, at this stage in my life?"

"It can happen to anybody."

There was a loud knock on the door.

"Cerrada!" shouted Elvira. "Closed. Fermé! Chiusa!"

"We must leave for the funeral. I must change into my clothes. And then we can talk about what you must do."

She walked up a very narrow spiral staircase. Margot went behind the bar and poured herself a large cognac.

Her mobile 'phone rang. It was Archie.

"Good morning?" with a brilliantly executed interrogatory tone which gave nothing of her mood away. "I slept in the studio last night. Did you get my message? I am with Elvira... we are leaving in five minutes... walking – it's a beautiful day. Elvira is changing into her nineteenth century finest."

Archie told her that he was bringing the car so that they could go together to the wake afterwards. He hadn't listened to his answering machine.

"I'm not sure that I am going to be up for that, Archie, but I'll come with you if you really insist." Margot deliberately disguised her decision. She was not going to be at the wake, she was determined to meet Laura.

He said they would discuss it at the cemetery.

※

*What did I really know about Xavier? Is he a murderer? Most of my evidence is superficial. He knew Paolo. He knew Domatilla. He knew Archie (I wonder, why didn't Archie tell me? Old wounds perhaps? No need). He knows about video art. I suppose I still need to give some harder, more concrete evidence. Obviously, his apartment had supplied some clues about his bizarre sexuality but then there are hordes of people who behave weirdly in private and are not murderers. Paolo had described his teacher's behaviour when he taught at the school in Scotland, but very much from his own narrow perspective. Robert was very secretive about Xavier but I assumed that was because he wanted to tease me. His charisma, the sex and his taste in art gave something away but on the whole, like so many other acquaintances, we don't know that much in detail about the people we meet casually. Was he ever married, were his parents alive, did he have siblings, how did he make a living? Simple, mundane, historical facts which make up the minutiae of our sociological DNA are rarely at the forefront of our conversation when we explore someone new in our lives. And yet for me, it is usually those facts which are vital in my ability to provide the psychological help my patients so desperately yearn for.*

*When I begin my probe into their minds, I make a point of asking the simplest of questions. Where were you born? What does your mother look like? What does your father do for a living? Do you like your brother? How old is your sister? Who was your best friend when you were at kindergarten? What clothes did you wear when you were a teenager? Did you enjoy your school holidays? What were your favourite television programmes? All are easy to answer and subsequently give so much vital information in building a picture of their personalities. The facts alone are useful but equally useful is the way those facts are trotted out and what observations they are the catalyst for. Normally, I am quick to use this process, oh-so-innocently, when I meet someone new socially. They never seem like the sort of questions I might be asking in the context of therapy, they are disguised as chit-chat but they often disarm a new acquaintance at first because they are forced to refresh their memories. Oddly enough, despite the need for an awkward dip into the past, most people quite enjoy the process and are oblivious to the degree I can glean information about them while they answer. Sneaky? I suppose so. But because of the apparent simplicity and innocence of each interchange, an immediate and intimate rapport is set up which is economic and often very entertaining. Anecdotes. Character analysis. Nostalgia. Genealogical history. Family strife. Rites of passage.*

*Why did I fail to go through this process with Xavier? The power of his sexual charisma had disarmed me on such a monumental scale that my usual faculties of curiosity, my usual need to bring my analytical talent into my personal life, had been abandoned. And so I know so little about him in that context. Does it matter? Perhaps not? On the other hand, my ignorance about him added a frisson to his mysterious aura which he must have enjoyed exploiting. In that sense, he was displaying some of the classic traits of a dominant, but he did not ally these with any form of the familiar consistent dominant characteristics. Even the traditional sado-masochistic paraphernalia was somewhat idiosyncratic, to say the least, and the way he tutored me in his games deviated from traditional role-playing techniques. It was quirkier. It hadn't been formulaic.*

*Of course, I could piece together a superficial portrait of him based on his behaviour but I suspect that the usual simply-gathered information that I would have gleaned from anybody else within minutes of knowing them should, in his case, have provided some vital context.*

*Is he a psychopath? Is he mad? He certainly isn't schizophrenic in the clinical definition of that word. Sexually perverse, certainly. Does this control him and his need to control others with it? And if this is the case, does the perversity tip over into psychopathy? If so, he is a very dangerous man and poses a serious threat to me and anybody else he controls. Clearly the Jungian theories about animus and anima come to mind – this is a man who trades in sexual ambiguity and enjoys playing with both sides of his lovers' sexuality. Paolo, Tilly and I can attest to that in spades. Obsessive? For sure, the bizarre nature of his apartment, the paraphernalia, the thoroughness of his collection in surgical instruments, for example, indicate obsessive and pedantic leanings. But the same could be said of a philatelist or a lepidopterist. Xavier is certainly unique – a frog-loving opera buff, who uses surgical instruments as sex toys and has a predilection for perverted performance art. Nina Simone.*

*Maybe that is at the root of my fascination for him. I cannot pigeonhole him as I can with my clients, and equally I cannot pigeonhole my own responses in any rational way. Smell, taste, looks, brain, touch,*

*sounds. All of it. Was I frightened? No more or less than Elvira was of*
*Carlos, or any other woman who was at the mercy of her sexual desires*
*with a man who was taking advantage of them for his own pleasure.*

*But a paedophile! How do I come to terms with that appalling fact?*
*Had this monster stolen Paolo's life? And Tilly's? And if Archie knows*
*him, why did he hide that from me?*

Elvira's high heels finally clicked their way slowly down the spiral
staircase. She looked magnificent. Not a trace of any make-up. A
simple veil. Sleek silk black dress. The only splash of colour came from
the third finger on her right hand where she wore a large, aquamarine
ring.

"What a beautiful ring!"

"Paolo and Tilly gave it to me on my birthday last year."

They slipped under the slatted iron protective door at the front
of the café and walked across Las Ramblas into the Raval. The Raval
was busy and the narrow streets were full of the hustle bustle of its
predominantly Arab quarter. Elvira and Margot knew every alleyway,
all the short cuts. They walked quickly and Elvira talked without
drawing breath. They walked along Carrer de l'Arc del Teatro, across
the Parallel and climbed the Poeta Cabanes, the steep cobbled street
with a beautiful name, which also housed one of Barcelona's oldest
family owned tapas bars called *Quimet e Quimet*. The proprietor, who
knew the women well, looked aghast as they snubbed his jolly greeting.
They waved by way of apology, but only just. This street led past some
ancient villas, including Margot's apartment block, and up to a set of
steps on the banks of the Montjuic. The Montjuic had been the site of
a Roman shrine to their god Jupiter, the God of Light and the protector
of the state and its laws. A favourite dinner party quip used by Archie

to explain their decision to live on it.

"Why on earth did Archie want to take the car today?"

They swept past the ancient castell and up to the wide avenues built for the Anella Olympica and the magnificent swimming pool Margot used at weekends. Both of them knew each of the magnificent views over the old Arsenal and the Port from here. Normally they would have stopped and enjoyed them – Margot had a favourite spot where there is a solitary bench; she had spent hours thinking about her clients in that very spot. Today, she didn't even notice it. As if inspired by Jupiter's status as a lawmaker, Elvira's advice was brutal on that count. She took Margot through a smattering of Carlos' unsolved cases and a few of the solved murders. They all led to one conclusion: if there was one man on earth she should trust, it was Carlos, and he would be sensitive to her predicaments. If there was any chance that her instincts about Xavier were right, she had no alternative.

"You must tell Carlos everything you know."

Margot slowed her pace. Her heart was beating fast. She stopped walking and stared at her friend, who just smiled. Elvira was right, of course.

# Chapter Twenty

The Cementiria del Sud Ouest lies below the circular road between the stadium and the Mediterranean. There are two entrances. Its main gate is within yards of Barcelona's massive industrial port and a taxi ride from the Colom. The funeral cortege had wound its way from the hospital on the Barceloneta past cranes, refineries and containers and was now processing at a snail's pace down the small hill which leads towards the public crematorium, a beautifully designed, sleek, white-walled futuristic building, at odds with the rest of this vast, unique cemetery.

Margot and Elvira's walk up the Montjuic and through the Olympic stadia had led them to the cemetery's other, less prepossessing gate in front of a disused training track. Thousands of graves, tombstones, mausoleums and chapels are literally carved into the stark, light brown cliffs which loom above the vast industrial seaport opposite the South face of the little mountain. At the summit, black marble gravestones, stone crosses and statues of Christ and the Virgin Mary clash with industrial silhouettes of cranes and container ships, another layer in a magnificent tableau stretching across the azure, backlit Mediterranean landscape. Thick stone columns are the guardians of rows and rows of memorials and coffins encased into carefully marked, square sealed cabinets, the final resting place for thousands of Barcelona's dead. Tiny square plaques are neatly sculptured into walls of stone stretching up and down the undulating hillside like strange vestiges of an ancient civilisation. Dried flowers, faded photos, and effigies of The Holy Virgin are encased into small, sealed glass promontories which give each cubicle, (not unlike the cubicle in a morgue), a poignant, idiosyncratic atmosphere – a little personal identity which keeps them from being desperate and uniform.

As Elvira and Margot walked around the corner of the last of the endless array of cypress tree-lined avenues, they heard the sad, forlorn sound of a solitary set of bagpipes in the wind, which had already begun to whip itself up into the early stages of one of the city's celebrated Mediterranean storms. The piper was playing a beautiful Caledonian lament. (Paolo had loved the bagpipes, which he had learnt to play at school in Scotland.) It seemed to be louder, closer. The cedar trees lining the avenues all the way to the summit of this extraordinary cemetery, were beginning to sway in the strong breeze, blocking out the bleak industrial sprawl which lies beyond the cemetery to the West.

Around the corner of the small road leading past the chapels of the richer families, a kilted piper came into sight ahead of a slow-moving black hearse. They were moving towards the entrance of the glistening white façade of the crematorium. Margot recognised the piper: Robert, in full tartan regalia. Behind the hearse, came a phalanx of mourners and the now crawling clump of cars. The entire ex-patriot community in Barcelona was determined to share in this exotic event.

A police car, a small blue and white Seat, was parked rather obviously away from the entrance. Carlos emerged and walked over to Elvira and Margot who had slipped behind the other mourners. He kissed Elvira on the cheeks and kissed Margot's hand.

"Buenos Dias, señoras."

He was dressed in his formal police uniform, which included a rather peculiar, ill-fitting helmet.

About half the mourners were under twenty-five, dressed colourfully and eccentrically. The balancing, older group was dressed in traditional black, sombre funereal clothes. This mixture of age groups gave the entire event a poetic poignancy. Paolo had been very popular amongst his peers and adored by his parents' friends alike. A small group of men, the pallbearers, hovered around the hearse which was now parked in front of the steel doors of the post-modern chapel, housed in the crematorium building. One of them looked remarkably like Paolo. His brother. The cemetery workers, dressed in bright yellow boiler suits, were smoking a discreet distance away from the chapel entrance, their white tractor at the ready to follow the hearse and cortege after the service. Paolo was destined for a plot which would require their modern mechanised diggers and tractors. The coffin slid out of the glass compartment at the rear of the hearse.

As Margot and Elvira watched this unfold, Margot grasped Elvira's hand. Dressed in an immaculate morning suit, as devastatingly good-looking and elegant as ever, Xavier, as one of the pallbearers, was lifting a corner of the coffin to his shoulders.

"He is one of the pallbearers!" Margot hissed her anguish.

Elvira was baffled. "Pallbearers?"

"The men carrying the coffin. The tall Englishman. That's Xavier!"

She clutched Elvira tighter. Elvira immediately said something to Carlos. He nodded and left them to follow the cortege into the chapel of the crematorium. Carlos instructed the policeman videoing the scene and then trotted back to join the women. Elvira went over to chat to another of the officers and Margot looked around for Archie. He was waiting in the reception area of the glass and concrete building. The chrome and white marble of its geometric design blended awkwardly with the strange collection of mourners. It was a bright spring morning – a mixture of trendy tee-shirts and black lace blouses, pony-tailed young men in jeans and be-suited dignitaries in morning suits. There was a clutch of young Muslims – jaballahs, fez and yashmak. Beautiful brown eyes. And plenty of expensive wraparound sunglasses.

In the courtyard, was a small, circular fountain which hadn't been serviced properly – old winter leaves had clogged it and a pungent smell mingled with the incense burners carried by the two altar boys accompanying a mauve-robed priest who was hovering rather awkwardly near a couple of multi-coloured vending machines inside the foyer. One of the boys was trying to buy a Coke but the machine was out of order. Archie signalled discreetly to Margot to join him and pass through the foyer and into the chapel. As they entered the air-conditioned auditorium, they walked past a small quartet of musicians who were playing a beautiful selection of seventeenth century ecclesiastical music.

"How are Tarquin and Sabrina coping?"

"Badly. They want to talk to you. They think that you must have some idea of what Tilly and Paolo were up to. Sabrina is very angry. She says it's all your fault. She has been drinking, inevitably."

"I've been worried sick about that. But I can't tell them anything. As you know."

"Where were you last night?"

"I slept in the studio. Archie, I can't tell them anything. Please can you explain that to them? I am happy to see them…"

Hugo was handing out a service sheet. His eyes welled up as he welcomed Margot and Archie with a bear-hug of relief.

"Thank you for picking up Mum and Dad. I just couldn't face them. We picked Emma's folks up yesterday. I hope Mum didn't give you a hard time. She has been drinking, as usual."

Archie was as comforting as he could be. "Don't worry, Hugo, it's always a pleasure to see them. Your Mum was relatively calm. They insisted on coming here with Paolo's mother. They are all staying at the Grand."

"Emma is reading a poem... She would love to come with you to the 'wake', if that's what we are calling it. Personally, I hate the word."

"Of course she can. I will look after her."

"Thank you, Archie."

Archie and Margot moved in. The chapel seating was organised around a small 'altar', a black slab, that was obviously disguising the technology which took oak coffins towards the furnaces below. This chic form of purgatory was surrounded by four groups of raked, black leather chairs, which looked like the seats you might find in a luxurious private screening room. They had red-lined backs in the shape of a small cello. A striking black woman, dressed in a very short yellow dress, made way to allow Archie, Margot and Elvira to shuffle into their seats in the centre, clustering opposite the perfectly proportioned lectern with an adjustable Sennheiser microphone. Archie kissed Elvira, and as Carlos joined them, shook his hand.

"The quartet are Jordi Savall's protégés; they are playing part of the mass of Cristobal de Morales, one of the great Catalan composers..."

Archie could be counted upon to know these details. To many in the chapel they had great significance. Jordi Savall had single-handedly championed the Catalan musical tradition with his phenomenal musical energy and talents. His wife, Montserrat Figueras, was one of Spain's great sopranos and a heroine for Paolo – he had a very large collection of the music Jordi had recorded with his family of musicians with their orchestra, La Capella Reial de Catalunya. He had been obsessively to every concert they had ever given and Archie had organised Paolo and Tilly's visit to la Collegiata del Castillo de Cardona to hear them record. They had even been to the cathedral in Valencia for a performance, which Paolo had recorded to use in one of his videos. Maestro Savall and his beautiful, dark-haired wife sat on the other side of the chapel. The harpist sitting near the altar was Arianna, their lovely daughter. Margot and Archie had asked her to play at their wedding.

"Le tout Barcelona!" Archie remarked.

Robert had parked his pipes and shuffled along the row to sit next to Elvira. He leant over to Margot. "I didn't know that my friend Xavier knew Paolo. Such a small world!"

"Xavier? A friend?" Archie was irritated.

Margot studied his face. What was he hiding and why?

"One of my oldest friends," explained Robert. "We played cricket together after Oxford. He teaches in a language school here now. I introduced him to Margot at *Lucia* the other night... Are we going to the wake together?" Archie nodded as if he vaguely remembered Robert talking about him.

Margot wanted to scream. All these men with secrets in their past! Elvira squeezed her left hand as if she knew.

"Of course we are," Archie whispered, "I brought the car."

"You will also need the car to go to the burial. Their family plot is half way up the hill."

Margot had managed to stay externally calm and bleated out something about the music.

"I think that's Emma... one of the musicians."

The singer began. A simple French chanson written by Josquin de Prés. *Mille Regretz.*

*Mille regretz de vous abandoner*
*Et deslonger, vostre fache amoureuse.*
*J'ai si grand deuil et paine douloureuse,*

*Qu'on me verra brief me jours definer.*
*(One thousand pangs of sadness and regret. I am so distraught at the*
*idea of leaving you. My sense of loss and despair is so powerful that*
*it won't be long before my days are numbered.)*

The priest entered from the foyer and into the teak-roofed amphitheatre, flanked by his two altar boys, complete with swinging incense burners. Everyone stood up. The coffin had begun its short journey down the tiny aisle of the chapel and was laid down somewhat precariously on the black marble tablet designed for it, opposite the priest who now looked flustered. He kept looking anxiously at the entrance. The soprano had finished the chanson and a small choir on the opposite corner of the chapel began to sing from Cristobal de Morales' Requiem Mass. Agnes Dei. "Lamb of God who takest away the sins of the world, have mercy on us. Lamb of God, who takes away the sins of the world, grant us peace."

When they had finished, there was a very long, awkward silence. The front seats on two sides of the chapel were ominously empty. They had obviously been reserved for the families. The rest of the arena was packed, standing room only. Tilly's parents had agreed that the service should be as much a memorial for her as it would be for Paolo. Margot caught Xavier's eyes. He was standing with the other pallbearers to the right of the priest. Was Xavier really waiting to carry the body of his victim to his grave? Another of his hideous, perverse and depraved scenarios, no doubt? Margot looked down and closed her eyes – she was feeling so ashamed that she had succumbed to this monster. Elvira whispered to her.

"I cannot believe this!"

A commotion behind the congregation signalled the entrance of another group. Paolo's parents had arrived and were making their way in front of the lectern to their seats. His mother was flanked by Eusebio and Gianni, her third husband. They were followed by another exquisitely dressed quartet. Tilly's father Tarquin, awkwardly dressed in a black morning coat, her mother Sabrina, veiled in a black smock, Hugo, Tilly's brother, in black jeans and black tee shirt and finally Emma, chic in black ear-rings and a black zipper jacket over her dress. Laura and her husband Reggie, a tall, rather awkwardly-dressed, heavily set man with a red face, followed behind Eusebio.

Paolo had been very accurate when he had described his mother and her third husband to Margot. Gianni was tall, with a beautifully trimmed dark beard. He wore half glasses, which were often hung around his neck, and when he removed them, his small, brown piercing eyes were surrounded by pencil-thin eyebrows, giving him an enquiring gaze, which could be very intimidating. Today these eyes looked ahead – sad and grave. Eusebio looked dignified and wore dark glasses. Paolo's mother, Alicia, was the most beautiful woman in the chapel. With her raven hair, she could have passed as Tilly's older sister. Statuesque and with a perfectly formed neck, her pale face elegantly enveloped her large blue eyes. Not a trace of make-up. She smiled shyly at a couple of friends she recognised and shook the priest's hand. Xavier walked over to shake Eusebio's hand and kissed Alicia's cheeks. Had she also been one of his lovers? She introduced him quickly to Tarquin and Sabrina.

Margot was overcome by a desire to leave, but Elvira restrained her. She was right, of course – whatever circumstantial evidence she was harbouring about Xavier, it had been totally compromised by this outrageous display of brazen hypocrisy. Nobody would believe her and to leave would be discourteous and mysterious. Margot tried to catch his eyes. In vain. For all his urbane charm and intelligence, is this man evil? Had his behaviour extended her definition of that word 'evil' beyond any of the extremes that she could have imagined, in studying the plethora of evil behaviour which came regularly as examples in her work with her clients? If he had been responsible for Paolo's death, he would surely never have showed up as a pallbearer.

Archie held strong views about the word. He had taught a class on the subject of evil – particularly in the context of the Inquisition as it applied to the Holocaust and the genocides in Africa. Archie believed evil to be an individual phenomenon, not a collective one and for that reason he had no sympathy with anyone who argued that an entire nation could individually let themselves off the hook for their behaviour by hiding behind the notion that they had all behaved irrationally under some kind of subconscious collective hypnosis. Hitler was evil, but so were his cohorts, and those who were Nazis were evil. "An evil man is a man who commits an evil act when he knows that it is evil. We all know the difference. It isn't difficult to differentiate between good and evil!"

Margot's approach was more humanitarian, more forgiving. Her work constantly provided her with mitigating factors, which could provide rational explanations for irrational behaviour. She was more inclined to forgive, to reconcile. Margot also had powerful convictions about the subconscious mind. Her decade exploring Jung and his disciples had been the bedrock of her approach to life, and to her work. Archie had never really accepted her unstinting hero-worship. He was uncompromising, reactionary. "We are all responsible for our own actions." Even subconscious behaviour, or collective hysteria, whatever excuse could be usefully invoked in this context, were all manifestations of that same phenomenon.

Margot knew that Archie would use his address to the congregation to expose this attitude to some extent. Tastefully. With subtlety. After the priest had welcomed everyone and said a simple introductory prayer, Archie walked to the lectern to replace him in front of the microphone, which he adjusted for his height. He then began what was the first of a series of short eulogies, readings and musical tributes from friends and family in both Paolo's and Tilly's honour. Predictably, Archie read a passage from the last book of *Paradise Lost*, a book Paolo had adored. They used to enjoy long sessions reciting passages from the poem and argue about its meaning. His theory was that Milton, for all his Puritan ethics and moral turpitude, was actually a hip, cool guy who had wanted to write a story debunking our idea that Satan was necessarily an unsympathetic character. Archie explained this and read the section where Adam and Eve re-enter Paradise.

While these moving tributes built up a strong picture of Paolo's special status, particularly amongst his group of young friends, Margot tried to find a way to distract herself from the grotesque realities of her situation. The quartet began to play a medley – their own, simplified versions of Paolo's bizarre taste in music. This raised a laugh or two. Bach's Cello Suites and Beethoven's Choral Fantasia blended rather incongruously with The Beastie Boys, The Sex Pistols and Mark Anthony Turnage. Nina Simone – Margot couldn't help shooting a fleeting glance at Xavier. He was laughing. They rounded off the medley with a sensationally moving rendition of the adagio from the Fourth movement of Mahler's *Resurrection*. Margot noticed that Xavier now had tears in his eyes. Evil men cry, too; crocodile tears?

Desperate to avoid thinking about the grotesque tableau before her, Margot began to play a mind-game to be played in Church at weddings and funerals, which she had learnt from Archie – *what a great liar he is*. Play was the wrong, frivolous word. She used the game to distract herself. Choose a couple of painters. Look around the congregation and then imagine the way that painter might have depicted the scene. William Blake and Tintoretto. Blake was easy – his visions of Dante's *Inferno* and *Paradiso* being easy to conjure up. Tintoretto more difficult – so many masterpieces. Stick to his painting in Venice, the *Scuola San Rocco*. Margot looked up at the teak roofing for some inspiration.

By now, Emma was reading a beautiful passage in English from *The Prophet*. She had removed her zipper jacket. She wore a tight black and grey body stocking under a flimsy, short black skirt, covered with a transparent, gossamer sheath which looked like a veil, and her only concession to colour – red high heels with red leather anklet straps. She struggled through the poetry and then finally broke down, staring out at the congregation, helpless. Sobbing. Hugo stood up and ushered her back to her seat, as Xavier replaced her at the lectern.

"This man is a creep!" Archie whispered, incensed.

Margot looked down at her husband's shiny black shoes and squeezed Elvira's hand until the blood drained from her fingers. Xavier waited until Emma was re-seated comfortably.

"I first met Paolo when he came into my classroom at a small boarding school in Edinburgh."

His voice oozed a quiet, reverential charm. Almost in the fashion of second-rate television pundits, he gave certain words an unnecessary emphasis, which added to the theatricality and pretentiousness of his address.

"He came straight up to me and in perfect French told me that it would be a waste of time to attend my classes but he would like me to teach him how to sing the songs of the French pop star Johnny Halliday and recite the poetry of Verlaine. I laughed at him and told him that his voice sounded more like Edith Piaf – he was not much more than a little boy – I explained that Verlaine's poems were complicated, and unsuitable! 'Piaf was a collaborator!' he hissed back at me and at the end of the first lesson he stood up in front of the class and sang in perfect French a poem by *Paul Verlaine* which had been turned into a song by *Claude Debussy*.

*"The poem is en français..."*

Xavier's voice was smooth and his French accent impeccable.

*Dans le vieux parc solitaire et glacé,*
*Deux formes ont tout à l'heure passé.*

*Leurs yeux sont morts et leurs lèvres sont molles,*
*Et l'on entend à peine leurs paroles.*
*Dans le vieux parc solitaire et glacé,*
*Deux spectres ont évoqué le passé.*

*'Te souvient-il de notre extase ancienne?'*
*'Pourquoi voulez-vous donc qu'il m'en souvienne?'*

*'Ton Coeur bât-il toujours a mon seul nom?*
*Toujours vois-tu mon âme en rêve? – Non.*

*'Ah! Les beaux jours de bonheur indicible*
*Ou nous joignons nos bouches! – C'est possible.*

*'Qu'il était bleu, le ciel, et grand, l'espoir!*
*'L'espoir a fui, vaincu, vers le ciel noir.*

*Tels ils marchaient dans les avoines folles,*
*Et la nuit seule entendit leurs paroles.*

Margot looked at Hugo. He was impassive. Emma tearful. Paolo's mother, Alicia, was looking down. Eusebio stared ahead. Xavier stared out at the coffin. Even the purr of the air-conditioning unit seemed to be holding its breath. And then another mobile 'phone, or perhaps the same one, began to ring incessantly.

"Paolo!" Robert quipped in a loud voice. He had moved up to replace Xavier to speak. The congregation laughed except Margot, Elvira and the girl with the yellow dress who stood up abruptly, slid through the length of her row and marched up to the lectern as Xavier was about to leave it. She slapped his face with her left hand, her right hand, and then walked slowly out of the chapel. Xavier stood there silently for a moment or two with as much dignity as anyone might muster under the circumstances, before walking back to his seat while Robert replaced him at the lectern. He mumbled a few awkward words of apology about his joke and spoke a simple prayer in Latin and quickly walked out in the direction of the girl with the yellow dress. The priest returned to the microphone, shrugged sympathetically at the family and began a blessing which ended in a chanted rendition of the Dresden 'Amen'! Paolo's body descended into the bowels of the crematorium and the congregation ambled slowly out of the auditorium.

*Who was the girl in the yellow dress?* Nobody seemed to know. Robert had followed her out – he obviously knew her. Every funeral has its idiosyncrasies. At this cemetery the procedures largely varied according to the status of the family involved. Money, of course, could intervene. As far as Paolo's family was concerned, there were no issues on either front but his mother and stepfathers had made their wishes very clear. Everybody was invited to the memorial site at the top of the hill. As soon as the congregation had discovered this, a phalanx began to form behind a tractor and an old-fashioned, small, glass-covered hearse which had been attached to it. The kind pulled by horses in the nineteenth century. Four officials with yellow boiler suits emerged from the side of the crematorium, carrying the coffin which had now been sealed.

"I thought he was going to be cremated."

"Paolo hated the idea of being burnt."

Archie looked anxious. Margot ignored him at first. She was looking for Xavier who had vanished. She caught Laura's eyes. She acknowledged her gently with a smile and mouthed, "See you later." This gave Margot her excuse.

"I am so sorry but I have a client this afternoon, Archie. I can't make the wake. But I need to talk to you."

"A client today?"

"I can't let her down. I made a promise. She has insisted that it had to be today."

"You must at the very least come to the burial. It would be regarded as unacceptably disrespectful not to. I can give you a lift back into town after that."

"I will come to the burial but I can walk back to my office, thank you..."

A small motorcade wound up the steep hill to the Lorca family memorial mausoleum, a small chapel looking out towards the Mediterranean. Paolo's mother's grandfather had built this before the First World War. There was a small, private burial ground nearby with a few crosses and a fresh open grave. The wind had become stronger, whipping up a series of dust flurries. A mechanical crane lifted the coffin tastefully off the trolley which had been hitched to a motorised hearse. Four more yellow-suited cemetery officials carried it efficiently over to the small throng around the grave. They lowered it awkwardly and then, to the family's stunned incredulity, the coffin refused to descend. The gravediggers had misjudged the size of the coffin. They tried every angle; they tilted the box and managed to lower a corner into the grave, but everything they tried was doomed to failure. It just didn't fit. Finally, Eusebio whispered something to the priest, who in turn whispered a few sentences to the pallbearers and they carried the coffin into the small chapel. Margot used this diversion as her opportunity to leave and hugged each member of Paolo's family. She kissed Archie, who repeated his offer to drive her to her office.

"I will walk there, thank you, darling."

※

*I know that at some stage I will have to tell Archie everything. Not yet. But the beautiful girl with the yellow dress... and I need to talk to Robert.*

# Chapter Twenty One

Laura was waiting outside the building in the square. Margot noticed that she had applied some pink lipstick and was playing with her wristband, the way Muslims play with worry beads when they are anxious. She followed Margot upstairs. When they had settled down opposite each other in her room, Margot looked more carefully at Laura's left wrist. She was wearing a simple cord bracelet, a replica of the one Xavier had cut from her own wrist. She tried to disguise her feeling of nausea.

"I love your bracelet. Did you make it yourself?"

Laura was startled and fingered it nervously. "No, no! It was a silly gift from a sweet little girl who made it at my daughter's school."

Her first lie. Margot knew it.

"I know... I know. I suppose you think that it looks suspiciously like the remnants of some shady relationship!" Laura unnecessarily volunteered with a laugh. That part of her answer was possibly true.

"No! I would never dream of second-guessing anything about you at such an early stage! We need time."

Margot was now pretty certain that the man who had become her obsession was the same man her new client had come to talk about. She asked Laura if she would mind if she went to the bathroom. It sounded like a feeble excuse. She grabbed her mobile phone and went into the small cubicle, where she sat and collected her thoughts. She was shaking and couldn't help thinking back to the last time she felt like this, in Xavier's apartment. She sent a text to Archie, asking him to be at home early. She washed her face and returned to Laura, who seemed to have accepted her superficial reason for needing to leave the room so soon after they had sat down. Had she been a therapist, she would have guessed something was up.

"Okay. Sorry about that..."

"Please don't worry. My plane to London doesn't leave until nine tonight."

"Are you going on holiday?"

"Business. Our annual conference is always in April. That's why I had to see you this evening. Thank you. I know it must have been difficult after that funeral."

And then rather nonchalantly she asked the obvious question that anybody at the funeral would have asked: "Who was that woman in the yellow dress?"

"I have no idea. I have never seen her before."

"Do you know Xavier? That man the strange girl in the yellow dress slapped at the funeral?" Margot was impressed. Butter wouldn't melt in her mouth.

"Robert Eliot, the editor of the local ex-pat rag, introduced me once at the opera. But no, not really..."

Laura didn't flinch, but there was an awkward pause. And then Laura laughed imperiously. A little too heartily.

"Robert! Oh, of course, that Robert! Robert once tried to seduce me at a party! He is spectacularly unattractive. I have always had the upper hand in all my dealings with the opposite sex. I remember reading a story by an Italian writer, Moravia I think, describing the kind of relationship the young woman at the centre of his tale, a story about madness really..." and she faltered, "...a relationship she was having with her father who was for her the ideal lover, but only in her fantasy life... I don't know why I am telling you this."

Here was the familiar pattern. New patients enjoy passing on information which has no relevance on the surface. A subtle way of boasting about their intelligence or their intellectual prowess. Margot made a note of this, but was really desperately trying to hide her horror at the significance of the rope bracelet, although she still had no hard evidence. Did Laura really think she had negotiated her way out of the trap that she had stupidly set up for herself by bringing up the incident between girl in the yellow dress and Xavier? Perhaps she had thought that by raising the subject, it would deflect any possible thought that she knew Xavier. Margot encouraged her to carry on talking.

"And your father?"

"I have kept my father at arms' length in the same way that the woman in the Moravia novel did. I hated the idea that he should have in anyway spoilt my relationships, my dealings with men. I suppose I bought into all those early feminist theories which were so chic when I was at Oxford. But to tell the truth, I had always believed that I was beyond even that kind of simplistic politicisation. I wanted to be me."

The eight-minute rule: everyone she knew who had been to Oxford or Cambridge always dropped this fact into their opening salvos, and always within the first ten minutes!

Laura had a strange, disjointed way of talking. She would pause and wait a couple of beats as if she was expecting an answer or an interruption. Margot kept silent during these pauses.

"And in that way, any man who posed even the tiniest threat, through his sexuality or any other peculiarity of his masculinity... any man who has tried to destabilise me or threaten my need to be in control... any man, all men like that have been the object of immediate scorn from my point of view, of contempt... or have just been just completely ignored. I go cold with these types. I know they are going to be trouble

214

and I give them a very wide berth. I have always chosen to be with men who were happy to submit to my terms of business... Does this all seem rather cold to you?"

She recognised all these elements of Laura's somewhat cerebral self-analysis and identified with her desire to buck the clichés of male domination without the usual annoying, pseudo-feminist political rhetoric. Nothing new!

"Having said all that, I have no desire to be a dominatrix! No masochistic tendencies ever show up when I am making love, having sex. I like to give pleasure as much I like to receive it... My partners never complained, and in my husband's case, our sex life has been and still is great – loving... Sensual... full of regular orgasms. He is a great lover and he always says that I am too, which I believe because he so clearly enjoys it... I have never liked the idea of pain much, being hurt during sexual interplay... Spankings are not for me... no German shepherd fantasies. When so much of it is so pleasurable anyway, what is the need, or the point in having somebody hurt you? Never got it! Understood it existed, powerfully, but never got it, personally..."

Margot had heard variations of this story before and knew what Laura was leading to. At Chicago, she had spent time reading around what were loosely called gender issues and sexual denial. She had spent one long, agonising summer reading the somewhat impenetrable theories of the French structural psychologist Jacques Lacan, who believed that women had become irretrievably sexually subjugated by men. Lacan saw conflict even in the signs used outside public toilets to delineate the entrance to the separate facilities for men and women. That summer, Margot had embarked on an elaborate mission to analyse women in this context. Interviews with victims of domestic violence. Visits to meet convicted rapists. Case studies about men who visit dominamatrixes. She spent a two-week period attending the trial of a pimp and then privately interviewed all the prostitutes who had testified against him. And then there were the many 'ordinary' women, suffering in secret because they chose to turn their fantasies into reality, victims of extreme forms of sexual deviation. Violent fantasies. Bestiality. Rape fantasy and simulation. Sado-masochism. Role-play. Many of these women Margot interviewed had happy, fulfilled marriages and successful careers. They just lived duplicitous secret lives. Her new client was quite probably another example.

Laura then, quite suddenly, changed tack and began to ask Margot a series of almost rhetorical technical questions… almost as though she knew that Margot had not been particularly surprised by what she had been telling her. It was time she moved to the next stage. She was going to dip her toes into murkier, less penetrable waters.

"Am I allowed to ask you personal questions?"

"You can ask them but I am very unlikely to answer them if they are about me. You are the client. I am analysing you here! But ask away, so long as you know that I will obviously want to know why you want to know these things."

The tension was unbearable.

"Is our body, and I mean the female body, designed to accommodate hardcore sex?"

"What do you mean by hardcore?"

"Perverse, unnatural hard core sex. Anal penetration, for example?"

"I am afraid that my psychotherapeutic experience in that area is limited but I know a little about the psychology." She concealed her experience with as much insouciance as she could muster.

"You have never had anal sex?"

"What are you trying to establish, Laura? Are you interested in my own experience, and if so, why? Obviously many women have pleasure from anal sex."

"I am looking for some common bond if you like... And what about rape... or a rape fantasy?"

"Again I am trying to understand why this is important to you..."

"What would you say if I told you that I have been raped voluntarily every week of my life for the last six months?"

Margot quickly absorbed the almost laughable shock value of Laura's confession.

"Rape is a criminal act and I would have thought that the concept of rape per se makes the idea of it being voluntary somewhat contradictory."

"If a man is threatening to kill you..." Laura paused, as if collecting her thoughts, "...and you agree to allow him to fuck you involuntarily, I would call that rape, wouldn't you?"

"Yes, I probably would. But every week of your life?"

"Sometimes I see him twice a week."

"Threatening to kill you twice a week?"

"I suppose the word is 'rape'... He rapes me every time we meet each other and part of that is a violent threat... I suppose the word 'kill' is a little melodramatic. But that is what it feels like to me. He petrifies me."

"I am sorry, Laura, but I am not quite taking this in. You meet this man twice a week. And during the course of the time you spend with him, he rapes you? Why do you meet him if the rape seems almost voluntary?"

Margot realised that this was an important question and at the same time the first truly prurient, non-professional question. She wanted to know her answer so badly. Laura paused. She continued to stroke her makeshift bracelet.

Margot was also rummaging through the database in her mind; she kept remembering Freud's patient, the eighteen-year-old Dora. Margot had never really bought into his convoluted arguments about Dora's compliance when she confessed that she had been raped by an older man, the husband of her father's mistress. Freud maintained, needless to say, that Dora must have wanted him to 'rape' her and let it happen, albeit involuntarily, on the surface. And if she took Freud's scientific analysis to its extreme, Laura would be trying to seduce her right now. Freud believed quite seriously that he was the object of Dora's desire during his sessions of analysis with her. Dora had wanted to seduce her father's friend and in turn seduce him. Transference! But of course, in Freud's case, the analyst was a man and the last thing Laura was doing right now was in any shape or form some deeply disguised form of lesbian seduction! Superficially, his theories about Dora's secret desires and sexual frustration might certainly apply to Laura but this would take hours of therapy to analyse conscientiously. And Dora brutally abandoned Freud early in her analysis, incensed by his patronising assumptions. Innocent dreams about her misplaced jewellery box, a gift from her father, became according to Freud, incestuous desires and repressed sexuality. But Margot was hooked. She realised that this patient represented a new departure. Laura had ignored her last question, or had no answer for it.

"How do you feel about this? Where did you meet him?" Margot couldn't really believe that she had asked such banal questions but her personal curiosity had exceeded her usual rigorous professional responsibilities.

"We were both waiting to go into the loo at MACBA. I go there on Thursdays to sit in the small café. I like watching the surfboarders. I feel safe inside the plate glass windows. When I have finished my coffee, I amble through the galleries, and look at the paintings. I adore Antoni Tapies, they have a great collection of his work..."

Laura looked away for a second.

" ...And I sometimes say things to the person who is next to me, taking in a picture. Usually just a word or two. And one day I said to this man, I made some silly remark, I said that I had always about wanted to own one of his paintings. A Tapies.

"He replied with a pretentious but rather poetic philosophical quotation. I looked at him blankly. This was his opening gambit, if you like. I giggled like a schoolgirl. He was gorgeous and it was such a funny line. He explained that it was the only phrase he knew written by some rather obscure French semiologist called Jacques Lacan who was referring to the 'Men' and 'Women' signs which separate the sexes outside toilets everywhere... What that had to do with Tapies I had chosen to ignore."

Margot couldn't help smiling. And of course, had calmly registered the Lacan reference and the MACBA link.

"Why are you smiling?"

"I have also read Jacques Lacan."

And then the inevitable thunderbolt as if Margot had wished this on her from the beginning of their session.

"He likes me to call him by the name of an animal. His real name is Xavier. He was at the funeral. He sang the French song."

Margot's heart missed a couple of beats. She managed to choke back a gasp, and then recovered enough to avoid registering any obvious shock at what Laura had confessed. No form of professional training had equipped her to deal with what she now faced. She tried to freeze her own brain while she listened to Laura's description of Xavier, as if she was still at her most sympathetic and rigorous. Obviously in any normal professional context, what Laura was revealing was controversial enough and professionally irresistible, but on a personal level it was devastating. How could she continue to disguise that personal prurience without revealing a powerful conflict of interest, without confessing her own guilt? Her characteristic, evenly suspended attention was about to be tested on a monumental scale. The rules of her profession and the kind of therapy she practised completely forbade any engagement with 'insider knowledge'. She was screaming internally. *My Xavier. Not your Xavier.* She desperately wanted to share her experiences, and to immediately tell Laura that she knew Xavier. To probe in the way that she might have outside the 'room'.

"What do you mean by the name of an animal?"

"He thinks I am a peacock and gave me the Spanish name for a peacock. *Pavo real.* I call him *leopardo...*"

"Why does he think that you are a peacock and why is he a leopard?"

Margot needed to draw Laura out, persuade her to talk without interruption. This was the only way to handle it professionally. To do this, she knew that her reactions would have to seem totally normal, as surreal as the nature of their exchange had been. Laura was about to describe in detail the sexual relationship she was having with the same man with whom Margot had twice shared the most spectacular sexual experiences of her life, experiences she had already decided she wanted to repeat. A man who was jeopardising her life and her marriage, and a man the police would almost certainly regard as a prime suspect in the murder of Paolo and Domatilla, if Margot was to let them into her secret knowledge.

"I didn't have any choice. He quite literally ordered me to behave exactly in the way he dictated I should. Immediately after that first exchange, he insisted on taking me to one exhibit in the gallery... a very sexy, sensual painting of a young girl. He spoke with great authority about art and talked about his own work, which involved extensions of conventional art, extensions of even the more experimental forms of art, the cutting edge stuff that is drawing the crowds, installations and gimmicks. He talked about the American video artist Bill Viola. I have always loved Bill Viola. He said that he was redundant, bourgeois. He dismissed most of the great post-war American artists as poseurs and frauds. This might have been rather silly and reactionary but in his case he did so with such depth. He was so informed. His details, his analysis spanned centuries. We talked and talked, we couldn't stop. He took me to other paintings in the gallery and then he led me to a room which was very different – very few paintings on walls or sculptures laid out normally. This room had computers, LCD screens, and exhibits like the kind you might see in a natural history or science museum. It had a small screening room... it had video art running on a loop on small televisions. He led me into the screening room. At first I was fazed by the change from the brightly lit galleries to the darkened room. I stumbled in the dark and he held me. He was strong, powerful. I really don't know how or why this happened so quickly but he kissed me on the mouth as I recovered from the stumble. I responded and we sat down. His lips were soft, gentle. A black and white film was being projected onto the cinema screen. It was a slightly scratchy, probably sixteen millimetre film, no sound. It looked as if it had been professionally filmed but the camerawork was done so it was like just observing what was in front of the lens. A man and a woman looked as if they were about to have sex. And then the man took his clothes off, and then the woman... she was thin. He was thin and tall. I suppose they would be called performance artists. Xavier just announced it, so casually: 'We have a special connection?' I had to admit that we did. And then he began to ask me some very personal questions about my body physically and my attitude to my body. 'I want you to show me your body,' he said. 'I want to see it in all its glory.' I allowed him to lead me on. At first I just laughed and teased him. 'Don't make me laugh!' He told me very firmly that he wasn't joking. And for some reason when he repeated his demands, I started to do what he told me to do. 'Watch!' he whispered.

"I watched the film... it was the most disgusting thing I had ever seen in my life! Way beyond anything I could have imagined being called art. And yet, as I watched it and as he explained it to me, I was more and more drawn to him physically and sexually, so much so that to this minute I am as obsessed with him now as I was back then..."

Margot listened to Laura, a trained lawyer, using her almost pedantic talent for description. She recognised almost every element of her seduction. She recognised the Günter Brus imagery of defecation and self-mutilation described by Tilly in her voice-over on the DVD Carlos had shown her. She recognised the charming and imperious manner Xavier used to advertise his idiosyncrasies, including of course the animal names. And what was very nearly the most difficult aspect to reconcile, she recognised the sexual excitement that she shared. His body, his hands, his frogs, his knives, his cock – Laura spared her nothing. Every gory detail, every sensuous moment.

What Margot did not recognise was the 'rape' element in Laura's experiences with Xavier, although of course she had come across rape fantasy many times before. This was a variation in Xavier's technique, yet in the context of his considerable power to exercise abusive control over his prey, 'rape' fantasies were obviously another useful weapon in his hideous, perverted arsenal. Finally, Laura was silent. She looked at Margot as if begging her to eradicate the memory of her story from her mind. She sobbed, quietly. All the bravado of her public persona was obliterated. She looked at her expensive Cartier.

"I suppose I have used up my therapeutic hour!"

"Don't worry about that, Laura. I can break the rule today – I don't have another client. What about you?"

Laura looked at her mobile carefully.

"My chauffeur is waiting for me in front of FNAC on the Catalunya. I still have a few minutes."

"Can I ask you some simple questions? They may help me to begin the process of helping you. This will inevitably be very painful at first. For both of us. Many of my clients underestimate this. It will change your life."

"Of course. Please do, go ahead. Ask. I totally understand. I am still embarrassed at my outburst when we met..."

"Don't worry, I have seen much worse."

The setting sun had begun to seep into the room and Laura now sat there looking like a character in a Diane Arbus photograph. Bizarre, a little defiant and very vulnerable, confused. By contrast, Margot felt like the female equivalent of Van Gogh in one his self-portraits. Deceptively contemplative, and insane. She composed herself by drawing the blind enough to take the sun out of Laura's eyes, and pouring two glasses of water. They both drank quickly.

"How have you been dealing with your husband?"

"Ironically enough, our lives have never been happier. We enjoy all that domestic stuff. The children are as adorably annoying as ever and our sex life is spectacular. I don't really even have a guilty conscience. Xavier seems so separate. Of course, the secrecy is thrilling. I love my

223

secret. But I have come to see you. I have been dying for some help. I realise that what is going on is not normal."

*Xavier! My Xavier! Her Xavier!*

"How do you feel when you leave him?"

"I feel exhilarated. Liberated. Excited."

"A little ashamed?"

"No!"

"And how do you feel on the day you have planned to see him?"

"Butterflies. The kind of fear that I remember the day before I had an exam when I was at Oxford, or the day when I had to wear a new dress at a big party at the Union. Or just before I took a dive from a high board in our local pool. Those last few steps and then a plunge into the air."

Margot knew exactly how she felt. She was describing exactly what she had experienced. She wanted to hear Laura articulate it in detail.

"What do you feel about him... about this man?" She so nearly used his name.

"I know that he is abusing me. I realise that he is in control. He doesn't disgust me and the physical pleasure I have from him more than compensates for the feeling that he is some sad, perverted, desperate man. I suppose the only time I really begin to worry is when he begins to frighten me."

"Physically?"

"We have an agreed system. If he is going too far, I have a failsafe system. I can rein him back. We have a sign for a complete 'stop'! But on one occasion he didn't, and I had to repeat my emergency signals. He said that he hadn't seen the signs. I was terrified but he managed to pacify me, eventually."

"And after sex?... How do you feel afterwards?"

"I feel ashamed, disgusted, filthy, cheap. For an hour or two. And then I want him again."

Laura stopped talking and looked again at her watch.

"I must go."

"Laura, one last question before you leave. Do you want to see him again?"

Of course, Margot knew that she had seen him at the funeral.

"That's my problem. I desperately need to see him again. I think about him every minute of my day. I wake up and all I think about is planning my next meeting."

Again, Margot knew exactly how she felt. She allowed Laura to pay her fee, hugged her and then looked searchingly into her eyes.

"Thank you, Margot, you have no idea how much I needed to talk to someone. I will ring you from London to arrange my next visit if that is okay?"

"You are most welcome, Laura. Have a great trip. Ring me anytime. Here, take this. And I mean anytime." She handed Laura a card from her desk, and when the click-clack of Laura's Fratelli shoes had disappeared across the square, she sat down and stared at the brown envelope with the script and the DVD. The 'phone rang. Archie would have known that the session had finished. She clicked the answer machine to listen to his message.

"Darling, please come home as soon as you can. I know you are upset. I will buy some goodies for supper."

And then there was another message, from Xavier.

"I need to see you! Soon!"

※

*Should I feel jealous about Laura? I feel protective, desperate, wired and strangely attracted to Laura. Almost sexually so. Certainly not jealous. Does Laura suspect that Xavier had anything to do with Paolo's and Tilly's deaths? Unlikely.*

*I can't rope Elvira into this, is there anyone else? Archie? No way! I am much too ashamed. He would never understand, never forgive me. It would crush him. He doesn't need to know so why should I upset him? I certainly don't want to ruin my marriage. I am sure that I can control the information, hold it back in the same way that I have done in the past when he has asked me about my clients – they are all people we come across from time to time. Carlos and Elvira are much more of a problem. He is a very good detective and she is my friend. I cannot lie to either of them, but to let them into my secrets would have catastrophic consequences for me and would almost certainly lead to Xavier's exposure.*

*I have enough circumstantial evidence to put him well and truly in Carlos' frame. But I can't prove a thing, let alone point my finger. He doesn't appear in the DVD. Is the voice coaxing and asking questions off-camera really Xavier? It sounded a little like him but I couldn't be absolutely sure. And anyway the first question Carlos or Archie would ask me would be – "How do you know this man?" And this would open up a very different can of worms. Sex with him was indeed violent and perverted, spectacular, but he didn't harm me and didn't try anything which would suggest that he was a murderer. A morbid interest in surgical instruments, chisels, extremely kinky sexual behaviour, and the rest? Carlos wouldn't understand that in a strange, peculiar way it was safe, I felt in control despite the degree to which I was dominated by Xavier. The truth is that the sex was so explosively good that I want more of it... dangerous, compulsive, and inevitable. But this is no longer just an exquisite secret.*

*Xavier has been the catalyst for unlocking a side to me which I have clearly been suppressing. Why him? And of course, why do I now have this uncontrollable need to explore the darkest sides of my psyche at this stage in my life, when everything seems so ordered and safe? Until now, they have been so safely harboured in the minds of the sickest of my patients. Trying to apply the rules and methodologies of my professional training is useless, unsatisfactory and frustrating. I have glib answers to every question. My perfect parents and my abusive uncle are surely only one side of the picture. Maybe there is something in my own psychology, a genetic flaw.*

*I want to see Xavier immediately and confront him, but I know that the second that I see him, the moment he holds me in his arms, his charming imperious manner – all of this will lead on to the inevitable. I will succumb to these newfound sexual urges. I will want him to be inside me again, and I am sure he will take me into unmanageable areas; he is a dangerous man and was involved somehow in the deaths of P. and T. But is he really a killer? Maybe I was too hasty when I dismissed the idea of a double suicide. Maybe Paolo and Tilly were indeed producing some sort of sick pseudo 'snuff' movie and the process went horribly wrong? Or maybe they were at the end of their tether and had decided on a romantic death pact. Paolo was a wilful boy, capable of trying everything. Tilly shared her life with him. Perhaps my initial instinct about 'murder' had been wrong.*

*But the more rational and professional part of me is, of course, at odds with all of these feelings. I am a trained analyst, I know my clients. I was thorough and rigorous with them in the way I am with everyone. When Tilly told me of her suicide attempts, I identified them for what they were: desperate attempts to seek attention. She admitted this, and we went on to discuss suicide at great length. She would quote from her favourite book, Le Myth de Sisyphe, Albert Camus' great existential tract which deals with the absurd nature of life and our need to find some way to deal with the temptation of suicide. She had always maintained that Camus had persuaded her that suicide could no longer be an option for her. Paolo also made his position quite clear. He loved life. He just wanted to enjoy as many experiences as he could. Why waste the opportunity? He used to joke that he hated to spend too much time asleep. He didn't accept that the subconscious experience of sleep could be as exciting as the conscious waking experiences we can engineer for ourselves. Had Xavier been taking advantage of Paolo's needs in that sense? He certainly qualified.*

*Carlos gave me the script and the DVD because he wants me to look more carefully at them. For clues. I don't really need the clues. Like Carlos, I need facts and evidence. Perhaps I can look carefully at the DVD with a view to empowering Carlos with information that he can use to arrive at his own conclusions. Leads. Connections. I could talk about the Brus exhibit at MACBA. Or point him to a website. None of this leads to Xavier, but it would give him something to work with.*

*Robert?*

# Chapter Twenty Two

Rain.

Margot usually enjoyed the rain in Barcelona. Especially prolonged, consistent Mediterranean downpours which were so rare at home in California.

Margot wasted no more time. She collected the DVD and the script, wrapped herself in the rainwear she used for her cycling jaunts with Archie, and headed for the huge FNAC store on the side of the Plaça Catalunya. After a rather frustrating discussion about the apparently redundant technology of her ancient office computer, she bought a small DVD player and asked the salesman to recommend a mini Hi-Fi speaker system which would give her the very best sound reproduction. He sold her an expensive Bose home movie system, reassuring her that it was top of the range, and 'idiot proof' in its setting up. To explain and justify her reasons for this eccentric, spur-of-the moment shopping spree – this was a very uncharacteristic purchase and she shared a credit card account with Archie – she bought a smattering of DVDs and CDs. Archie would never lend his books, DVDs, CDs nor his precious vinyl records. He was pathologically anal about his music and so Margot felt he would 'buy into' her seemingly fresh desire to have a good audio visual system of her own in the studio, for entertainment and relaxation in fallow periods between clients. He had often suggested it before.

"Buy the best; don't skimp!"

Not that she ever had much time for anything other than writing up notes and case studies. Margot was very popular and had reached her limit – four clients per weekday, five when a client was coming more than once a week. She never saw clients on Sundays but she was always available on call at anytime except during her 'break' periods, very rigidly applied holidays; one in the spring for two weeks over Easter, one during the summer for four weeks, and another two week break at Christmas. Even then there was a system to deal with emergencies.

She walked home from FNAC through the back streets of the Raval. She could feel the ghosts from the world of Jean Genet in *The Diary of A Thief* which was written in the cafes and bars in this quarter. Some of them were shuttered up. Others had one or two lights on – it was dark from the almost black sky. Bar L'Angleterre, with its art deco, wrought iron and long, inviting bar, had one or two customers, soaked from the downpour with the perfect excuse for a glass of Cava or a beer. Those still in the streets were scurrying into other dingy, dark, dry havens. Thieves. Pimps. Pickpockets. Murderers. Male prostitutes. Hookers. Artists. Poets. Dali. Bunuel.

In her heightened state of awareness, she indulged this heady atmosphere as much as she had ever done. She stumbled into a tiny bar with dark green walls and simple wooden bar stools. She ordered a large cognac from the rather attractive, English-speaking Dutch barman. She gulped it down and headed south; she was on a mission.

It was still pouring with rain, so she bought a cheap umbrella from an old Algerian woman selling them on the street corner opposite the Sikh temple. There was a police car in front of the temple and a small crowd behind a cordon. Another murder? A family disagreement? Violence. Margot shivered. She trotted past without lingering and scurried down a tiny alley leading through to her beloved but now windswept, palm tree-lined avenue, Las Ramblas del Raval, which was totally deserted. She knew that at the end of the avenue, down the connecting street she used every morning, there was a Pakistani-owned barber-shop with a telephone booth and an internet facility – one of her clients had told her that you could make calls there which wouldn't show up on any records. She needed to make an untraceable call to Xavier. She was relieved it was open; often they were shuttered in the rain. She headed straight to the booths which lined the tiled walls. The modern telephone had been neatly constructed above the old basin of what had once been part of the salon. Arabic graffiti littered the white walls along with a card advertising a prostitute.

Margot dialled; he answered after two rings.

"Xavier, I received your message. I need to see you, too."

"Come around tonight, Margot."

"I can't tonight. Tomorrow morning? Early."

"Seven?"

"Seven at your apartment… please!"

"See you tomorrow. Je t'embrasse!"

Without any hesitation, Margot replied, "Toi aussi!"

She hung up, paused in the claustrophobia of the booth and began to cry uncontrollably. Apologising in Arabic, the Pakistani barber left his only client and helped Margot gently out of the booth. He apologised again, this time in English, and fetched her a glass of tea and also gave one to his young Spanish client, who nodded with a polite 'Gracias'.

"How can I help you, please? Don't worry about him. He is an old school friend. I cut his hair for nothing. Free! I could cut your hair free too!" He smiled sensitively.

"I am so, so sorry. I am okay. Thank you. Thank you. I don't know why I am like this. Please don't worry about me. I am okay. Really. Please, carry on. I am fine!"

The kindness of strangers. Margot remembered the Tennessee Williams phrase, and wanted to kiss him. The Pakistani went back to cutting his friend's long, dark hair. She drank her tea gratefully and left, promising to come back. She thrust a hundred Euros into his hands.

"God bless you! Imshallah!" he shouted after her.

She ran awkwardly down the wet cobbled streets with her FNAC bags. Once at her studio, she showered quickly and then went to the desk dressed only in her raincoat. The storm had taken the daylight away from the evening earlier than usual. Margot loved this kind of half-light. She shook with excitement as she took the new machinery and speakers out of their packaging. She didn't need the instructions – the shop assistant had been right about how simple the system was to assemble – and within a minute or two, boxes sprawled over the desk, the blue glow of her Panasonic screen had become the only light in her studio.

She scrambled for the DVD and inserted it quickly into the machine. The 'phone rang again. Archie. She ignored it. Margot pressed the play button and when she had control of the machine she used the fast forward control to bring her to the moment she had left the DVD when Carlos had first shown it to her. Tilly was sitting on the floor and a voice was coaxing her, 'off camera'. The rather tiny sound from the DVD player wasn't good enough so, carefully and methodically following the simple instruction booklet, Margot placed the Bose speaker around the desk. She went back to the player and pressed. The voice was not Paolo's voice. Paolo's accent was unmistakeable. This voice was an older man's, speaking in fluent Ancient Catalan. She increased the volume, reversed the images back to the beginning of the scene and again pressed play. She was now absolutely sure who owned this voice. Xavier had been the guiding mind behind Tilly's film. She played it back repeatedly and memorised the phrases like an actress, practising for an important audition. Archie would translate it for her.

Outside, it was still pouring with rain. Margot tidied her desk, putting the DVD together with the script in the envelope Carlos had given her. She called a cab and while she waited for it to arrive, she neatly dressed herself in the sombre black suit she had been wearing at the funeral. As she closed the shutters, she noticed a tall man sheltering in a doorway opposite her building. At first, she thought it looked a little like Robert. He seemed to be looking up at her studio, but almost as if he had seen her, he trotted away towards the small archway that led towards the port. He was caught in the lights of the cab as it came into the square, honking its horn at the man as he slipped between the car and the ancient wall.

Margot took Carlos's envelope from the desk, hurried out of the building and into the cab. Its windows were steamed up. She gave the driver her address and when she had settled in and he had reversed out of the small square, he remarked that he had nearly run over a man earlier, as he drove into the Plaça to pick her up. Margot asked him what he looked like. Bushy eyebrows were the only significant characteristics he had been able to pick out in the shadows. And tall. She shivered.

# Chapter Twenty Three

Archie was in a very strange mood; he was irritated with Margot.

"Why are you so late? Your client must have left you hours ago."

He very rarely asked her to account for her time and he certainly never challenged her about it.

"You don't normally spend so much time writing up your notes. I've been waiting for you."

Margot apologised and went into the kitchen. Archie had laid out the table for the supper he was preparing; sausages, fagioli beans with a simple green salad, followed by hard cheese and dates, along with a bottle of an unfamiliar Catalan red wine.

Margot played with her food and, much to his annoyance put one of her sausages onto his plate. She left some of the beans but she drained the wine. "This is delicious wine. Is there another bottle?"

"It's a new one on me. As it happens, I bought a case of it." He went towards his wine rack, pulled out another bottle, uncorked it and filled her glass.

"What was the wake like?" Margot asked.

"Awful. It was a very good thing you didn't come. Tilly's parents were more than a little upset. The funeral had been a bit too much for them. They knew that Paolo was a strange one but they had assumed you were keeping Tilly from any serious harm. Apparently, she had cast you in the role of being her protector, her safe confidante. They think you let them down very badly. Especially Sabrina, who was drunk, as usual."

"They can't blame me. I was her therapist, not her bodyguard."

"They thought that you had been her safety net. Tarquin was very angry and even he became very drunk. He started shouting at Eusebio at one stage. He wanted to know why Tilly couldn't be buried next to Paolo. Something to do with her citizenship, apparently. Sabrina had to calm him down. It was very embarrassing. I left as soon as I could."

"Tilly and I had a great relationship. And Paolo. They loved me as much as I loved them. But I had no control over what they did."

Archie cleared the plates and began to eat some cheese. Margot poured another glass of wine, waiting for an opportunity to ask Archie about Xavier.

"People always blame the shrink! I can just hear Sabrina... 'They were shrunk,' she will have told you. Well, I didn't 'shrink' them. I gave them help. Help they didn't find from anybody else. They so desperately needed it. And help they needed because they had such shitty parents! And she was just as bad as Tarquin. Tilly used to tell me... Fucking hypocrites! I hate all those trustafarians – stuck in the past of all that privilege and power their families used to have, and never been able to move on from it!"

Margot very rarely swore and her emotional reactions were well outside the boundaries of her professional faculties which she had no intention of evoking. Archie continued to eat his cheese without flinching. Margot ate a date. She realised that she had so nearly broken her golden rule about client confidentiality. Holding her breath, and in a very casual, almost throwaway manner, she began to probe.

"By the way, I saw you yesterday after our mediaeval history jaunt at the cathedral. With Robert's friend. Xavier. I didn't know you knew him."

"Xavier?" Archie hesitated. "Oh, that Xavier! The pallbearer at Paolo's funeral? No. I hardly know the man."

"You were walking towards Las Ramblas. I am sure it was you."

"Not me. I went straight to the Metro... How do you know him? "

Margot was skating on very thin ice, but then Archie seemed to be equally cagey. She decided to deflect his lie with a convenient change of subject.

"How strange. The man he was with was a spitting image. Xavier shared Robert's box at the opera on Monday night. I didn't take to him much, but I suppose he was charming enough."

*Why is he lying? What is he hiding?* Margot drained her glass and poured herself another.

She continued almost too casually. "His eulogy seemed a little overheated," and then conveniently changed the subject. "Much more to the point, who was that girl in the yellow dress who slapped him? And why, for God's sake?"

"She's one of my students."

"No! Why was she there?"

"She attended the same language classes as Paolo and Tilly."

"Really? Wow! Who is she? What was that all about?"

"I don't really know much about her. She comes from Niger in the Sahel, south of the Sahara. She is frightfully clever. She will almost certainly get a first."

"What is her name?"

"She has an English name and an African Muslim surname. We all call her Isobel. Scottish name, really!"

Archie left the table and began to clear up. "The police have been interviewing Robert, of all people! And they want to interview me."

"I'll do the washing up, Archie."

She was becoming irritated.

"I have no idea what I can tell them that they don't already know."

Archie was now filling the basin and putting the dishes into the hot soapy water.

"You can go to bed, if you like. I'll sleep in the spare room tonight; I have to be up early."

He rather pointedly began to put on the yellow rubber gloves which were part of his ritual to establish what he called 'domestic brownie points'.

"I said I would do the fucking dishes, Archie!"

Margot was almost shouting at him. Archie looked at her wild eyes, shrugged and left the room. This was their first serious marital fight, ever. Margot sat in the kitchen, fighting back her tears, determined to avoid any mawkish apology. Archie put some jazz on the hi-fi, aware that Oscar Peterson's magical piano chords would percolate from the kitchen's Bose speakers. Margot loved his music. She blew out the candles. It had finally stopped raining and a full moon bathed the kitchen in an eerie glow. She sat in the dark, trying to make some sense out of what she had learnt about Xavier since meeting him only three days before.

What petrified her was that she was unable to rid herself of the overriding desire to allow him to sexually manipulate her. Remarkably, she was still prepared to allow him to treat her as badly as he had treated Laura. Rape her? Perhaps. Even that thought had begun to excite her again. She certainly didn't feel any competitive jealousy about his other lovers, and she was prepared to extend her threshold for pain and humiliation if that was what it took to see him again. She trembled at the thought of the seductive smell of his skin, the bittersweet taste of his semen, and the electricity of his fingers, along with the mellow imperiousness of his rich voice.

She went over it all again in her mind, turning it over and over and over. Her own extreme experiences, Paolo's story of what can only be described as sexual abuse, whatever spin he might have preferred to put on his 'romance' with Xavier when he was a boy. The clear cut connection between the DVD and the cord bracelet, Laura's description of her rape fantasies, and then the strange connection with Archie – all part of the accusatory ammunition she was determined to use to confront him when she saw him in the early morning. She needed to be purged of the fears she was nursing that Xavier, and now Archie, had in any way been involved in the murders. She had decided to delay any rational or logical reaction to his behaviour and was prepared to accept all his excuses and explanations. In that sense she had become his prey. He was, as ever, in complete control.

Archie returned to the kitchen. "What's going on my darling? I have never seen you like this."

Margot decided to change tack and be less defensive and less aggressive. She tried to sound as normal as possible under the circumstances.

"I am so sorry. I am just a little bit drunk, Archie. I am fine. Really... The funeral upset me more than I thought it would. I have been thinking about Paolo and Tilly. I am angry at Tarquin and Sabrina, but I suppose they might have a point. I have wracked my brains trying to think of anything Tilly might have told me which could have been the vaguest of hints that she was up to something unusual. Perverted, perhaps. But there was nothing I could find which would indicate any fear or anxiety. I can understand how her parents feel, Tilly was a wonderful girl. But I am at a loss, as much as they are. What happened came completely out of the blue. For all of us. But then, we all have our secrets."

"I know. I feel bad too. I also felt that I had failed them. Look, I fucked up. I tried to apologise to Tarquin, then... well, Sabrina just resorted to the bottle."

Archie had joined her at the kitchen table. Margot was desperately trying to avoid breaking down and spilling out for Archie what was really troubling her. She deflected her thoughts.

"I think I need to do my laps, get fit again. I am going to be there at dawn and swim for an hour or so in that Olympic pool at the top of the Montjuic. That pool is always empty when I like to go at first light. It's too far away for the early morning businessmen."

Archie stood up to leave. "I love you, Margot... You really don't have to sleep alone tonight. Come to bed... soon."

"As long as you don't mind me slipping out before dawn..."

"Have I ever before?"

"I love you too, Archie!" and there was no question in her mind about that, whatsoever.

She waited in the dark and listened while he opened the shutters in the drawing room, (they hated any fug and the storm had passed), turned off the jazz, brushed his teeth and shuffled with his leather slippers into their bedroom. She had a quick shower to shake off the grime of the rainstorm, and joined him. He was snoring. She was careful to slide under the duvet so as to avoid touching him. He was a very light sleeper. A little woozy from the red wine, she dozed off thinking about Laura. There was something that had bothered her about her need to leave their session so quickly. Perhaps she had been planning a *rendez-vous* with Xavier before catching her plane to London?

# Chapter Twenty Four

Margot slept through the piercing, intermittent whines of her alarm clock. The dawn chorus of birds finally woke her and she leapt out of bed as if a snake had bitten her, but she soon recovered. Although her first thought had been of Xavier's body, her stomach churned as she realised that what she was planning to do that morning might be the catalyst for disaster. She showered again but the excitement from the sexual anticipation of Xavier's two previous encounters did not recur. She dabbed a simple daytime perfume on her shoulders and slipped into blue jeans and a black tee-shirt. She kissed Archie on the forehead, wound her hair under her yellow helmet and took her bicycle towards the front stairs. She was late and couldn't afford the time to walk.

Archie called out to her, "Don't forget your towel and goggles."

Margot stopped in her tracks. She went back to the bathroom and took a small, chic mauve back-pack from its hook on the back of the door, checked it peremptorily and slung it onto her back.

"Have a great day, Archie. Let's have dinner out tonight."

"Okay. I'll call you at the studio. Maybe Robert might like to join us."

"No! I couldn't face Robert, and anyway, I have to see him this afternoon."

"I love you."

Archie really did love her. The idea that he had anything to do with Paolo and Tilly's murder had evaporated overnight.

Margot staggered down the stairs with her bike trailing behind her, and taking the Olympic roadway down to the Plaça Espanya, she peddled like a demented professional cyclist. As she cruised into the north end of the Barri Gotic, stragglers were leaving the Catedral after morning mass. Yet again, a police car was positioned on the wide pavement area opposite Xavier's apartment in the Plaça Santa Maria del Pi. More early risers were spilling out of the smaller church set into the corner of the square. Margot padlocked her bike against its railings. She rang the bell of Xavier's apartment firmly and waited. No response. Perhaps he was still asleep. She rang again. This time she waited about a minute. Was he playing another of his games of control?

She looked at her watch, she was at the most twenty minutes late. Her third attempt to raise Xavier was prolonged, insistent. Silence. She looked around. She was now internally hysterical, and also a little frightened. The square was empty again except for the police car. She left her bicycle and walked quickly down towards the Calle Ferran where she knew there would be an open café, and then remembered that of course Elvira would be in her bar. She quickly crossed the Plaça Reial and was soon on a stool in front of her friend who couldn't help noticing her desperation.

"So early! I will squeeze you some orange juice."

The noise of the juicing machine was unbearable. Margot was shaking.

"I have just been around to Xavier's house. He said that he would meet me there at seven. He didn't answer the bell. I rang three times."

"He was probably at the police station. Carlos was going to talk to him today, very early. Apparently this Xavier knew Paolo at his school in Scotland and there was some strange reason why he lost his job there. He said something about the results of some voice tests."

"How did Carlos find out about Scotland?"

Margot felt stupid asking this question because, of course, Carlos was an excellent detective. She gulped the juice and drank the strong coffee Elvira had gently pushed towards her.

"I suppose he looks into everything and everyone. He has a friend at Scotland Yard. He was very interested in what happened at the crematorium yesterday with that girl in the yellow dress. He suspects that your friend Robert might know more than he has been telling him."

Elvira left her position behind the bar and sat next to Margot. She took her hand.

"You must go and talk to Carlos. Tell him everything you told me yesterday."

"I know I must, but I can't. Not yet. I will, I promise. But I have to see Xavier again."

Elvira didn't need to ask her why. Margot's face told her everything she needed to know.

The two priests came into the bar.

"We saw your husband taking someone away earlier this morning," the older priest said to Elvira, as they made their way to their usual table. "The tall Englishman. He comes to Mass sometimes. He used to come every day with those two kids who were murdered. Always in the evening. He was teaching them Catalan."

Paolo spoke Catalan, but the priest wasn't to know that. This innocent anecdote re-enforced Margot's conviction. Despite all the indications, it still seemed inconceivable to her that Xavier was a killer, let alone Paolo's murderer.

"Apparently, the night watchman who found the bodies has disappeared."

This was news to Margot.

"What night watchman?" she whispered to Elvira.

"The man who found the bodies and 'phoned the police very late on Monday night. It's in the papers. The police are looking for him. He is their first official suspect."

Margot's mobile phone rang. She answered, told her caller to wait a minute and then went up the narrow, art deco spiral staircase to the small balcony, where she sat at a small round wooden table and a bench. She talked in a whisper.

"Where are you? I can't talk. I am in a bar... I was twenty minutes late... I am so sorry... But I must see you; I have to see you today, as soon as possible... I can't now. I have a client... lunch, but I will only have an hour, I have another client in the afternoon."

Another 'phone rang, this time in the bar. Margot looked down from the balcony, almost as a photographer might have, when framing a poignant picture. From her perspective, and this included the mirror image which allowed her see the entire café, the scene below had an abstract, unrealistic atmosphere, little pro-active life. A bubble. And in a strange way she felt safe there. Her sanctuary, no temptations or complications. The two priests had been joined by a couple of older tramps sitting at the bar drinking brandy. Elvira was on the 'phone and looked pre-occupied. She was the one person in the world who could probably be trusted to keep Margot's predicament secret, even from Carlos. But imparted secrets can be dangerous. They have the power to change lives, change perception, change behaviour, and alter friendships. Elvira looked up, said farewell to the caller and came upstairs.

"That was Carlos. He is very worried about you. I have told him nothing but he has interviewed Xavier and Robert. He wouldn't tell me anything about it, he never does. But he did tell me that he had no evidence. He needs to question you and your husband officially. At the headquarters building. I told him that was stupid and that he should see you in a relaxed place, with Archie. Both of you. And so he asked me to ask you if you would like to come to supper with us tonight instead. I will cook you my famous paella."

Elvira looked appealingly at her friend, who burst into tears. Elvira sat down and put her arms around Margot's shoulders. A man shouted from below in an English accent.

"Café, por favor!"

"That's Hugo's voice." Elvira went down immediately.

Hugo was alone. She gave him a solo. He sat at the bar, slurring his words.

"You knew my sister, Tilly, didn't you?" he asked in perfect Spanish.

"Many girls come here, Hugo."

"Domatilla."

"I cannot talk about Domatilla, señor. Except that I loved her and Paolo." Elvira used English.

"Me too. I didn't come to ask you anything. She loved this bar." Hugo sipped his solo. "I saw you at the funeral. Thank you for coming. My girlfriend Emma was Paolo's half-sister. I have to go to London for Tilly's funeral."

Margot watched all this from the balcony. She wanted to go down to Hugo and hug him, but she knew that she couldn't without becoming more involved than she could cope with this morning.

Hugo then began to gabble, almost as if talking to himself, half-monologue.

"The police finally took me out to the warehouse... Tilly was strange but she was happy. Her art was the most important thing for her. It was all weird but it was so beautiful. Videos... She put them on the Internet. Paolo was always in them. I am in one. She wanted to recreate a famous painting by Goya. She used me and all the other people in our language class. Isobel, the girl in the yellow dress who slapped Xavier... Xavier, our language tutor, used to use paintings as a way to help us to learn the language. Paintings and movies. But mainly paintings. Santa Eulalia. That was his idea. Isobel loved Tilly, too. She blames Xavier for giving them the idea..."

Elvira continued to wipe the glasses she had been washing.

"I just can't believe that they could have been so stupid."

He stared at his cup. He opened a sugar lump and ate it slowly. The priests were sitting there like frozen statues. This was better than anything they had heard in the confession box that week. One of the drunks was clumsily playing the fruit machine. Margot looked at her watch. Her first client wasn't due until ten.

"My husband is the policeman in charge of the case. He is confident that he will find the night watchman who is apparently their suspect."

"I don't think the night watchman did it! Why would he have called the police? I still think that they had decided to die together. Paolo always said that dying would give him the ultimate sexual high."

Hugo left his stool and put a few Euros on the counter.

"I told your husband that."

Elvira took the Euros. "Sometimes killers ring the police from the scene of the crime."

The drunk at the fruit machine had been listening, too. Hugo laughed and left the bar. Margot waited a minute or so and then went down to Elvira. They hugged without a word and Margot left, leaving the customary ten-Euro note, which Elvira today put into the charity box on the counter. Margot whispered in to her friend's ear.

"Ring your husband and tell him that I accept his invitation to supper this evening. Archie and I had plans to go out tonight. I will ring Carlos later. Maybe he can give me a lift? Archie can meet us there."

Elvira kissed her again. "Don't forget to ask Archie."

Margot lingered at the door and looked down. When she had gone, Elvira went over to the priests.

"You have stayed longer than you ever do this morning, monsignors. I am sure that you have a long queue of sinners waiting for you, to confess. All those horrible bankers that have been stealing from our bank accounts."

"They can wait today. Our Lord will forgive them in good time!"

The priests laughed and ordered another café solo each. Elvira rang Carlos.

"She has promised to see us this evening. Can you pick her up?... Vale... Adios!"

She watched Margot walk down the street. She had noticed the bags around her eyes and the ashen face when she mentioned Archie.

✳

*Archie. He is going to be devastated. He won't believe that I could have been so secretive. I tell him everything except the stuff I learn from my clients. Always have. He will be jealous and shocked. Angry. But Elvira is right. I must tell him everything and doing it with Carlos and Elvira there might make it a little easier.*

*I wonder, what have I done to earn Elvira's trust, her unfettered friendship? Ostensibly we have little in common with each other. She loved listening to all my stories, my childhood, about my parents. And in that sense, I told her many things about my lovely, lovely but boring life in La Jolla, stuff I haven't bothered to tell anybody else. Pointless facts about the kind of ice cream I liked in my milkshakes, the different* colours on the walls in my bedroom and the pretty clothes I wore. Frills and velvet. My mother bought patterns from a mail order company which advertised in the LA Times. The latest Paris fashions for children, that she cut out of the haute couture pages in Vogue or Harper's Bazaar. Always the more upmarket magazines. Mother would then make them up herself – the material was rigorously chosen to match the specifications and she would have at least one or two fittings with me before finalising the sewing and extraneous paraphernalia like the buttons and ribbons which again had to be 'just right'. Elvira adored all this. She said that her mother wouldn't have known the difference between haute couture and 'off the peg' and saved up to buy the cheapest second hand clothes she could find in the junk stalls which came into the village on market days.

Archie also bought into the Garden of Eden-like presentation of my life. He said that it gave him comfort and hope although he had always been very suspicious of the so-called American Dream. "Dreams for the rich, nightmares for the poor". But he loved me to be that perfect woman, and has always had me up on a pedestal. Little did he know what was brewing and bubbling up beneath that Barbie Doll exterior.

Obviously, much of what I told Elvira, I have also in some way or another talked about in the therapy I had to go through as part of my training. And of course, to Marie-Christine. She had probed and probed to no avail. They had both listened to my childhood memories of the stories I had been told by Uncle Ian, including one in particular about a family of five daughters. When they came home from school they had been ritualistically punished by their grandfather for minor transgressions – forgetting to shine their shoes, or being five minutes late for breakfast. He spanked them with a slipper and then fondled their nubile bodies by way of apology. Their mother had insisted that they watch their sisters going through this process. It was a horrible story and my uncle only told it to me by way of illustration but to a certain extent I shared in his excitement about it. And I felt so bad about that. Ashamed.

I had read a story in the newspaper about a man who had been arrested for sexual abuse and I wanted him to explain it to me. This was a form of trauma because, although I saw it as past history, I believed that perhaps I had inherited some genes from my ancestral family which would contribute to my personality in such a way as to allow me to identify with their more colourful, more volatile lives and so become more 'normal'. Marie Christine was sure that his stories were my own substitutes for traditional Freudian influences, and that they were also hiding traumas, fears that I had submerged. Perhaps. Shrinks are notoriously blind to their own problems. As much as I profoundly understood the basis for her enquiries and the patterns of her therapeutic techniques, I found it absolutely impossible to help her conclusively. We went around in circles and she eventually told me that she didn't feel that there was anything else she could do for me. I didn't seem to need it. This was a spectacular admission and both a relief and a sadness for me. And how wrong I was; I miss her so much now.

What seemed to have particularly pre-occupied her was the degree to which I so relentlessly hung onto my seemingly unblemished childhood. I didn't even allow her to deflate my fantasies about Uncle Ian – her theory was that he had been my first 'secret'. He had been my 'secret lover' and he had in a strange way 'abused' me. I was very angry at this and used all my wit and University learnt intellect to fight her on this point. She gave up. "Do you ever feel guilty about this, about your privileges, Margot?" she would ask, incredulously. At first this used to make me worried that I would be ill equipped at dealing with *the damaged minds of my clients. I so wanted to 'help' them, to give them a little of the kind of pleasure I experienced in my life. I wanted to make my patients' lives more comfortable, more palatable. I had so little direct personal experience of any abuse, or any 'messages' as they are so simplistically called in the analytical environment.*

*And so I rationalised my good fortune and decided that all this good without bad had been a positive factor as far as my chosen career was concerned. My vocation. I believed that this clean bill of mental health and a genuine innocence when it came to listening to all the tales from those clients within my research projects at Chicago, and in the hundreds of case studies I read, allowed me to maintain a scientific objectivity which I have always believed was the secret of my success as a psychotherapist.*

*Thankfully, I never had much capacity for being judgemental, despite my strict Catholic religious education. I could never have cast that first stone. This, of course, had been at the root of my need to pick an arena to study which would provide a balance for my sanitised upbringing. And so... Familial abuse. Sexual trauma. Rape victims. The study of all these horrors gave me some balance. Good can't exist without evil. Evil people cannot thrive unless there are good people to destroy, ruin. In traditional Freudian terms, I have to accept that I am a freak. I have no history of any of the symptoms Freud identified as consistent in everybody else's psychological footprints, I am absolutely sure of this. Even those earliest influences in my case seemed finally harmless. Or so it would seem from those hours and hours Marie-Christine spent in deep analysis, trying to find some trace of what she was convinced had to exist. And her concluding 'bill of mental health with one rider, of course! Uncle Ian!'*

*But then what is going on now? Am I at last resisting the notion that I am a 'goodie two-shoes', and educating myself into my darker side, which seems to be a 'sine qua non' of human nature? Initiating myself at last into that world everybody has been dealing with and which for some reason has passed me by, deflected by the bubble which I had created in my safe, cerebral life with Archie? Where has the dark side of my psyche been lurking, balancing the freak of nature which seemed to have submerged that side of life out of the bio-chemical make up of my brain cells? Do I now need to make myself deliberately bad? Make myself naughty, make myself normal? No, not needing to but being compulsively forced to. Normal? Xavier's games are hardly normal.*

*And I still want to play with him. Rather in the same way that I liked listening to my uncle Ian's stories.*

*Maybe that is what Elvira has picked up? Maybe she is some sort of personal protective angel? She is a very devout Catholic. She may have recognised instinctively that I was an endangered soul. Whatever it was, she adored listening to my stories of the idyll I had enjoyed as a child, and in that sense I represented a living example of Utopian citizen for her. America presents this image to so many people who know little about what it is really like to live there and be an American. Hollywood movies present fantasies – dreamlike distortions. Good triumphing over evil, threats being demolished. Cathartic exercises designed to woo us into a soporific sense of security about our special way of life. But realistically, we all have skeletons in our cupboards and we are all prey to the same need to join in with the allure of Satan's temptations. Paolo had loved Dante because he understood that more than most. He indulged it fatally. Is his fate to be my fate, too? I am at last living in the modern equivalent of Dante's Inferno. And which is Xavier? Beelzebub or Lucifer or Dis or Satan? They all apply.*

# Chapter Twenty Five

Margot tried to focus on her two morning clients. Saturday clients. Oddly enough, they provided her with a convenient diversion.

Apart from Italian cinema, Anthony loved football. He devoured the sports pages in all the English, Spanish and Catalan newspapers and magazines, absorbing each and every item with any connection to his beloved obsession. In particular, he was a massive fan of Barcelona's celebrated football team, an unlikely quirk for a boy brought up in Scunthorpe. He went to every home game and for away matches he would ply the Raval for enough 'tricks' to give him sufficient cash to afford the plane tickets and hotel costs. Apart from the barest of day-to-day living expenses, and the rent for a very cheap squat in the Barceloneta, his only other luxuries were regular visits to the cinematheque and the two sessions each week he religiously insisted on having with Margot. He had been her first client in Barcelona, and he never doubted that she had saved his life.

Anthony was one of the funniest men Margot had ever come across. If there was one relationship she would have loved to have seen blossom, it would have been a friendship between Ant, as she called him, and Archie. Ant was uneducated but an autodidact with a formidable memory for detail and a hungry appetite for all kinds of information. He was a brilliant prostitute – his clients felt relaxed and he was very good at the 'fancy waterworks', as he described his sexual dexterity. He was a good listener but at the same time, he was quite prepared to take over the role of a loquacious storyteller if the occasion suited him.

"Will you come to the Barça match next Sunday with me?" was

his opening gambit at ten seconds past ten o'clock that morning. He was also obsessively punctual. "My current number two has cried off," he continued. "I don't fancy number three anymore and number one doesn't fancy me. And so I thought of you."

"Number four?"

"Number one-oh-one, darling! You don't have the right bits, unless you have had a sex change since I saw you on the night before your wedding in that gorgeous bridal suite at The Arts. But if I were to be in serious stuck, I could always bring along some kit for you one evening and we could try it out!"

Margot laughed. "I didn't know that you saw all of me that night, by the way. But I am game for anything. Count me in for Sunday. As it happens, my usual lunch date has been cancelled and I have never been to a soccer game."

"The Barcelona stadium, Camp Nou, or Barça as I call it, is Paradise On Earth, darling. Imagine two teams, twenty-two gorgeous boys in tight body-hugging strips, all playing for you, for you and for a hundred thousand other people in the stadium, mostly boys. Apart from one in Brazil and one in Mexico, it's the biggest stadium in the world and was designed by a famous architect. I can never understand why there are so few girls around during the games. I am just a girlie, as you know, and I have to go at least twice each game to that lovely smelly lav so that I can toss myself off! There's so much exciting action happening in front of me – I go three times if one of the poor dears gets sent off the pitch for a foul."

Margot had always known that Ant was irreparably compulsive. She had managed to persuade him to understand this, and to understand some of the causes of this sometimes devastating behaviour. He was considerably less damaged now, and much more in control of his life than he had been when he had met her at her wedding five years ago. Perhaps here was an opportunity to probe some of the elements in his obsession for football in a way that could also help her to deal with Xavier. His obsession seemed to be as irrational as her own. She decided to tease him.

"There are all kinds of taboos. You know, of course, that some shrinks never visit their clients outside the consulting room. That is taboo in their book. Then another one is sex with clients. So that one is out too, Ant, I am sorry to say."

"I know – for them, maybe. Those shrinks are out of date and out of touch. But you are such a grown up girl and us grown up girls can do what we want. What harm could you possibly do to me? I am much more likely to damage you."

"I think that is why those rules exist."

"You are so deranged anyway, Margot. You always look so innocently at me when I tell you my naughty stories. Anybody that innocent has to be mad. Barça with me couldn't make it any worse. Only better."

"Ok, you win! I will come."

He jumped and screamed for joy. Margot wanted to ask him some questions, so she allowed him to calm down and then moved onto the area which she hoped could help her with Xavier.

"Do you mind if I ask you a couple of questions for a change?"

Margot remembered asking Laura the same thing. It was becoming a habit.

"Fire away..."

She framed the questions so that they would seem to concern him, and not herself.

"You have talked about your mother. You have talked about Monica Vitti. You have talked about at least twenty footballers. Is there anyone you have never talked about because you have done something with them that is both shameful in one way, and irresistibly sexy in another?"

"Margot, I can't believe that you have just asked that question. Every experience I have had is irresistibly sexy, and shameful!"

Ant looked her contemplatively. He was very still. She looked into his eyes and he looked away at first, but when he realised that she was on a serious mission, he looked back at her and without any irony or the customary banter, he said, "Yes! Once, for about six months, I came under someone's spell and I lost control!"

She wanted to throw her arms around Anthony and kiss him all over, but she also needed to stay focused, professionally. He had just delivered the most comforting sentence he could have uttered that morning, without having the slightest inkling as to why that was the case. She also felt a little guilty, but she was confident that she could make sure that whatever they might unearth of value for her, would have equal value for him. This was a familiar pattern in post-Freudian analysis, and she was superficially trying to convince herself that this strategy had her usual ethical justification.

"What do you mean by 'lost control'?"

"I couldn't resist it although I knew it was wrong in every way. It was so pleasurable. I craved the experience."

"Did it involve anything out of the ordinary for you?"

Anthony was quiet again. Without a trace of his normal ebullience he launched into a description of a teenage affair, a very perverted and violent, Sado-masochistic relationship with a much older woman. A woman he wouldn't identify at first. The Oedipal resonances seemed clichéd, until he described the initiation, the first time that sex had taken place, and Margot identified from his description the one significant and horrifying fact.

"Dad was next door! I could hear him snoring."

The woman Anthony was describing was his own mother.

Anthony broke down. He crumbled in the chair like a tiny child. Margot managed to calm him down, and when he recovered, he thanked her profusely. "I have wanted to tell you this for five years but have never had the courage to face it myself. Thank you, darling Margot. Thirty years and five minutes."

Anthony's mother had given him life and had stolen his life. Somehow, Margot had stumbled on the opportunity to deal with Anthony's problems in the context of her desperate need to solve her own.

*How did he deal with his shame? Who did he tell? How did he handle his secret?*

*Of course, there is one vital difference: Ant's mother was not a murderer, however appalling her behaviour.*

These moments of revelation, of 'breakthrough' as they are called, are few and far between. Rather like extraordinary co-incidences and moments of extreme intensity, the capacity to give them some external context with a phrase or sensible conversation is usually non-existent. Anthony was capable of a witty solution to almost anything, but on this occasion he could only resort to the one event that was important for him that week, Sunday's match.

"Are we still on for Barça?"

"Don't be silly, Ant. I wouldn't miss all those boys for anything! Where shall we meet?"

"Elizabets. Lunch. We can take the M to the stadium from Universitat. Twelve?"

"Twelve on Sunday at Elizabets."

Much to her surprise and disappointment, he leapt up and made it clear that he wanted to leave as soon as possible. He kissed Margot on the lips and left with a chuckle, leaving her without any solutions.

Before she could collect her thoughts beyond being aware of the butterflies nesting persistently deep down in her stomach, she heard her next client's powerful voice say "Gracias" and a car door slam, firmly. He came puffing into the room, heaving a shoulder bag onto the floor and taking off his long, leather coat. Gottfried was not just oversized, he was Gargantuan. Margot took his coat through to her study area and threw it on the desk.

"I was so sorry to hear about your clients."

"I didn't know that you knew they were my clients, Gottfried."

"I know everything."

He said this without any trace of irony. She couldn't resist asking him, "Did you know them?"

"No, but I knew Paolo's real father. He had a portfolio of investments looked after by our bank. Before he was killed, he would come into lunch with my father from time to time."

"How is your father?"

"I hate the man of course, and he's as ever… he's been annoying me more than usual. My brother came into the city and Father insisted on throwing a party for him. He asked me to organise it and then interfered with every decision I made."

"What decisions?"

"Everything. The venue was changed. I wanted to do it at The Arts, or another space which would have no family connections. My father wanted to do it on his yacht. I wanted to have a live DJ – the best in Barcelona, but my father insisted on flying in Julio Iglesias at vast expense. Julio Iglesias, for Christ's sake! He's an old friend. Stuff like that."

"Why on earth did he ask you to organise it?"

"I think he is trying to keep me away from some dodgy deal the bank is involved in to try to save its skin. We have had an army of Bulgarians through the doors. Bulgaria is the new Iceland."

There had been a constant battle for control of the family banking business. Gottfried was much smarter than his Dad and had proved his financial prowess to the banking community with a series of independently negotiated contracts made with three emergent Chinese industrialists. This precociousness had destroyed his father's conviction that Hans, Gottfried's younger brother, was the more talented son. On the back of the Chinese triumphs, Gottfried had been shifted to work on corporate identity and Hans had been despatched to New York where he could shine without his brother's competitive spirit stealing the corporate limelight.

Margot had been through many theories about Gottfried's relationship with his father but he still remained an enigma. Gottfried was a virgin. He rarely had any girlfriends, or boyfriends for that matter, but he was very sociable and loved parties and nightclubs. He lived alone in a suite in a tiny boutique hotel. What of his relationship with his mother? She lived in Madrid with her second husband, a famous chef who appeared on television in a very popular food show. At one stage, the idea that he was a repressed homosexual had some credibility, his vocal homophobia supporting this obvious theory. Was he quite simply a 'closet queen'? He seemed pathologically afraid of that particular line of enquiry and deflected Margot's probing whenever she had raised it. No matter, today Margot wanted to investigate Gottfried's apparently perverse need to revolve his life around his father's business, knowing that he didn't really need to on any level – financially, he could survive without it. Emotionally, his father caused him so much unnecessary stress. Again, she was using her client to research levels of obsessive and perverse behaviour in an attempt to analyse herself.

The session was fruitless and frustrating. However much Margot battled against it, Gottfried insisted on spending most of his hour describing the party and telling her how much better it would have been if he had been allowed to organise it without his father's interference. He needed to get this off his chest. Familiar and boring territory. When his fifty minutes was up, to the second, she retrieved his coat, took his cheque and sent him packing.

She now had exactly one hour to prepare for Xavier and walk to his apartment. She re-wound her answering machine.

Archie. Skip. Robert. Skip. Carlos: "Please call me as soon as you can – I hear we have plans but I still need you to come to the police headquarters. Procedure."

Hugo: "I so want to see you guys. Can we all come to Sunday lunch, please?"

Archie: skip. And then a young woman, a voice she had never heard before, with a French accent.

"Margot, my name is Isobel. I was Paolo's friend. I was the girl in the yellow dress at the funeral. Please can you call me? I want to see you as soon as possible. It is urgent."

She said the word as if she was speaking in French, somehow giving the word more punch. Margot dialled the number immediately.

"Isobel?... It's Margot..."

She listened for what seemed like a very long two minutes.

"Okay. I understand. Can you see me right now, this morning?... I will meet you wherever you want... give me somewhere in the Barri Gotic and I can be with you in twenty minutes, wherever... I know it well... I'll be there but I can only afford half an hour. Is that okay for you?"

She didn't want to take the risk of missing Xavier a second time, but she had enough time to see Isobel and make it in time. After ringing Robert to leave him a message to say that she was expecting him as usual at three that afternoon, she went over to the shutters to close them, and yet again she was absolutely sure that a man was watching her studio from the shadows opposite her building. He moved as soon as she caught sight of him. She closed the shutters, slipped off her jeans, showered, slipped into a red summer dress, ran out of her apartment, across the packed Reial, across Calle Ferran, now teaming with midday tourists, and along the tiny street to the old chocolate café Isobel had suggested for their meeting. It was relatively empty, and Isobel was already sitting at the back, wearing the same yellow dress she had worn at the funeral. Margot was struck by her simple beauty. Isobel twinkled at her with a shy, welcoming handshake.

"It's my favourite dress! Promise! Thank you for coming so quickly. I know where you live..."

Margot was breathless, but she knew instantly that this was a woman she could trust with her life. Isobel shook her hand affectionately.

"I am so sorry but I only have half an hour!"

"Xavier?"

It was almost as if she didn't need to ask the question.

"How do you know?"

Isobel smiled and began her story. She had a quiet, attractive voice. She spoke English fluently with a light French accent, which reminded Margot of Marie Christine. Margot allowed her to speak without interruption, practised as she was with listening to confessions and personal histories.

# Chapter Twenty Six

"Have you ever been to Niger? Non. We learn *le Français* in school... There are very few tall, beautiful white men in Niger except the arrogant *pieds noirs*. I like tall, beautiful English and Scottish white men. I fell in love with Xavier at first sight, which was a big problem for me because I am married to a very jealous man, also from Niger, which is my home country. I was married to him when I was fifteen.

"I met Xavier at the language classes. He was teaching English, and other languages. Catalan. He asked us all to stand up and tell everybody who we were and where we came from and why we were in Barcelona. (Paolo and Tilly were there – I didn't really understand why Tilly was there at first). I told the Catalan class, I suppose about twenty of us, the truth, that my English was poor, and they laughed at my clumsy words which I mixed with my perfect French. Xavier was very kind and corrected each mistake. He was very sensitive. He gave us all names. He called me 'le rossignol', the nightingale. Niger was a French colony which is why I speak such good French, but my husband is a King and he is very proud about his culture. In his kingdom, the King would have several wives. Obe only has me and I speak French, which makes it very difficult for his family!

"My family lives in Agadez, a small city in the north of my country. It is on the ancient salt route close to the Sahara desert. My father is an imam, my mother is a teacher and they gave me a great education. I won a scholarship to Le Sorbonne and I met Obe in Paris. He is very handsome and gave me a great time. He had money. When he asked me to marry him, I told him 'yes' but I wanted to be his only wife. He told me that he would accept, but if he could be my only husband. He told me that his family would kill me if I was ever unfaithful to him. He would kill me. He was not joking. He explained his position with all sorts of highly complicated religious and sociological justifications which I challenged – I thought that they were stupid – but *finalement* I said yes because I loved him so much, and so we were married in my home village. Until I met Xavier, I had never been interested in another man, physically, sexually. In Niger, in many homes, the young women have traditional sexual initiations when they are virgins. These can ruin a woman – they still circumcise many young girls. But my mother and father are progressives. They are what Obe calls radicals. Of course, he was surprised that I was a virgin but he liked that so much.

"After my first class with Xavier I had a coffee with Paolo and Tilly. They were so obviously interesting. Most people there were boring. *Banquiers. Hommes d'affaires.* Tilly had told us during the class that she was an artist, a film-maker. She made installations. Paolo had also been very funny. He said that he was the apprentice to the sorceress Domatilla. He made a joke about her name. More Dom than Tilly he said. We all laughed without really knowing why. Xavier explained the significance of Paolo's use of the word 'dom' to us. I had guessed. He did this in English, Spanish, Catalan, French, Italian and German. He explained 'domination'. He explained 'submission'. He explained sadism. He explained masochism. This was such a revolutionary way to teach us English. Incredible. Anyway, I decided to get to know Paolo and Domatilla. They fascinated me. They were so attractive. Fun. Dangerous, too, which I find interesting. So many people are so predictable. And so I asked them to come for a drink with me at my favourite cocktail bar. Gimlet? It is in the Born, a very small bar called Gimlet. Gimlet is an English drink made from gin and limes. Gordon's Gin and Rose's

Lime juice! I love it so much. Gimlet has this beautiful teak bar which looks like a very long – you call it sleek? – highly polished piano. It is also usually very empty at nine o'clock when our classes finish, and they play some great jazz music. They didn't know it then, but I know that they loved it too.

"Tilly explained her 'mission' as she called it. She was wanting to find interesting people, good subjects for her art. She wanted to use them in small movies that she was going to make and then put them on an internet site. They had to be very special people and they had to be prepared to 'break the boundaries'. I volunteered at once. I told to her that I had been encouraged by my parents to explore. I came from a very different culture and so whatever Tilly had prepared for me would be an adventure. She told me to look on her website and I would find some of the art she had 'made'! This was her word. 'Made'. I love that word so much. And then, out of the blue, Xavier joined us in the bar. I was so shocked. And shy. He explained... he spoke beautiful French... that he thought I was the only interesting woman he had in any of his classes since Tilly had arrived. I was now so excited. We were all so excited.

"I had come to Barcelona because Obe is studying Spanish law. He helped me get a place on your husband's course at the university because the principle reason we came to live here in this city is that Obe wants to practise law in South America. Barcelona is a gateway for many Brazilians. We have many Brazilian and Argentinean friends. So many, and they mostly talk in Spanish or Portuguese. And so Xavier, Paolo and Tilly were great. I could practise my English with them and of course I found Xavier very sexy. I like older men. White men. He explained that he had been introducing Tilly to some of the great paintings in the art galleries in Barcelona and that she had used these to inspire her, for her work. He loved *les cinéastes* who had used many paintings and art as inspirations. He told me about Derek Jarman. An English gay *metteur en scene* who had died of Sida, Aids. He said that he had made this beautiful film about Caravaggio. And another film about Christophe Marlowe, an English poet. Both these men had died very violently. But he told me that the films had beautiful images which had been inspired by great paintings. One of his films, an amazing music film called *War Requiem*, has a perfect movie image reproduction of a Piero del Francesca painting of St. George. Tilly had picked up on this idea and was using the people she found in Xavier's class to help her make short films which were like this. Recreations of paintings. I made a joke about Caravaggio's death. He was murdered. Xavier loved my joke. He said that he was fascinated by the circumstances of people's death. He talked about a famous pop singer who hanged himself in the hotel room in Australia. And an English journalist that suffocated himself to death in London during his attempt to have the perfect orgasm. I suppose I should have realised then that he was weird. But he had so much charm and I found him very sexually attractive. He told me that he would like to ask me and my husband out for dinner one night. I accepted cautiously, knowing that Obe would never have let me have *le diner* with another man, alone. (I would have preferred this.) But Xavier is very smart, very quick. He had known this."

A waitress brought Margot and Isobel a cup of a very dark, gooey chocolate concoction. A Barcelona speciality. Isobel waited until she had moved back to the serving counter at the front of the shop. She looked around nervously as she sipped the chocolate.

*The paintings on the website. Of course. I love her voice, her awkward accent, and her careful use of language. I can see why Xavier was so attracted to her. And of course, I can see why she was so attracted* to him. *Xavier was the antithesis of all the men she would have been used to meeting through her husband. Why did she want to see me so urgently? Where was this leading to?*

Isobel continued. "I needed to go home, to check out Tilly's website. *Tout de suite.* Obe went to bed and I told him that I had to check my emails. Tilly used a very complicated security system. She had given me a user name and a password. But it still took a long time to find the site. And when I finally found it, I watched all her work, I was stunned. I had imagined that she would have made maybe some simple recreations of famous paintings. Obvious. Naive. And, yes, each short film she had made had many references to paintings, by painters *très connus,* which I recognised. But there was much more. Tilly had used her imaginings and her talents to be very shocking. Her films were very violent, sexually provocative, and *très dangereux.* I was fascinated, and I have to admit that I was definitely aroused, sexually, by the idea of being in them. I watched them over and over. They were not pornographic. They were very sensual. Brilliant, really.

"But there was absolutely no way that I could ever tell Obe that I had agreed to be in one of her films. Obe would have been horrified. I realised that I would have to be very careful. And of course, at this stage, I now knew a bit more about Xavier's relationship with Tilly. What his work with her was really like.

"We all met again *pour diner* one evening. I told Obe that Xavier was charming and we could use him to practise our English. Xavier suggested Café L'Accademia. When he arrived, he told us that Paolo and Tilly were going to join us for dessert. I was thrilled in one way because it bore out the 'innocence' of my fantasies, but I was a little anxious. Tilly and Paolo were capable of anything.

"During dinner, Xavier was so charming to Obe and they talked about Brazilian football. Another of Obe's passions. During a break in courses, Obe went to the toilet and Xavier and I were alone for the first time. He didn't say anything but he knew what I was thinking. I told him that I had seen Tilly's website and that I had been shocked. He said that he thought that she was brilliant. I pretended. I said that I could never be in one of her films. But he knew. He knew that I had been aroused. He laughed. 'Of course you want to be in her films.' And then, almost as if I had no control over what I was saying, I told him that I was very attracted to him sexually. He laughed again and told me that he felt the same way about me. I told him that Obe would kill me if he were to find out. Xavier said that he could understand how he felt and paid me a series of beautiful compliments. He seemed almost excited at the idea of Obe's mortal threat. Outrageous? Just before Obe came back to the table, Paolo and Tilly arrived. My heart sank. They had been drinking. Too much. They wanted to go to Gimlet. When Obe finally returned, he apologised and said that he had an early start. He suggested that I should stay and go to Gimlet with them. He had obviously been charmed by Xavier's calm exterior and was amused by Tilly and Paolo. They hugged him generously. They were immediately affectionate towards him but he left quickly after paying the bill, and then we all walked through the Born to Gimlet where we got more drunk. I didn't want the evening to end. I was falling in love. And Xavier made it so easy. He insisted on helping me to sober up at his apartment..."

And this was the first moment that Isobel drew breath from her story. She paused.

"You have been there? I know you have been there... You know what it is like and what he is like. At first he was very cautious with me, kind, like a father, but then one thing led to another and that night he made love to me... That was almost one year ago but what happened that night drew me into his web, Paolo and Tilly's web. I had no control over it. I was out of control... I want to show you something."

Isobel stopped again and pulled a pocket digital camera out of her purse. She played with its technology for a few seconds and then showed Margot its display screen. "Xavier has maybe ten cameras rigged around his apartment. They are all wireless, linked up to his computer. This is what he showed to me when I told him on Tuesday that I could never see him again."

Margot watched the screen for about five minutes. A succession of beautifully edited mini movies. All of them were essentially pornographic records of Xavier's sexual exploits with Isobel. Graphic and unambiguous. And then one, quite staggeringly beautiful, short, moving picture of Tilly in a recreation of Rossetti's great Pre-Raphaelite image of Ophelia's suicide. Margot gasped.

"That is a Pre-Raphaelite painting. Oh my God!" And then very quietly, "He's a murderer! He coaxes them... because he needs to."

*Always images of people dying or at the instant of death. Paolo. And then Tilly. The scalpel. There is something hideously familiar about all this. Kant... Freud, the pleasure principle... Lacan.*

A series of essays she had studied in Chicago about the relationship between death and sex began to flash through her mind. Kant's story about the choice a man has between the opportunity of sexual intercourse with the woman of his dreams and the gallows. Freud's theories about the pleasure principle. And Lacan's brilliant seminars about jouissance.

Margot looked at her watch. She still had about ten minutes. She was ashen-faced.

Isobel looked intrigued and continued.

266

"All these movies are on the hard drive of his computer. Of course, we must find some way to destroy all these pictures. But the reason I wanted to see you is different. I need your help and I think that you need my help. When I saw him on Tuesday he made a mistake. He had left his laptop computer screen open on the kitchen table and I caught a glimpse of some images on the screen. They meant nothing to me at the time. I had seen hundreds of similar images..." She paused. To take in Margot's reaction... "And when I saw you at the funeral, I knew... Those pictures on the screen were you!"

Margot stared at Isobel. Isobel was defiant. She became cold. Perfunctory. And oddly naïve.

"Together we must trap him and steal those pictures. He had been doing another movie. They were all trying to recreate the English painter Waterhouse's painting of Santa Eulalia. Waterhouse was a friend of Rossetti who painted..."

"I know," Margot interjected. She was trying to recover. She squeezed Isobel's hand. She paused. Isobel's almost innocent naiveté was infectious.

"Why did you go on seeing him for so long?"

Isobel laughed. "I shouldn't have to answer that question. You know exactly why. I know you know."

Margot nodded, sheepishly.

"What if you are wrong about him? The police are interviewing Robert. And my husband."

"The police are interviewing Robert and your husband because they are stupid. Robert likes young girls. He likes me. He knew Paolo. He was trying to have an affair with Tilly. But no way is he a killer. Xavier will have given them some very clever explanation, an excuse... I think that they were probably disturbed when they were shooting the film.

267

Maybe the night-watchman."

"I don't think the police are stupid. Just doing their jobs. Have you ever been to that warehouse?"

"No! For all I know that was another one of his secrets."

"What do you want me to do? What about the police? They will need evidence. Surely he will have destroyed all the evidence?"

*There is something desperately silly about all this. But I can't resist it. It's almost as if this is part of one of Xavier's games. Ridiculous. Extreme. And yet compulsive. Almost sexy. Being with Isobel is also a little alluring. Seductive.*

"I think that we can trick him. But you must make me one solemn promise. When we find his computer, we must steal it. It can never become evidence. I don't think that he keeps any copies anywhere else and if there are, I can find out by checking from his computer log."

"Have no fear about that. If he has pictures of you, he will have pictures of me, too... I must call him if I am going to stay here any longer with you. We need some more time."

Margot pulled out her mobile 'phone and punched the keys. He answered.

"Xavier! I am running a little late. I will be with you in half an hour... À tout à l'heure! Je t'embrasse!"

Isobel smiled wryly at Margot's use of Xavier's favourite valedictory phrase.

"He seemed to be normal. I hope he hasn't smelt a rat."

"Smelt a rat?" Isobel looked confused.

"An English expression – it means that if he has smelt a rat he will have figured out what we are doing, in this case!"

Isobel smiled. "Our plan must not smell of any rats... It's very simple. We need to steal his laptop for long enough to destroy the pictures of us that he has. We can lure him into feeling safe. When you have done that, I can arrive and when he comes to fetch me, you can take it."

"That seems too simple. Where does he keep it? I have never really noticed it. I have only been there twice. And what happens..."

"It is always in the same place in the kitchen, by his projector."

"What if it isn't?"

They looked at each other anxiously, like two frightened schoolgirls plotting a midnight feast.

"I am sure that it will be in the same place. Why not?"

"What do we do then? I can record him. I have a tape recorder on my cell phone."

Margot was now petrified but she decided to go along with the plan. All the psychological detective work she had been trained to do seemed hopelessly redundant and she knew that Isobel was right. This was a golden opportunity to trap Xavier; she trusted her new friend's instincts. It seemed simple enough and with two of them working together, the risks and inherent danger were diminished. She was also absolutely clear in her mind about Xavier's mental make up.

Isobel reminded Margot of the layout of the apartment by going through it in great detail, detail Margot found easy to remember. They hurriedly rehearsed a schedule which included a strategy for Margot's behaviour when she was alone with Xavier, before Isobel was to ring the doorbell.

"Are you sure we shouldn't just go straight to Carlos? To the police."

"I cannot risk that until I know we have my pictures on his computer."

"He may have copies."

"I doubt it. He is very careful to hide everything. Everything is very secret. He did not want to give Tilly or Paolo anything; he refused to let me have my copies but he transferred these onto this camera for my birthday gift last year because he knew he was safe because of my husband's jealousy..."

"Blackmail."

Margot paused for a few seconds while she collected her thoughts. Isobel played with the sugar cubes on the side of her saucer.

"And what about Paolo and Tilly?"

"I am sure that he was responsible for their deaths."

"You think that he murdered them? "

"I think that he will have many questions to answer."

"He is a very dangerous man."

Margot paid the check. Isobel was going to give Margot about ten minutes with Xavier alone and so she was going to wait behind in the café for a little longer. Ten minutes to keep him at bay, enough time to find the computer and distract him. They exchanged and checked cell phone numbers – their 'phones were to be their only alarm system. They also agreed that Isobel would go straight into the church when she arrived, to avoid any unwelcome curiosity. It would be easier to wait there for Margot's signal.

"One last question... Did Xavier ever mention that he knew Archie, my husband?"

"I don't think so, but then everyone knows your husband, Margot. He's adorable."

Margot felt vaguely reassured. They shook hands – a prolonged gesture – and then Margot left.

Isobel looked lonely and afraid when Margot looked back at her from outside the café. She blew her a comforting, but inevitably forlorn, kiss and set off towards the Plaça Santa Maria feeling mysteriously ambiguous about her mission. Quite suddenly, all her previous feelings for Xavier returned as powerfully as they had ever been. Margot had to find a way to subjugate them. They were so obviously perverse and inappropriate. Despite herself, she had been seduced by a paedophile, and by a man who was also almost certainly a killer. To nurse any residual feelings for a man like this seemed to be so outside the boundaries of normal behaviour. The image of Tilly floating as if dead within Paolo's recreation of Rossetti's autumnal leaves was certainly powerful visual evidence. It suggested premeditation. It suggested complicity. But even the Pre-Raphaelite connection could be afforded a simple explanation. She remembered one of their Sunday lunches. Paolo and Tilly had been intrigued when Archie had shared with them his enthusiasm for their work, and had so cogently explained the connection between late Victorian painting and Raphael.

She hardly needed to rehearse in her mind other specific accusations she would level against him – Xavier was a self-confessed paedophile for a start – Paolo had made that quite clear. His antics as 'Guy' were a matter of public record. These facts alone should have been enough to trigger Margot's disgust and anger. But what if he had a powerful and subtle defence to that, too? Some cunning explanation about reform and apology? Or some cock and bull story about Archie. As she walked towards the square, she wrestled with the cold-blooded facts and the analytical details which nailed Xavier so specifically. She hated herself for her weakness. She hated herself for being suspicious about Archie. She felt ashamed, and strangely felt almost like a guilty accomplice. She and Isobel had been part of the world he had constructed for all his victims.

*We had been his 'special friends'.*

Was Archie part of all that, too? His accomplice.

She shivered at the thought. Finally, she managed to come to terms with one inescapable fact: whichever way he or she might try to rationalise or justify his behaviour, Paolo's and Tilly's lives had been horrendously sacrificed as part of Xavier's blatantly evil and unacceptable *modus operandi*. She had to hang onto that fact and any fear or apprehensions disappeared. The images of their dead bodies, of the violence and the blood which must have been part of that fatal, horrendous ritual. These neurotic thoughts thankfully helped to destroy any vestiges of her lust. She could finally become clinically cold-hearted in her purpose. When she arrived, she noticed that the police car had gone. The shops were opening and there were one or two tourists outside the church. She recognised the owner of the Indian restaurant where Archie had taken her last summer, sweeping away some broken glass in front of his doorway. She said hello, and he returned her greeting with a smile. A young couple emerged from Xavier's apartment building.

Margot immediately thought of Isobel. She hoped that she would be lucky and there would be no difficulty when she arrived which might divert Xavier. She rang the bell forcefully. No immediate reply. She rang the bell again. Nothing. She used the mobile 'phone this time. She rang Xavier's number. No reply. She left a message. "Xavier, I am waiting outside. Where are you?"

She didn't panic at first. She rang Isobel. No reply. She rang Xavier again. The 'phone switched off message' was in Catalan. She waited to hear the English version to confirm that Xavier had indeed turned off his mobile. She looked around. The restaurateur asked her if she was okay? She said, "Yes, thank you," rather curtly and hurried off towards the church.

She tried Isobel again; still no reply. She went into the church. Perhaps she had left a little earlier and Margot had taken longer to walk to the square than she had imagined she would? She had ambled there, lost in her thoughts. She noticed that a policeman had followed her into the church. Coincidence, surely. But now she was nervous. She looked around. She even wandered past the confessional boxes and walked up to the altar. She crossed herself. No sign of Isobel, so she decided to wait. She tried Xavier again. In vain. She felt sure that the policeman was watching her.

After twenty minutes, she gave up and walked quickly back to her office. She played back her messages. Nothing from Xavier. She went over to the window, opened the shutters and saw the policeman who had been in the church. He was on the 'phone.

And then it happened again. Walking hurriedly towards the tiny alley that led through to Las Ramblas – the unmistakeable form of Xavier. With Archie. There was absolutely no doubt in her mind. He was wearing the bow tie she had given him as a Christmas gift.

They were arguing. In a split second of cold, unemotional clarity, she rang Carlos.

# Chapter Twenty Seven

Barcelona's modern central police headquarters building was located towards the Mediterranean end of Las Ramblas on the perimeter of Raval, where traditionally the criminal community was based during the heady days of the city's mercantile and naval power. It is now surrounded by what has become the apex of the city's tourist industry. Without the heavily armed sentry guards and its very modern surveillance cameras, its gates could almost be mistaken for the entrance to a television studio or modern office block.

Carlos had asked Margot if she wanted to be picked up by a police car but she decided to walk the tiny distance from the church where she had made her call. She noticed that she was being followed by a policeman who kept a very discreet distance behind her.

Catalonia has two police forces, both separated from Spain's national justice system. One deals with civil and domestic matters, *Guardia Urbana*. The other, Barcelona's autonomous extension of Spain's very efficient and effective criminal investigation system and is responsible to Catalonia's Ministry of Justice, which in turn is part of the Catalan separatist political structure. It is called the *Mossos D'Esquadros*. Both forces have different uniforms, and differing infrastructures.

Senior officers in the Mossos, like Carlos, are highly respected for many reasons. They have to undertake a very rigorous training to qualify for their work at the vast Police Academy in Barcelona, the newest and best equipped in Europe. They also enjoy a high level of success in curbing Catalonia's crime. In Barcelona particularly, they have managed to obliterate the appalling image that the Franco regime's policing system left behind. During the Olympic games in 1992, there were fewer reported crimes than in any city in Europe during that year and since then the Mossos, given its full policing powers in 1994, has managed to control the influx of international criminals who have flocked into the city as it has prospered into the twenty-first century. Of course, like everywhere in the world, there is an unacceptable level of violent organised crime, particularly in the ports of cities like Barcelona and Valencia, convenient trading gateways for both North Africa and the Middle East.

The city's broad-based racial mix, particularly amongst the poorer immigrant community, has inevitably been a catalyst for tensions and exploitative crime – prostitution, the white slave business and the narcotics trades. These were the normal, more familiar arenas for Carlos' investigative work.

The Santa Eulalia murder, as it was now known, was unique. Carlos had never been in charge of an investigation into a murder which was so difficult to categorise, but he would merit each investigation at least the same amount of rigorous and meticulous application. The murder of Paolo and Domatilla was particularly poignant because his beloved son was Paolo's direct contemporary, and because of course, Elvira had known the victims.

When Margot walked into the sparse modernity of the interview room, Carlos decided that his junior investigating colleague should ask most of the questions – he needed to go through the procedures and he was sure that their evening dinner would be the most likely opportunity to provide him with the most crucial information. He also knew that Margot would undoubtedly be very stubborn about the issue of client confidentiality. What he had not been prepared for, was the level of information she seemed to be happy to present for him, volunteered.

In his opinion, when people do that, they are usually hiding something darker, withholding another secret.

After thanking him for the invitation to dinner, Margot began by asking a question.

"Have you found the night watchman?"

Carlos and his colleague, Sub Inspector Luis Ramon, looked at her blankly.

"Come on, Carlos. This is hardly a state secret. Have you found the man who reported the crime?"

There was a hint of desperation in her voice. Margot knew that if they had found him, he would have been another factor to help them piece together what had happened while Tilly was dying. Surely he would have tried to help her, to save her?

"Yes, we have. His body was found early this morning, washed up on the shores of the large reservoir near the airport. We are waiting for the results of the post mortem from our colleagues in the ABP which controls the outer regions of the city."

Luis, like Carlos, spoke perfect English.

"You know that I have a duty towards my clients and that the information I have about them is confidential. Has a judge been appointed for the investigation?"

Margot knew a little about the Catalonian judiciary. Before any criminal investigation could go forward, a judge had to be appointed.

"A judge will be appointed if we need to make an arrest. My boss, Major Montaner, has informed the British consul and he is personally co-ordinating the Strategic Planning Division. He was at school with Paolo's step-father, Eusebio Casals, and is a family friend. The Mossos are very careful about the murder of any tourist or foreigner. Our tourist industry is a source of great pride in Barcelona. I am in charge of the preliminary investigation. *'On the ground!'*" Carlos was proud of his command of English colloquial phrases. "In Spain, we have the same procedure as in your country when we need to request confidential information. In police matters, it is customary that reputable doctors and psychotherapists help us do our job without betraying any part of their professional obligations to their clients. Especially in a murder case. And this is definitely a murder case."

"I am aware of my obligations personally, but I don't know much about Catalan law. I understand that it is much the same here as in the US." Margot made it clear that she was resigned to that. Carlos explained that in Barcelona, like in the US, the legal system was particularly hampered by very similar and strict procedural bureaucracy.

"At Chicago, questions of client confidentiality and the ethical and moral implications of privileged knowledge were important issues, fiercely debated. But we were always to be encouraged to be as helpful as we could with the police."

"You are not, of course, a suspect. We are absolutely certain that you had no direct connection to the deaths of your clients. My colleague, Luis, needs to ask you questions which will help us trace their killer."

"I will give him as much help as I can. Who are the suspects?"

There was a fresh, almost cold, confidence in Margot's voice, as if she had regained control of her destiny, and no longer needed help from anyone. She knew that she had to be very careful. With the new knowledge she had learnt from Isobel, for Isobel's sake. She also had to protect Laura, and she felt a strong sense of responsibility towards Robert (his relationship with Tilly was a secret), and of course, to Paolo and Tilly's parents. But she also knew that Carlos was a professional and apart from his own investigative work, which would have thrown up information at least as effective as some of the knowledge she had gleaned more privately, Carlos would also be ruthless in his determination to prise from her everything she knew. She wanted to give him and his colleague the impression that whatever she told him now would be as much as he would need to lead him to Xavier without revealing anything whatsoever about her relationship with him. Her main problem was that her only known public encounter with him had been at the Liceu with Robert. To that extent, Carlos would hardly have known that she had any special knowledge about Xavier. Even her notes about Paolo and Tilly made no reference to him. And then there was the thorny new factor – Archie's connection.

"The only official suspect at this early stage is an English journalist, a Mr Alton. And we have been interviewing your husband."

Margot smiled at Luis. *Robert and Archie?*

Luis began with a series of simple perfunctory questions about her job and her clients. Background more than anything else. He wanted to know first if she ever mixed with her clients socially.

"Yes, I do! Many therapists are stricter than I am. In the small community of British and American ex-patriots, it would be very difficult to avoid overlap. I have found a way to make it work for my clients and for my own peace of mind. It is sometimes awkward. But Tilly became my client because her father was my husband's best friend..."

Carlos and Luis knew that they didn't need to establish her connection, but this of course allowed them to ask questions about Paolo and Tilly that had roots in her social connection with them, as opposed to their professional relationship. This in turn gave Margot the opportunity to pass them a series of useful facts and connections. The obsession about Pre-Raphaelite painting. The enthusiasm for digital work. The language school. Catalan history. Even Xavier's past in the context of the language school (although she had to hold back the knowledge that Paolo had been taught by Xavier at the same school he had been fired from. Xavier had told her that. Not Paolo). Her volunteered information about Xavier went strangely unnoticed at first. Neither policeman seemed particularly interested.

"Did you know that Tilly's arms were mutilated, scarred? Self-inflicted."

"No, but I saw her do what she did on the DVD."

This was true. Tilly had obviously been very clever and like most self-harmers, had covered the evidence. She wore long-sleeved tops to all her sessions with Margot.

"Why did she do this awful thing to herself?"

"She took her artistic projects very seriously."

"Who would have told her about the Austrian artist, Günter Brus? It might have been your husband?"

"MACBA had an exhibition of his work."

"Why would she have known about this?"

"They were very inquisitive artists. They would have been fascinated."

"Is there anyone else you know who might have shared their enthusiasm for this kind of perverted behaviour, under the guise of 'art'?"

"No!" she lied for the first time. Robert, of course. And Xavier.

"Did Tilly ever discuss this with you?"

"No!" This was true, of course.

"How long were they your clients? Why did Paolo want to stop coming?"

These were all legitimate questions. Routine. Margot answered them efficiently. She wanted to find a simple mechanism which could lead them to Xavier without directly incriminating him. In this first round of questions there had been no opportunity.

But Carlos had been waiting to ask her the one inevitable question she had hoped he would ask.

"Do you know Xavier Innes-Hopkins?"

"I have met him once at the opera house. He is a friend of one of my clients."

"What do you know about his relationship with your clients?"

Margot paused.

"As far as I was aware, in looking through my notes, and from my sessions with them, they never mentioned Xavier. But of course, he was obviously helping them with their art projects." Again this was true, but Carlos was no fool.

"We asked him to come in here this morning which he did very willingly. He told us that he had a long and complicated relationship with both Domatilla and, of course, with Paolo. We have a register here in Spain, of people who might have committed crimes in another country, bad crimes, of suspected paedophiles, for example. Mr Innes-Hopkins was the subject of a long, unsuccessful investigation by the Scottish police. Paolo was taught by him at the boarding school which eventually fired him for suspected homosexual relationships with his pupils. He is on our list. And a list they have at the consulate."

"Is he a suspect?"

"Of course, but so are many others. We had thought that the night watchman was the major suspect until this morning. And then there is your friend and client, Señor Robert Alton."

"I heard that the night watchman had 'phoned the ambulance."

"You need to meet our criminal psychologist, Olivia. He will tell you that many killers, psychopaths particularly, 'phone somebody from the scene of their crime."

At this point, Margot seized her opportunity to point them in the right direction. The Mossos had obviously been very thorough and she was able to help them with her own work as a sleuth.

Without hinting at her secret relationship with Xavier in any way at all, she explained that using the DVD and the script, and her husband's knowledge of both Pre-Raphaelite art and Catalan history, she worked out that Paolo and Tilly's artwork had involved someone else, another person whose boundaries were broader. After the funeral, she had watched the DVD again, paying attention to every detail rather like a detective, and in particular she had amplified the off-camera voice, which she had thought was familiar. She was pretty sure that the voice on the DVD was the same voice she had heard somewhere else. One of her clients had asked her about Xavier and the strange moment at the crematorium. Robert had mentioned Xavier's school of languages connection and she had then realised that in all the time the couple had been seeing her professionally, Paolo and Domatilla had deliberately, mysteriously disguised and hidden one crucial relationship in their lives. Why? Putting two and two together, she surmised they had been hiding something, very uncharacteristically. She played the tape once more, and then knew that the off-camera voice was Xavier. Looking at the script, she also realised that to complete it, they would have had to involve somebody else. A third person to visualise their demise?

"But the script is only about Santa Eulalia. There is no mention of Paolo. Or a young man being nailed to a cross... Paolo and Tilly could have done all this on their own."

Margot looked down. Until then she had been able to separate the grisly details from the realities of Paolo and Tilly. She composed herself, as the police officer continued.

"Señor Inns-Hopkins confirmed everything you have suspected. He admitted that he had helped in the shooting of parts of Tilly's film. But he denies any involvement in their deaths. He also has a powerful alibi for Monday night. He tells me that Señor Alton left the Liceu before you."

Luis was determined to trick Margot into giving up some of her privileged secrets. He doggedly pitched in again. His voice had the tone of a man who sensed that he was dealing with a liar. Margot tried to judge her situation objectively. This was a police investigation, for God's sake! Her two favourite clients had died violently, almost certainly aided and abetted by her lover, and they were trying to lay the blame on one of her husband's oldest friends.

"We are confident that he has told us the truth. We had hoped that you might have had some more information which could have come from your notes. Do you use tape recordings?"

"Not always, but yes, sometimes. It depends on the client. With Paolo, yes. Not for Tilly."

"Do you know Mrs Isobel Komura?" The question she had most dreaded. What did they know?

"No! I don't. Who is she?" Another lie.

"You know who she is. She is the woman who slapped Señor Alton's face in the crematorium."

"Oh, yes! Extraordinary... Have you talked to her?" she asked very casually.

"No, not yet. We have been interviewing everybody at the language school who knew the victims. She is on our list for tomorrow's interrogation."

Interrogation? Both men were silent as if they were waiting for her to tell them something. Margot needed time. She had told them what she had thought would be enough to nail Xavier. All to no avail. But she was determined to hold back.

"Why are you interviewing my husband?"

The two policeman looked at each other.

"I would have thought that would have been obvious. He was Domatilla's godfather, and he had taught at the same school as Paolo."

Margot looked dumbfounded. "The same school? Where?"

"In Scotland. And with Mister Inns-Hopkins."

"Impossible!"

"True"

"Paolo was not taught by my husband."

"But he definitely taught at the same school. We have done our research."

Carlos shrugged and stood up. Luis pushed a button to turn off his tape recorder, and began to rewind.

Margot used the toilet as her excuse to be on her own. As she sat in the chrome and porcelain of the cubicle, a couple of women were washing their hands, chatting in Catalan. She sent a text to Archie.

*"Don't forget dinner tonight. I have a surprise for you. Please ring asap. Love, Me xx."*

✳

So Archie had known Xavier in Scotland. Was there some reason why he had hidden this from her? Perhaps it had never really arisen. What part of his past did Xavier represent? What did Xavier know about Archie that she didn't? What did Archie know about Xavier that she didn't? Was there something about her husband's past that he had been desperate to keep secret from her? Surely not. She remembered the studies that she had made in Chicago chronicling the perverse private rituals and secret bonds endemic in the British public school 'old boys networks' throughout the latter part of the twentieth century. Useful research for her dissertation on child abuses in the Roman Catholic church. Archie's early life and work certainly overlapped this entire forty-year, post war era.

She returned to the reception area where Carlos and Luis were waiting for her.

"Let me enjoy the privilege of showing you around our organisation. We are very proud of it."

"I would love that."

Margot's third lie! She was desperate to be alone.

Carlos picked up a 'phone and within a minute, a smart officer in a more formal blue uniform, with the familiar Catalonian shield badge and three talons on his shoulder, delineating his rank, marched in, saluted and ushered Carlos and Margot away from the reception area.

"See you this evening!" was Luis' parting shot. He was busy replaying the tapes. Margot looked at him, quizzically. She hadn't until then realised the significance of the supper meeting that evening. This was not the social engagement it had been disguised as, it was going to be a continuation of her interrogation. Carlos was a cunning old fox, and had obviously also asked his colleague, Luis, to join them for dinner. Margot's need to string out the police investigation enough to find a way to deal with her infidelity now seemed a silly, insignificant ploy. She was going to use the supper as much as the police had intended to.

Her exhaustive tour of the Mossos D'Esquadros Central ABP, as the headquarters are known in police parlance, included the Criminal Investigation Division and its highly scientific technical facilities, the

General Investigation Office with a phalanx of computer screens and young, fashionably dressed investigators behind them, the Central Co-ordination and Liaison Office, the Regional Control Room which like the outside of the building, looked like a state-of-the-art television newsroom, the Support Office, more serious personnel and their Regional Investigation Area. All of these areas seemed to operate at least as efficiently and calmly as the corporate headquarters of a well-run international conglomerate. Sergeant Diaz was obviously trained to know exactly how to pinpoint the glories of the Mossos organisation. Margot wondered if this display of professional pride was Inspector Carlos Mendoza's subtle way of letting her know that he was fully aware that she was withholding at least one important fact and that he had the resources to winkle it out by hook or by crook. But this didn't really solve her problem.

When the young corporal had completed their tour, Carlos told Margot that he had been asked to show her something, part of the murder investigation, which would probably upset her. They walked down another corridor of strip lighting and chrome fittings, arriving at a laboratory.

"Have you ever been inside a modern laboratory for post mortem examinations before?"

Carlos asked her to put a white robe over her clothes, and to wear a mask which covered her nose and mouth. A security card and a voice identity triggered the electronic system, allowing them clearance to enter the chilly, pristine environment. More chrome and glass, and a sweet stench which reminded Margot of the crematorium. Of course – dead bodies. Within seconds, she was looking at Tilly's naked body.

At first she felt nothing, uninvolved. This was a new experience and her inquisitive mind wanted to absorb the details objectively, however disturbing. She took refuge by trying to think about what she was seeing from a psychological standpoint. She remembered reading an exhaustive study by a zoologist about the naked female form. Apparently one of Henry VIII's wives had a third breast. Freud had written about dead bodies. *Is this how soldiers feel when they come across their dead friends on the battlefield?* But within seconds, this chilling, detached intellectuality disappeared and was replaced by a feeling Margot had experienced only once before, when she had said goodbye to her dying uncle at his funeral. This was the Tilly she had nursed through hours and hours of the painful agony of a young woman whose childhood had been desperately lonely and unhappy. Loveless. Isolated. This was the Tilly whom Margot had loved in the way that mothers love their daughters. She looked around the room, oblivious to the pathologist and her corporal's attentions. She sat down on the nearest chair she could find and cried without any inhibition. Quietly.

The corporal brought her a glass of water, which she drank quickly. Carlos was impassive.

"I want to look at her again."

Tilly's red hair was flaying behind her beautiful face. Her eyes were closed. Millais' Ophelia, indeed.

The pathologist came over with a polite simple request.

"Please, could you look at her arms? We removed the tattoos which were there on both arms after taking photographs of them."

Margot realised that she had never seen much of Tilly's arms, she always wore sleeves, or cardigans. She had never mentioned tattoos, either, for that matter.

Each arm bore a series of neat scars and several relatively fresh wounds, which had obviously been patched up. *Brus, the self-inflicting artist. No, this was evidence of much more than an artistic adventure.*

Margot felt ashamed, remembering Tilly's long-sleeved black coat on the day she died.

*How could I have missed this obvious evidence of such a revealing and definitive element in Tilly's disturbed psychological condition? Why didn't I make this connection? Self-mutilation!*

"I had never noticed these before," she said, truthfully. "She had told me about this problem in her childhood but she convinced me that she was no longer doing this."

"The victim was a 'cutter'. Is this the term you use in your profession?"

"Yes."

Margot looked more carefully at the unmistakeable evidence on Tilly's arms. This was beyond the form of self-infliction which had characterised Brus's artistic experiments, although there were analogies. Margot had come across cutters before. Like anorexics and bulimics they were a phenomenon, which the therapeutic and psychiatric world had initially baulked at, and often refused to treat. Not for the best of reasons. Many therapists at first refused to accept that this perverse behaviour, at least as prevalent in the Western World as familiar compulsive disorders, had roots in same the kind of psychological frameworks with which they struggled, and in some cases were ill-equipped to deal with. They were baffled and refused to treat people who showed them their self-inflicted wounds, their 'cuts'. They argued that they were evidence of serious mental disorders beyond any form of therapeutic remedies, the product of truly sick minds.

Margot had met one of the pioneers in this specialised field at a conference at the University Of Texas who had given a comprehensive analysis of the illness. She couldn't understand why her profession refused to categorise this behaviour as a disorder. She had also explained that self-mutilators often show signs of other, more familiar personality or eating disorders like anorexia or bulimia nervosa. They were also usually superstitious, compulsive and finally, most poignant of all, she described cutters as lonely individuals who find it difficult to make lasting attachments. But when they find someone to latch onto, they become compulsive. Paolo, in Tilly's case.

*How did I miss all this with Tilly? Why did I fail to recognise her symptoms? All those obsessive showers in the studio at the beginning and end of each session? She talked about those endlessly but I didn't really understand their context. The tattoos? She kept those secret. But of course, cutters are notoriously secret about their habit. And suicidal. Some of those wounds were fresh. Why had she returned to it? Xavier.*

Tilly's lifeless, naked body had revealed to the police secrets which Margot had failed to discover about her sad life. Secrets which Xavier must have been privy to. Carlos was using every professional weapon at his disposal to apply a very gentle but persuasive professional pressure. He needed to know more of Margot's secrets. The corporal offered her a lift home, but Margot explained that she would rather walk to her office. Carlos walked her to the gates of the police station on Las Ramblas and then insisted on accompanying her home.

Out in the street, the Saturday night crowd was out in force. Tourists. A 'hen night' of women dressed in British policewoman's uniforms. Fanatical Barça fans. The policeman joshed with the transvestites on their early evening break. When they arrived in front of her apartment, Carlos hugged her spontaneously. And then, as if embarrassed, proffered his hand, which Margot took affectionately.

"Thank you."

"This girl you saw, your client, was the same age as Luis's sister."

Carlos, of course, had known how upset she had been by the

image of Tilly's corpse, and he also knew how ruthless he had been in eliminating one of his prime suspects in this way, but Margot was now in the clear, as far as the police were concerned.

*Tilly had become the model client. At first, after she had arrived in Barcelona, she had resented me. She had been very quiet and polite. She had answered my questions economically but she refused to describe her family set-up. I tried hard to persuade her to describe her mother, for instance. She told me a story about the embarrassment she had experienced when her mother had appeared in the room one night, completely naked, dancing seductively for the family. On another occasion, when Tilly had come down to the kitchen to fetch a glass of milk when her parents were having a dinner party, she had caught her mother kissing one of the dinner guests. But she had been very quiet about the time she spent away from them, in the scullery with the servants, or in the nursery with her brother. "He drew Viking ships on the blackboard and I would use the coloured chalks to draw the women and children in the villages they burnt down. Mum would rub all that off angrily and replace it with butterfly drawings and Latin."*

*She hadn't ever bonded with her mother, and barely saw her father. He spent most of his time at his office or playing tennis at his club during the day and retired to his bedroom, separate bedroom, to watch recorded current affairs programmes, and then listen to his tape-recorded books. Her mother supervised their diets and paid fleeting visits at mealtimes, having spent the mornings in bed, and Tilly never really knew what she did during the rest of the day, but remembered how she smelt of perfume and alcohol when she came to kiss them goodnight.*

*All this reticence changed when Paolo came into one of the sessions – I had very reluctantly agreed to this and insisted that it was going to be a very special 'one off' exception. I explained that I had to be able to concentrate on each of them individually, but on this occasion, as if Paolo empowered her, she began to open up. She described in detail the story of her childhood rape by the butler, and she explained her feelings about her brother, Hugo. She also went into detail about the bullying she had experienced at school, and as this picture of her bizarre, abusive childhood emerged, I was able to slowly gain more of her trust. In that sense, Paolo's presence had been an advantage – he had remained totally silent. Why and how did she keep the new burst of cutting from me? And conceal it so effectively? Again, Xavier must have manipulated her into it in the same way that he manipulated Paolo into a ritual which was to lead him to an agonising death. Jouissance!*

# Chapter Twenty Eight

Margot rang Archie to tell him that they had been invited to supper with Carlos and Elvira. He seemed a little surprised, but went along with the idea and offered to drive them to their apartment in Tibidado. They agreed to meet at Elvira's bar.

Isobel's cell 'phone was still switched off.

It was nearly dark. Deep shadows. She went over to draw the curtains and noticed that the same tall policeman who had been there the night before was positioned across the square, this time in a peaked cap. They all have so many uniforms! She smiled. Carlos was doing his job, looking after her. She poured herself a large glass of malt whisky, listened to her answer phone messages, writing a list as they came off the tape.

Laura: "Thank you. See you when I get back next week."

Hugo: "Lunch? I need you, Margot."

Archie: "Where are you?"

Emma and Eusebio: "We love you."

Carlos, cheerful: "Thank you for coming in. I hope you like tapas; I am going to the Boqueria. Catalan wine."

A referral from a shrink in London. A long message from her Mom, explaining their plans for the summer.

"Hello!" from Dad.

Robert: "Opera and dinner on me next week? Stella is coming in from London on Sunday. I think she is having another affair – I need to come in to see you as usual next week. And I want to talk about Tilly!"

No name. Caller hangs up.

No name. Caller hangs up.

Isobel: "I am so sorry. I am so, so sorry... I will call you later on to explain." She sounded desperate, nervy. She sounded panic-stricken.

No name. Caller hangs up.

She couldn't ask Archie, but perhaps Hugo would know how to contact Isobel's husband. She left him a message accepting his lunch invitation and asked him to call her.

She then dialled Marie Christine in France. She was the only person in the world who could help her now. Marie Christine, herself, answered. At long last, Margot could enjoy her comforting voice, and her wise words. She nearly burst out crying at the relief she felt and then tactfully established with her that she was well enough to talk.

"I need at least an hour of your time on the 'phone... you are the only person..."

And with that, Margot told her absolutely everything she could remember with any relevance to the events Barcelona that week. All her secrets. When she finally hung up, two hours later, exhausted and emotionally drained, Marie-Christine had clarified everything to her complete satisfaction. Margot thanked her profusely and promised to visit see her as soon as she could. She now knew exactly what she had to do – she was going to have to tell the police and Archie everything.

She then left some cash on the desk in an envelope for her cleaner, who came on weekends. She closed the shutters, turned off the light in the consulting room, went to the bathroom to put on some lipstick, and just before she left, clicked the answer–machine to the message system. She walked quickly through the seductive, early evening bustle of the Barri Gotic. Looking over her shoulder, she thought that she noticed the policeman again.

Archie had already arrived at Elvira's bar, and was sitting on a bar stool drinking Coca Cola with Elvira. Margot greeted her friend with a kiss.

"Elvira, I need to talk to Archie alone. Do you mind if we go upstairs for a few minutes?"

"Please go. I will bring you a drink. What would you like?"

"I am fine, thank you. We will come down when we've done, and then Archie can drive us up to your house. Carlos left me a message – he's doing tapas!"

Elvira laughed. "I can close everything down."

Margot then led Archie upstairs to the balcony and to the small wooden table next to the washrooms.

"Archie, you know that I absolutely adore you, don't you?"

"Yes, I do."

She took a sip from his glass of Coke.

"You are going to learn something tonight which I never wanted you to know. Things about me which I did not know existed. Bad things... And I am so sorry about this. I am so sorry that you have to know this. I thought that I could hide it all, but I can't."

Archie was silent.

"I have been involved in something this week which I have not been able to understand. It has all been beyond my control. I have gone into psychological territories which are impossible to rationalise. I have behaved badly. Very badly."

Archie remained quiet.

"I am out of my depth. Frightened. Petrified. I desperately need you to understand how important you are for me, and you must promise me that as much as you may be angry about what I am going to tell you or not tell you, or hurt by it, you will try to forgive me."

Finally, Archie took her hands. "I have always accepted that we must have secrets. Of course. I have my secrets too. And this week has been bloody for all of us. You have behaved very well under the circumstances."

"Archie, these are not normal secrets. And, no, I have not behaved at all well."

"Why are you telling me this now, and here?"

"Because I am going to tell Carlos things tonight at supper which you will hear about for the first time, and they will upset you so much. But Carlos has to know about it. And if he knows, I need you to know. This is different from my work."

Archie paused. To have supper with Carlos was odd enough. To have your wife provide a public confessional was extraordinary.

"Okay. I understand the need to tell Carlos stuff. Frankly, I would have thought that he would want you to do this formally, at the police station, or wherever he does these things. But you don't have to tell me anything I don't need to know. I would rather that you kept anything really grisly to yourself. You know how much I trust you."

"I was at the police office in Las Ramblas. This afternoon. I can't keep this stuff to myself any longer but I didn't want to have to go through it twice. I wanted you there. You will understand tonight why. Carlos has asked another policeman to be there. It's odd but then this whole saga..."

She was about to ask him what he had been doing with Xavier but Elvira had switched off the main lights in the bar and only the toilet fluorescent gave any expression to Archie's face in the half-light. Archie looked baffled. He was searching her frightened, vulnerable face. He trusted Margot's judgement as much as she trusted his, but she knew that he was going to be very hurt.

"Would you like a drink before we go?" Elvira called up to them.

"No, we are coming."

In the car they were silent and listened to one of Archie's collection of jazz. The journey was uphill and long-winded through the rush hour in the gathering dusk.

*Am I a coward? Surely the proper thing to do would be to tell Archie everything, privately. But I want to be just as honest with Carlos, and I want to make sure that I tell them exactly the same information. Carlos, in that sense, can be my filtering device or censor for Archie and Archie will be my witness for Carlos. I won't have to repeat anything. And I won't have to go into any graphic details about the sex.*

When they arrived at the policeman's home, they shuffled in awkwardly, almost reluctantly. Elvira defused the tensions by showing them all her son's graduation album. Carlos was by turns both officious and charming but wanted to move onto the professional business. Luis hovered in the shadows of the living room like a predatory lion. Elvira finally insisted that they all sit outside on the terrace which looked down across the parallel 'new city' of Puig, and Montaner and Gaudi, the Barri Gotic glowing with the excitement of a city about to have dinner, and then towards the port – the twinkling gaudy luxury of floating gin palaces and the majesty of the floodlit Colom.

*I love Barcelona so much.*

Margot helped Carlos carry through the tapas he had been preparing from their small kitchen. Anchovies. Chorizo. Peppers. Cheese. And an assortment of grilled fish. Elvira was pointing out to Archie the house where she had been born and the Church where she and Carlos had married. Margot told Carlos that she needed to use the bathroom – her excuse. She needed to talk to him in a private space.

She whispered, "I am going to tell you a few stories tonight... now. About me. And about Tilly and Paolo."

"In front of Archie?"

"I have to do it now. Here. Is that okay?"

"Of course. But Luis will have to use his tape recorder."

"Okay."

Carlos hugged her and went into his office. The old fox had been hoping for this.

When they returned to the terrace, Elvira and Archie were sitting quietly, looking out towards the city. Margot sat next to Archie and squeezed his hand. Carlos sat opposite her, while Luis positioned his small tape machine and checked that it was working properly. Carlos then delivered a small official speech, making Margot aware that what she was doing had official status, and that she was doing so voluntarily, in the relaxed arena of his home but that at some later stage, she may have to repeat all of her statement again for a judge. Archie snaffled an anchovy tapas and laughed nervously. Elvira smiled. Carlos and Luis were solemn.

And so she began her story again. There was no need to insist on any confidentiality at this stage. What she was about to divulge was so outside the bounds of any normal and rational behaviour. She understood the consequences, and had decided to accept them. She was emotionally exhausted and felt strangely comforted by the eccentric situation. The couple of hours she had spent on the 'phone with Marie Christine had been an inadequate dress rehearsal – talking privately to a woman you trust about sex and eroticism had been so much easier. She spoke slowly, without interruption for an hour and chose her words very carefully. She avoided any explicit detail except when it was relevant. Of course, the details of the sex were vital for Carlos, the connections. She tried to modify the level of sexual excitement for Archie's sake but to explain the degree of her obsession was impossible without revealing her emotional and physical hysteria. She used the days of the week as her chronological and technical staging posts. Robert. The opera. Tilly and Paolo. Xavier's appeal. His apartment. The sex. Laura. And finally, the girl with the yellow dress. Isobel.

Carlos stopped her at that stage.

"Do you know where Isobel is?"

"No. Why?"

He went quickly to the 'phone in his office. Luis switched off the tape recorder. Margot, Elvira and Archie sat silently. The food was cold, untouched. Archie was ashen-faced. When Carlos returned, his mood had changed. He was obviously distracted.

"I must go. I am so sorry. Please, can you come to see me again early tomorrow morning? I need a statement for the judge."

Margot agreed immediately. She was shaking. Archie said that he had an early start and started to leave. Margot said a polite thank you to Elvira and Carlos. No hugs. They left immediately.

"In Barcelona, they need to persuade a judge to agree before they can make an arrest."

This was Archie's only comment for about ten minutes as he wound the car down the dark, narrow streets to the larger floodlit avenues in the Diagonal. His silence was violent. Brutal. Savage. The pain was excruciating. When they were close to the north end of the Plaça Catalunya, Margot asked Archie to drop her at the Corte Ingles department store corner. She said that she needed to have an hour or so on her own in the studio, but Archie begged her to come home.

"I need to tell you my story. Please!"

"I don't think I can cope with it now."

He ignored her and drove the car into a side street. His voice took on another, firmer tone. "You are going to fucking well sit here and listen to it!"

Margot turned on the inside passenger light. Archie spoke quietly, as he began his own story.

"At Strathalmond School in the seventies, and throughout the private educational community, homosexuality was rife – amongst boys, and teachers... During my own boarding school days, adolescent sexual desires had confused me. I was never really sure whether I preferred men or women. Repressed sexuality had been so part of everyone's childhood in those days. When I left school, I had one or two encounters with men of my own age but unlike many other masters, I was never, ever attracted to young boys. And then I fell in love with the matron there. She and I had a fling and I knew then that I was definitely heterosexual. I have never looked at a man or boy since then with any form of homoerotic desire. But I was a very popular teacher, and I exploited that. The boys adored me. Callum, a sweet, but confused young man, fell prey to that. I was his hero. He worshipped me and developed a crush. When I rejected him, he was very angry and his scorn was my undoing. He disrupted my lessons. He was rude and he was soon to be seduced by a new arrival – a much younger master... This precipitated a disaster which I had no control over at all.

"During a visit to the sanatorium, the school doctor discovered that Callum had been abused, buggered, and reported it to the governors. In the investigation which followed, Callum pointed the finger at me. I was absolutely defenceless – no proof one way or another. Just his word against mine. I was forced to resign. I had to leave immediately. After ten years in the British public school system, notoriously protective, my career was in ruins – I decided to make a break and emigrate to the US and join academia. Just before I left for Chicago, Callum came to my home to apologise, telling me that he had been persuaded to lie to save the skin of his lover, also a teacher. He was terribly upset. He never recovered, emotionally, and some years later I learned that, towards the end of his school career, he had died. Suicide. I would never be able to prove my innocence... That new young master, a Spanish teacher, his lover, was your lover. Xavier."

They sat in silence. A couple of football drunks performed a macabre little dance for them in the street. Archie turned off the light.

"Why did you lie to me about seeing him the other morning? Twice?"

"I hadn't seen him for years. I barely had known him at Strathalmond. He sought me out when he arrived in Barcelona and asked me to give him a reference for his job application at the language school. I sent him packing at first. But then I realised a bizarre, uncomfortable coincidence. Within months of all this, Paolo was sent to Strathalmond, too (his father had been there), and he became a junior contemporary of Callum's. I hadn't taught or met him, I had left before that. But this connection was rearing its ugly head again. I wanted to avoid any chance that this loathsome man could rake up any of the past – his distorted, dishonest version of the past. The ex-pats don't necessarily all have to hang out together but as you know, the opportunities for horrible gossip always exist. And so I decided to meet Xavier again and we made a pact to avoid each other here in Barcelona in return for the good job reference I gave him. I didn't want anything to do with him and didn't want to risk stirring up the past. I think he had sensed that. And so we sort of avoided each other. I was appalled at his hypocritical speech at the funeral and then we'd bumped into each other in the street just after you and I had been at the Cathedral. Quite by chance. He was revoltingly over-friendly. I just walked away without saying anything...

"Why did I keep it from you when we met each other in Chicago? I had hidden the whole horrible secret for so long. I had no proof. It had been so much in my past, it seemed irrelevant. I never thought that I would come across him again. And there is always that fear that you might have thought that I had been covering up something more sinister..."

"Why did you see Xavier a third time?" Margot realised the irony of her question.

Archie looked at her quizzically and then realised that he would have to continue. No more lies. No point.

"He hunted me down when he heard that the police were going to interview me. He said that if I kept quiet about his past, he would about my own. I lost it and shouted at him. I went bonkers. I told him what Callum had confessed to me. This vile man had ruined my life in Scotland! He had abused a brilliant young pupil to the point of suicide, and now I began to suspect that he had been involved in Paolo's death and the murder of my goddaughter. I was damned if this awful paedophile was going to get away with it anymore! I knew that I would have to tell you at some stage, but I wanted the police to know as soon as I could get to them. The trouble is, Xavier had got to them first and so my interview with Carlos was embarrassing. Rather predictably his assistant, the corporal, gave me a very hard time. 'If all this is true, why didn't you come to see us straight away?' he bleated... I couldn't give him a reasonable argument. He didn't seem to accept my story about Callum. The cultural boundaries were being stretched. For all I know, you won't believe me either. Oddly enough, I think that Carlos knew I was telling the truth."

"Of course I would have believed you! Why didn't you tell me?"

Another excruciating silence.

"If I had known that Xavier had also been fucking my wife, I would have been much less forthcoming with the police and would have planned to kill him!"

"No, you wouldn't. You don't have a violent bone in your body, Archie."

Margot's tender rebuke fell on stony ground.

"You fucking patronising bitch! You know so little about me! You have used me and abused my trust."

There was hatred in his eyes.

Margot got out of the car. He rolled down the window and shouted after her.

"How will you get home?"

There was more than a hint of mistrust in his voice. Desperation and anger.

"I will call a cab, thank you, Archie... I am so, so sorry."

She was disgusted with herself, ashamed. She hated herself.

*I have betrayed Archie. I have betrayed my clients. I have betrayed my friends. I have betrayed myself.*

# Chapter Twenty Nine

Margot walked quickly down Las Ramblas, deliberately avoiding the central areas of the Barri Gotic. Plaça Joaquim Xirau was empty. Only the pulsating throb of techno music coming from one of the balconies echoed around the otherwise darkened apartments. She walked quickly up the stairs to the first floor of her building, fumbled for her keys and hurried into her studio. She opened the shutters and looked across the small square. No policeman.

And then a hand touched the nape of her neck, the fingers squeezed gently, and an arm firmly pulled her body around at the waist. She didn't have to see his face. It was Xavier.

For a fleeting moment, Margot felt that same erotic desire which had so overwhelmed her in the opera house when she had first felt him behind her, but it almost simultaneously transformed, like metamorphosis, into terror and anguish. The very same sensations which had so seduced her were now repulsive and nauseous. The blade of his small, surgical knife rested on her throat. His voice was quiet and resolute. He was dressed in a policeman's uniform.

"Don't scream, Margot, please don't scream or shout. If you do, I will have to kill you instantly. I have absolutely nothing to lose."

"I promise I won't scream."

Margot had too much to lose.

He picked her up and carried her to the Eames chair in her consulting room. She tried to resist but he skilfully and forcefully tied her to it with four lengths of black and hooked elasticised binding ropes, those used by cyclists to tie luggage to the back of their bicycles.

He cut every shred of clothing from her body with his knife and then sat in the patient's chair. He methodically unbuttoned the tunic he was wearing, and removed the small helmet.

Margot's mind focused immediately on detail. The buttons. The texture of the material. His vest. She knew instinctively that to react with any suggestion of the hysteria she was experiencing internally, would be fatal. She watched him calmly. He had been tracking her in the disguise of the uniform used by the city's civil police, the Guardia Urbana, a completely separate policing organisation to the Mossos D'Esquadros, and not involved in criminal investigations. Of course, she had no reason to have particularly noticed this distinction until now because he had been the 'policeman' who had given her a false sense of security all week.

The floor of her studio had been covered with PVC sheets. She noticed a neat bundle in the corridor. It looked like a small body wrapped in a blood-soaked shroud. It reminded Margot of Saint Eulalia. *Isobel?*

# Chapter Thirty

Xavier talked slowly and quietly, without any aggression.

"I am very, very tired. I haven't slept this week. Patches. This is all finally catching up on me."

Silence. He looked at her and smiled. "I don't suppose you've read a collection of essays written by a relatively obscure French intellectual, Georges Bataille, called *Eroticisme?*"

Margot shook her head. "No, I haven't."

Even if she had, she had no desire to engage with him in any phoney academic discourse. She was numb with horror, yet she was also disarmed by his chatty, supercilious tone. She was much more concerned, however, with what he intended to do with her, and how she could prevent him.

"Bataille makes some very powerful arguments about the uneasy relationship that exists between animals and human beings, between taboos and transgression, between violence and sexuality. Murder and eroticism. *Tout homme a dans son coeur un cochon qui sommeille.* He believed that we rather conveniently suspend the taboos to do with death for spurious religious reasons, as part of the natural order of our patterns of behaviour. Human sacrifices, for example. Bataille's theories about the reasons we go to war are fascinating. He writes about the laughable hypocrisies of Christianity's acceptance of the Ten Commandments. *Thou shalt not kill...* He says that human violence is never cold calculation. It is the result of emotions – anger, fear and, of course, desire. A taboo exists so that it can be violated. Priests can bless armies chanting the *Te Deum...* He also has some interesting, and subversive theories about the Marquis de Sade. In de Sade's books, pleasure is greater if it is criminal, and the worse the crime, the greater the pleasure. *There is nothing that can set bounds to licentiousness.* Bataille rationalises de Sade's seemingly anti-social philosophy by arguing that if crime leads men to the pinnacle of sensual ecstasy, 'the fulfilment of the most powerful desires' then, in de Sade's opinion, all efforts to prevent the enjoyment of such pleasure had to be resisted at all costs."

He wasn't going to let up on the intellectual tosh. Where was it leading? Margot was familiar with the long-winded, intellectual justifications her clients would use to try to rationalise their bad behaviour. Xavier was no exception in that sense, but he was using some powerful and grotesque logic to arrive at his theories. Margot employed all her emotional disciplines to counterbalance the terror she was experiencing, and tried to listen to him with a cold, calculating intellectuality. She wanted to know what was in the blood-soaked shroud. She could feel beads of sweat beginning to creep down her spine between her naked body and the leather of the chair. There was none of the sensuality of her previous encounters with him, just cold-hearted revulsion. Did she need to talk to him in the way that she might if he had been a client?

"Do you recommend that I read him? I have read some of de Sade's books. *La nouvelle Justine and One Hundred and Twenty Days of Sodom.*"

Margot had been very wary of the fashionable theories about de Sade's, that his demented posturing represented a useful research tool in the treatment of sexually disturbed psychopaths, for instance. She summoned as much of her academic dexterity as she could to find some instinctive way of deflecting Xavier. Who could possibly believe that the kind of violent depravity used by de Sade's most monstrous of creations, in his lust for violent death and extreme sensuality, was somehow divine or sacred and somehow, therefore, representative of some deeply hidden, dark element in all of us? Ironically, this was probably at the root of Margot's own psychological dilemmas – that nobody would deny the inevitable link that exists between intense sensuality and the desires to inflict pain or to kill or be the victim of torture and death.

But this did not concern her now. She desperately needed to find a way to survive.

"I have read everything he wrote. The manuscript of *One Hundred and Twenty Days of Sodom* disappeared when he was moved from the Bastille at the time of the Terror and wasn't rediscovered until 1900 or so."

Like an untimely death knell, the 'phone in the office rang, interrupting his flow. The answering machine clicked into action. It was a very distraught Archie.

"Darling, please ring me as soon as you can... Please come home. I know we have so much to talk about... Carlos has just rung me. He tried to reach you on your mobile. Do you remember that girl with the yellow dress at the funeral? The police have found the body of her husband in the wasteland above the Olympic stadium... he's dead... battered... they think she has been murdered too, by Xavier. Please don't walk home. Take a cab. Or 'phone the police – Carlos offered when I told him where you were. Apparently her last call was to your office 'phone... or 'phone me. I can come with the car... I love you... Nothing you told me matters... I know you love me, too..."

"What a great guy!"

He mimicked Archie's accent expertly; Xavier's sarcasm was

repugnant. Margot had always liked Archie's voice – his peculiar heightened accent, an imperfect blend of well-enunciated Queen's English with a light Scottish brogue and the languorous vowels of classical Venetian, was in such sharp contrast to the purring licentiousness of Xavier's. She shivered. No wonder her new friend Isobel had let her down. She must have been followed by Xavier, no doubt manifesting the maniacal characteristics of de Sade's warped, murderous heroes. She was obviously his next victim. Margot had one forlorn hope: if Archie knew that she was at the studio, he would know that she would normally pick up in the middle of the message, or 'phone straight back. Perhaps, just perhaps, he would know that something was askew. It was a very remote possibility that he might decide to come down to fetch her now. Xavier left his chair and went into the office area of her studio to silence the answering machine, which was bleeping intermittently with its programmed alarm, signalling the terrifying warning from Archie. She heard him fasten the shutters. He walked back behind her. Her body tightened and her shoulders contracted. He enveloped her and sat on her lap. His breath was stale, and smelt of fish. He tried to kiss her on the lips. She bit his lip viciously. He laughed as he licked the slither of blood.

"I met Isobel this morning, Xavier."

"I know you did."

"She was obsessed by you."

He moved off her knees and took up his position in her client's armchair. His mood had changed, he seemed resigned.

"I must tell you about Tilly and Paolo."

Margot knew that she might have made a mistake, but she had to keep him talking.

"I loved them as much as you did."

"I loved Paolo, particularly... I always had a special relationship with him. And Paolo's death was what he wanted. I know that you are going to find it difficult to believe me, but when the police finally see the footage, they will be able to confirm that. I wanted to allow him everything. Ecstatic experiences he wanted to have. I did not want to harm him. We were such good friends. He was one of my special friends. What we did together at first was just a bit of harmless fun..."

"How old was he when you met him first, Xavier?" Margot tried to maintain the interrogatory tone. What she really wanted to say to this despicable paedophile was at odds with the tone she needed to preserve to keep him friendly. And she sensed that he expected her to play his game, his way.

"I can't really remember. He was a very mature young boy."

Margot shuddered as she remembered that Paolo had been twelve years old when 'Guy' had first abused him.

"And did you fall in love with him then?"

"Ancient Greece had an elegant system for the moral and sexual education of their youth. Plato describes it in *The Symposium*. Young boys were willingly initiated by older men. I had a mentor in that sense when I was a boy and was never harmed by his care and affection for me. Paolo and I had a very similar relationship... we would invent exotic games to play. Not unlike the games you and I have been enjoying this week."

Margot shivered again. Well-read paedophiles often evoke Plato's dubious elitist and misogynist treatise about love and sexual initiation. She couldn't help thinking about the agony Paolo must have been put through when he was being nailed to the cross in the horrendous re-enactment which formed part of Tilly's DVD. Did this evil man really believe that he had not harmed him? That a crucifixion was part of a harmless exotic game?

He sat back in the chair. Margot tried to engage his eyes, but he seemed a little drowsy. She remembered that on a couple of other occasions, in particularly intimate, psychosexual exchanges, her patients had unwittingly entered a trance, an almost subconscious psychological state, and then had fallen asleep. She realised that Xavier was beginning to show similar mannerisms. She remained calm.

"And Tilly? Where did she fit in?"

"I loved Tilly, too. In the way that I have loved all the women who are my special friends. Tilly had a delightful attitude to life. She adored you too, Margot. She told me that you had been so helpful and kind to her. When she arrived in Barcelona, Paolo became confused about our friendship and we stopped seeing each other for a while. But then he brought Tilly to my classes and I discovered that she and I shared a passion for paintings, and for video art. She was happy to become a character in the amusing diversions Paolo and I were devising. And then she began to make them part of her own work. She also shared in my theories of eroticism and about violence and the connections between death and sexual pleasure..."

Xavier was struggling with his eyes, which were closing intermittently, as if he had been given a slow-acting sleeping draft.

"...I am so sorry, Margot. I am fighting with a strange sort of drowsy feeling. I am so tired. I want you to challenge me. I want you to talk to me... I like taking to you..."

The complexities of this sick man were completely outside the boundaries of the macabre situation, but Margot realised that Xavier had never talked to anyone about his experiences in this arena. He had obviously been able to separate and compartmentalise his relationships, and juggle them. He was obviously brilliant at controlling people's emotions, manipulating them and, fatally, Paolo and Tilly must have enjoyed a privileged position in his life.

"And Isobel?"

He revived a little and straightened up.

"My God, I was almost asleep! Do you have this effect on other patients, Margot?"

"Sometimes."

Margot continued to play along. She realised that she might have found her only escape route, but she had to disguise it; Xavier was very smart.

"...How amazing... Isobel made the mistake of falling in love with me. I explained to her that I loved her too, but that I loved many people. Tilly and Paolo. She wouldn't join in our games. She was under a spell... you enjoyed playing my games..."

"I did, Xavier. You overwhelmed me. You have that power..."

"Tilly wanted to die with Paolo. She and Paolo believed that they would achieve a romantic mythological immortality if they died together... Ecstasy... And agony... I encouraged it but when I realised that they were using the film they were making about St Eulalia's martyrdom as the vehicle for these theories, I tried to talk them out of it. But they were determined. And when I realised that they were actually putting it into operation... Paolo, particularly Paolo, insisted on it all... The Cross... the Pain... the Blood... Tilly began to cut her arms and she went into a trance and lost consciousness. Almost as if she had taken drugs... It all got out of control when the night watchman found us."

Tilly's trance was completely consistent with the behaviour of self-mutilators. Her suicidal tendencies blended with Paolo's self-destructive euphoria were their horrifying, lethal concoction. Their choice. Their secret. And now Margot's most unwelcome secret. They had wanted to die and no one except Xavier had known. They chose to die.

What sort of a man could be involved in such a satanic nightmare? Allow it to happen? Encourage it, enjoy it... This was not a religious ritual, this was the physical manifestation of three very sick minds. And Xavier was beyond any form of redemption, finally culpable. Margot battled against her instincts. She wanted to scream and protest, and she wanted to begin a powerful diatribe, destroying all his delusional fantasies about his behaviour. What she might have asked a client at this juncture seemed redundant. This man was a psychopath. Stick to known facts. Characters. Move the story on. The blood-stained shroud lying in the corner.

"And the night watchman? And what is that in the sheet? Isobel?"

"The night watchman gave me no alternative. I remember reading a description of a killing by Ian Fleming. He had found it very difficult to kill a man for the first time... this was during his wartime exploits in naval intelligence... In fact, I found it very easy. He made it easy for me."

*He enjoyed it. He gave me no alternative...* Margot repressed a gasp. *I give him no alternative.*

"Did you find it easy enough to come to the opera to meet me, knowing the way I felt about Paolo and Domatilla?"

"You had to become one of my special friends. I loved them as much as you did. And I trusted you when I met you. I trusted you, Margot... until I saw you with Isobel. I wanted to trust you... I wanted to love you in the way Paolo loved Tilly..."

"Did you want me to die too, Xavier?"

He was battling with his drowsiness again. Margot looked at the side table with its box of tissues, used by her clients. There was a dark, soft leather pouch next the box, with an elegant locking device in the style of an expensive cigar or pen wallet. *Maybe he will fall asleep.* His eyes were closing. She almost whispered, gently. Testing him. Another furtive glance over to the bloody shroud.

"And Isobel?"

"In Niger, where Isobel comes from, they kill women if they are caught being unfaithful to their husbands. She had to be punished. I did him a favour. It was very, very beautiful. Almost as beautiful as Paolo's death. Tristan und Isolde. Yes, *jouissance*, if you like..."

He hardly opened his eyes and his head was drooping; he was barely conscious.

"Silence!" he said quietly.

Is he asleep?

Margot thought she heard a car pull up in the Plaça below. Unusual at this time of night, unless it was a taxi. No car doors. No voices. The shutters were closed.

*If this is by some tiny chance Archie, he will know that I always work at night with my shutters closed if I have a client and that I have a rule that he can never disturb me here. Did Xavier lock the door? Is Xavier really asleep? Does Archie know where to find the spare key?*

Footsteps. Brouhaha. And then Xavier's eyes snapped open.

"Paolo and Tilly? Tilly didn't really want to die as much, but I insisted that we had to take it all to that extreme limit. That was the idea. That was their pact. St. Eulalia. The painting. The crucifix. The cords. That is what we had agreed to do – rather like that game of chicken in that James Dean movie... If there had been a priest here right now, I would have had too many sins to confess. You could have been my Mother Confessor. Paolo's death pains... the most beautiful sight I have ever experienced." He laughed quietly.

"A priest?..."

Xavier was slurring his words as if under the influence of some kind of narcotic.

"You could have read me the last rites! A lustful man... a reasonable man... given the choice of ravishing the object of his powerful lust and going to the gallows, or controlling his passions and surviving... I choose to submit to my darkest desires. I have possessed the men and women of my dreams. I have savoured their bodies, living and dying... Paolo and Tilly were the most beautiful. Ecstatic, immortal... You would have been so lovely, too... blinded but alive... And so I must pay for the pleasure I have had in Hell, and maybe indulge in the ultimate pleasure like them and die on my own, rather sophisticated equivalent of the gallows... *Jouissance...*"

He glanced at Margot and reached for the small leather wallet. He opened it quickly, efficiently and pulled out a surgical knife.

"No! Xavier! No, no Xavier!"

She shouted and then screamed.

Xavier continued to watch her from the comfort of his armchair, smiled, and then without shifting his body, and with one smooth, uninterrupted gesture, cut his throat and neck from one side to the other. Each of the carotid arteries vomited blood like a fireworks display. His head slumped onto his chest. Margot's hysterical screams matched the horror of what she had been so calculatedly forced to watch.

Within seconds, Archie, Carlos and a handful of policemen had battered their way into the studio. Margot continued to scream as Archie and Carlos untied her from the chair and Archie cradled her in his arms. It took him about five minutes to calm her down enough to loosen her tight grip from his enveloping body. The policeman had unwrapped the shroud. Isobel's beautiful body had been mutilated.

Margot was still whimpering when Archie wrapped her in the winter coat he found in the studio closet, and with Carlos, led her downstairs and into the back of his car. A phalanx of police officers began to fill the room. A large crowd had gathered on the pavement outside, and were cordoned off behind a police ribbon.

# Chapter Thirty One

Archie sat in the back of the car. He knew that there was absolutely nothing to say. They sat for about five minutes before a uniformed policeman offered to drive them home. It was the same officer who had shown Margot around the Las Ramblas headquarters that afternoon. Archie said thank you and gave him his car keys.

"All that blood... He didn't touch me again, Archie."

"I know, my sweet Margot... I am so sorry. I shouldn't have left you."

"It was not your fault. I wanted to be on my own. I wonder how Xavier got in without a key?"

A gurney was being wheeled out. Isobel's body. Margot noticed a car parked in the corner of the Plaça, surrounded by white tape. The same black sedan that had been parked near the Santa Maria.

*Of course. This was no police car. It was Xavier's old Citroën.*

Archie gave the police driver some concise directions in his fluent Catalan. It was after ten o'clock, and the streets seethed with Saturday night traffic. The policeman asked Archie in English if he would like him to arrange a doctor for his wife. Margot thanked him and very politely explained that she would be fine. They sat in silence, looking out of the side windows now spattered with rain. Blurred images.

*Red neon lights be damned... How did he get into my studio? All the blood. And that ghastly bundle in the corner – he must have dragged it up the stairs? I wish I could cry...*

Margot slowly closed her eyelids, welcoming the abstraction of that dark, unfathomable galaxy which confronts the mind when our eyes are closed.

*Blindness?*

The last time she remembered this kind of blindness had been during her last orgasm when she was blindfolded in Xavier's apartment. She shivered, then began to shake.

"I can hardly breathe!"

"Stop the car! *Aturi el cotxe immediatament!*"

Archie yelled at the driver, who pulled into the side of the steep road which wound up the Montjuic.

"I can't breathe. I feel so cold. I can't stop shaking... My whole body is shaking. Cold. "

Margot was indeed shaking.

Archie was dumbstruck and helpless. "Shall we go to a hospital?"

"No! No! Please, Archie, no! I think am having a panic attack. I just wish I could stop shaking."

Archie put his arms around her and she gradually became still and quiet once more.

"I think I am okay now. Thank you. We can go home now."

The driver asked Archie whether he should take her to the hospital, but Archie explained that she had been having a panic attack and told him to drive on.

When they arrived at the apartment, Archie ushered her in like an invalid and gently guided her into their bedroom. He then ran a hot bath. Margot changed into a large, woolly dressing gown and sat on the edge of the bed. And then she sobbed, quietly. Archie returned and led her towards the tub.

"I'll be back. We don't need to talk."

"I can't talk now. Too much to talk about. But I will in time... I love you, Archie."

Margot edged her way slowly into the warm water and lay there, absorbing the luxury of the huge tub and the lavender bath salts which Archie had sprinkled into the bath. She closed her eyes. She desperately needed a diversion.

*I wonder if Anthony can get another ticket for Archie and then he can come to the football game with us next week? He would love that, and so would I.*

Her mind went blank. Archie came back with a goblet of brandy for her and his own glass of wine. She smiled, gratefully.

"Thank you, darling Archie... Will you stay and have a shave, and then you can have my bath. I need you here."

This was a familiar ritual they had established.

"That's what I had been planning."

The phone rang. "I'll just go and unplug that 'phone. I don't care who it is!"

Margot hoped that Archie wouldn't put any music on. He didn't. He came back to the bathroom, kissed her on the lips and on her eyes. He then began to lather his shaving bowl with the expensive badger hair brush she had given him last Christmas.

One of the taps was dripping. Archie tightened it. Silence, except the excited, happy screams of children playing in the street.

"It must be awful to be suspected of a crime you didn't commit."

Archie's face was covered with soap. He reached for his razor and started to shave, slowly and methodically.

"It was so many years ago. He was the only person who knew the truth. Xavier."

Margot didn't want to react. What is Truth, said jesting Pilate; and would not stay for an answer. She remembered that she had used that mantra once for Xavier – one of her father's favourite witticisms.

"I must ring my Dad!"

## Acknowledgements:

*The editorial guidance and inspiration from Tim Binding, Loo Brealey, Samantha Hill, Caroline Michel, Alice Sandeman-Allen and Franc Roddam was crucial for this, my first novel, and I also owe a special debt of gratitude to Dr. Jill Vites whose wisdom and professional brilliance steered me personally away from a very dark place psycholgically towards the idea of writing it in the first place. And of course my wife Hilly who has had the perverse role of living with me through its creation.*

*Dr Janet Reibstein read a very early draft and generously gave her professional observations about contemporary practice amongst respected therapists. This was invaluable and helped me fashion Margot's idiosyncratic modus operandi.*